COLD-BL

"I want to verify a c

"Things that could get   a new trial."

"What new trial?"

"If I find evidence . . ."

"Evidence ain't gonna do her a swill a good. When she's caught, she's going to fry. Everyone says so."

"They don't fry prisoners anymore, Gary."

"Yeah. Too bad." He smiled. "New trial? You're crazy, honey. Me, I'm wishin' about now that there was no death penalty."

"Really? Why is that?"

"Rona Leigh's got nothin' to lose. If she's of a mind, she really will come and kill me."

"But maybe she didn't kill Melody and James. Maybe she's not a killer."

"Listen to me, FBI. You can't spring her. Y'all are wastin' your time. There ain't nothin' I could tell you, because everybody knows what I done."

"What do you mean by that?"

"Here's what I mean. I wanted Rona Leigh to kill Melody. Believe me, I did. But the thing is, what I wanted I never believed could happen. Not for a minute . . ."

More outstanding praise for *Love Her Madly*

"Halfway through the book, Tirone Smith presents a tour-de-force. Then she shocks us even more with a stunning turn of events. Suffice it to say, Poppy encounters some surprises before the story's over."

—*Hartfor Courant*

"A skillful writer and an artful plotter."

—*Arizona Daily Star*

Also by Mary-Ann Tirone Smith

LOVE HER MADLY

MARY-ANN TIRONE SMITH

PINNACLE BOOKS
Kensington Publishing Corp.
http://www.kensingtonbooks.com

*This book is dedicated
to six literary guerrillas—
Sybil Steinberg
John Coyne
Michael Anderson
Dan Doyle
Molly Friedrich
and
Elizabeth Stein*

1

This was the first call I made. Houston Police Department. Asked them to track down the dispatcher working out of the Thirty-first Precinct seventeen years ago, third shift, on duty from eleven to seven.

Very efficient force down there, cop called me back twenty minutes later.

He said, "Now have I got Agent Penelope Rice of the FBI here?"

He did.

"Count yourself fortunate, ma'am. Officer Melvin Hightower dispatcher seventeen years ago Thirty-first Precinct is still dispatchin' still workin' the third shift don't ask me why. He's home asleep till five. Don't need to sleep far as I can tell. Melvin's famous for the amount of rest he gets on the job."

He gave me Melvin's home phone number. I thanked him.

"Always a pleasure helpin' out the feds, ma'am."

Yeah, sure.

At five o'clock Officer Hightower answered his phone on the first ring. He didn't say hello, he said, "FBI?"

So I said, "Officer Hightower?"

Him: "Agent Rice?"

I let it go. "Yes, this is Agent Rice. Sorry to bother you at home."

"Expect it's urgent."

Very urgent. "Yes, it is. I need you to recall the work you did the night Melody Scott and James Munter were killed."

"You and everybody else. That little guttersnipe. . . . Well, her number's just about up, ain't it?"

He wasn't looking for an answer so why bother?

"About to get the big stick. I'll tell ya, it's all been comin' back to me like it happened last night, like I got a picture show in my head. I'd be more'n happy to share my recollections with you, Agent, but I do find myself wonderin' what interest the FBI might be havin' at this late date. I mean, when it's too late to change a thing."

"Let's just call it a spot check, Officer. We were involved in the case before it went to trial."

"That so? Never heard that. But who am I? Dispatcher, is all. So here I go: See, that night? I get two calls concernin' the crime. From the same guy. 'Course, he was fool enough to try to deepen his voice second time. First voice, regular voice, guy tells me two people got beat up, gives me an address, a motel, and then I get dead air. Couple minutes later he's Mr. Deep Voice and says two people, armed and dangerous, high on illegal drugs, are causin' a fuss and gives me another address, a residence, then more dead air.

"I figure it's just some fool with an ax to grind. . . . Hey, now, I didn't quite mean to say that, did I?"

"I guess you didn't."

"I don't take none of it lightly, Agent."

"I'm sure."

"Where was I? Oh. I send two cars out, two boys in each, hear from my second car ten minutes later. Officer says, 'Melvin, we got a coupla naked, stoned kids standin' in a bathtub fulla bloody water.' More blood than water, he tells me. Says, 'Ain't their blood neither. Some, but most of it came *off* them, not outa them. And there's a pile a clothes on the bathroom floor saturated with blood.' Says, 'Melvin? A violent crime's been committed real recent, some other location. You keep your ears peeled, hear?'

"Then as I remember he said he wouldn't be gettin' much outa the two kids till he brings 'em in. Says, 'Make a real big pot a coffee, Melvin, 'cause I can see I'll be needin' six cups myself. Figure these hopheads'll choose my squad car to puke up all the shit they been takin'.'

"Two kids, Agent, are Rona Leigh Glueck and her boyfriend, Lloyd whatever-his-name-was. Forget. Officers come in, Rona Leigh wrapped in a blanket, and she's laughin' and laughin'. First sensible thing we make outa her is, 'I had me so much fun killin' that bitch I got a pop ever' time the ax chopped her.' Then she goes totally berserk, like a blind dog in a butcher shop, starts carryin' on, screamin' and cryin' and laughin' all at once. Pukes right then. Never puked in the squad car, oh, no, she waits till she gets in fronta my desk. Toss her in the lockup with all the hookers, and they're like to kick the shit outa her 'cause she's still pukin' her brains out. But then they recognize her as one a their own and clean her up. The boyfriend, he never said a damn thing.

"Then the other shoe drops. Two officers I sent to that motel? Here's their story. They knock on a lotta doors, put up with a lotta grief from the other guests, who figure they was bein' arrested and don't know what for. Then they find the right room. The boy's room."

Time to let him come up for air. "James Munter."

"Yeah, Munter, that was it. His room was unlocked. Officers open the door, flip on the light, first thing they can make out? The handle a that ax. Where it wasn't slick with blood said the wood was almost white. The light comin' through the door behind them had lit it up, is what that poor rookie kept sayin' to anyone who would listen. Said the ax handle looked like it had a lightbulb in it.

"The blade was embedded in the female victim's upper chest. Senior officer says to me, 'You wouldn'ta believed it, Melvin. A drip fell right down on my shoe like suddenly it's rainin' blood.' Ma'am, our two boys look up at this big red splash on the ceilin' and then they step back real quick so's they won't get dripped on further. And then they just go steppin' on back and steppin' on back till they was out the door again. Rookie told me he just slammed it, liked to make it all go away. Ya with me, Agent?"

"I am."

"Could understand his feelin'. Been there, done that, which is why I choose to dispatch. Two boys run to the cruiser and call the precinct for help. Get me. I remember listenin' to botha them talkin' so fast, so crazy, I could smell sulfur. I said to them, 'You boys best calm yourselves right down 'cause I can't make out one word y'all're tryin' to say.' So they did, and I know to quick send out another car, call the man in charge, wake him up, and then, a course, all hell breaks loose. Real soon, you got your newspaper boys, you got your TV lights, you got your rubberneckers, ex cetra. With a homicide word flies fast, never mind what happens when you got a double ax murder, you know what I'm sayin', ma'am?"

"I know." I said to the dispatcher, "Did the officer who found the bodies get the names of the people staying at the motel?"

"No, ma'am. Let's just say those folks had the foresight to check out real fast—long as you call runnin' out the back door checkin' out."

"What about other people in the neighborhood? Did any witnesses come forward?"

"Ma'am, that neighborhood is so low-down you don't want to know who your neighbor might be, never mind listen to what he has to say. Nobody seen or heard a thing. We figured right away, Forget about witnesses."

"Were you able to trace the calls?"

"What calls?"

"From the puppeteer?"

"What the hell is that, FBI talk? Did you say *puppeteer?*"

"The man who called you twice. Disguised his voice."

"Oh, him. Nope. Nobody saw to tracin' that call."

"I find that impossible to believe."

He chose not to respond.

"Who destroyed your trace?"

"Ma'am, thought you said this was a spot check?"

"That's right."

"Hey, Agent, you're a pisser, you don't mind my sayin'. You want to talk to someone else in the department? That'll be fine. But you take it from this old geezer, who's been around a lot longer than you, it is too late for stirrin' up shit. She dies in—what is it? Couple weeks?"

"Ten days."

"Ten days? You see? There's no point. Now I got to get movin'. Got plenty to do before I report to work tonight."

Yeah. He had plenty to do. Had to get back on the phone the minute I hung up and report my call to someone. The bastard.

∞

Here is what led to my calling Melvin Hightower. Last night I'd settled down on my sofa to watch the tape I'd made of the *Evening News with Dan Rather.* I am a dysfunctional sleeper. I wake up three hours after I go to bed and can't fall asleep again until my alarm makes that little click immediately preceding the voice of Don Imus telling me the President is a moron. So my VCR is set to tape Dan, and when I find myself staring at the ceiling at 2 A.M. I get up, go to my living room, and watch the news.

Last night, before going to the tape, I went to my fridge and selected a bottle of nail polish called Drop Dead Red from one of the twelve little holders that are supposed to keep eggs. I don't have anything else on tap except in the freezer section, where I've stowed a bottle of Grey Goose and a crystal spritzer of Worth, both of which I use during DC summers when, even with my hair up and the air conditioner blowing on my neck, I can't cool off.

As I painted my left hand, Dan prepared to interview Rona Leigh Glueck, condemned ax murderer, about to become the first woman put to death by the people of Texas since the Civil War. Dan explained that in 1862, in the town of Mesquite, the previous woman executed was hanged by the neck. Her crime had been her manner of payment for a newly purchased horse: three bullets to the trader's face. There was some talk the man had raped her, but so what? She was a Mexican.

I half listened, half watched, and finished my left hand while Dan chatted with his guest, her smile so winsome, her manner so charming. She explained how Jesus had taught her the value of human life. She said, "I have taken human life, and I know what a horrible thing it is to do that. Jesus teaches us that murder, abortion, mercy killin', and the death penalty are all evil." Dan nodded in his fatherly way. "Though I am happy to accept a state of glory—if that is what must come to pass—I know that He is not ready for me yet. He wishes my life to be spared so I can spend the rest of my natural days preachin' against the takin' a lives. In a divine revelation, Jesus has offered me a ministry."

Sure.

I was about to start on my right hand when the camera panned down to Rona Leigh Glueck's own hands, very small, her nails trimmed and neat but not painted. I paused the frame. Her wrists were exceptionally delicate, the size you can encircle with your thumb and forefinger.

So maybe it was a lightweight ax.

I screwed the top of Drop Dead Red back onto the bottle and went to my FBI office–connected computer that is on a card table in my dining room, where I don't dine. I've been meaning to call in a desk since I moved to DC, but I haven't gotten around to it yet. It's only been five years, though, no problem. I keyed in the name RONA LEIGH GLUECK and got a one-line message:

CASE #8037568-8233. DATA NOT ENTERED.

Shit.

DATA NOT ENTERED meant a file existed, but I'd have to deal with it on paper. My fault. It was taking an inordinate amount of time to get all the files entered into our computer system. That's because I figured my personal attention to each would be a good chance to separate out the cases that should be reinvestigated.

My first assistant—previous to the present one I'd hired myself—said, "Reinvestigated? How about we just burn all the files?"

That initial week on the job, each time I brought up a problem the advice was either *burn it, toss it, shred it,* or *lose it.* I fired that first assistant and just about everyone else. As the new crime lab director, I cleared the decks. Got rid of the lazy louts with their patronage jobs and restarted the engine with no-nonsense peace officers, disciplined investigators, and the most talented chemists I could scrounge—out of academia and, even better, the pharmaceutical companies. People who needed something more meaningful in their lives than collecting stock options. People who were willing to dedicate themselves to fighting crime and seeking justice. Whistle-blowers. People like me.

I made a lot of new enemies in addition to the enemies I'd made as a prosecutor in Florida and, before that, as a district attorney in the Bronx. But I figure those kinds of enemies were impotent to begin with, so why worry?

Once I'd gotten everything sorted out, I sat behind my top-of-the-line desk and took in my corner office above all of DC, and then I went in to have a talk with my director. I told him I wasn't meant for office work; I needed to be out in the field.

He immediately said, "Within the FBI, though."

"Yes."

I could see he was glad of that. Then he protested my leaving the lab but in such a way as to show me how much he'd appreciated my work. He said, "Poppy, you turned a sinking trawler—infested with a lot of rats, I might add—into one sleek nuclear-powered yacht."

I said, "Thank you."

"Did you have something specific in mind?"

"Yes."

He smiled at me. "I'm listening."

That's what I wanted to be sure of: him listening. "You know all those files I separated out, the ones that need a good district attorney to reinvestigate them? We need a full-time pseudo–district attorney."

"You."

"Yes."

The man puts justice ahead of troublesome mechanics. He said, "Write out the job description and get it to me. Then I'll do what I have to do to make it official. Essentially, reassure everyone that the crime lab is now functioning perfectly. That there's nothing more you can bring to it and that other departments need Poppy Rice more."

What a combination. Though he was a superb politician, he respected me.

"I'd like to keep some space here."

"You got it."

"And I want my assistant."

"I could use her."

"Everyone could use her."

So now here I was, out in the field with my home base my sofa. I took another look at Rona Leigh's hands, I got up, put on a raincoat over my Victoria's Secret pajamas, a gift from a fellow whose name I no longer recall, and pushed my bare feet into sneakers.

FBI headquarters in Quantico looks like a space station. FBI headquarters in downtown DC looks like an extravagant art museum designed by I. M. Pei.

Our security guard said to me, "You really gotta tie those sneakers, Poppy, ma'am."

I said, "Who's got time?"

He said, "I got all night. I'll tie 'em for you."

I said, "Thanks, Bobby. I'll do it." I bent down to tie the sneakers.

He never said a word about what I was now just noticing—I had a New Balance running shoe on one foot and a Nike tennis sneaker on the other.

I looked up at him from my squat position. "I put them on in the dark, all right?"

"What happens when you don't pay your electric."

"Oh, shut up, Bobby."

"Hope you didn't tip your manicure lady either."

Bobby has a great gap-toothed smile.

I said, "Why don't you apply for a job as an agent, Bobby, you're so damned observant."

He shrugged. "Security guards got to be observant too. Pay us to stay on our toes."

I stood. His smile was gone. "Sorry. Didn't mean to condescend."

He chose not to forgive me. He said, "Body gets used to it."

"I said I was sorry."

"Least you people don't call me Boy no more."

He'd started working as a security guard in 1957. He'd been fourteen but lied about his age. Had reached his full height, over six-two, so nobody questioned his statistics.

I went in, got the file on Rona Leigh, went back out, told Bobby I loved him, which I did, and dashed back home. Back in front of the tube again, I pressed play and looked at the ax murderer on the screen and then down at the mug shot of Rona Leigh Glueck tucked into the inside cover of the folder. She was seventeen the night Melody Scott and James Munter were murdered. She was scrawny and obviously still high as a kite when the picture was taken, though it was hours after she'd been brought in. Her thick hair was tangled. She hadn't had a chance to comb it after her bloody shower.

Rona Leigh Glueck had lived in prison for as long as she'd lived out of prison.

I fast-forwarded past the ads. The *Evening News* continued. As Dan interviewed her I found it hard to believe, just like everyone else, that this lovely soft-spoken woman with eyes as large and warm and brown as Bambi's was the same woman in the mug shot.

But that was because she had thrown off Satan and accepted Jesus as her savior.

Don't they all?

Rona Leigh was not a Mexican like the woman executed in 1862. She was white. And she was saying to Dan, "I do so appreciate this honor you have bestowed upon me, Mr. Rather. Letting me speak with you here on the TV in order for people to understand that I have been asked by Jesus Christ, our Lord and Savior who has covered me in the armor of salvation, to pursue a very, very special mission in His Holy Name."

I noted that she spoke these words with her eyes fixed deeply into the camera's lens while at the same time showing that fetching dimpled smile and raising her slender fingers in a small wave, a gesture of *Hello there, y'all.* She could do these three things all at once because a good born-again Christian must master such choreography in order to snooker people in.

Like everyone else on death row, Rona Leigh may have found Jesus, but her conversion wasn't the real reason why a cavalcade of white knights—from the pope to Jerry Falwell—were charging in to save her. The real reason was that she was a pretty woman. Chivalry had come into play as it always does with a pretty woman, arms full of bundles, trying to open a door. A man will knock himself out to help her. If the woman's ugly, she can have two broken arms and the same man will barge past and let the door slam in her face.

Ergo, if a pretty woman is an object placed on a pedestal, how does that square with murdering one in cold blood while two dozen people watch the killing, listening attentively for the death rattle, like they're second-graders waiting for instructions on how to make art out of macaroni. It didn't square. Let us take our lesson from Jesus, who stopped a gang of fellows from stoning an adulteress to death. An adulteress who was, I'll bet, pretty. Jesus was a gentleman.

So the upstanding men of religion using the example of Jesus Christ had all come banging on the door of the good governor of Texas, beseeching him to stop the public stoning of Rona Leigh Glueck. But the handsome good-ol'-boy governor found himself in a bind. There were seven other women on death row in his state, and all of them were black. How ever would he get around denying their pleas for clemency if he granted Rona Leigh the stay she requested?

Just a week or so ago my assistant and I were chatting about this very development. She'd said, "Hell, it's all feminist backlash. Just another way of keepin' us in our place. Let's save girl killers from execution because, after all, they have nothing in the brains department so they aren't responsible for their numbskull behavior. If the governor of Texas was a right-wing extremist instead of this new-style Republican we're seein'— happy-go-lucky instead of . . ." She searched for the words.

"Instead of a mannerless goon," I suggested.

"Yeah, instead of an asshole—then Reba Lou might have a shot of slipping out of the noose."

"Rona Leigh."

"Whichever."

I'd brought up Rona Leigh with my buddy Joe Barnow. Joe is chief field adviser at the Department of Guys, the ATF: Alcohol, Tobacco and Firearms. He said, "Clemency for Jesus-finding is in violation of the first amendment, separation of church and state. Also, Poppy old girl, just who should get to decide if a prisoner really has found Jesus or is faking it?"

Then Joe became a redneck prisoner on death row. He said, "Ah b'lieve I have found Jesus. He's right there!" Joe pointed dramatically toward a big plant draped with twinkly lights standing in the corner of his living room, romantic decorator that he is.

I shaded my eyes and searched. "Where? Ah ain't seein' Jesus."

He grabbed me and turned me to the plant. "Right yonder beside that mesquite tree. Ah found Him! Ah have found the Lord. Now set me free!"

I squinted, and then I smacked his shoulder. "Y'all did not find Him. That there's a possum!"

It was Spike, his cat.

Then I left our much-loved make-believe role-playing game behind because I got depressed. "Shit, Joe, imagine some African American dude wearing one of those little white caps telling a clemency board, 'I have found Allah!' And all the board people mumbling to each other, 'Says he found what?'"

He laughed. I didn't. Joe didn't know I was depressed. There are some aspects of my thoughts I keep from him.

All the same, here was Dan Rather talking to Rona Leigh Glueck as though she were a child instead of a condemned prisoner, convicted of murdering two people in cold blood, fighting for her life, and I was finding I understood his going all soft. It was not just those big eyes of hers blinking innocently, it was the pre-makeover Paula Jones matted bangs, a drooping lifeless clump of chemically permed, dyed-black curls. A style that makes a woman look defective and in need of a good man's charity, even though bad men see those same fake curls as a neon sign flashing the message: *Anybody want a blow job?*

Dan Rather, as we all know, is the former kind of guy.

I leaned back into my sofa. We just don't have that hairdo in DC.

I looked to the file on my lap and took out the envelope with the crime scene photos, pictures of forms and objects—the bodies, the mattress, a phone—all coated with dark red blood.

In a far corner untouched were ten beer cans, eight down, two upright, a balled-up pair of socks among them. I looked for some forensic notes. None were in reference to what I guessed—that the victims had set up a makeshift bowling alley before they were killed, the game interrupted just after one of them left a seven-ten split. They'd been playing before they would have gone ahead and had sex—just before they would be murdered—rolling the ball from the mattress to their tenpins. Reminded me of Joe pretending to be a prisoner, with me jumping right in as straight man, the kind of game *we* played before settling in.

At a murder scene, one element of the horror and gore, the pathos, is what causes maybe one tear to leap to our eyes before we can head the rest off.

I went back to the bodies. One didn't really look like a body; its torso had been axed flat. That was Melody, the picture taken after the ax had been removed.

Dan Rather distracted me. I looked up again. He was wishing Rona Leigh well. She smiled calmly, gave that little wave, and then Dan said good night to his audience, looking completely abashed as if he couldn't understand how anyone would want to see his sweet little guest dead.

I turned off the TV. In the light of the streetlamp— I don't have any sort of blinds yet—I polished the fingernails on the other hand while I mused on it all. I was waving that hand in the air when I saw a naked man standing in front of me. Not entirely naked: The dial on his watch glowed green. He said, "You intend to get any sleep at all tonight?"

I said, "What in the world are you doing here?"

"You invited me." He glanced at the green dial. "And about six hours ago we made love."

"Oh, yeah. I forgot. I'm sorry, Joe."

The pieces of furniture in my living room are a sofa to sit on and a coffee table to put my feet up. Plus the TV. I patted the cushion next to me. Joe sat down.

When Joe Barnow's agents aren't ferreting out smugglers and drug lords, they're shooting and firebombing babies in Waco and Idaho with the help of the FBI, not my section. Joe says when a criminal resists arrest, threatens his agents with guns, lobs *grenades* at them, the responsibility for the repulsive results of the measures required to protect themselves lies with the criminals.

He says, "If those people want to hide behind their babies' cribs while they're trying to kill ATF agents, they're the ones who cause the deaths of the innocents, not us. Rules of engagement. You want to engage us, learn the rules. Your choice, whether to be compliant or hostile, and if you pick hostile, get ready to find out that your house isn't your castle after all."

He doesn't say, *And I drink too much so I can keep saying shit like this. But then I still can't live with myself so I drink some more.* The man is a mess. I don't hold it against him.

He put his feet up next to mine on the coffee table. I glanced at his lap. His relaxed state of affairs was too precious.

He glanced at my lap, too.

"Whose file?"

"Rona Leigh Glueck's."

"Why?"

"I couldn't sleep. I just watched Dan Rather interview her. He inspired me to run downtown and get the file."

"Poppy, you've got to learn to delegate—"

"I know, I know. But she's got ten or eleven days left, depending on whether you call three A.M. today."

"Where does your interest lie, Agent Rice?"

"In her wrists. They're as tiny as a child's. How much does an ax weigh?"

"Depends on the ax." He took the file from me and covered his lap, alas. He rifled through and took out a page. "Twenty-four pounds."

"Fairly heavy, no?"

"But she was young and strong."

"Young, yes; strong, no." I reached over and took out

the medical report. "Upon her arrest she was five feet two, eighty-eight pounds, and suffering from drug addiction, alcoholism, chlamydia, and malnutrition."

He said, "Well, I weigh around one-eighty. You got a calculator?"

"Not on me."

"Don't get up. Twenty-four pounds is a little more than a quarter of her body weight at the time. A quarter of mine is forty-five pounds. I could swing a forty-five-pound ax, no problem."

"Your ratio isn't figuring in the malnutrition, disease, all the rest. And what strength would you need to pull the ax back out of a chest if it's sunk in all the way through, lodged in the ribs and breastbone, say? Probably even more."

"Probably a lot more." He shuffled through the pictures and reports. "A dozen chops. Have you read this cop's notes?"

I looked over. "Not yet."

He read what I was to hear the next day from Dispatcher Melvin Hightower. "Cop says when she confessed she was laughing. She said she enjoyed killing . . . let's see . . . Melody Scott. Said she had a pop every time the ax hit home. What's that, an orgasm?"

"Must be what they call them in Texas. But she was lying. Bragging."

"She was?"

"Murderers in a frenzy don't take a break to concentrate on having orgasms. It's myth anyway, multiple orgasms. One, and your heart's pounding, your muscles are contracting, and you have to struggle to catch your breath. A few in a row would blow the top of your head off."

"Want to get in a frenzy and try?"

I picked up the file from his lap and looked. A change had come over Joe. We had nice frenzied sex there on the sofa. On the sofa and on the floor too, and during some of it we were apparently airborne. But I couldn't concentrate. I faked the orgasm. Joe didn't mind, though, because he said he never knows the difference anyway and because I told him it can be fun to fake an orgasm. One time we were making love and he started making all these noises and doing God knows what and I asked him what was going on and he told me he was faking an orgasm. I laughed so hard I had hiccups for an hour. I do enjoy this man.

Now Joe went off to my bed. I put my Victoria's Secrets back on and read a little more of the report. The little more I read was unbelievable. I went into my bedroom and got in with Joe. I felt bad waking him.

"Joe?"

"What, baby?"

"You faking sleep?"

"Yes."

I put on the bedside lamp. "Joe, the jury sentenced Rona Leigh to death rather than life in prison because of the testimony of the prosecutor's key witness"—I waved a paper I'd brought with me in front of his face—"a *forensic physician*. What the hell is that?"

"No such animal. You're either a pathologist or a coroner."

"That's what I always thought. This expert witness said . . . let's see . . . he said, 'Diabolical effort and determination was necessary in order for the accused to keep pulling the ax out of Melody Scott's chest in order to swing it again and again and again.'

"Now get this, Joe. When Rona Leigh's defender questioned him as to how she managed to do such a thing, considering her weight and condition, he said glee gave her the strength, rather than muscle. *Glee*. Now there's a forensic determination."

I noticed Joe's eyes were shut.

"Can I tell you more thing?"

He mumbled, "Sure."

"The forensic physician topped off his testimony by telling the court that the evidence wasn't entirely circumstantial. That Rona Leigh's *odor* was still on the ax handle."

His eyes opened. He said, "Objection," and then he closed them again.

"I certainly hope there was an objection. Even so, the jury got to hear what he said."

Jurors love doctors. They love expert coroners hired by the prosecution. They admire what they think is scientific evidence. That's because they flunked high school chemistry just like the lawyers. People go into law because they can't figure out the business end of a Bunsen burner. But here was a new one on me. A physician testifying in a court of law, under oath, that a killer's odor was left on the evidence.

"Joe, pretrial, the public defender sent a letter to my lab when it was under the direction of my predecessor, may he die of leprosy. The defender wanted to know if someone of his client's height, body weight, and physical condition was capable of committing the crime. He'd seen what I saw tonight on TV. A copy of the letter is in the fucking file, and it's stamped INADEQUATE PROCEDURE. The original was returned unanswered, unless you count a rubber stamp as an answer. Son of a bitch."

Joe patted my thigh with the strength of an ant. I let him sleep.

The crime lab had been an ongoing travesty for a very long time. Agents used to feel free to use rubber stamps at whim without taking the trouble to explain to querying law officers the procedures for filling out the proper forms when seeking assistance from the FBI. Those seeking assistance who were not deemed worthy of response never followed up, since public defenders like the one assigned to Rona Leigh were either inexperienced, incompetent, or burdened by unrealistic workloads.

I climbed out of bed, went back to my computer, and put case # 8037568-8233 at the top of my list. I would find out the answer Rona Leigh's public defender didn't get seventeen years ago from the FBI.

Then I got back in with Joe. He mumbled something.

"What, sweetie?"

"I'll bet you're figurin' the boyfriend maybe did it."

"Why not? Tells her she did it, she believes him, and then the cops remove any doubts that might crop up in her pathetic head. That way they kill two birds with one stone. Worked. I imagine the boyfriend must have been executed at some point."

"I think I read he died in jail. Poppy, honey?"

"What?"

"Before you take this one on, see if there's something else besides her weak physical condition. Just that won't cut it."

He was right. "I've got Dr. Glee."

"One more besides. Three is always a convincing number."

Three would happen the next day, when police dispatcher Melvin Hightower revealed a puppeteer.

I gazed at my ceiling. Joe's breathing had become regular. I dropped the papers on the floor, switched off the light, slid down under the sheet, burrowed into Joe, and closed my eyes. I fell into a deep sleep. Three seconds later I heard the click of my clock radio, followed by the voice of Don Imus telling me the President was a moron.

2

After I had my chat with Melvin, the Houston police dispatcher, I went in to see my director. We meet fairly regularly and I keep him informed as to what I'm working on, while he counts on my assistant when he needs to reach me in the field. Once in a while he has a few ideas of his own as to who belongs on my list, and I respect that. Then there are the occasional favors we ask of each other.

Not too long after I started my new job, he figured I owed him a little something. He called me in.

"I need a week from you, Poppy."

"When?"

"Now."

He described a "special concern" of his boss. That would be the President. The President had a very dear friend who needed help. From the FBI. The dear friend was a Catholic cardinal—someone was dipping into his till.

I asked, "How come me? I don't need to waste time swatting at gnats."

"I know. But I have to have someone who won't make a mistake and who will know to step lightly, since lightly is what is so called for here."

"Give him Auerbach. He's the best technician we've got. That anybody's got. He's never made a mistake in

his life. Tell him to wear sneakers instead of those gunboats he's always clumping around in, and I'm sure—"

"You can take a man out of his gunboats, but you
can't—"

"Shit."

"Poppy, we're dealing with a powerful and prominent man here. One *all* politicians have utmost regard
for. A household name, which makes things even stick-
ier. Sometimes I have to balance all that in. Of course,
you know that too. You'll find the little Judas in their
midst with no trouble."

"Why don't they handle Judas internally the way
Jesus did?"

"They tried. They went to the Jesuits. The Jesuits suggested the FBI."

"Too busy cracking Vatican bank scandals."

"Apparently."

He stood and handed me the report he'd received
and called out to my back, "Thanks, Poppy."

The household name was Beltrán María Cardinal de
la Cruz y García, the recently named very colorful
prelate of the Archdiocese of New York. The new pope
had traveled to Miami in order to harvest the most
conservative of conservatives and plant him on Fifth
Avenue. After he'd been in residence for about a year,
he was informed that someone had been helping himself to the contents of the collection plate to the tune
of ten million dollars in twelve years.

I consulted with Auerbach. He got together the software I'd need. He said, "At least it's New York. You'll
get to see a play or something."

"Anything good on Broadway these days?"

He gaped at me as if I were speaking Swahili.

It's hard to remember Auerbach doesn't know everything.

I went to New York and was welcomed by the cardi-

nal with so much grace that I forgave my director and
got the software going then and there. In two minutes
I'd set up a vertical balance sheet and watched where
it refused to remain vertical. Typical Ponzi scheme: Replace stolen old money with new money and then fake
the balances. I said to the cardinal, "Have we got any
priests or staff living the high life? A deacon with a
house in the Caymans? Secretary with gambling debts?
Mistress holed up at the Plaza? Bastard children squir-
reled away in the suburbs?"

He smiled. "If we did, we wouldn't have needed the
FBI." The smile faded. "I don't like this any more than
you do. Find him."

I apologized for being rude.

He said, "I accept your apology. But I understand
why you are annoyed, Agent. I have taken advantage of
my position. I hope you will forgive me that."

Why not?

Took me more than a week though. Two weeks. The
cardinal's bookkeeper, a very old priest, tiny and shy
and kindly—so happy to help me—believed the
Church in South America kept the peasants oppressed
so the bishops could maintain their standing as the
hemisphere's nobility. So he'd set up a very tidy laun-
dry and diverted a goodly number of contributions to
Chilean revolutionaries.

When all was said and done, the little bookkeeper
was transferred to his new parish on a Hopi reservation
in New Mexico, though I suggested jail. But cardinals
are above the law. Their own law, preventing scandals,
is paramount. He blessed me in the name of the Father, the Son, and the Holy Ghost and held out his ring
to be kissed.

Then he said, "I hope that someday there may come
a time when I can do a favor for you, Miss Rice."

I said, "Eminence, just keep praying for me. I'm sure I need it."

So now I got to remind my director of that mission. "You know how you insisted I go to New York awhile back? To do the favor for Cardinal de la Cruz?"

"I certainly do. And you didn't fail us."

"I have to spend a solid block of time in Texas." I told him about my interest in Rona Leigh Glueck.

"How long a block?"

"Ten days, max."

He raised an eyebrow. "I guess there's no worry of your stretching it out to two weeks, is there?"

"No, sir, there isn't."

He leaned way back into his big comfortable leather director's chair. "Poppy, it is not our job to find innocents on death row. Call that professor and his students out in Chicago—he's springing guys left and right."

"But it's not his job either. Sir, it's no one's job. There is no regulatory commission to see that the condemned haven't been victims of a corrupt system. I want a job like this because I have the equipment. The professor doesn't. He only has chutzpah. It's time for the authorities, for the law, to set an example and not leave it to volunteer do-gooders, God bless them all the same."

"There is legislation—"

"Ten days, sir."

I plunked the letter on the desk, the one from Rona Leigh Glueck's public defender with the piss-off message stamped on it. He read it. He sighed. He gazed across his expanse of desk at me.

"Is there more to this?"

"Excuse me, sir?"

"I'm wondering, since there's so little time. Not a DNA situation either. And the governor of Texas . . . Jesus. You trying to prove something here, Poppy? Something personal with you I don't know about?"

Shrewd man.

"No."

"All right, then. So exactly why do you think the ax murderer might not have done it?"

I was past the hard part. Good.

"*One,* she couldn't physically swing the ax: too weak, too small, too sick. *B,* there were no eyewitnesses except the wacko who was with her, and he's dead. *Three,* she showed the cops she was a hard-hearted bitch and they found her attitude offensive. *D,* she was a braggart; in her state of mind at the time she thought it was cool to say she loved the act of murder. *Five,* Texas law authorities have a reputation for reveling in high success rates. They probably encouraged the bragging until they got her to sign a confession to same. *F,* a story was created and accepted, and juries like to believe that official stories are the true ones, that people don't make false accusations, that—"

"Poppy, no need to give me philosophy. *One* through *F* were plenty. So, was your glib mix of numbers and letters meant to tell me that no one looked into whether or not she had the strength to lift the ax?"

"Well, one guy did. He came to us. You just saw the response he got. And there's something beyond the *One* through *F* that I really wanted to get to."

"What?"

"Rona Leigh and her boyfriend may have had a fuse lit under them, and the fuse lighter hasn't paid any price. Little pet peeve I have."

"Oh. The ulterior motive I was wondering about."

Not quite.

He pressed his fingertips together and thought for a moment. "Poppy, it wasn't under my watch."

"Of course it wasn't, sir."

He stood. "Please let me wish you well. I don't like holding my hand out to your back."

"Sorry, sir."

We shook hands.

⚭

That night, while I was packing my suitcase, Joe called.

"How're you going to handle this, Poppy?"

"If she agrees to see me I'll be direct. I'll ask her for the details of the crime as she saw them, and then I'll go from there, check a few people out, see if I can put together a plausible explanation of what could well have happened as opposed to what she confessed to."

"And then you'll go to the governor with the new version."

"As long as I feel I have enough in hand, that's what I'll do."

"He's never granted a single condemned killer a reprieve during all the years he's held office. He will never allow this crime to be reinvestigated."

"There's always a first time."

"It's such a long shot. Poppy . . ."

"What?"

"Listen, if you ever need to spill anything, feel free to spill it on me. I'm your friend."

"You are. And I'm glad of it."

"That's all I'll ever need to hear from you. Call in if you can."

If. Good man. "If I can I will, Joe."

⚭

Before I saw Rona Leigh I needed to know more about glee. Might not be necessary to see her at all if I determined that under the influence of glee, or drugs or alcohol, she was perfectly capable of committing the crime she was to die for and had consequently enjoyed committing it after all. So during the flight to Waco, I called this friend of mine, a shrink who specializes in sociopathic behavior. I'd met him at a conference in London. He was having trouble with job ethics. If the patient says, "Tomorrow I shoot my boss," is the guy fantasizing or will he do it? Should the shrink notify the boss and the police or not? My friend burned out, took a job offer from Stanford, and moved to San Fran. I begged him to sign on with us instead. He's the best. But he refused to be on our payroll even as a consultant. He'd had enough of dealing with the law. However, he told me I could consult him whenever I liked.

Through the crackling static, he said, "Poppy, we've not a connection, have we?"

I said, "Not in the cards, sweetie. Sorry."

He said, "I was speaking of the phone connection. I've resolved myself to the sad truth that I'll never be the great love of your life, though you remain mine."

"You're very sweet. Listen, I'm at thirty thousand feet."

"Ah-hah. And where are we off to? West Coast, I hope?"

"No, dear. I'm landing in Waco in one hour."

"Will that anarchy business never go away?"

"No, it won't. But anarchy isn't my purpose. Waco is also the place where Texas sends women sentenced to die. I'm going to visit Rona Leigh Glueck. Have you been following all that?"

"Most obviously. We Brits love a good murder, particularly when murder happens to be one's specialty. Besides, she's the latest media darling, so there's really no avoiding her, is there? Climbing on the bandwagon, are we, Poppy? Joining in to make a mockery of the U.S. askewery of liberty and justice for all?"

"You don't like it, go back to the razzle-dazzle of Liverpool or wherever."

He cleared his throat. "Ah, loyalty. A cultural virtue that is just so much horseshit. But let us not argue and be distracted from your purpose. How can I be of help?"

"Listen, Doc, you know those stories you read in the tabloids about a mom who lifts a Chevy Suburban off her child after he's been hit? Is that kind of thing really possible?"

"Indeed it is. Rare but verified. The mothers crack their vertebrae, wrench and even rip muscles, break blood vessels in their eyes, but they're able to perform Olympic-quality bench presses long enough for someone to pull the child out. But let us also give fathers their due. In one case, a father was killed because he'd taken on the weight of the car with his back, and once the child was out he let go and was crushed."

"Jesus."

"Yes. Jesus."

"So are there other examples of superhuman strength?"

"Why be hypothetical? What exactly do you want to know?"

I said, "That's why we've not a connection, Doc. You cut to the charge while I scope the battle."

"Well, it's what I have to do. I can't help myself."

"Yes, you could."

He laughed. "I didn't win you, Poppy, and I never will because I don't make the effort required, do I? Bloody hell."

"Now, now. You're—"

"No protest, please. This is business and I'm all ears. Tell me the problem."

"I'm wondering if sexual frenzy is as potent as the need to save your child's life. Can it get you to do something along the same lines as lifting a car? Say, if you weighed eighty-eight pounds."

"Not so far as to heft a car, but a sexual frenzy—if it

has religious overtones—can allow an ordinary person to accomplish superhuman feats."

"What religion are we talking here?"

"All of them. All religions that repress people sexually. In voodoo, people get themselves into such a state they strangle chickens, drink blood, pass out. Now, with Catholicism, the phenomenon is called ecstasy. People have been canonized because they perform extraordinary feats, which the saints attribute to Jesus thrusting His golden sword up through their bodies; with each thrust a feeling of mightiness, invincibility, comes over them and they are able to go out and raise an army, dig a well with their bare hands to water the troops' horses, lead the crusade, conquer nations. That kind of thing."

"Jesus doesn't have a golden sword."

"He does when you're having an orgasmic dream. There was the popular saint, Theresa, who wrote in her diary about the feeling of waking up to a sword being thrust into her body, the sword of Jesus plunging into her again and again. She was obviously having an orgasmic dream, and it woke her up. Religious ecstasy is often orgasmic. Now, if you were a religious person who knew nothing of orgasms and you had your first one in your sleep, you could well think God had something to do with it. Why, the first time I had one . . . well! If I'd thought for one minute that it had anything to do with Jesus, the vicar would never have gotten me out of the church."

"The first time I had one I thought it was cancer."

He laughed. He wasn't touching that one, though.

I said, "But do people *kill* in ecstasy? Outside the War of the Roses?"

"Yes. You've heard the verb *to smite,* haven't you?"

"But you don't think someone could dig a well in a

sexual frenzy alone? I mean, without believing that God commanded it?"

"We're talking about Rona Leigh Glueck, are we not?"

"Yes, we are."

"I don't personally know of it. But I can get a couple of opinions for you. By the way, I ask if it's Rona Leigh we're talking about because presumably you'd want those opinions right away."

"She'll be executed in nine days."

"Poppy, you think she mightn't have done it, is that right? You want to preclude such things as superhuman strength because you question whether she might have had the strength required?"

"Yes. Exactly. Perhaps she wasn't physically or mentally able to do it. But before I go making an ass of myself, it sure would help to find out that she didn't have some *unaccountable* physical abilities. Then I have to convince myself and a lot of others that maybe her boyfriend accomplished all the ax swinging on his own and manipulated her into thinking she did it."

"Far more likely than lifting cars off toddlers. Sociopaths are the grand masters of manipulation. If I were a gambler, I'd take the odds on the boyfriend."

"If you *weren't* a gambler you wouldn't use a Vegas term like *take the odds,* Doc."

"Wouldn't I? We don't say that in the U.K.?"

"No, we don't."

"Poppy, I am entitled to lose a wad in a casino now and again."

"Never said you weren't."

"Would you like to lose a wad with me next time? Come to Vegas. We'll stay at the Bellagio and pretend we're in a Borghese palace."

"Call me a week before you plan to go and we'll see."

He laughed some more. "You're such a good sport. You know that, don't you, darling?"

"I do know that. And I like the sound of *good sport* so much more than *slut*. Thanks for everything, Doc. Appreciate it."

"Always a pleasure. And you must never be hard on yourself, Poppy, my girl. Always boring, that."

He was right. I don't know how I slipped.

"Poppy?"

"Yes, Doc?"

"Whence cometh the bug in your bonnet? Surely there are others who—"

I told him we were about to land and hung up. Wasn't about to let him analyze me.

༄

When I'd called Rona Leigh's warden from DC, described my spot check, and asked if I could speak with her, he said, "Come on down. My door is always open to the feds." Just as accommodating as Dispatcher Melvin. He knew, though, that he didn't actually have to grant permission. I could arrive at his door equipped with the legal papers sidestepping any objections. We understood each other.

My plane arrived an hour late because the pilot was not a stud. He took wind-shear advisories as a personal threat to his life rather than as a challenge. The agent who was there to get me to my car wasn't too terribly annoyed, but something was on his mind, I could see. Before he got it off his chest he first gave me the good news that I didn't have to go into Waco to get to the prison.

The agent said, "Yes, ma'am, count your blessings. Waco is always jammed full of pilgrims who think the remains of the Branch Davidian compound are on

Main Street. All David Koresh could afford was an empty dried-out field miles out of town."

I didn't tell him I'd considered a pilgrimage myself. Joe got nicked in the shootout right when the agent next to him took a bullet through the neck, leaned over onto Joe like he was going to whisper something in his ear, and died. The agent was twenty-four years old. That was when Joe let loose and firebombed the place. When the FBI said they hadn't firebombed anything, they weren't lying. Joe did it. The surge of guilt he felt later will never go away. He thought the Davidians would come running out in order to save their babies. But they didn't, and the babies died too. Too bad he had to learn the hard way that maternal instinct is a myth. My friend the British shrink verified. "But members of a cult replace the love and loyalty one normally feels for one's child with devotion to their god, in this case, Mr. Koresh."

The agent who met me—"Agent Northrup, ma'am"—said, "It's a pretty drive to Gatesville. You head south on the interstate but you curve off into a little arm of hill country that heads right directly to the Mountain View Unit, which is the place Rona Leigh's been callin' home since they built it for her. Nothin' like settlin' into an FM road in Texas and enjoyin' Mother Nature at her finest."

Texans do love Texas. "What's an FM road? You're not allowed to listen to oldies on AM?"

"Ha-ha. No. Farm to Market."

"Sounds slow."

"It ain't. You'll be the only car on the road, trust me, and the highway patrol don't bother patrollin' them."

"A prison is a unit?"

"That's right."

"Most places it's facility. Which is worse?"

"A tie. Better when we just had place names. Or nicknames. Folsom. Angola. Sing Sing."

"Alcatraz."

"Now that was a lulu. Just don't dare refer to the men's death house as Huntsville. Huntsville is a city, not a prison. There's just no romance anymore, is there, Miz Rice?"

Miz. Some segments of society have been calling women Ms. since the beginning of time. Just spelled it differently.

"None. So the death row holding Rona Leigh must be a fairly small place."

"Used to be real small when she was the only one. Now it's caterin' to several more gals, all makin' their way down the path to the death house."

"Well, I guess I need me a map about now."

"You makin' fun?"

"No. I just can't help joinin' in. Y'all."

"Y'all is plural."

Oh.

He handed me the keys and then he took gentle hold of my elbow. I turned and faced him directly. Now he was ready to tell me what was bothering him.

"What?"

"We do routine checks fairly regularly. On our cars."

"I should think so."

He blushed. "Well there's something you should know. . . ."

"I should know everything."

"That's true. Excuse me for allowin' you to think I meant otherwise. Ma'am, someone went and took the spare tire out of the car we'd intended for you."

"So maybe the last person who drove the car had a flat and forgot—"

"And there was a skinny little nail drove into the left

rear tire of that car. Someone intended to inconvenience you. I'm sorry."

"Who's the someone?"

"We're lookin' into that right now."

"Have you got anyone here I transferred out of the DC crime lab?"

"We got two."

"How long before you find out which one?"

"We been told to find the sucker by tonight or our chief is goin' to transfer every last one of us to Timbuktu."

"You'll let me know within the minute of finding out, won't you, Northrup?"

"Yes, ma'am. We'll bring his head to you on a platter. I'm real sorry. We're all great admirers of yours, Miz Rice."

"Thanks."

Jesus. This was nice.

When I turned on the ignition the car didn't blow up. I pulled out of the lot and glanced back at Agent Northrup waving, his ass on the line.

Then he turned, shoulders slumped.

Damned auspicious start.

∽∽∽

Waco lies in what is referred to as the post oaks area of East Texas, though the post oaks were cleared long ago, the land denuded. I read that in the tourist guide the agent gave me along with the map. It lay opened on the passenger seat.

The eight-lane highway out of the airport was clogged, the brown ground on both sides as ugly as *denuded* implies and then add strip malls. But my exit came right up and within a few minutes green hills seemed to rise up out of nowhere, one after the other, and I did realize the beauty and serenity of the hill country just as Northrup had said.

I found a station playing oldies on AM. My stepfather loved rock 'n' roll. So did I.

It was early fall, the hills lush with vegetation, and atop each one a vista, always a little bit different from the previous one. Some hills shot straight up like mossy cliffs, and some were a series of rounded stepping-stones, bare on top. Each hid something new: Fort Hood, a thriving military community that covered 340 square miles with the largest collection of soldiers and fighting machines in the world; next to it a stretched-out piece of land so flat a bulldozer might have leveled it, and in the center a town called Flat. Then, in the distance beyond Flat, I could see a perfect mound, not a hill. From a crest in the road it looked to be so symmetrical it was as though a giant's child had filled a cake mold with damp sand and turned it over. Atop the mound, directly on its apex, a town called Mold.

While I drove, I pictured Rona Leigh looking out from the Mountain View Unit window at a view of Mount Rushmore. Funny how your mind drifts when you drive by yourself with no one to bother you and only the sound of The Doors in your ears. The mountain Rona Leigh viewed—if prisons had viewing windows, which they don't—was no Mount Rushmore, judging from my ride through hill country.

All the tiny towns I passed were identical, all the same as Thalia in *The Last Picture Show.* They were beat-up but quaint. Each had a movie house too, no longer abandoned since Texas was enjoying an economic boom. The picture shows themselves hadn't returned; the theaters were now banks or gun stores or real estate offices or, mostly, churches. Churches called The New Church of Jesus' Love.

People preferred the twelve choices they got at the

Cineplex to the one choice they'd had at the picture show.

I passed hills that had areas of chalk exposed, and then I came upon a causeway taking me over a long blue lake edged with the whitest sand that turned out to be more chalk. A sign said BELTON LAKE, and my guidebook told me it was man-made, "an impoundment of the Leon River and several creeks that flow through the area." That was a nice idea. There were a few small boats, people fishing.

At the end of the unnamed drive, I passed an unobtrusive sign that read TEXAS INSTRUMENTS and got a glimpse of the low sprawling buildings of a corporate headquarters hidden amid the hills. Pretty. I wondered where the employees lived. Mold, maybe.

Then just rolling landscape, mile after mile, and at about the time I began to wonder where the hell this damned Gatesville was I saw a road sign right in front of the Last Supper Cemetery. Five miles to go.

I passed over an expressway, the speedy route to Waco. And then a turn past a drive-in movie that was showing four feature films. The drive-in marked the head of Main Street, Gatesville, which was not the least bit beat-up, and then there was the old movie house, spruced up, showing four more. This town hadn't closed its movie house; it never even had to close its drive-in.

Gatesville was glossy, picturesque—shiny new banks and stores and small businesses, a new elementary school, and a renovated courthouse, "one of the finest remaining examples of Romanesque Renaissance Revival of hand-cut and carved limestone." First I'd heard of that particular revival. The guidebook didn't tell me what the brown trim was, but it was stone and as beautifully grained as marble. At first I thought it was polished mahogany and, when I got closer, petrified redwood.

I pulled up in front of the library, which is always a great place to talk to someone with a brain who can give you dependable directions. Librarians never say, Don't worry, you can't miss it. They make clear how to avoid missing it.

When I turned off my ignition, I finally saw something I hadn't seen since I'd left DC: human beings outside their cars. Traveling through Texas it soon becomes clear that people exist in brief glimpses dashing from their cars or pickups into a store or bank. No one walks from one place to another, and certainly no one goes for a stroll. There is no casual meandering that I could detect. There are these famous road signs all over Texas warning drivers they are in a prison area and shouldn't pick up hitchhikers. There were several such signs on the way to Gatesville. I never saw a hitchhiker, because all hitchhikers are escaped cons. If they weren't, they'd be in a vehicle.

In the library I went to the checkout desk and asked about a map of the town, something handed out with abandon at libraries compliments of the advertisers, another plus when you need dependable directions.

The librarian immediately held one out. "Y'all lost?"

Plural. Maybe she thought I had friends out in my car. "Not yet. I hope this will help."

"*I'd* be glad to help, ma'am," she said, big friendly Texas grin.

"I've got a reservation at the Holiday Inn. But before I ask you how to get there, I wondered if there's a real hotel. Here in the center of town."

"No, ma'am, there is not. We've only got the motel chains. Most visitors to Gatesville—well, they like their anonymity."

She'd broken the ice, enabling me to segue right into the questions I needed to ask.

"Is the prison in that direction then? Where the motels are?"

"Which prison are you interested in?"

"You've got more than one?"

"We've got six."

"Oh. The women's prison."

"Four of the six are women's prisons."

"The Mountain View Unit."

She didn't bat an eye, just took the map from me, opened it, and spread it out on the counter. "The women's prisons are in a cluster just here." I leaned in. "A quarter mile down State School Road, which is two blocks up Main, that way." She pointed.

"A quarter mile?"

"That's right."

"Kind of close."

"Kind of convenient. This is a company town."

"Is there a state school there too?"

She smiled. "That was what they told us we were gettin' years ago when the Texas Criminal Justice Department came on up here one day and cut a quarter-mile drive from Main Street to a big old farm they'd gone and bought. When we found out they were buildin' medium-security jailhouses, it was too late to do anything about it. So we named the road State School Road out of spite."

"The Mountain View Unit can't be medium security."

"That's right. It's got its own designation. Death row is considered something beyond maximum security, since the only prisoners inside are sentenced to lethal injection."

She said *lethal injection* in the same timbre I'd use for *community service*.

"You'll know it when you see it because it's the only unit with razor ribbon goin' round."

"Seven women are housed there, is what I've been told."

"I don't know the exact number. I know it's small, but then I hear it keeps growin' all the time. If you want my advice, ma'am, you'll stay at the Best Western. It's newest and it's the closest to the prison, right by the entrance to the bypass. Think you'll do better there than at the Holiday Inn."

"Thanks. Is the bypass a road?"

"Yes, ma'am. The department decided they wanted a bypass to the Waco highway."

"What does it bypass?"

"The town. Which is good. We don't get the prison traffic anymore."

"I guess you're expecting a lot of traffic pretty soon."

"That's right. Anything else?"

I didn't want to leave her on a down note. Keep your librarians happy. "What's the reason the bypass doesn't have a name?"

"Town couldn't decide who to name it after. Every town meeting forever after has been a fight over what to call it."

"Who would you like it named after?"

"Emily Morgan."

"Who was . . . ?"

"She was a whore who kept Santa Anna so busy that the Texas Rangers were able to turn around and defeat his army after he took the Alamo. Never would have been a Republic without her."

Texans have such a sense of humor. As opposed to couth. I decided to get a rise out of her.

"Could I walk from the Best Western to the prison?"

"Walk?"

"Yes."

"No, ma'am, you can't. No sidewalks."

"I don't mind walking along the side of the road."

"You mind getting picked up by the Highway Patrol? They'll figure you just strolled off the fields. But if you don't like drivin' you could ride."

"There's a bus?"

"I meant a horse." She was having fun with me too.

"I don't have one."

"Want to hire one?"

"I'll drive."

We shook hands and I thanked her for the map. I took a look through it. Holiday Inn should reconsider their decision not to advertise there like Best Western did.

I drove two blocks and took a left onto State School Road. There in back of Main Street was a little cluster of houses, the first Gatesville housing development. The closer I got to the prisons, the newer the developments, small houses neatly tended. The Texas Department of Criminal Justice, Institutional Division, employs more personnel than any other business in the state. Learned that in my guidebook.

I drove up over a hill where I could see a collection of buildings not unlike the Texas Instruments headquarters, except the surrounding area had been cleared of any trees and foliage. To my right was a sign that directed visitors to a boxlike reception building. I bypassed it.

Tilled fields spread out to a far distance, and women in loose white gauzy tops and white pants—thin fabric blowing in the wind—were hoeing. A few were on horseback. The prisoners appeared to be supervised by their own. There must have been several hundred women farming. I think only one of them wasn't black or Hispanic. She could have been, though, with her hair dyed blond.

Glittering in the sunshine was coiled razor ribbon

atop the only fence, a fence encircling just one of the buildings, like the librarian said. But there was no mountain in sight of the Mountain View Women's Unit. No Mount Rushmore for sure. The tallest thing I could see was a two-story guard tower by the gate in the fence. I turned into a short driveway that led to a parking lot directly in front of the gate. Another sign. This one was black with red letters: WARNING! ONCE YOU CROSS THIS POINT YOU HAVE CONSENTED TO A SEARCH.

Four cars were parked in the lot, with room for maybe a dozen more. I angled into a space and watched the women in the fields. They didn't look at me, they worked. The sky was bright autumn blue; there was no sound. All was calm and peaceful.

I got out and walked up the short sidewalk to the gate. At the head of the sidewalk, yet another sign, same colors as the last: BEWARE! YOU ARE ENTERING AN AREA WHERE COMMUNICABLE DISEASES INCLUDING HIV ARE PRESENT.

Something told me I wouldn't have found the signs of this prison industrial complex on the driveway entering the corporate industrial complex that was Texas Instruments.

3

The guard in the tower did not look my way as I approached the gate. Security was not what I expected. Maybe when a prison is the size of a beach bungalow, things get scaled down. I rang a bell. A second guard came out of the low building. I identified myself, showed him my ID, and told him I was there to see the warden. He introduced himself. "Corrections Officer Captain Harley Shank, Agent. Pleased to make your acquaintance."

He told me the warden was in his home. He pointed. On the other side of the Mountain View Unit, almost hidden by the only grove of trees left standing, was an old farmhouse, yellow with white shutters. I thanked him.

"More than welcome, ma'am. Uh . . . Agent."

I could have walked to the house, but as my existence hadn't aroused anyone's particular interest, since obviously word had been passed that I was coming, I didn't want to act suspicious. I got back in the car.

The warden wasn't home. The woman who answered the door was apologetic. She wore the same white clothes as the women in the fields. House slave.

She said, "Sorry, ma'am, warden been called away. He back in one hour, give or take. He say, tell you to visit with the chaplain if you like. 'Fore he gets back. Reverend Lacker. Chaplain expectin' you."

"Where would I find the chaplain?"

"He livin' in town now. In a rented room."

"Why is that?"

"You might ask the man, ma'am."

She gave me an address on a slip of paper. Reverend Lacker lived on Main Street. Before I'd left for Texas, I learned that Rona Leigh's chaplain was her husband, had married her some time ago. I drove back into town, retracing my route up State School Road.

⁂

A large and battered Bible was situated front and center on the coffee table next to a bowl of Wheat Thins and a pitcher of lemonade. He poured two glasses.

He said, "Though I like to think my guidance has prevailed, Rona Leigh's acceptance of Jesus Christ as her savior is the thing that showed her what makes up a human being. Showed her what a human being *is*. How a human being *acts*. How a human being should *be*. This is something she had to learn, since she'd never been taught what the rest of us are taught before we go on to take such things for granted. She has worked long and prayed hard to become a human being.

"Previous to her spiritual rebirth, she was not a human being but, instead, an empty vessel inhabited by Satan. The devil made her his den. His cave. When Rona Leigh put herself into the hands of our Lord and Savior, Jesus Christ, she threw off Satan and was born again, praise God."

Of course. He smiled. Benevolently, I'd have to say. Made me think of the Beatles, Paul McCartney, cherubic but smooth. Full of smiles. Beaming relentlessly. How everyone had loved the precious mopheads. The Christian right had noted the phenomenon.

I said to the radiant chaplain, "Reverend Lacker—"

He interrupted me. "Excuse me, ma'am, but I have been temporarily relieved of my duty as the unit chaplain while I guide my wife. Until my ministry is returned to me I prefer your calling me by my first name, Vernon. Not Reverend Lacker, thank you."

He smiled a new smile, contrite.

Now I knew of three Vernons—Elvis's father, Vernon Jordan, and this one, Rona Leigh Glueck's husband.

I said, "Well, then, Vernon, you can call me Poppy."

I could tell by his face that he wouldn't. He didn't.

This third Vernon said, "To put things more simply where it concerns my wife, Miz Rice, let me use the purest words of Jesus Christ through the witness of John, chapter three, verses five through seven: *'I say to thee, unless a man be born again of water and the Spirit, he cannot enter into the kingdom of God. That which is born of the flesh is flesh; and that which is born of the Spirit is spirit. Do not wonder that I said to thee, 'You must be born again.'"*

I listened politely. It is so absolutely amazing that men have gotten away with disregarding women's sole role in childbirth in order to bestow the real credit upon the baptizers—themselves.

Vernon reached into the bowl of Wheat Thins. He grabbed up a handful and started munching. I was relieved that the bowl hadn't been filled with pork rinds. I can only handle so many clichés. But I needed to ingratiate myself with him. I needed trusted access to his wife.

"Vernon, why should it be as simple as that? How could anyone accused of such a bloody and brutal crime find redemption with such ease?"

He took my words in. Something registered in his eyes. Surprise. His gaze took me in. Me the human being, not me the nonentity he intended to blow off with scripture. The smile plastered on his face eased up. He said, "Could it be you came here meaning to take me seriously?"

"Why wouldn't I?"

He studied my eyes. He said, "I fear people like you . . . women like you . . . Excuse me." He breathed in deeply, gave a long look skyward through the ceiling, and then his eyes met mine again.

"I pray to the Lord God to help me keep from sliding into the sin of the naysayer. For making judgments I must leave to Him. *Judge not lest ye be judged.* I neglect to heed His words, may He forgive me my limitations. But . . . well, you see, ma'am, women who are as worldly as yourself treat me with derision."

I had to make this guy my friend. "Their loss, reverend."

He didn't correct me this time. "Let me be candid, ma'am. Those very women happen to frighten me. As do you, though you resist making judgments, a Christian virtue I surely need to pray for more deliberately, as I just said."

"My job is to resist making judgments till all the facts are in. Making sure *all* the facts are in and that the facts are true."

"And that is my job as well. But I didn't mean to say—"

"Reverend Lacker, tell me please, what specifically do you fear? I don't understand."

"Literally?"

I wondered what that was supposed to mean. I didn't ask. "Yes."

"I fear that you will freeze my sperm and render me obsolete."

Now I couldn't help but smile, just as he couldn't help the serious look that accompanied his solemn words. I said, "How is that literal? Frankly, it's about as metaphoric as I can imagine."

The smile came back, smaller, though. "An evangelical preacher does not speak metaphorically. There is not one thing Jesus said, nothing in the New Testament, that is metaphoric. It is fundamental. There is no need to interpret. It is all there for us to see, plain as day."

He picked up the Bible next to the Wheat Thins.

I said, "I cannot believe that women taking over the world and annihilating the male gender is a real possibility to you. How can you trust Jesus to the exclusion of human dignity?"

His eyes were very dark brown, almost black. Up until this moment, soft. But now he wanted me to see him. "Miz Rice, you are not just an FBI agent, you are a theologian. I would like to talk to you about human dignity, the lack of which is what happens when Satan infiltrates a person. I would like to do that because I forget that sometimes the drama of the pulpit is out of place in a conversation. But there is no time for the two of us to try to understand each other. I feel, though, that you and I want the same thing: that which is right and just."

I'd give him that. I joined him in a few Wheat Thins.

"For ten years I have been chaplain to women condemned to die and to women serving hard time for felonies. And here is what I have witnessed. At some point during their incarceration, the gravity of what they've done just hits them like a bolt of lightning. In almost all cases the women are convinced the bolt was sent by Jesus. And when they experience that encounter with the Holy Spirit, they feel terrible . . . terrible. Mortified.

"They feel huge and grievous guilt. They experience remorse. And, finally, they repent. Although I give credit to the Lord, I know that He didn't send any lightning bolts. I am not blind to the benefits these women receive from a life of order when previous to their time in prison they didn't know order. I do not deny the humanizing

effects of education on them, the learning available to
them here, minimal though it may be.

"The point is, they come to accept their punishment
fully. They learn to live with it, they *welcome* it as their
due. When the bolt of lightning strikes, they suffer severe depression, and what takes them out of that
depression is their need to give back. It drives them. It
replaces their previous driving force—rage."

He'd finally put the Bible back down. His cheeks
were pink, and now his hands clenched together.

I said, "So what do they do about it?"

"There are women here making afghans for the poor
and knitting booties for foster babies during every spare
moment they can find. But they need better means of
giving back, of physically demonstrating remorse.

"There are none. Rona Leigh is one of those women.
She tried to organize a cooperative, to unify a group to
create beautiful objects. Those same afghans but ones
they designed themselves. And quilts. Dolls. All to be
sold at a profit so that the money could go to shelters
for battered women. To help take care of crack babies.
Whatever. But she was stymied at every turn and was in
fact forced to dissolve the network she'd formed with
other prisons all over the state." He smiled. "Many ad-
dictions here have been replaced with another: e-mail.

"Miz Rice, I fell in love with the human being Rona
Leigh has become. She is no longer evil. I want her life
spared not because women shouldn't be executed
while men should, not because I'm against the death
penalty, not because her victims were scum to begin
with and were no loss to society whatsoever, not because of any of that. Though I see it is God's will that
this particular woman should be spared, the larger reason for me is this—and may God forgive me that I do
not have the meekness he commands—I don't want to
lose her. I love her."

Ah, love.

I said, "Let me tell you what I think about love. I think people fall in love not because of the individual who has come along and made their hearts go pitter-pat but because of the timing. When you're ready for love . . . looking for love . . . you zero in on the very first person who comes along. Unless, of course, that person looks like Quasimodo. Then it's the second person to come along."

This was true of myself but not anyone else I've ever met. Somewhere along the line, I realized I didn't want to be married to the guy who happened to beat out Quasimodo due to fortuitous timing.

Vernon gathered up some more Wheat Thins and started popping them into his mouth whole. He said, "I pray you are not correct about that."

C'mon, Vernon, old boy, stand up for your love for Rona Leigh. "Vernon, I wish I weren't. But it explains why so many people find love in the wrong places. Because we go to the wrong place when we're feeling the need for love."

"When we feel the need for love, we should go to church."

"That's not where you went. You went to death row in a women's prison. Perhaps Jesus led you there."

He could keep his voice steady, but he kept shoving fistfuls of Wheat Thins down his throat. He said, "I am almost afraid to ask. I worry that I am sinning if I ask. But I will. Do you see the Lord, then, as a manipulator?"

"I don't believe in the Lord."

He choked a little. He cleared his throat. He said, "You blaspheme."

I didn't respond, but I held his gaze. Then he looked away, wounded, down at his Wheat Thins. Finally, he came back. "The Lord God is real. But it's not a matter of belief. It's faith. You haven't faith. I will pray for you."

"Vernon, you claim to appreciate my honesty. Faith, as far as I'm concerned, is the need to believe what those in authority tell you is true. Once I had faith in the Tooth Fairy. I had faith because when I was five years old I lost a tooth and I found a quarter under my pillow the next morning. The preposterous tale my parents told me was true. But the next year, when I was six, I made believe I was asleep so I could peek at the Tooth Fairy as she exchanged my molar for a quarter. She turned out to be my dad." Who was not a light-footed fellow. "At six I learned there wasn't a Tooth Fairy or, for that matter, a Santa Claus, and probably not a God either. Faith to me is buying into bullshit—excuse me—when you're a child and then, as an adult, refusing to accept that you were hoodwinked. By your parents, no less."

Now I waited. I expected self-righteousness and, I hoped, anger. Then I could get him to speak about Rona Leigh from the point of view of reality. Reality was the only thing that might possibly mean a new trial for the woman. But I didn't get either. I got compassion. I got a benevolent smile.

"Excuse me, ma'am, but you are wrong. There is faith and there is trust. They are not the same. But now I know something I didn't know before. I can trust you, Miz Rice. You are honest and direct. To admit to atheism requires grand courage. But Lucifer lurks within you, and I will beg God with my very being to protect me from him as he is crouching so close by. And I will pray for your conversion more fervently than I have ever prayed for anything in my life. I believe it could well be harder to save your soul than to save the life of my wife. Not her soul . . . it's already been saved. Her life is my more pressing need. So tell me exactly what you must know. Ask me and I will be direct with you. What can we do?"

"We can go to the governor with something more than redemption."

"But what else is there?"

"Two things. There is the strong possibility that she didn't receive a fair trial. I'm gathering up several pieces that I intend to put together for the governor. And another thing is the truth about the crime itself. The truth of the actual crime that might never have been considered to begin with. Vernon, has Rona Leigh ever told you that she didn't kill Melody Scott?"

His eyes grew wide. Such a question amazed him. "No. Of course not. She has maintained her guilt from the start. And then—through the grand gift of the Lord Jesus—she came to take responsibility."

"Has she ever said she didn't remember what happened that night?"

"No. She remembers each directive Satan ordered."

"Has she ever revealed a motivation for killing beyond the drugged and drunken state she was in?"

"No. When Satan controls you, there is no other explanation for your actions."

"Have *you* ever thought she didn't commit the crime?"

"I never knew the vessel she was when she was inhabited by the devil. I only know the woman she became, the woman she is today, a woman who sees a spider and won't kill it. Who asks a corrections officer to take it outside. The saintly woman my wife became once released from Satan's iron grip. Now she can't kill anything. Not even a spider, let alone a human being."

I leaned forward. I put my hand out to him, placed it over his. I said, "I'll ask you again. Have you ever thought that she didn't kill Melody Scott and James Munter?"

I could tell by the expression that came over him that he hadn't. Ever. Or maybe he never wanted to. If such was the case, I would confirm his fear that his sin

lay in the absence of any meekness. I waited. I wouldn't
prod any further.

He said, "But . . . Rona Leigh *confessed.*"

"I know. Vernon, people confess all the time to
crimes they didn't commit. They confess because they
want to be famous. Or because they're alone and confused. Because they're being threatened or tortured,
or, if they're young, they want to please those in authority. Conversely, sometimes when they're young
they need to brag about how tough they are. There are
a lot of reasons why people confess. Perhaps Rona
Leigh confessed because she had faith in the authority
who told her to confess. Faith, or maybe . . . trust."

"But who else could have done it?"

"Lloyd Bailey."

His chest puffed out. He pulled his hand out from
under mine. He found a foothold. "They were equally
guilty."

"Is she guilty if he convinced her that she'd committed the crime when she hadn't? So he could get a
lighter sentence? What if the police got her to admit
it by reinforcing what he told her? She was in with-
drawal. What if she confessed because she was
promised drugs?

"Reverend Lacker, you never answered the first question I asked you. How did she find redemption with such
ease? Perhaps the answer is because she's innocent."

He leaned way back into the sofa. Sank himself into
the cushions. His eyes filled. "Ma'am, please. She was
besieged by Satan. What difference does it make
whether Lloyd killed them or she did? She was there
with him, in the room where the killing happened.
The point is that they became one evil entity in a marriage of degradation. They had been joined by the
devil. The details of who did exactly what are pointless.
They committed the crime together."

If Rona Leigh didn't do it, he couldn't give his hero, Jesus Christ, credit for saving her.

But I had to make amends and do it fast. I said, "Pray for me."

With a stinking great heap of humility, he said, "I will."

Little son of a bitch.

❧

The warden had an office-cum-sitting room on the third floor of the house under the eaves. He was probably more comfortable in his home than in an official office. That's because he was, in effect, a plantation owner, the prison fields his land, the prisoners his chattel.

He sported formal cowboy wear: white shirt, black string tie with a silver ornament, pressed jeans, and boots. The boots were chestnut brown, the leather shiny but with a patina that muted the shine to a lovely warm glow. A nice leather jacket hung on a hook behind him, and a Stetson, a perfect sculpture, white and solid as if carved from bone, rested on the shelf above.

I hoped I'd be able to see a view of the mountain from the window—we were just high enough to see over the top of the post oaks. On the map I got from the library, I noticed that the highest elevation in the Gatesville area had in fact been something called South Mountain. Through the window, I looked south. The highest hill seemed ever so slightly higher than the second highest.

I said to the warden, "Is that South Mountain?"

"Yes, Agent, it is."

I'd say the elevation of South Mountain was maybe nine hundred inches. There was no mountain. Someone gave the women's death row its name as a joke.

Beyond the prison complex I made out a narrow line of muddy water, one of those creeks the army engineers had impounded and turned into Belton Lake.

The prison fields were surrounded by a wetland that spread out into the far distance. State School Road had been laid across a swamp, the houses on either side built on fill.

The warden said, "So you've come to speak to the prisoner."

I turned from the window. "Yes, I have. But there are a few things I'd like to know before I do."

"For instance?"

"When will she be transported to Huntsville?"

"Rona Leigh's not goin' anywhere."

"I'm sorry? I understood . . ."

"The death house in Huntsville is smack in the center of town. It's a big brick box, takes up two city blocks. The Walls. Nickname 'cause that's what you see: walls. The holding pen is in the Walls too. We've decided we can't send her to a unit where the population is entirely men. If we do they will become, let's say, agitated. The law says executions shall be carried out at the Walls. However, the wording doesn't say *women* shall be executed there, it says *men*. So we were able to get around it. Rona Leigh will die right here at her home, something all of us wish for when it comes time for our own passin'. It'll be real hard on my corrections officers. The guards. They've all come to know her. Whereas at the Walls, the boys execute strangers. So I've had to make clear to our own boys that they're just cogs in the wheels. The people responsible for the execution of Rona Leigh Glueck are her jury, her arrestin' officers, ex cetra. The governor himself.

"The holding pen is in our death house, in the same building as the execution chamber. The execution will be carried out on my turf, and I intend to do my turf proud."

He sounded like the father of the bride.

I said, "Will the details be the same? I mean, the holding pen, for example. Is it a cage?"

"Nothing could describe it better. It just arrived from the manufacturer three days ago."

"Where is the building?"

He rose and joined me at the window. He pointed.

"See just inside the front gate? The little bungalow? Used to be a rest station for the watch guards, if they needed a little nap during their break. It's been converted to a death house. It's not quite ready. End of the week."

"May I have a look?"

"Can't see why not."

He took a key from a wall safe and grabbed his Stetson. Same one that the Texas Rangers wear. He set it on his head at a perfect angle without having to look in a mirror.

Outside, we climbed into his pickup for the fifty-yard trip. I asked him, "Have you spent much time with her?"

"Yes, Agent, I certainly have. She is allowed to ask to speak to her warden. I have accommodated Rona Leigh as to all reasonable requests, just as I have accommodated yours. And that brings me to a request of my own. Strictly based on curiosity. I think I am entitled to know what your aim is here, considerin' my hospitality."

I would be honest. Why not? "Rona Leigh Glueck's defense requested information from the FBI pretrial. Through a bureaucratic laxity, they didn't get the information. I have it. I want to determine if it would have had any bearing on the outcome of the trial."

"You aim to spring Rona Leigh?"

He was half smiling at me.

"I aim to know the truth."

"Ain't got a hell of a lotta time, have you?"

"No, I don't."

"You know, ma'am, I have had to call on her many times without her askin'. I had to lay down ground rules throughout this past year when all the other do-gooders decided to come to her rescue."

I was a do-gooder. I'd been demoted from *agent* to *ma'am.*

"She isn't deserving of rescue is your feeling?"

"My feeling? My feeling doesn't enter into it. I am not paid to cross the courts, no matter what my feeling might be."

"Warden, why do you think there is such a clamor to save her? The do-gooders aren't your typical anti-death-penalty people. Many of the people who are calling for the governor to save her life support the death penalty."

"All but one of 'em: the pope. He ain't for the death penalty. But the rest of them—Pat Robertson, Jerry Fal-well, each and every member of the Christian Coalition—they are. But them and the typical do-gooders like that Morley Safer, say, or the guy from *20-20 Vision,* all those fools think Rona Leigh isn't a murderer anymore. She was, sure, but now she's a woman-aglow-with-Jesus instead. Hell's bells.

"A murderer stays a murderer, no matter what she's like years after she committed the crime. And all murderers are actors, I'll tell you that right now. Some movie producer ought to cast these killers for their pictures. A psycho can act any role he wants to. Rona Leigh Glueck has spent every wakin' minute playin' a part. That sweet-as-molasses smile a hers? An act. You ever see a picture of that Catholic statue, ma'am? The one with Mary holding Jesus across her lap after they took him down from the cross?"

"Yes." I didn't say I'd seen the statue itself. "The *Pietà.*"

"That's the one. Who built that?"

"Michelangelo."

"Right. I was readin' about that statue one day in *Christianity Today*. Long time ago, someone asked Michelangelo why he'd given his statue the face of a young girl. And he said that the mother of Jesus was chaste, a virgin; he was a Roman Catholic, after all. He said, Therefore she don't age.

"Rona Leigh, at her trial? She was still in her teens, but she had the face of a played-out, drugged-up, alcohol-sodden, hooker killer, which is what she was. Inside a few months, once Rona Leigh was dried out? She didn't want to be in prison anymore. She figured it would take a miracle to get her off death row. So that's what she decided to go for: a miracle. Honest to Pete, she put on the face of the actual mother of Jesus, like Michelangelo's statue. No lines, no wrinkles, pure white skin, and she's stayed the same even now and she's no spring chicken.

"I'm sure you know, ma'am, the power a psycho can call upon. Besides that power, she was able to make the most of her hookin' skills to create something a lotta johns paid good money for. She became young, innocent, a darlin' child who could pray with a sincere and heartfelt fervor.

"Now, ma'am, you're FBI. I know I can't shock you. So I'll tell you that not long after she got here her sister came to visit. Rona Leigh had the corrections officer tell the girl she was too busy prayin' to have any visits. Sister raised a little fuss so I got called over—girl was goin' on about how she'd come all the way from Houston and Rona Leigh wouldn't see her. Girl told me her sister's prayers were nothin' but fake. Said lots of times the johns'd make 'em kneel in prayer, their eyes lifted to the heavens, their hands folded. Have them recitin' the Lord's Prayer while they was—excuse me—fuckin' 'em up the ass. The sister said Rona Leigh sure knew how to pray good. Real good. They all do. Hookers, I mean.

"In my mind, Rona Leigh has played that role, on her knees, eyes lifted to heaven, prayin', managin' to fool 'em all, for seventeen years. And you want to know somethin'? She hasn't slipped once. Hasn't lost her cool, hasn't got mad, hasn't told us all to go do somethin' unmentionable to ourselves when each of her appeals to the board was tossed out. I admit I thought she would. In fact, I thought she'd end up like a pig on a wet deck, slippin' and slidin' back to what she was.

"But who knows? Pat Robertson is a highly educated man. Maybe he's right, but I don't think so. My feelin' is that Pat Robertson is a fool just like all the rest."

Warden had feelings after all. All right to have them as long as they don't stray across a court's verdict.

The bungalow was right next to the gate. It was no more than twenty feet from State School Road.

The same four cars were in the lot. The warden said, "This here's where the corrections officers park. There's a big lot for visitors back up the road at the main entrance to the complex, and that's what the media'll have to be content with, come Rona Leigh's date. We have shuttle buses for visitors, but the newspaper and TV folk are goin' to have to walk." He smirked to himself, probably imagining Morley Safer made a fool of.

I said, "You're going to have a crowd right outside these windows, aren't you?"

"The windows have shades. The night of the execution, we'll put up barricades at the end of the drive to keep the protesters and the cheerleaders out."

He pressed the bell at the gate. The guard who came out was the same one I'd spoken to earlier. The warden introduced him to me.

"I already had the pleasure." I shook hands with Captain Shank.

The warden looked at me from beneath the exquisite curve of the Stetson brim. "You been by here already, Agent?"

I would be Agent in front of the underlings.

"I came here first. I thought your office would be in the . . . unit."

He and the guard caught each other's eye. They both laughed. Captain Shank said to me, "We don't put our wardens in the death house." Then he turned back to his boss. "I love these Yankees, I surely do." They laughed some more. I joined in. I'm not a Yankee, but no Texan considers Washington, DC, as being south of the Mason-Dixon line.

The guard let us through the fence and the warden took out his key.

There were three rooms carved out of the bungalow, all in a row, identical signs on each door: OUT OF BOUNDS. Inside the first of them was the mesh cage, the holding pen, centered exactly in the middle of the room, no different from the one the men have. Rona Leigh would spend the end of her life like a zoo animal.

We walked back out to the hallway and went in the next door. It was the death chamber, and it was set to go.

The slim cot was the lone object in the room, its two paddles extending straight out at right angles, solidly primed to embrace its victim. A final embrace.

There were no such paddles on the first cots. But they would become a necessity. It's hard enough to get an IV drip into a relaxed still arm, let alone a flailing one. When I'd watched a condemned man secured to an identical cot and paddles, the whole scene took on the feel of a new-age crucifixion. Crucifixions for the millennium, an epidemic of them. I'd been part of the epidemic.

Now a woman would be crucified.

Seven wide brown leather straps hung down from the

cot, heavy brass buckles dangling from each. One would be laid across her shoulders, one over her rib cage, one across her hips, and one each for her wrists and ankles.

I asked the warden, "How many men on your tie-down team?"

"Regulations say five. But I'm thinkin' one guard and the medical technician'll get the job done fine. The doc and me can always help, but I can't see the need. Prisoner don't weigh but a hundred pounds."

Directly behind the head of the cot was what once had been a closet. The door was narrow and, just to its left, an opening had been chipped out of the cinder block. They'd put a plate over it with a hole for the IV tube. The nurse would be behind the door so she wouldn't have to stand next to the prisoner while she killed her.

We went into the closet. There was a stand for the IV bag, a cupboard for the bag itself and for the tubing and syringes. Next to the cupboard, a little refrigerator.

"For the chemicals?"

"We're expectin' those any day."

"Who checks the expiration dates?"

He smiled. "You ain't lettin' me forget I got a big-time agent from the FBI here as my guest, are ya? Don't you worry, Agent, I'm sure that detail will be taken care of. Chemicals'll be kept in my office until they're transferred here. Check the expiration dates myself, how's that?"

I smiled back. "Where's the computer?"

"We're hands-on in Texas."

Maybe my jaw fell, I don't know, but his smirk was a little expression of victory for him. No computer. No line of keys to tap in order to release the parade of poisons.

I said, "The nurse will use a hypodermic? Directly into the IV line?"

"That's right. Wouldn't want a computer with some kind of virus in it giving the condemned the flu."

A big, big grin.

I said, "You've never been in command of an execution before, have you?"

"No, I have not. But I've witnessed my share, and I intend to see that in Texas we give all killers the same treatment, men and women alike."

We left the little closet.

We went back into the death chamber.

One wall held a large window that looked onto the witness room. There were new draperies tied back on either side. Immediately after the condemned is pronounced dead and the doctor declares the time of death, the curtains are drawn shut. The witnesses do not see the body bagged. During the days of electrocutions, the draperies were introduced because it was deemed necessary to begin preautopsy procedures right away, there in the death chamber. The speculation is that the immediate start to the autopsy became a priority in order to kill the prisoner when 2,000 volts didn't get the job done.

The warden said, "We're still waitin' on the folding chairs."

Another departure. "Chairs?" At executions the witnesses simply crowd up to the window.

"All's I need is for someone to faint and crack his head open. Once I saw a witness faint but someone caught her. I'm takin' no chances."

"How many witnesses can Rona Leigh have?"

"Six."

"Has she chosen them?"

"She's got five so far. But she can change her mind right up to the last. The men don't change their minds. We'll see if there's a difference. With a woman.

Since, as we all know, a woman's prerogative is to change her mind."

He was still smiling, his hat still angled so perfectly, string tie neat and black against the white shirt, just a touch of embroidery at the pocket.

I was now officially sick of Wyatt Earp.

"May I see Rona Leigh?"

"Sure can."

We went out and crossed the small yard to the main building. I didn't ask why we weren't driving.

Instead, I sprang my question when he wasn't expecting any more of them.

"Warden?"

"Yes, ma'am?"

"Seeing as how Rona Leigh never slipped once, have you ever considered that she might not have done it? I mean, I know you're not paid to cross the court's decisions, but maybe such a consideration doesn't quite do that."

He stopped. He pushed his Stetson back one inch with the knuckle of his forefinger. "And what would be the point of my considerin' any such thing?"

"Point? No point. But did it ever *occur* to you?"

He folded his arms across his chest. Captain Shank at his post gave us a sideways glance. "Truthfully, ma'am, there were a couple of times I *wished* she hadn't done it. This is a real tricky business we got happenin' here. We are usherin' in an era of executin' women. Lotsa red tape and headaches. I got enough ribs on the fire without wonderin' whether any of my prisoners committed the crimes they were found guilty of. I say again, I respect the justice system of the great state of Texas."

"But have you—"

He held up his hand, palm in my face. Maybe he'd begun his career as a traffic cop.

"Enough, ma'am. Enough." He turned on his heel. I followed him.

And I wondered about the comfort that lies in faith. I wondered how comfort could possibly override consideration of the truth.

I felt my heels digging in a little further.

Before the warden left me, he said, "Agent, the woman is a killer. She's a psycho, and as far as I'm concerned she's downright brainwashed."

"Who'd have brainwashed her? Her husband?"

He hooted. "That little boy? No, ma'am. Mind, now, their marriage was not consummated. To my mind it ain't a real marriage. No conjugal visits on death row. Ask me, even Rona Leigh wouldn't want to do it with that pinhead. So here's who brainwashed my prisoner: She brainwashed herself. All that self-help business. *I am a good person. People like me. I like me. I am no longer in the hold of Satan. I am a saint.* Damn them all."

He looked at his watch. He was almost through. "Rona Leigh has finally become the character she's acted over all these years. Brainwashed into thinkin' she's the RC virgin. Now let me ask you somethin', Agent Rice of the FBI, 'fore I take my leave. What do y'all want from us? The law don't account for any presto-chango killers. Gal may sound like a saint, might act like an angel. But it don't make her any less a killer. Innocent people are dead, and they were made dead at her hand. The court has spoken."

"The court didn't get all the evidence that could have been made available to them."

"Who says?"

"I do."

He took me in. "But you, ma'am, are an outsider."

4

I was an outsider, but I wasn't bound to rules and regulations when it came to visiting a prisoner in Texas, though Corrections Officer Captain Harley Shank thought I might be interested in knowing what they were. Shank was inside now, a different guard at the fence. Positions had shifted. He handed me a pamphlet to read while I waited for Rona Leigh to come out. There were two categories: what visitors were not allowed to wear and what they weren't allowed to bring in. First category: no hats, belts, sweaters, jackets, vests, coats, boots, hair ornaments, or jewelry. Within that category also fell handbags, briefcases, bags, cameras, and computers. Second category: no food (including gum, candy, and drinks); no medications, cigarettes, cigars, newspapers, books, magazines, paper of any sort, pencils, pens, gifts, or money.

I put the pamphlet down on the ledge in front of me. The Plexiglas was spotless, the metal mesh embedded within it as thick as chain link. The room was wired for sound. This would not be a private conversation.

Shank escorted her in. She was manacled, ankles and wrists, and she wore a bright orange jumpsuit. When Shank got her seated, he walked a few feet away and took up a position behind her against the wall. She wiggled her fingers at him and he wiggled his fingers back, and then she turned to me.

Most people have three names, but only a certain class of Southerners goes by all of them. Miss America will never be Jane Doe because southern girls win. She'll always be Jane Laureen Doe. I was reminded of that when Rona Leigh and I greeted each other. She smiled and said, "Please call me by my first name."

Fine. "I'm glad to meet you, Rona. I'm Poppy Rice."

And she chirped, "Begging your pardon, ma'am, it's Rona Leigh."

I said, "Excuse me. Rona Leigh."

Her skin was indeed as smooth as marble. But Michelangelo notwithstanding, the sun hadn't touched her face in seventeen years.

She said, smiling, "I don't know why the FBI has sent someone to see me. I just spoke on the phone with my husband, and he said, 'No, Rona Leigh, the Lord sent her.' He said that if you feel I have truly repented, you will make a case for me to the governor."

I apologized again. "I'm sorry, that's not accurate. I will make a case to the governor if I feel there is evidence that you didn't have a fair trial."

The smile, which reflected curiosity, became benevolent. "Though I appreciate the effort you are making, I can tell you right now that I did evil. I deserve to pay for my crime, Miz Rice, an eye for an eye. But all the same, God has singled me out. He wants to make me an example—that in delivering to us His only Son, in sacrificing Him, He meant to teach us repentance and forgiveness. He meant to give us an alternative to retribution."

"That really has nothing to do with the role I see for myself. I know that . . ."

She leaned forward, still smiling. "I only know this: If there is still some chance that our good governor will spare me, I will spend the rest of my days in prayer and praise of the Lord and in work for good causes."

I looked into the lovely eyes of the condemned and asked Rona Leigh Glueck why she thought she had been chosen, why she thought she should be spared.

"I cannot question Jesus but only put myself in His mighty hands. When we give our lives over to the Lord, we must trust His judgment and not question it. I thank Him every day for my fate. I thank God for the gift He has given me. I know in my heart that the Lord Jesus never makes a mistake. I must follow where He leads me.

"He has allowed me to understand there has been reason for my tribulations. Just part of the path I have had to travel so that I could reveal His blessed message. I don't understand what you think you can do for me, but God has told me to listen to you. Ma'am, at first I told my husband I didn't see the purpose in havin' a visit with you because even if you find some mitigatin' circumstances that mean I shouldn't be put to death, it will be of no use. You may be the FBI, but you ain't Texas. I hold no hope that anything you find will sway the parole board or the governor when it comes to paying for the crime I committed."

I would try to get her to see where I was coming from. "Rona Leigh, I'm not talking about mitigating circumstances. What if there is something of substance? Something that might shed suspicion on the decision to convict you?"

"Well, then, they'd kill me all the faster. Matter of pride. But none of that matters. I'm not innocent. I did it. I have taken responsibility for what I have done, even if you find that some lawyer forgot to enter in a piece of evidence." She turned to Captain Shank. "Ain't that true, Harley?"

He nodded. "It is."

"Why don't you explain it to the agent for me?"

Shank walked to the Plexiglas and stood next to her chair. He said, "Ma'am, this is a state where even if you was fourteen and mentally retarded and you killed somebody? Forget it. You're dead as a can a corned beef. Why, in the old days, somethin' like that happened? It was considered a little bitty oversight. Police would have brought the slow-witted child back home and bid his daddy and mama to put a few extra locks on the attic door. But now? You fourteen and don't know how to cross the street without help? And you get ahold a your daddy's peashooter and kill the mailman? Why, you goin' to find your butt smack on the rookie end a death row. We got a coupla gals here can't tie their own shoelaces. Not that they got shoelaces to tie."

I looked from Shank to his prisoner. I wasn't there to be humored.

"Rona Leigh, I am considering *actual* innocence. I am not speaking about mitigating factors or legal errors. The file we have contains discrepancies which could lead to evidence—"

"Miz Rice, I have no chance for another trial no matter what discrepancy you dug up. In Texas you got thirty days from your conviction to come up with new evidence. Tomorrow, if fifty witnesses came along and said they was lookin' through that motel window seventeen years ago and the girl that killed those two kids wasn't me, it'd be too late."

I said, "The law giving you thirty days can be tested. If the evidence is not new, if it has been there all along. . . . I see that as your lifeline to the governor. I want to get that reprieve, a new thirty days. That's all we can try for."

She put her elbows up on her own ledge. Her little hands had been in her lap. Now they were out there, dwarfed by the wide cuffs. She said, "Here is the lifeline that Vernon and I see. Although we will continue to rely on prayer, continue to hope that the governor listens to Jesus, we are not going to put aside other ways that Jesus might place before us.

"You are a woman in power. You are from the FBI in Washington, DC. We're thinkin' that maybe you got ways to get the governor unstuck from the path he has chosen. You know. . . . What's the word? You could intimidate him. By throwin' him off his stride, you could maybe convince him that he has made a serious mistake in refusin' to consider my plea for clemency."

Intimidate the governor. Wonderful. "Playing games with the governor is not my plan. If justice was not served in your case, the rest of us weren't served either. I want to go to him with something substantive. Realistically—"

The smile interrupted me. "My husband thinks you might be my only chance to live. My story ain't pretty. But the things that make a young girl a maniac? When those things are taken away, when she's cut off from them, then the girl's essential nature *can* return. Vernon says the Lord wants to show the governor that repentance is kin to DNA. He says the governor needs to know that if there was a test like that on my essential nature, the test would show I am not the Rona Leigh Glueck who killed two people seventeen years ago."

I imagine the flabbergasted look on my face brought on by the new and ever-so-condescending smile.

"See, Miz Rice, Jesus has given me back the DNA that was taken, and I am beholden. In His name, I will do whatever He asks me to do. Vernon says Jesus has asked me to give you my heart so that you can bring it to the governor. He wants you to make the governor understand the woman that Texas wants to execute is already dead."

Sometimes, even I can be rendered speechless.

"Ma'am, I was born with drugs and alcohol in my DNA. My mother put whiskey in my baby bottles so's I'd sleep. I did hard drugs, me and my mother and sisters together, from the time I was conceived. Then she introduced me to her johns. Drugs and alcohol and havin' sex as a child transformed my nature. Poisoned my DNA.

"Through Jesus' love I have recognized what was stolen from me and have gotten it back, because Jesus is by my side. I battled Satan so's I could find out who I was before he fouled me in my mother's womb.

"By trusting in the Lord Jesus, I have found that person. I am not a killer. I am not a drug user. I am not a drunk. I am not a prostitute. That was someone else. I am not that other person anymore. I am born again."

She spoke with enormous conviction. She'd become a preacher. But the tone, the woeful tone, was one I'd heard before: the tone of a convict who needs you to understand that he or she didn't kill anybody, rob anybody, rape anybody, slash anybody's face.

I said to her, "Even if the woman I am talking to now represents a rebirth, there are people who have suffered as much negligence and abuse as you have—more—who *didn't* grow up to become prostitutes or addicts, let alone killers. I need to convince the governor with facts, not a sob story. Excuse my harshness here. We need to—"

She leaned forward. "Harsh? Ma'am, harsh don't bother me none. Jesus has stepped in to protect me from harshness. Jesus wants you to be my witness. The woman you are looking at is innocent. The Rona Leigh I once was has been vanquished by my acceptance of Jesus Christ as Lord and Master. Jesus has baptized me with His love. He has helped me to root out that other Rona Leigh. I am sorry for what these hands have done. But these hands are now clean, *clean*. Washed by Jesus, may I be forever deserving."

She held out her hands to me to see how clean they were, her delicate hands. Then she pushed her chair back. "I don't understand why you have chosen to make this effort for me. I have confessed my crime. I—"

She would never understand. "Rona Leigh, yes, you have confessed. But a confession doesn't mean you did it."

Her eyes opened wide just the way her husband's had. What an amazing thing for anyone to say. She smiled down at me. She said, "Exactly right. Exactly what I been tellin' everyone. I confessed, but I didn't do it. Satan did it." She straightened her back. "Tell the governor I am a *lady*. I now have the DNA of a lady, thanks to the Lord whose arms enfold me now. That is what will sway the governor. Never mind your facts. The governor is a Christian, a good Texas boy. He will not kill a lady."

And she took on an air of remove, a haughtiness. Indeed, she was a lady, the kind of lady recognized in such places as Texas. We don't have them in DC. Just like we don't have the hairdo.

Captain Shank stepped forward to escort his prisoner back to the other ladies on death row, and she flashed him a beatific smile. The little creases that had come into her forehead in the last ten minutes melted away. All aflutter, she said to him, "We will pray for this peace officer today, Harley. She will crusade for us with Jesus by her side."

He said quietly, "Amen," and they were gone.

Was she utterly deranged? At least now there was no doubt in my mind that she could well have been set up to kill, was convinced she did kill, and then agreed to sign a confession. But derangement didn't matter, as Captain Shank had made clear.

I checked out of the Holiday Inn and into the Best Western. I put my stuff in the closet, in the drawers, into the bathroom. And then there was a knock at the door. I opened it.

A Texas Ranger filled the doorway, Nick Nolte in a white Stetson.

He said, "Max Scraggs. May I come in, Agent?"

"How did you know I was here?"

"My job."

"What job is that?"

"The job to see this execution through. To see that chaos doesn't break out. But if it does, we want you to know that there is someone on the scene you can turn to."

My, my. "Come on in."

I invited him to sit down. He took the chair. I took the edge of the bed.

I asked him, "What the hell are you talkin' about?"

"I'm talkin' about this. Every day, more and more people are turnin' up to support Rona Leigh. She's becoming some kind of holy martyr. Now, turns out, we got a big-time FBI agent in town who could maybe give them the hope they need to cause us some serious trouble. But you're doin' your job and that's that. If trouble breaks, you need a cop? You come to me. If some other trouble of a more personal nature gets aimed your way? Trouble from people who don't like the thought of Rona Leigh bein' a martyr, embarrassin' people? I want you to know we will be happy to be of assistance, ma'am."

He stood up. He touched the brim of the Stetson. "You need a cop for any reason whatsoever, come to me."

I suppose I might have told him to watch the tires of my car. But instead I thanked him and he left.

I could see that I'd reached a point in my day where

I needed to talk to a familiar voice. So I called my assistant. It was quarter to five, her time.

"You checkin' on me, boss?"

"If I were, I'd be calling twenty minutes from now. The day you answer the phone at five after five, I'll know it's time for me to race back there and take your temperature."

My assistant's name is Delby Jones. When I interviewed her I asked her why the name on her social security card was not Delby Jones. She said, "You were actually the first to notice."

She made up the name, she said, when she was a singer. She left the band because that line of work wouldn't pay for Pampers and the complete works of Dr. Seuss. The name Delby Jones had grown on her.

I liked that. Imaginative way to clear the past out of your system while still holding on to the dream.

In addition, Delby has great reasoning skills and can keep a boss, an office, and herself finely organized. Mostly, she doesn't miss a trick. Impeccable instincts. So in the end, her terms were worth it. Her terms meant she'd pick up her girls at our day care every day at one minute past five. And besides the five o'clock thing, at one minute before noon, she leaves to have lunch with them. Once, the President was in my office and so was she. She cleared her throat to serve me notice that it was the children's lunchtime. The President ended up going to the day care center with her. Like me, he knows that the value of devotion is much more visceral than loyalty. So off he went with Delby while the Secret Service scrambled into formation and followed. I was left with a couple of technicians staring at their backs. After lunch, the President said to me, "I forgot how good a peanut butter and jelly sandwich can be." Delby told me he'd left his carrot sticks on the plate just like all the kids.

Now, on the phone, she said, "You want to know something fast, right?"

"I do. But first, real quick, did that fabric sample I gave you, let's see . . ."—I looked at the notes on my computer screen—"number eight-four-two, did it come back?"

"'Course it did. You'd be here kickin' ass for a week if it didn't."

"So what was that stuff?"

I heard her clicking away at her own computer. By the time I'd finished the question, she had the answer. She's like that guy Radar on *M*A*S*H*.

"Let's see. We got mostly sugar, gelatin, fumaric acid, an artificial flavoring agent, disodium phosphate, sodium citrate, couple of coloring agents—yellow five and blue one—and BHA. Says here, the only thing differentiating the sample from lime Jell-O is a woven elastogen agent." Then she hmphed and said, "Well, I am really pissed off now, boss. Don't it kill you that lime Jell-O has no lime in it? I ain't buyin' it anymore."

"Me neither. When I get back, I'll make us some gin and tonics and we'll throw in a couple of genuine limes apiece."

"And when might that be?"

"Could be tomorrow, at the rate I'm going."

"Tomorrow? That's good to know. People never can understand why I don't have your schedule. I tell 'em, Because you don't know it yourself. For example, how come you're not at the Holiday Inn?"

"Found someplace better."

"Okay."

"How much time have I got?"

"Thirty seconds."

"Delby, can you send me everything there is on two of the guys I had reassigned? The two who ended up in the Houston office?"

"Sure."

"I mean, can you do it now?"

"Honey, it'll get done. You sure you don't want me to know where you are? I just got through tellin' an agent from the Waco office to quit pesterin' me, and I'd let him know where you are as soon as you call in."

"Send the stuff I need to the hotel where I'm supposed to be. The pest can do his own work. And thanks, Delby."

"Welcome. And where'm I sendin' the lime Jell-O analysis to?"

"Nearest trash can."

"Right." She hung up.

It'll get done meant she'd order someone else to do it as she ran out the door. Someone unlike herself who was always looking for work after hours to avoid going home to where the hard work was.

⁂

Joe found me. He always does. I wondered if he'd met a cop named Max Scraggs when he was camped in Waco.

I said, "Joe, those edible underpants you bought me?"

"Yeah?"

"You'll be pleased to know they were really edible."

"I could have cared less."

"I know. I was worried all the same. I tested the residue. Lime Jell-O."

"I hope the taxpayers find out about that test."

"Me too. But there's something else you should know."

"What?"

"Jell-O doesn't have real fruit in it."

"There's a right time for junk food."

"Listen, I might come home tomorrow. I hope we can get together, okay?"

"Okay? Nothing could make me merrier. So did you see Rona Leigh?"

"Her, the chaplain at the prison—her husband—and her warden."

"How'd it go?"

"None of them want to discuss the possibility that she might not have committed the crime, not even her."

"How come?"

"Cowed by Texas law. The thirty-day rule. Do you know about that?"

He said, "The law is a deliberate one. A lot of feeling out there that a few sacrifices have to be made since, as we all know, the death penalty lowers the crime rate."

"Out where?"

"Out in any roomful of men when they're in their Jurassic dinosaur-hunting mode. Kill a few marginal ones, if that's what it takes to eliminate the bad ones. They say things like that when there are no women around to point out that they're all a bunch of ass-holes."

"Joe?"

"Yeah?"

"When did you become a feminist?"

"At that dinner at the White House. The night Kool and the Gang played."

The night we met. Joe was a he-man. But the night that Kool and the Gang played the White House he told me twenty thousand things that revealed his soft side, one of which was that the death penalty was capricious.

"Poppy, it says in the Post this morning that William F. Buckley thinks the death penalty is appropriate because murder victims deserve respect and dignity posthumously."

"How does the state killing a mentally retarded

teenager give anyone respect and dignity? William F. Buckley is, always has been, and always will be full of shit."

"Well, that's what I thought when I read it. What's the matter, Poppy? Why so hung up lately? What the hell is bothering you?"

I chose not to tell him about the letter I'd gotten a couple of weeks ago. "I don't like this."

"What *this*?"

"This execution. Rona Leigh. . . . I mean, she thinks she's an angel. She is angelic, really. Joe, I do believe the governor might well have given her a stay if she was about to be electrocuted rather than euthanized. Or if she were going to be hanged or stood up against a wall to be shot. The clean lines of lethal injection are what is preventing the stay. So maybe if we're going to have capital punishment, it should be messy. When you throw a switch that sends a zillion volts of electricity through a live human being, the witnesses can smell hair burning. And the reason for the blindfold is that poached eyes explode. People think blindfolds lend a note of glory—the romance of the firing squad. Women being executed ended firing squads. Mata Hari steps up, takes off her clothes, and where are the guys supposed to aim?

"This upgrade to death by injection. Finally there's a way to kill where the condemned only feel terror, not pain. Therefore the gender issue is gone. She'll just close her eyes and fade away."

"Poppy—"

"You know why all those priests and bishops and Puritans loved burning women at the stake? Because their clothes burned off first. They got to see naked bodies incinerate."

"So it's all connected to sex. Executing women."

"Yes. Therefore, you can't do that kind of thing to

someone who looks like Rona Leigh. Who looks like an angel. Maybe if they shaved her head and starved her first. . . . Joe, she's a *lady*. She told me so. You don't force a lady onto a table, tie her down, and kill her. That's what all those people coming to her rescue have been trying to cram down the governor's throat."

"Ergo?"

"I think the man is probably so angry he's thrown out the baby with the bathwater. I'm beginning to wonder what I'll do if he won't even consider actual innocence."

"You'll just have to threaten him."

"Excuse me?"

"Tell him you intend to carry on the investigation even if he doesn't grant the reprieve. Even if she's already been executed."

"But that goes without saying."

He laughed. "Not to him, I'll bet. Listen, darlin', I've got beepers going off left and right here. I have to run."

"Wait. Joe, I shouldn't come back. I've got too much to do here."

"I was thinking you'd come to that conclusion. I miss you."

"Well . . . turn off your beeper. Make a little time for phone sex."

Silence. Then he laughed. "Beeper is now off. Ladies first. You just close your eyes, honey, and lay back in my ever-lovin' arms."

Joe has the right sensibilities. I do love our long meetings of the minds followed by our meetings of the bodies, even if we have to settle for such meetings via the wires sometimes.

He was damn good.

I watched the *Evening News* live, for a change. Pat Robertson was interviewed. He told Dan that Rona Leigh Glueck was a lady.

I called Max Scraggs and invited him to dinner. I needed the Texas law after all.

He said, "You happy with just edible food, or do you need real food?"

"Real."

"Good. I just got to Waco. I'll have somebody bring you here to a restaurant I have in mind. When can you be ready?"

"I'm ready."

"Five minutes. You'll hear a knock on the door."

The young cop who drove me to the restaurant in Waco told me he knew of me. I thanked him for the compliment.

It was a German restaurant.

Scraggs said, "Some Bavarian prince was given a chunk of land by the Republic of Texas in exchange for—I don't know—the cachet. One of his descendents opened this restaurant. We have even more diversity than meets the eye, Agent."

"Poppy."

"Poppy. The descendent is a great chef."

The great chef came to the table to greet his steady customer. Scraggs introduced me and then said, "Just fire your best meal on us, Billy."

I said, "I'm glad his name wasn't Hansel. I can only take so much diversity."

Immediately, a waitress banged two mugs of beer on the table.

"Hope you like beer."

"I do. Officer—"

"Scraggs. Max. Whichever."

"Scraggs, I thought you might have some advice for me. Here's what I'm dealing with. Rona Leigh Glueck—

and, as of tonight, Pat Robertson—claim she's now a lady. She says that being a Christian gentleman, the governor will grant her a reprieve if only he can be convinced of this conversion—from lowlife to lady—in addition to the one he already knows about."

Scraggs said, "The governor may be a Christian gentleman, but that doesn't give him scrambled eggs for brains. Beer'll taste better if you chug it."

I'd been sipping. I drained off two inches. He was right. "I want this case reopened. I'd like it reopened before she's executed. I have evidence he needs to see. I need him to understand that I'm coming to him with facts, not bullshit."

"He won't see you. No matter what you've got."

"How do you know that?"

"Man told me as much."

"What?"

"Ma'am. . . . Scratch that. Poppy. Here's what it's like. The governor of Texas is a figurehead. Our legislature meets four and half months every two years. During the other nineteen and a half months, the politicians do their politicking while they're bellying up to the nearest bar. That's where—"

"Hold up. They meet how often?"

"You heard right. The legislature carries out business off-season, and the governor isn't invited. The virtual governor is the president of the state senate, elected, not appointed, who leaves the ribbon-cutting and ambition toward national politics to the figurehead. Then the senator knows he'll be rewarded—maybe a cabinet position. His most important job is to make sure the governor looks good, dazzles in the klieg lights, and he also makes sure he doesn't have enough information about laws and legislation to say anything wrong."

"I find this astonishing."

"We don't blast the information from the rooftops."

"Scraggs, the governor's big thing is that condemned prisoners in his state have not been denied access to the courts. He always says that in the past tense because they only have thirty days after conviction for access."

"And that loophole is closed tight. Try your dumplings."

All right. I took a break. I ate a dumpling, best one I've had since I was in Munich. "What if I show him that her original access to the court was made null by corrupt evidence, make clear that I'm not looking for clemency, just a reprieve. To give us a chance to look more closely at justice denied her."

"The man believes she's a cold-blooded killer. She dies in . . . let's see . . . nine days. He sees no point in listening to what you might have to say. He wants her dead, plain and simple."

I ate another dumpling. I said, "Scraggs, how do you get rid of your garbage in Texas?"

"'S'cuse me?"

"Landfills?"

He laughed. "In Texas? Use our *range* to let *garbage* sit and rot? We incinerate it."

"When I flew into Waco I wondered what the layer of brown was. Now I know. Anyway, I'm just going to have to threaten him, then."

He stopped chewing, even though his mouth was full. I disconcerted him and now I leaned into his face.

"You can tell that governor of yours I will continue my investigation even if Rona Leigh is executed. And if I show actual innocence, that she was innocent of the crime she died for, then his political aspirations beyond the present biannual four-month leadership of the state of Texas will end up in the nearest incinerator."

He chewed some more and he swallowed. He chose to hold his temper. He did allow himself to be a bit caustic, however. "Ma'am, even if I was your messenger boy, which I'm not, I couldn't make such a threat on your behalf. Governor won't see me either. He's in seclusion at his ranch—until after the execution."

The dumplings were gone. There were chunks of some kind of meat in front of me now. I stabbed one of them and put the whole thing in my mouth. I couldn't taste it. I tried to hear Scraggs's talk about the fine autumn weather. Neither of us enjoyed the following five courses.

He drove me back to Gatesville himself. He said, "You wanted my advice. Here it is. Pick another condemned killer. Governor's got too much at stake here. He's got political reasons for seeing to Rona Leigh Glueck's death. You're from DC. You know how it is. Politics rules."

I said, "Only if you let it. You made your choice, I'm making mine."

I guess I'd have to call our goodbyes icy.

⟋⟋⟍⟍⟍⟍⟋⟍⟋

The next morning I called my director for what I hoped would be better advice than what I'd gotten from Scraggs. I expressed my frustration. "Sir, how can the governor seclude himself? I mean, what if twenty witnesses suddenly turn up and say Rona Leigh didn't do it?"

He said, "Politics. The governor's washed his hands because he knows there won't be any twenty witnesses turning up. There won't be one. Last-minute phone calls from the governor as the prisoner is about to breathe his last only happen in the movies. Nobody's going to hear from that guy unless the press gets wind of something juicy."

"Got any ideas?"

"Yes, as a matter of fact, I do. I've just heard from

our office in Waco. Seems they're having trouble with car tires."

"Who told you?"

"My man in Waco called me because they wanted you to know that the two guys from your lab were not involuntary transfers. When things got crazy in DC they asked if they could return to their former stomping grounds, which happened to be Houston. I cleared that with Delby. She remembered that you actually liked the two guys but you could tell they were burnt out so you wished them well.

"I asked Waco why it was so important for you to know about the burnouts, and that's when they told me about the nail in your tire. They've concluded that some guy in the lot meant to change the tire and got involved with something else. So here's what I told Waco. If we so much as *think* someone is trying to stop you from looking into this matter, I'm going to the governor myself. But in the meantime, if you decide you have something to take to the man, here's the number to call. Soon as you tell the fellow on the other end who you are, the governor will at least talk to you."

What a guy.

"And Poppy?"

"Sir?"

"Had a chat with Cardinal de la Cruz. He wants to speak to you."

"Don't tell me someone else is dipping into the till."

"I don't know. He said it was a personal matter. Here's his secretary's number. Meanwhile, you watch your back."

5

I'd found Cardinal de la Cruz to be an intriguing man. His lineage might have been the family-tree diagram on the first page of an epic historical novel. On his mother's side, it traced back through Queen Isabella to the Moors; it was her branch that ended up in Cuba. The cardinal's father had been Batista's Minister of Culture, meaning he kept Havana's casinos and sex shows up to snuff. The night Fidel took over, Batista saw to it that the de la Cruz family was on the first plane out, right after his own. In Miami, Signora de la Cruz continued the job she'd begun in Havana—praying for her son's vocation. Her prayers were answered.

The cardinal's secretary was very friendly, still grateful to me on behalf of the Archdiocese of New York. After a minute of general gushing, he said, "His Eminence would like to ask a favor of you."

Did they think I was now at their beck and call? The priest read my mind.

"He doesn't need you to investigate another matter. The favor has to do with the work you have undertaken on behalf of the condemned woman Rona Leigh Glueck."

I wondered how many people my director had mentioned my work to. The priest read my mind yet again.

"Forgive me for not being more forthcoming, but all

I can tell you is that we learned of your work via an angel. The cardinal, as it happens, is in Texas right now. He will celebrate the marriage of his niece at the cathedral in Laredo, the city where the girl's family lives. A private matter no one will hear of until they read the society pages the next day.

"His Eminence wonders if it would be possible for you to meet him there. He regrets having to ask you to go out of your way for him, but he feels it is an urgent matter that he wants to discuss with you face-to-face."

"Laredo. On the Mexican border, isn't it?"

"Yes. It is a very personal matter that has been on his mind, and he is in a dilemma. He feels he could make a sound decision if he exposes his thoughts to you and would respect your opinion on the matter. He could go to others, but this same angel is telling him that you are the one he needs. He begs your indulgence, Miss Rice."

I said, "Actually, talking to him might help me in a dilemma I find myself in."

"I will pray then that both of you will benefit from such a respite from your physical labors."

Then he blessed me in the name of the Father, Son, and Holy Ghost.

I called Delby and told her I needed a handle on the cardinal's Texas connections. She faxed me a bio.

Post-Cuba, the de la Cruz family spent a dozen years deciding exactly where to settle permanently. They tested out their European properties for a while, making their greatest effort in Madrid, but never felt at home there. After all, it hadn't been home for three centuries. Then they'd spent several years in Mexico City but realized that what they missed was their countrymen and finally decided on the newly burgeoning metropolis formerly known as Miami, now Little Havana. But Beltrán's oldest sister had started school in Mexico City and begged her parents to allow her to stay on. Since Señor de la Cruz still had business there, illegal but productive, he thought it might be a good idea for a member of the family to be retained across the U.S. southern border. Years later, when that segment of his enterprise petered out, Beltrán's sister emigrated once again, this time to Texas—to Laredo—and married a man who was now the mayor. The approaching wedding of her daughter was in fact making the newspapers, not because the cardinal would officiate, which was being kept secret, but because his niece was marrying the first baseman for the Houston Astros, who happened to be a recent Cuban refugee. Cubans are a tight group.

I found I couldn't get back to Waco the same night so I told the clerk at Best Western I'd be away till the next day but that I was keeping the room. She said, "Our cleaning staff does enjoy hearing news like that."

The flight from Waco was two hours.

In the early evening, Cardinal de la Cruz met me in an anteroom off the lobby of La Posada, a hotel across the plaza from the Laredo cathedral. Like the cathedral, the hotel was old and dowdy, but it was festooned with flowers and lights in the Mexican tradition. He fit me in during the time the wedding party was dressing. I guessed it had taken only minutes for him to dress, as he was wearing the robes of the Franciscans, his order. That meant he looked like Friar Tuck rather than a prince of the Church. No miter or gold-embroidered vestments. Instead, he was covered in brown homespun tied with a rope and wore a pair of sandals on his feet. I told him I didn't know cardinals could do that. He smiled at me and said in his cosmopolitan accent, "There is no one to question certain decisions of mine but the pope, and he is in Rome."

There were two guards stationed at the open doorway of the anteroom, and they managed to keep everyone out except for five little flower girls in white tulle appliquéd with lace butterflies, their heads wreathed in hydrangea. They flitted in around the legs of the guards, who looked like a pair of colossi trying to rein in fairies. The cardinal encircled the children in his arms and his gaze, blessed them, and shooed them off toward their mortified parents, now standing in the doorway. He smiled and gestured to them, and the parents knew enough to come in, kneel, and kiss his ring. Once they'd slunk away, little girls in tow, he said, "It is divine that you and I start our discussion in a moment of innocent beauty and purity. Ironic, too."

I waited.

"Miss Rice, I see myself as having been assigned an important mission, one completely unexpected but certainly fulfilling a long-held wish. In recent days, God has called upon me to demonstrate the strength of a morality that lies within the teaching of the Church, a morality swept to the side, out of sight, by many. My issue has to do with the Church's stand on the death penalty. We are strongly, very strongly, opposed. We are opposed to the taking of life, any life, all life, whether it is the life of an innocent, such as an unborn child, or the guilty, such as a murderer incarcerated. Upon my investiture as cardinal, God bestowed upon me a clear duty to see that Catholics understand that in condoning the death penalty they commit an act of accessory to murder. And so I have been meditating over the past few days while in this lovely place."

He looked into my eyes. But of course I had nothing to say. Not yet, anyway.

"Miss Rice, I need you to be my messenger."

"Not to God, I hope."

He laughed. "I have plenty of messengers for that purpose. No, to Rona Leigh Glueck."

I didn't understand.

"You have been speaking with her, is that correct?"

"Yes."

"I want you to ask her something on my behalf. I want you to ask her if she will agree to my acting as her spiritual counselor. I need you to explain to her that I am doing this not out of personal humility, I am ashamed to say, but rather at the command of the Lord."

I got it. "You need a bully pulpit, Eminence. In addition to the pulpit on Fifth Avenue."

"Exactly so. It seems an ideal way to remind Catholics that they must join those who are just now realizing it is wrong to support—even to show enthusiasm for—the death penalty. Catholics are required by doctrine to be in strong opposition rather than act as rooters. Catholics should not be the last to give voice to the truth that executing killers does not deter killing but adds to it, an unpopular opinion, which until recently seemed inviolate. Catholics should have been the first to voice this truth, but if they are the last . . . well, I'm sure you know what Jesus said about the strength the last might find in their laxity."

He looked up to the Lord and then to me. "And also, I admit to curiosity. Miss Glueck says she has found Jesus. What those words mean to me is that she has done penance and Jesus has forgiven her. To Catholics, it is Jesus who finds *us*, not vice versa. The sentiment is the same, though.

"I want to examine what is required for God to bless a killer with His forgiveness. If that is what has happened, it would be an enormous privilege to ease this woman's journey from this life to the next. And if she didn't, as she puts it, find Jesus—if it is all an act of self-preservation—perhaps she will allow me to help her let Jesus find her as she faces the state's retribution.

"Finally, Miss Rice, so that you understand my strongest attraction to this mission, I am simply continuing the Lord's directive to visit the infirm and the imprisoned, which I do regularly in my own parish."

He slipped his hands comfortably into the folds of the brown homespun. He was through.

I said, "Your Eminence, I will be happy to give your request to Rona Leigh, along with your reasons. I assume that's why you told me what they were. You want her to understand them."

"Yes. Again, I am grateful for your clear-sightedness. And since you are so clear-sighted, I know you will wonder why I did not choose to say all this to you on the telephone. It is my lack of humility. I thought you would perhaps be more successful in your own mission as well as mine if you permitted me to personally bestow upon you the blessings of Jesus Christ our Lord so that you may succeed in your own efforts."

He took his hands out of the folds. He put his right hand on my head and blessed me: Father, Son, and Holy Ghost called into action yet again in the space of a very short time. And then he said, "Go in peace," and offered me his ring. I kissed it, and when I lifted my head, he said, "I have complete faith that you will find the necessary path to pave my way and your own as well."

That meant he was giving me permission to carry out whatever manipulating I'd have to do in order for him to use Rona Leigh to his own purposes. Realizing that, lights began to flash in my head.

"Your Eminence, if Rona Leigh agrees to your request, would you give me the opportunity to tell the governor of your plan? Before *you* let anyone know about it? If he hears it from me rather than from an aide reading the news to him from the morning headlines, I will have the advantage I am looking for in convincing him that Rona Leigh's case should be reexamined."

It was hard to tell what went on behind Beltrán Cardinal María de la Cruz y García's eyes. They were pitch. He asked me, "What is the advantage you hope for?"

"His agreeing to grant me a meeting with him."

"A meeting on Rona Leigh Glueck's behalf?"

"Yes."

He smiled. The black eyes twinkled. "We both know the weight a face-to-face appeal provides. Once, I said to you that I hoped I could do a favor for you as you had done for me. I believe I can grant you what you ask. We are on the same wave, are we not?"

"Wavelength."

He laughed. "I acknowledge and appreciate the correction. I wish more people had the—now there is a better word than the one I was about to use—the *chutzpah* to correct some of my mangling of my second language."

And then he stood, thanked me, and went off to preside at his niece's wedding.

Well.

I was ready for a drink. The bar at the hotel had been taken over by ballplayers. I let one of them buy me a margarita. I considered scouting them, but they'd all be off to the wedding shortly. As they knocked down their drinks, a few told me to come along, they'd find room for me, but crashing weddings was not appealing, so when they had to leave I went up to my room instead.

My view was the Rio Grande and the walking bridge to Nuevo Laredo. In the last light of evening, the border guards were changing shifts. The new ones were bringing fresh German shepherds out of their kennels. I watched as a dozen or so Mexicans on the other side shed their clothes, hung them on branches, and waded into the water. I waited for the whistles and bells and barking to start. But the border guards ignored them.

They were not crossing the border illegally, they were bathing after a day's work in the United States.

There were no fences, no barbed wire, no anything. In fact, beyond the hotel was a little playground on our side. There were probably so many illegal immigrants keeping La Posada and all the rest of Texas running that any effort to keep the Mexicans out was a show. The sun had set. I was bored.

I went outside to the plaza, bought a guava ice-cream cone, and sat on a bench with two maids from the hotel. The night was warm and humid. We watched the wedding party come out of the hotel entrance serenaded by a mariachi band, the little flower girls fireflies now, darting about in the glow from the hundreds of strands of lights hanging from the trees. The bride on her father's arm had on a Mexican wedding gown, flower-bedecked, flounced, and banded, her long mantilla no doubt passed down from Isabella herself. The mayor's tuxedo was impeccably tailored, elegant in contrast.

Her mother was the tallest woman there and wore black: a pants suit with flowing white lace collar and equally flowing cuffs dripping down from the bottom of her narrow sleeves. The lace covered her hands but not the gleam of her rings. Her heels were so high she towered. There was no question that if Beltrán de la Cruz's sister had been born a male child, the family could well have had two cardinals.

I always cry at weddings, relieved with my decision never to marry. Just the way I get misty-eyed when Delby brings her girls to the office on Bring-Your-Daughter-to-Work Day. They put their plastic barrettes in my hair. They keep me stocked in nail polish. I adore them. I also know I would no more consider lunching with children down in the day care center than going for a swim in the Potomac.

I wiped the tears from my cheeks and the ice cream off my chin with a Kleenex one of the maids passed along to me.

Much later that night when I woke up at 2 A.M. and didn't have a tape of the news on me, I went back to the hotel bar. It was empty except for one of the ballplayers, who apparently hadn't been in the mood to dance till dawn. I took a stool.

He said, "Whatcha drinkin'?"

I said I'd have a Grey Goose on the rocks and one of whatever he was having.

He said, "You like to mix and match, darlin'?"

"It's a good way to get to know a stranger."

He said to the bartender, "We'll have a C.C. Manhattan and two Grey Geese on the rocks."

He wanted to get to know me too. He was depressed. He was on the fifteen-day disabled list. After we'd enjoyed some conversation, laughed, we went to my room.

Disabled, my eye.

༄

I woke up the next morning happy to find the ballplayer was no longer in my bed. He'd left a note on my pillow, though. *Sometimes you get lucky and make a connection. Thanks.* He was right. On the road, once in a blue moon, the night turns out to be not so lonely.

Before I got myself back to Gatesville, I called Delby to see if anything of note had come in.

"Found a big development soon as I walked in the door."

"Go ahead."

"That dispatcher from the Houston cops made an anonymous call to us last night about three A.M. Must think we're ninnies. Told the office that the guy who called the Thirty-first Precinct twice on the night of the ax murders was the victim's husband. Name, Gary

Scott. Owns a dive called the AstroBar in Houston. When the murders took place he only worked there. Then it was called Pee-Wee's. Think the dispatcher's got the guilts?"

"I wonder. Or maybe he likes stirring up shit."

She said, "Or office politics. Needs to get even with someone. We'll never know, though. Thought you were coming back today."

"I thought so too. Things have gotten interesting. I'm thinking I'll visit the scene of the crime: Houston."

"Wondered when you would decide it was time. I'm smellin' progress. Good luck, boss."

I got out my map. Three hours to Houston. I'd drive.

I opened my laptop and keyed in to Yahoo. Tried AS-TROBAR. Nothing. Tried PEE-WEE'S. I got one response, an article in a Houston alternative weekly called *Badass Houston*. Three years ago *Badass Houston* hailed Pee-Wee's as serving the most dangerous food in all Houston—in all Texas, they'd bet. The food column read:

> *We doubted the ribs we ate at Pee-Wee's had been refrigerated before they were tossed on the grill. Tasted like wild boar, not that we've ever had wild boar. The charcoal grill was not vented to the outside, another reason we use the word "dangerous." If the food doesn't kill you, the fumes will.*

The food critic suggested going to the bathroom after dinner, sticking your finger down your throat, and throwing up. Then he added a disclaimer:

> *Be aware that the bathroom is the outside rear wall of the bar with a spigot that's two feet off the ground, unconnected to any water source.*

He concluded by advising diners to drink their beer from the glasses rather than out of the bottles, even though the glasses were filthy.

> *We couldn't help but notice the rain of mouse droppings stuck to the beer caps.*

Definitely time for a foray into the Houston demi-monde. Time to torment the puppeteer. Maybe Delby's and my reactions were a combination of the dispatcher's motive. Maybe the dispatcher felt the way I did, had a need to shake up a guilty party who had avoided getting his hands dirty.

∽∽∽

Front door to back, the AstroBar was maybe twenty feet long and not more than ten feet wide. There was the bar and the line of stools. One small table was jammed into a corner. A pair of unmatched chairs stacked one on the other were on top of the table. Line-dancing was out of the question in this Texas bar, and movie stars rode mechanical bulls elsewhere. I was actually hoping to see one in person, since I've always been fascinated by a twenty-year-old forensic mystery just recently solved—and by one of the geniuses I hired myself. Autopsies performed on Texas males from age eighteen and up have revealed a preponderance of healed and unhealed hairline fractures of the thumbs. That's what happens from hanging onto a mechanical bull for dear life.

Besides the new name, no charcoal grill. *Badass Houston* needed to update. Food, I observed, was limited to the yellow sludge that plops out of a heating machine onto a cardboard nest of tortilla chips. On second glance I was wrong about that. The machine was unplugged. Didn't work. Someone has to clean those contraptions now and again or they get gummed up. This one had been overloaded once too often. The cracked dried-up overflow of gunk, now orange, coated the outside of the machine as well as the sur-rounding counter space.

And *Badass Houston* never noted the supply of liquor behind the counter. The bottles lacked a single recog-nizable label. If I were drinking, I'd probably have been unable to resist Neck Oil American Whiskey. I did see vodka. The bottle's simple green label read Potato Vodka. Amid the liquor sat a radio. Forced to identify the music coming out of it, I'd try *easy country church*.

The back wall of the bar was a tattered curtain. An otherworldly blue glow showed out through the rips and tears. A tanning bed had been installed in the bar's storage room, and someone was using it. Cowboys who aren't real cowboys, the ones who feel more at home in bars rather than where the deer and the an-telope roam, pay a few dollars at places like the AstroBar so they can look like they'd just moseyed in from the range.

There were four of those men leaning on the bar, choosing not to sit on the stools. Only three had on cowboy hats, the other an old Houston Oilers cap. Didn't accept the loss of the franchise. The heads didn't turn toward me as I came in the door. It took them a few seconds before they registered an alien presence, and then their conversation stopped and they about-faced together. Their weapons weren't con-cealed.

I got myself on a bar stool and I said, "Are any of you Gary Scott?"

First all four snickered. Then one said, "Nope," two gestured toward the rear curtain, and the fourth called out, "Gary, you got a customer here."

The blue light went out. A minute later a fellow

parted the curtain while buttoning his shirt. He didn't
have on a hat. He had instead large hair, black, blown
into the shape of either the *Niña,* the *Pinta,* or the
Santa María, then lacquered into place in a patent-
leather shine. He was very tan. He said something to
me as he made his way behind the bar, but I had no
idea what it was.

"Mr. Scott?"

Now I got just a grunt, but it seemed affirmative.

Gary leaned over directly into my face and smiled.
Teeth, white and even. Not the originals. He spoke
clearly now. "You're the prettiest reporter so far. What
paper you from?"

The cowboys and the nostalgic football fan watched
intently.

I said, "I'm from the FBI. My name is Poppy Rice."

I made sure my jacket fell open enough to reveal the
black leather strap leading to my own weapon. "I'm
looking into some irregularities concerning the prosecution of Rona Leigh Glueck."

I flashed my badge instead of my ID card.

"You with the FBI?"

My stepfather used to have a pet peeve. When he was
mowing the lawn the guy next door would make a
point to come out and say, "Mowin' the lawn?" It made
him crazy. I've inherited a lot of my stepfather's tics.

I slid the badge out of its case and held it to his nose.
The men at the bar tried to see it too. I put the badge
back and flipped the case closed.

Gary came out from around the bar, walked past me,
untangled the two chairs, and dropped them on either
side of the table. He said to the men, "Anybody comes
in, get him what he wants." And he said to me, "Ma'am,
you can join me right here."

I slid off the stool and joined him. He wasn't going
to ask if I wanted a drink. He took a pack of Newports

out of his shirt pocket, shook one out, and didn't offer me one of those either. He lit up and threw the match on the floor. Finally, he squinted through his smoke and he said, "Here's about the only thing I got to say to you or anybody else about Rona Leigh Glueck. One week from today, when I'm settin' in that jail they got up by Waco watchin' her die, I'll be experiencin' the best five minutes a my life."

He dragged on the cigarette and blew smoke out of the corner of his mouth, one small gesture of consideration, perhaps.

"Mr. Scott, what will be accomplished through Ms. Glueck's execution?"

He sneered. Picked off a bit of nonexistent tobacco from his tongue. "Wish all the questions I been gettin' were that easy." He dropped the cigarette to the vicinity of the match and squashed it under his boot. Decided not to let smoking distract him from his point. "Here's what executin' *Ms. Glueck* will accomplish. My little girl'll get to give *Ms. Glueck* exactly what she got comin' to her."

The riff he'd developed for any media person who would listen to him had been worked out to its most dramatic potential.

"Melody, my wife, the gal whose heart that little bitch laid open, will be standin' up there next to Saint Peter—and maybe Jesus too, if He can make time—just waitin' on *Ms. Glueck* with an ax of gold. Before the devil can drag *Ms. Glueck's ass* down into hell with him, Melody'll chop her up from here to kingdom come. Then she'll—"

"So you're telling me that revenge and punishment are the reasons Rona Leigh should be executed."

He said, "Excuse me, ma'am, but what other reasons might there be?"

"Deterrence, for one. Do you feel that the threat of lethal injection deters crime?"

"You mean would it've kept the bitch from cuttin' anyone else if nobody'd caught her?"

Gary didn't know the difference between deterrence and recidivism.

I said, "Not exactly. I mean the theory that executing murderers might make others think twice before killing someone. Warn them as to what would happen if they did. Scare them off. Would her execution serve to do that?"

Now he laughed. The guys at the bar, louder. Gary explained the theory away very carefully to be sure I understood. "Well, little lady, let me tell you the way that goes. See, when somebody gets your goat and you want to smash their nose on up into their brain, you don't stop on it to think, *Hey, I might get myself executed for killin' this sacka shit.* Damn foolish, is what I'd say. What do you boys say?"

He held up his hand as if leading a band and the cowboys responded with vigorous nodding, with the Oilers cap adding, "You got that damn right!"

I lowered my voice, but not low enough to exclude the cowboys from the conversation. "Melody was cheating on you, isn't that right? I mean, on a regular basis, not just the night she was killed."

In a single motion the enthusiastic men at the bar wiped the grins off their faces and turned away.

Gary said, "What Melody or me was doin' would be no business of yours."

"I mentioned I was looking for irregularities. Why was Melody sleeping with James Munter if she was married to you? I mean, shouldn't I assume . . . ?"

He leaned forward. "Assume nuthin'. And I don't appreciate nobody takin' a crap on my wife's name." I didn't get a *ma'am* this time.

"It's actually more a matter of understanding the connections rather than any intention on my part to insult your late wife. Was there a connection between you and Lloyd Bailey? How well did you know James Munter? And what about Rona Leigh, was she a friend of yours? What makes you so enthusiastic about watching Rona Leigh die for your wife's murder when she was killed while in bed with the other victim? Some men might think a wife—"

"My wife wasn't cheatin' on me, you hear?"

"Melody and James were just having a sleepover the night they were killed?"

The cowboys hunched up like a row of vultures. Gary leaned forward. So did I. We were nose to nose.

"Now you listen up. We keep to different ways down here from what you tight-ass Yankees got. You ain't got no right struttin' into my bar like you was the goddamn queen of—"

I said, "You would agree with our former President then? That sex isn't necessarily sex?"

I could smell his breath, that foul odor of tobacco with hints of Listerine. Drinkers like Gary love Listerine, as it's nearly half alcohol. He said, "As a matter of fact that's about the *only* goddamn thing I'd agree with him on. Gettin' a blow job ain't nuthin' but showing a bitch who's boss. A lesson you could stand yourself is something I'd lay good money on."

I breathed back on him. "Then what about the woman deriving sexual pleasure through oral sex? From a man who's not her husband. Would *that* be cheating on her part?"

He leaned away and folded his arms tight across his chest as if to contain the urge to smash my nose up into my brain. He stared into my eyes. He said, "Eatin' pussy is for braggin' rights. And about now, honey, you are beginnin' to make me hot. *Real* hot. So how come talkin' about fuckin' don't seem to bother you? It would bother a Texas gal. A Texas gal might be a A-One piece a ass, but she don't try to talk the way a man talks. You want a chance to show me you're as good as you talk?"

I stood up. "If ever you find employment with the FBI and, say, if someone kills me? Then you can go out and ask around if you want that information. I appreciate your time, Mr. Scott." I grasped a straw. "One more thing, though. I'd like to ask you about where you found the money to buy this bar?"

He jumped up and knocked against the table. "You can just get the hell outa my establishment right now. I don't have to take shit from you. Since you ain't got your storm troopers with you, you heed my words or you'll be wishin' you never came within a mile a me."

I was at least six inches taller than Gary Scott. It was plain why he'd changed the name of the bar. The blood that had risen to his face had turned his tan purple. I strutted out of his establishment like I was the goddamn queen of wherever.

I waited at the corner, three empty storefronts or so down from the AstroBar. I glanced at my watch every thirty seconds and kept looking impatiently up and down the street. Just an average everyday woman waiting for a ride. I don't know if anyone noticed my performance since there wasn't a soul to be seen and not a single car came down the dried-out edge-of-Houston road, where clumps of dirt and bits and pieces of litter blew along the gutters. There were only the five pickup trucks in front of, beside, and on the dirt in front of Gary's bar. My car, which I'd parked around the corner, was out of sight.

I didn't have to wait long. One of the cowboys came out of the bar. He got in a truck and headed my way.

Cowboys in Texas are basically blind. Either too

much squinting into the sun or not bothering to wear goggles when stretched out on a tanning bed. This cowboy was directly in front of me when I stepped out into the road. He spotted the hundred-dollar bill I was holding at chest level just the way limo drivers at airports hold up their riders' names. With the new bills, it's much easier to spot Ben Franklin than it used to be. The truck scrunched to a stop.

He leaned over to squint through the passenger window and smiled at me. He said, "Needin' a lift?"

He threw open the door and I climbed in. The cowboy plucked the bill from my hand and stuffed it into his shirt pocket as efficiently as if he did this sort of thing every day of his life.

I said, "Why don't we drive around a little, and then you can take me back to my car. It's around the corner. I just want to talk to you about a couple of things I didn't get from Gary."

He said, "Fine by me," and he shifted gears and rumbled down the road. His boots were red.

I said, "I'm going to name some people. I'd like you to tell me what you know about Gary's relationship with each of them."

"Shoot."

"Melody Scott."

"She's dead."

"I already know that."

"She was Gary's wife."

"What about her?"

"She decided to marry one short, ugly, no-'count loser because it was the best way to show her daddy what she thought of him."

"What did she think of him?"

"Figured he reined her in just a little too tight. If she married Gary, maybe he'd give it a rest. Worked just like she thought. Her daddy cut her loose. Melody was freed up."

"Did Gary know her reason for marrying him?"

"Could a cared less. Pretty piece a ass at his beck 'n' call was fine with him. 'Cept Melody was at everyone else's beck 'n' call too."

"What about James Munter? And I already know he's dead."

"He was nobody. Melody picked up guys just to rile Gary. James was a retard. Couldn't teach a hen to cluck."

"Lloyd Bailey?"

He laughed. "Him too. Put to bed with a pick and shovel."

"Right."

"Lloyd was just one of a buncha guys, come in, buy whatever junk Gary's got on hand. Till he met Rona Leigh. She recognized that Lloyd did okay for hisself. Lloyd was one of those people, dumb as a sacka rocks, couldn't read or write, but he worked on vehicles, see? He could fix anything wrong with any truck, car, or bike you brought by him. And he was fast. Listen to your engine for five seconds, tell you what you needed by way of parts, then you bring him the parts plus your own tools and he fixes your problem. Right out on the street. People'd say if Lloyd crawled under your rig and then you looked under it, you wouldn't see hide nor hair a him. He'd be wrigglin' around inside the engine like a worm in a Snickers Bar.

"Boys was willin' to pay Lloyd for his feel and his speed. All you had to do was find him. And if he was in the mood, needed a few bucks, you counted your blessings. Besides good and fast, he was cheap. Lloyd had no overhead and he was America's guest."

"What does that mean?"

"Didn't concern himself with the tax man. But once

Lloyd took up with Rona Leigh, he gave her every cent he had, every cent he earned, to do with as she pleased, so long as she'd quit hookin' and just service him. Rona Leigh knew a good thing."

"Why'd they kill Melody and James?"

He smiled. "All Lloyd wanted was his chopper back. Got stolen a few days before. But that night, when Lloyd stood next to James's bed holdin' the ax over his head, James told him he never stole no bike. Then—too bad for James—he insulted Lloyd. Big mistake. Lloyd was one jumpy little stud. You didn't want to cross him. Temper like a basket a snakes. Man had no rudder, I'll tell ya. And when Lloyd was drugged up and you crossed him? Well, you just took your life in your hands.

"That night, James made the most biggest, god-awful mistake a his life. I don't know what he coulda been thinkin'. 'Course, he was a halfwit, so he probably wasn't thinkin' at all. And he was in the middle a fuckin' Gary's wife so he mighta been a teeny-tiny bit distracted."

"How do you know all this?"

"Heard it from someone who visited Lloyd. In prison."

"Lloyd tell his lawyer any of this?"

"'Course not. He said the only thing he could say. That Rona Leigh made him do it."

"He thought that would get him off?"

"So they told him. Get him a life sentence, insteada what he got, is what they told him."

"That obviously backfired."

"Yeah, it did. Still, we all thought the jury would take pity on him. But the jury figured you want to accuse someone of stealing your bike, you do it man-to-man, not while the guy's in a position that would make some other guy look bad. When he's fuckin' the other guy's wife, ya know?"

Of course. "Lloyd basically killed Melody because she was a witness, then?"

The cowboy didn't bat an eyelash. "I don't know as he much cared about that. If Melody'd gotten outa there, she wouldn'ta said nuthin'. I suspect it was just a case a her gettin' caught in the crossfire."

"But he did kill her?"

"He did."

"Rona Leigh didn't swing the ax?"

He laughed. "You got to be kiddin'. She couldn'ta swung a toothpick."

"She's going to die for something she didn't do, then."

"Never said that. Rona Leigh played things a little too close to the vest. You got to watch your ass, and she didn't."

I looked out at the skyline of downtown Houston in the distance. The smog hovered just above the buildings, hadn't settled to the streets on this particular day.

I said, "So did James steal Lloyd's motorcycle?"

"Nope."

"Do you know who did?"

"'Course. Aaron Granger stole it."

"And is he dead?"

"Aaron? Hell, no. Back then, after the murders, he just scrammed outa town. James got family."

"I take it this Granger would have had reason to fear James's family."

"Better to be safe than sorry. But he's back. Things cooled off and all, when Lloyd died in prison. AIDS. Turned homo, what with no women." He looked me over. "Now can I ask you somethin', FBI?"

"Sure."

"How come you decided to come down here just to jar Gary? You got a personal stake in any a this?"

I lied. "Not personal, no. What's your name?"

"How's Chuck?"

"Chuck's fine. One more thing, Chuck."

"Shoot."

"Why did Lloyd think James Munter stole his bike?"

He banged his steering wheel with the heel of his hand and hooted. "Now that's the question I been waitin' on you to ask! Wondered when you'd make it around to gettin' your money's worth. See, that there part of it, that's the funny part. Melody was a piece a work. When Melody let it be known that she was about to take James out back and fuck 'im, Gary was pissed. But when he figured the two of them had took off together Gary was like to kill her, just how you said it should be back at the bar. She'd crossed the line. Everyone was laughin' at him. In his face matter of fact. Big joke.

"So Gary calls Lloyd, tells Lloyd that the man what stole his bike was presently fuckin' his wife. Told him the guy's name was James Munter and where to find him. Gary knew Lloyd would stop whatever he mighta been doin', go to James Munter's place, and find Melody in James's bed. He figures when Lloyd beats the hell outa James, it'll give Melody the shits. Maybe Melody'll take a few licks too.

"But like you said, FBI, it backfired."

"How do you know Gary called Lloyd?"

"The guy owned the bar back then? Even more of a shrimp than Gary, shaved off at the pockets. He heard him make that call. Not the only one, either. But Gary didn't want Melody knocked around bad, just wanted to put a scare in her. So he tells Lloyd that Melody has the hots for him. Man! Just one more fuckin' backfire. Gary forgot about Rona Leigh. No girl would even look at Lloyd once Rona Leigh teamed up with him. *Whoo!*"

"You just said Rona Leigh couldn't have swung the ax."

"That's right. She got Lloyd to whack Melody."

"Chuck, how do you know that?"

"Don't. Educated guess."

"One last thing."

"You got it."

"Where'd Gary get the money to buy the bar from Pee-Wee?"

He stared straight out at the road.

I took another hundred-dollar bill out of my wallet and held it out. He took it.

"Gary inherited the money."

"From who?"

"From his dead wife, who else?" He removed his hat so he could slick back his hair, the world's most nervous gesture.

"And who knew that? Everybody?"

He turned his face toward mine. He squinted. He said, "I didn't."

"Did Gary know he'd inherit money from his wife when she died?"

He looked back to the road. "See, ma'am, that's the one thing no one wants to know. No points for knowin' that. I ain't stealin' your money, neither. No one knows. Matter a not crossin' the line."

"Which line?"

"Which line? You learn anything a-tall in FBI school, ma'am?"

Yeah, I did. Follow the money.

6

I called Rona Leigh's warden, asked if I could see her the next day.

He said, "Her dance card is full. You can come on by, though. She asked me if I'd heard from you. I expect she'd see you in a minute. I'll call you back."

He did. I could see her next morning at ten.

It was late afternoon. I headed toward the airport. As the plane lifted and became immediately engulfed in smog, I asked the man in the string tie next to me what the governor intended to do about the pollution in Houston. He said, "Shoot it."

The clerk at the Best Western said, "Cop's been lookin' for you. Ranger."

"A Ranger? Well, then, I guess he'll find me."

～～～

The next morning I arrived at the Mountain View visitors' lounge fifteen minutes early. There were a dozen people there, all reporters. Rona Leigh was presently with two guys from *People*. Soon as the prison van arrived back with them, I'd get shuttled to the bungalow.

Rona Leigh now lived in the pen. Unlike the men on death row, she wouldn't be transferred the day of the execution. Another executive decision by the warden. He told the press he had to consider his other girls, how riled they'd be on that last day. Didn't want them to see Rona Leigh marched past them. Goodbyes would send them out of control. So he'd snuck Rona Leigh out when they were asleep.

The *People* people stayed past their allotted time. I went outside when the van came into view. I recognized the reporter and his photographer. The photographer specialized in crime. He'd taken my picture several times.

Instead of hello, I said, "You guys are on my time."

"Hey, Poppy Rice. Rona Leigh gave your time to us."

"Promised her a cover, didn't you?"

"Sure."

"It'll come out before the execution, I take it."

The reporter's name was Frank. Their top dog. "Comes out in two days."

Three days before the execution, the spiritual adviser arrives. The cardinal would coincide with the *People* magazine story on Rona Leigh. Perfect.

Then Frank said, "Just to piss you off further, she eliminated the guy before us so we got his time too."

"Who?"

"U.S. News and World Report."

I got up on the shuttle steps. "She knows which side her bread is buttered on."

Frank said, "Tell us what she says to you, and I'll put in whatever the hell it is you're doing here. You got an angle you want publicized, just say the word."

"Hang around. There's a good chance I'll have something for you."

"Something new? If not, I'm gone. Story has to be in the hopper at midnight. I'm telling you, I feel like I'm working for the fucking *Wall Street Journal* on this one. Our Rona Leigh deadline is tight."

The photographer, taking my picture, said from behind his lens, "That's 'cause *she's* got a deadline."

The van started to move.

The corrections officer riding with me was Harley Shank.

"How's it goin', Agent?"

"All right. How's Rona Leigh?"

"Not that great."

As he led me across the grass he said, "She's gettin' a little crazy. I'm real glad you're here. She feels you're a special friend to her, Agent, sent by the Lord. Her only other friends are the girls on death row, and they can't help her anymore now that she's in the pen."

I suppose there was no harm in letting the woman think my purpose was to help her rather than support the Constitution.

There was a window cut into the wall of the room with the holding pen where there hadn't been one before, a chair in front of it for me and another one on the other side for her. Rona Leigh was in the cage crying. The guard inside opened the cage and she stood and came out. This room wasn't wired; we each had a phone receiver. I picked mine up. She sat down and did the same.

I said, "Hello, Rona Leigh."

She sniffed. "Hello, ma'am. S'cuse me." She took out a Kleenex. "That man from the magazine asked me how I'd felt when I packed my things. What things? I told him I had no things. I have a bar of soap. He asked me how I was goin' to feel on my date. How I'd feel when the needle punctured my arm."

"I'm sorry."

She began rubbing her arm where the needle would go in.

"I tried to stay strong for Jesus, Miz Rice. I tried. Those two men wanted me to be grateful that they would be running my picture, but the reporter was not interested in the mission Jesus has for me."

"How did you answer his questions?"

"I didn't. I just kept explaining the divine plan Jesus Christ has chosen. I kept telling him about my true self that was robbed by Satan and then given back by the Lord." She tried to blink back her tears. "I'm glad you're here. I was wishin' you'd come back, and then I figured that, by wishin' for it, I was wishin' the days away. I don't want these days to pass. I don't want to fail Jesus."

My plan had been to confront her with what Chuck told me. Tell her that no one thinks she could have swung the ax. Ask her if she recalled telling Lloyd to kill Melody. But she was somewhere else. The governor would hear it instead.

"You're not going to fail him, Rona Leigh. Jesus has sent someone who will see to it that you don't."

"Jesus?" A tear fell down her cheek.

"Awhile back I did some work in New York. For the cardinal at the Catholic cathedral. He—"

"Cardinal de la Cruz?"

"Yes. You know of him?"

Her chin trembled. "I do." Too bad the photographer was missing the visuals. "Cardinal de la Cruz wrote me a letter a long time ago. He told me he was praying for me, and he wrote out a Catholic blessing."

"I didn't know that."

"Some things I keep to myself. He didn't go to some newspaper to say he was praying for me, neither. He only told me, nobody else. I wrote back. I thanked him."

She slumped a little.

"Rona Leigh, I spoke to him yesterday."

Now she perked up. "Did he ask after me?"

"He did better than just ask after you. The cardinal wants you to do something for him."

"He does?"

She was exactly like a little kid eager to understand

what the surprise is going to be. The little kid she keeps telling everyone she never got to be.

"He wants permission to act as your spiritual counsel. He wants to come out here and be with you."

She didn't understand. I saw a look of disappointment, and I thought I saw the beginning of anger; a spark came to her eye. And then she saw the possibilities. I knew that because her back was straight again.

"He wants to stand by me?"

"Yes."

"And the governor will learn this?"

"Right away."

"He'll learn it from you, won't he?"

"That's right."

Her eyes narrowed just a bit. A flicker of distrust.

"Rona Leigh, if I can tell the cardinal you agree, I can tell the governor the same thing. And I think I'll also be able to tell the governor that in a very short time *People* magazine will break the story, which probably means the cardinal will be on their cover, not you."

She smiled. She said, "I been on plenty of covers. Only thing is, Vernon might not be too happy. He'll have to tell Reverend Robertson. Reverend Robertson was going to send a representative to advise me. But never mind. I think the cardinal is closer to God. I mean, a Catholic has to make big sacrifices to be a priest. Jesus appreciates sacrifice more than anything else."

Her shoulders rose. She grinned. "We're goin' to do this, Miz Rice, we are. With the cardinal in his backyard the governor will grant me my reprieve. I know it'll be only thirty extra days, but—well, a miracle could happen."

That's what I thought, though my idea of a miracle was not hers.

"Rona Leigh."

"What?"

"Don't tell the warden about this. The governor has to know before anyone else does."

"Okay."

"Don't tell anybody."

"All right."

She put her fingertips up to the glass, as close to a touch as she could give a visitor. She said, "I do thank you, Miz Rice, I do. Will you tell Harley I am not going to see anyone else today? I need to pray."

I turned and relayed the message to Captain Shank.

He said, "Amen," and looked down at her with great reverence.

She stood, and the guard at her side walked her into the cage.

I watched the foggy imprints of her fingertips fade from the glass.

Back at the lounge, I told Frank to come with me to the phone and listen in on my conversation. I put the receiver between our two ears. The photographer rolled his eyes. I called the cardinal's secretary. He told me how anxiously they'd been awaiting word from me.

I said, "Rona Leigh has agreed to Cardinal de la Cruz's request. She is happy he made such an offer. I will tell the warden she has consented to the cardinal's being her spiritual adviser. He will be with her when she is executed."

Frank grabbed my arm. He couldn't help himself. I asked the secretary if he thought the cardinal might change his mind, and I moved so that the receiver was full to Frank's ear. He took in the priest's one-word answer and bit his lip.

Then I said into the phone, "Father, may I be the one to break the news to the media?"

He said, "To the benefit of Rona Leigh?"

"To the service of justice."

A little pause. "Then certainly. The cardinal will not

object. But let me know when it will happen so he can have a press conference ready to go."

"It will break in two days. Hold on a minute, Father." I put my hand over the mouthpiece.

"Frank, what time will *People* hit the grocery stores?"

"When they open the doors."

I said to the priest, "The best thing would be for the cardinal to have the press conference at La Guardia, the morning he leaves for Texas."

He agreed and I received yet another blessing.

I hung up. In a strangled whisper Frank filled the photographer in, grabbed the phone, and started jabbing numbers. I pressed my finger on the little mechanism that gave him a dial tone.

"What? What?"

"Do not tell your editor who your source was, just that it's one hundred percent reliable. Have him call the cardinal's office for verification." I gave him the secretary's number.

The photographer, hovering over us, said, "Don't call from here, Frank. Call from the car."

Frank said to me, "What's this secretary's fucking name?"

"Watch the mouth. He's a priest."

The photographer said, "This is great. I get to go back to New York. I've never taken a shot of a cardinal before."

I went to Best Western and waited an hour. I called the cardinal's secretary back. Yes, the *People* editor had spoken to him. He told me he wondered at my speed. I said, "Speed is one of the things they pay me for, Father."

"We know that. It took you two weeks to find what we'd spent six months on to no avail."

"You knew someone was robbing you for *six months?*"

"I suppose we hadn't told you that. We were too embarrassed."

Oh.

I dialed the number my director had given me. A receptionist sang, "Secretary of State." I identified myself and asked to speak to the secretary. Without a hint of hesitation she asked me if she should call him out of his meeting. I told her yes, and she told me it would be just a couple of minutes. It took one minute.

"Agent Rice, what can I do for you?"

I described the news that was about to come down in two days and, no, I wouldn't say which publication, just that it was national and it was big. Then I asked him if the governor could fit in a meeting with me right away, preferably tomorrow.

He asked me where I was.

"Gatesville." I gave him my number.

"I'll get back to you."

I told him, "If I don't hear from you tonight, say by eight o'clock, I'll call the *New York Times* one minute after eight."

He didn't get back to me and neither did the governor. The governor's wife called me at seven-forty-five instead. She inquired as to how I was enjoying Texas. I told her I loved it, I'd been to so many places, and I was entirely smitten with Laredo.

She said, "Me, too!" Then, "I'm also wonderin' if you can make it down to Austin tomorrow. We're havin' a barbecue here at the house, and the governor and myself would love it if you'd join us."

Good. I was finally going to get an authentic Texas barbecue.

I went to the Best Western desk and asked the clerk if I'd have to go to Waco to get the best boots around.

"No, ma'am, you just head right into town. Man who makes the warden's boots'll make yours."

She gave me the address.

I drove into the center of Gatesville. I asked the boot-maker, "How long have you been out?"

He said, "Not long enough, buttercup."

Boots cost six hundred and fifty dollars. Another hundred for the rush.

෴

There were around forty people gathered in the back-yard of the governor's mansion, and none were uniformed guards. Just a couple of Texas Rangers in full dress stationed at the gate. I spotted another Ranger not in full dress. He was a guest. Max Scraggs. He gave me a nod.

I was surprised at the lack of security, just as I'd been surprised when I came upon the prisons in Gatesville where all the prisoners were out hoeing, unattended. Just as surprised as I'd been in Laredo, watching the Mexicans bathe in the Rio Grande. The governor's mansion had a fence around it, but it was decorative wrought iron. The mansion stood on probably an eighth of an acre of grass, and across the street a rising lawn led to the capitol, sitting on a crest. Aside from that view there was no other. The mansion was sur-rounded on three sides by soaring new office buildings.

I mentioned the lack of security to my assigned es-cort guide.

He said, "We really don't need much. I guess it's be-cause everybody round here is packin' a rod. If some cowboy with a weakness north of the ears looks like he's trying to get into the governor's house uninvited, why, the postman will nail him."

That was good to know.

The mansion was a pretty white house with columns in front and swings at either end of the wide front porch.

But it wasn't a terribly big house, four rooms down, four up, with a four-room addition in the back. My escort explained that seventy-five years ago a governor had moved in with eleven children, hence the addition. There was a basketball hoop in the driveway and a little patio where the governor's cat snoozed on one of several worn and comfortable-looking wicker rockers. The cat's fur was shaved over his backside. The escort told me the cat tended to roam and had come in a few nights ago with a couple of bites out of his hindquarters.

"A retreat injury. If his head were bitten, that would be an injury of aggression and he'd be showin' off his stitches. He's one embarrassed wimp of a cat."

Then he complimented me on my boots.

The governor came right over as soon as he spotted me. He was as gracious as he was attractive. In his forties, trim, his hair graying ever so classically at the temples. Tanned and tall. He wanted me to feel comfortable in his home, he told me. He introduced me to several Texas legislators whose wives were on the other side of the lawn, chatting. The guys did a lot of back-slapping and laughing, maneuvering me along what was pretty much a reception line until I was funneled to the wives.

Along the way I was introduced to Commander Scraggs. He shook my hand. "Nice to see you, Agent."

I said, "Likewise," and moved on.

The ladies welcomed me into the conversations about their jobs and the juggling they did to keep up the domestic ends of their lives, about politics, religion, and everything that mattered, while the boys went back to the pressing matter of a crucial playoff game.

Then we were all handed plastic bibs that said, I ATE RIBS WITH THE GOVERNOR.

Once we dug in, the governor's wife kept plying me with Handi-Wipes until she was assured I didn't mind eating ribs without the use of utensils and could fall right into sucking the sauce off my fingers along with the locals. I told her the rest of the country didn't know the meaning of barbecue. She said, "The secret is just a few blocks away. A restaurant called Stubbs. They cater, God love them. Stubbs makes our favorite sauce. If you have time, you can stop by and get a few jars to stick in your suitcase."

I would try so I could take the sauce to Joe, and he'd duplicate her feast.

The governor ambled over to us, leaned toward me, and said, "You and me will just sneak away shortly. Have that little powwow you'd like before dessert's served."

He'd do his best to blow me off in the few minutes between courses.

His wife led me to a bathroom so I could have a "scrub." Just before she dropped me off in the library—"the governor's favorite room"—she said, "You do know that the Bible instructs us, *An eye for an eye.*"

Now where had I heard that before? I was about to protest, tell her the issue I was concerned with was not the death penalty but rather ferreting out corruption. But I felt like playing her idiotic game.

I said, "I interpret that scripture as meaning a crime deserves punishment but not that the punishment should be the same act as the crime. If someone is raped, you don't rape the rapist. So I believe it should be left to the Lord concerning the ultimate punishment, since the Bible commands ten things in particular, one of them, *Thou shalt not kill.*"

Her response was a little cough. She escaped as quickly as she could, depositing me at the library door. Inside was a small antique cabinet with very old books, the bindings faded and cracked. That was the extent of the library's collection.

I went in and sat on one of the chairs across from the

sofa. An aide led the governor in, I stood, and he waved me back into the chair. Then he waved the aide out. He settled comfortably into the sofa, a coffee service on the table between us. He poured. Next to the coffee service he'd set the glass of scotch he'd carried in. It was half empty. He picked that up, rather than the cup of coffee, and polished it off.

His handsome laugh lines were now worry lines. He looked ten years older than he did while shmoozing out on the line. He took me in.

"Been enjoyin' yourself, Agent?"

"I have."

"Everyone treat you good?"

"Everyone. Your wife went out of her way."

"She can sense when to do that and she can sense when she needn't bother. She is aware that you did us one very crucial favor. Knowing news that will affect me as strongly as this will. . . . You have allowed that I will maintain the upper hand. Besides that, made me realize I shouldn't be seen as hidin' out. Time to throw a little party. So I owe you and I will listen to you. But I have to tell you that I don't expect anything you can say will influence the decision I've made. Only reasonable I should say that. I have made up my mind as regards the condemned prisoner. However, I will hear you out if you wish to proceed."

He looked at his empty glass, decided on the coffee after all. He leaned back into the cushy sofa with his cup in hand and waited.

I said, "Governor, I do wish to proceed, and I want to start by saying people in this country, as you know, have begun to feel uneasy about the escalating numbers of executions. They're feeling especially uneasy about the mounting number of mistakes. Considering the impact of DNA testing—"

"I have considered that impact. But very few people

in Texas, according to the polls we've taken, are feeling uneasy. And they certainly know as I do that there's no mistake when it comes to Rona Leigh Glueck. As their representative, my understanding of the law is that contrition is not a criterion for overthrowing a sentence of death. Contrition is not DNA. That woman is as cold-blooded a killer as ever there was. I know there are people who have decided that Jesus has saved Rona Leigh Glueck's soul and that I should save her life. They are in the minority."

I tried again. "What I'm saying to you has nothing to do with any of that. I am not here protecting Rona Leigh. I am here because, unfortunately, there is no test the equivalent of DNA that can say a prisoner was a victim of false evidence, police tampering, or a lawyer who fell asleep at the wheel. Giving such a victim a second chance at—"

"Wait right there. Giving a second chance to a condemned killer is a sign of weakness, as far as I can see. Weakness is a political liability, sure as anything. As many people as there are who need to think Jesus wants me to change Rona Leigh's death sentence to life in prison, twice as many do not. I am not a wimp, Miz Rice."

"I am talking about a reprieve, not a commutation of her sentence."

"It's all the same. People are watching to see if I am tough enough to put a woman to death. Well, I surely am." He stood up and picked up his empty glass. "Think I'll have another one of these. Care to join me?"

"Thank you. Yes."

He went to a little cabinet, took out a decanter and a glass, and poured. There was no ice around. He refilled his own glass.

He handed me the glass of scotch and sat down again. I took a sip. Man knew how to drink.

While he slugged it down, I took advantage. "Governor, I've come to learn several things about the crime Rona Leigh Glueck was convicted of, which, in other states, would be conditions for a reprieve, for a new investigation. But the reason I am here to see you personally, the reason I needed to see the governor of Texas, is because the evidence I've found would allow you to determine whether or not she had a fair trial."

He snorted. "First off, what other states do or don't do makes no matter to me. And second, I am only duty-bound to consider two factors: whether there's any doubt about the inmate's guilt—and the only doubt would arise from a DNA test—and whether that inmate had access to the courts."

"But fairness is—"

"Court says guilty, that's it. It's a contradiction to say the condemned is innocent of a crime he's been condemned to die for because otherwise he wouldn't be condemned."

I think he got the line of double-speak he'd memorized mixed up. Single malt scotch will do that.

"I'm afraid I don't understand your point."

Neither did he. "Listen, nobody raped anybody here. Nobody left their telltale body fluids behind, and what a relief that is." He raised his glass. "I believe I will drink to that fact."

"You are disdainful of the fact that DNA testing has exonerated innocent men convicted of rape and murder?"

"Maybe I am. My mama used to say you could judge a man by his friends. You're suspected of rape? Then you are probably a no-'count. If we execute a few rotten apples, a few losers who bring nothing to the society that feeds them, what difference does it make?"

He leaned back into his sofa cushions and the smirk

became a grin. The governor of Texas was drunk. He started blathering the way drunks tend to do.

"And I am perfectly aware, Miz Rice, of the rumor that Rona Leigh's boyfriend committed the crime and then put the ax in her hand. But I am sure you understand that if you take part in a crime, even if you don't strike the blow, you are just as guilty of first-degree murder."

"First degree? Only if you were part of a deadly intent."

"Intent? Girl was there, wasn't she? If some piece of garbage in prison with Lloyd Bailey goes around saying Lloyd told him on his deathbed that Rona Leigh just stood there not knowin' what the hell was goin' on, then fuck him."

I do love it when the gloves come off. I knocked down the rest of my scotch.

"Governor, I am not fool enough to come here and think I can convince you of an unproven theory as to what took place in a motel room seventeen years ago when two people were axed to death. But if you give her a thirty-day stay, I know I will produce evidence that will—"

"The paroles board grants stays, not me."

"They're your appointees. You tell them what to do."

"Listen, there's too much red tape, if you want to know the truth. We've got 459 prisoners on death row, and I can't be—"

"They'll cut the red tape on your say-so."

He squinted, took another slug of scotch, and looked at his watch. "Much as I like drinkin' with a mighty fine-lookin' woman, I am a busy man. Is there anything else you have to say? I mean, without repeatin' yourself?"

Prick. "Yes. There are circumstances surrounding the condemned that haven't—"

"Stop right there. Don't go thinking child-abuse stuff carries any weight with me. It don't give you the excuse to kill somebody once you grow up."

"Actually, she was still a child when the crime was committed."

"Not in Texas, she wasn't."

"Governor, there's an important detail that never came out at the trial."

"Why tell me about it? Have her lawyer file an appeal based on your information."

"Because as you point out we're in Texas. Thirty days has passed since her conviction, hasn't it? And legislation to change such a travesty has been vetoed three times. By you."

"You aimin' to get personal here?"

I kept at him. "No. I'm not. How do you feel about entrapment?"

"There was no entrapment during her trial." *During her trial?* "Nothing came out as to—"

"Melody Scott's husband set up his own wife to be attacked. He told Lloyd—"

He put his hand up. "All bullshit. Gossip."

"Mr. Scott knew—"

"Don't matter a damn about Mr. Scott. See, I heard it all. I am not moved. And that RC cardinal won't move me either, rest assured." He drained his glass.

"Governor, how can it not matter? Gary Scott knew he would inherit money upon his wife's death. Were you aware—"

"Hardly any money at all. In fact, peanuts. Agent, I already know everything you came here to tell me. But I will not go around granting reprieves based on the shenanigans of white trash."

"So you'll let her die even if she was set up? Even if she—"

"I can see I am not gettin' anywhere with you, Agent.

My wife has probably started serving her pies. So this is the last thing I'm sayin'. In Texas, you get arrested, you have full access to the courts, and that is all you deserve. She has lost all her appeals. The law has ruled against your killer. Her time is officially up."

"Excuse me, *my* killer? You're going to get personal with me now?"

He stood up. "You have outstayed your welcome, Agent. I suggest—"

I stood up too. "A prisoner requesting clemency or a reprieve from her governor is not exercising the right to an appeal. The governor isn't the court, isn't the clemency board, he's—"

"I know what the governor is. I *am* the governor. I will not second-guess my courts. Or my board. I leave their affairs to them."

"But it's not a matter of second-guessing. It's your *duty* as governor. A singular duty. You are the only one with the right to consider whether a punishment is fair. That's the key concept I keep trying to bring up to you: *fairness.* Even if you dislike having to be fair when it comes to white trash. Fairness isn't considered by prosecutors and judges and juries and boards. In fact there are state legislatures trying to prevent that right of the governor, trying to take it upon themselves to determine the fairness of a penalty. Now I can certainly see why. You—"

He put his finger in my face. "This is my state! Here, the law is the law. In my state, if you're fool enough to get your ass in the way of the law, then expect to pay the price. My *duty* is to see that the laws of the land are carried out. I will not stand in the way of the will of the people of Texas!"

"Their will for blood?"

He waved his glass in the air. He bellowed, "For justice!"

And I chose to speak barely above a whisper. "Governor, the slant you've chosen to take on your duty is a perversion of the power granted to you by the people of Texas, even if the people of Texas are too stupid to know where your power lies. It's a hell of a lot easier to say you are powerless than it is to *exercise* power. You are not a wimp. You're worse. You're impotent."

He started to sputter. The door opened.

Now I raised my voice. "The possibility that *my killer* is innocent flies in the face of what you rely on. Order and establishment. Because you're afraid of the responsibility inherent in the breakdown of order if it flies in the face of the truth! You don't want any part of the truth—and you're the *governor!* You should be ashamed."

He threw the glass against the wall behind my head. Shards flew. The door swung open. Men surrounded us. He pushed the closest one back and pointed his finger at me again. "Now you hear me, girl. You can go around exercising all the power you want. Be my fucking guest. But you are a fool. Rona Leigh Glueck will be executed. She has killed in cold blood. Or she stood by and watched her lover do the same. The punishment is *fair.* An eye for an eye, goddamn it. I am the Christian, not that piece of dirt. An eye for a fucking eye."

He stopped. His lips remained parted but he didn't speak. He was thinking.

And then came the famous grin. "In fact, next week, I intend to show the stuff I am made of. I will witness the execution myself. Personally. I can only hope you'll be there too so's together we can watch the woman pay for her crime. What do you say?"

"Oh, I'll be there, Governor." I ripped out my last card and played it. "But that won't be the end of it. I will carry on this investigation after she's dead if that's what I determine is required. I love exercising my power."

He squinted. Slumped a little. But he wouldn't say any more because his aides were managing to drag him out. The one who stayed behind said to me, "You'd better hope the man doesn't end up in Washington someday, because, ma'am, you'll be out of a job sure."

I had now antagonized two men in Texas to the point of hysteria, one the scum of the earth, the other a greater scum, even if he was the governor.

Max Scraggs had designated himself to be the one to get me out of the mansion via a side door. He'd put his hat on for the occasion. He said, "You mean business, don't you?"

"I always mean business."

"What are you going to do?"

I looked up at him. The curve of that brim, the solidity of a Stetson. . . .

I said, "For now, I'm going to buy a hat. Need one to go with the boots."

I stalked off. I got in my car and drove the block and a half to my hotel. I said to the concierge, "Where can I buy a Stetson?"

She said, "Boot Hill."

I guess I just stared at her.

She smiled. "The store, not the cemetery. Corner of Seventeenth and Wilson."

"How far is that?"

"Straight on down the street we're on. I'll call your car back."

"How far down the street exactly?"

"Two blocks."

I walked out of the lobby and strode the two blocks. To be in a city and have an entire sidewalk to yourself almost calmed me down.

Inside Boot Hill, the fragrance of cowboy hats calmed me further. I told the salesman I needed a hat.

He looked me up and down. "I imagine you do." Then he went into his pitch. "Now, ma'am, let me just say that a Stetson is made of felt and the best Stetsons are made of beaver felt. Would you be interested in the latter?"

I asked, "Do they kill the beavers?"

With a perfectly straight face, he said, "No, ma'am."

I put on the Stetson nearest me. I looked like the flying nun. He said, "Wrong size, for starters."

He measured my head. He said, "You have a prominent occipital bone."

He went into the back room and brought out a hat and laid it on the glass counter. It was jet black and sleek. It looked like a beaver that had just come out of the water. He said, "You need a hat like this. You'll get away with it when you wear it back east. It's a real nice style, smaller crown than a ten-gallon. And, course, it's black. I mean, your bein' blond and all."

He touched the hat gently, with reverence.

"What is it, an eight-gallon?"

He said, "It's the Gambler, ma'am."

I shouldn't take my frustration out on a salesman. I said, "I'm sorry, I was just joking."

"I can take a joke."

He slid the inside door of his counter back. Under the glass were what I thought were necklaces. They were hatbands. He lifted out a strand of small silver ovals, said, "You'll like this one," and hooked it around the hat.

Then he picked up the hat like it was a tiara and placed it on my head. He tipped it a little here and there and then studied me. "Turn around, ma'am."

I did. The wall behind me was all mirror. The Gambler was one fabulous hat. I looked very good. I turned back. "Wrap it up."

He smiled. "You know, I figured you wouldn't ask me how much. I knew that when I saw the boots comin' through the door. Other thing you need is a belt, and I got some beauties right over here."

He fixed me up with a jeans belt with various images of armadillos etched into the leather and a silver buckle with "the finest scrollwork you'll find anywhere in Texas."

Then, his turn to joke, he said, "'Course, you'll need a gun."

I held back my jacket.

He said, "Well, I am duly impressed."

He took my hat and my belt and came back with a big red-and-black Stetson box and a little bag for the belt. He held the door for me. He asked me if I had any plans that evening. No, but the man didn't quite thrill me.

"Next time I'm in town," I told him.

He smiled but shrugged. Good sport.

꿍

I headed back to the hotel, had dinner from room service, and rented a movie during which I fell asleep. The next morning, *People* magazine was out, the cardinal was featured on the *Today Show,* and the governor had scheduled a press conference for 10 A.M. Outdoors, on his porch.

So I went.

The mansion was surrounded by demonstrators protesting the execution of Rona Leigh. They were circled by a parade of pickup trucks, the drivers and riders hooting obscenities at them. The governor stepped out on the porch and horns started to blow. He smiled and waved at the pickups and the honking stopped. He bent his head to the mike and his demeanor grew serious.

He said, "I thank you all for coming here today to express the strength of your feelings concerning the sentence of death for the prisoner, Rona Leigh Glueck, which will be carried out in a matter of days. I, in good conscience, cannot grant Miss Glueck the reprieve she seeks. She has had her day in court, and she was found guilty of a heinous crime, the brutal murder of two innocents. It is my duty as governor to consider whether or not the sentence handed down to her by a jury of her peers was fair.

"Well, it was. It was a fair sentence. The most harsh sentence to match the most harsh crime one human being can commit against another. The Old Testament commands: An eye for an eye."

A woman somewhere began singing "Amazing Grace." The rest of the demonstrators joined in.

The governor raised his voice. "It is not a simple thing to put a woman to death. I pray for the clemency board who made a good and sound decision not to grant her the clemency she sought; I pray for the jury who found her guilty; for the prosecutor; and for the police officers who arrested her. I pray for her warden and for her executioner. But I pray most of all for the families of her victims.

"Cardinal de la Cruz will stand by her and pray for her as she meets her maker. And I will stand by the people I have just mentioned, the people *I* am praying for. I will stand by those heroes who saw to it that Rona Leigh Glueck would be held accountable for her crime, and I will stand by those who have suffered terrible loss. I will be there for them. I will be there *with* them. I will stand witness to the execution of the killer. I will be there at the Mountain View Unit in Gatesville when that woman's time comes—as it should.

"Thank you very much, God bless y'all, and God bless America."

Maybe if I'd worn the Gambler, my boots, my new belt, and my jeans I wouldn't have been noticed. As soon as the word *America* came out of the governor's mouth, I heard a loud *clunk*. It was the sound of something heavy coming down on my head. The *clunk* was immediately followed by an explosion. The bright Texas sun went out.

7

Not very long after the sound of the *clunk* I heard a siren. I opened my eyes. I was on my stomach, face to the side. Out of the corner of my eye I saw a video camera two inches from my nose. I tried to push myself up but hands were all over me keeping me prone while anti-death-penalty ladies kept telling me to lie still and try not to speak. I must have been trying to speak.

The paramedics broke the crowd apart, cradled my head, rolled me over, and lifted me onto a stretcher. The sun came on again. I said, "The sun in my eyes isn't helping here."

And then my eyes were shaded by a white Stetson. Max Scraggs. He accompanied me to the hospital in the ambulance.

Like the ladies, he also advised me not to talk and then he advised me once I could talk that he was the one I needed to talk to most.

The ER doctor who examined me said that with a concussion, even a mild one, it was best to submit to a twenty-four-hour observation. I told him a mild concussion was a headache. A little Tylenol and I'd be fine. Hovering above my head, he said, "Well, now, what say first things first? First, instead of shavin' a circle around that cut, I'm takin' advantage of your long hair. Lovely hair and we'll see the blood's washed out soon's I'm finished."

He employed a creative nonstitching technique, taking four strands of hair from either side of the split in my scalp and then tying a knot. He repeated each knot ten times.

He said, "Double sheet bend."

I said, "What?"

"Sailing knot. Use it when you want to be extra sure the line'll hold but look neat at the same time."

Next time I needed stitches I'd remember to ask for a doctor who owned a ketch.

While he knotted, Scraggs said, "We've got four witnesses willin' to identify the fellow who put you out. Don't really need 'em. Got the action on amateur film several times over."

I said, "Then what are you doing here? Go after him."

"We're hopin' to find him before the *Austin Constitution* gets put to bed."

"This is going to make the papers?" It wasn't a real question. I knew the answer.

"We're seein' to it that you will still be referred to as an unidentified woman. Some people, of course, will recognize you. Tomorrow is another day. So you'll have time to reveal yourself as the identified woman to those you see fit to inform."

"Thanks, Scraggs."

The doctor said, "What've I got here, a movie star?"

I thanked the doctor sailor for the compliment.

Scraggs said, "Tomorrow morning, I'm goin' to need to talk to you."

"Give me a ride back to my hotel, and you can talk to me in five minutes."

He looked at the doctor, who nodded.

Then a half-dozen stricken faces appeared in the

doorway. FBI. The locals had amassed for a fallen fellow. Behind them, white Stetsons.

The doctor looked a little stricken too. Figured he'd just closed up the head of one dangerous con. "Nurse, we are through. Let's pack up our riggin' and go where we're needed. Have an aide clean her head." He said to me, "I get a mild concussion every time the boom hits me. Hits me three or four times per sail. But hear me, ma'am. If you throw up or faint? Y'all come back." Plural. Figured I always traveled with a Ranger.

He left and I sat up. I did not wince at the pain. I said to the gathered state and federal law enforcers, "Here's the thing, guys. Whoever your infiltrators are, fire them. They're supposed to tell you things like *Someone intends to put Joe Blow out of commission.* And then you're supposed to see that Joe Blow *doesn't* get put out of commission. And, plus, you *warn* Joe Blow. Then you find out when the deed is planned for and you lie in wait and arrest the perp when he comes waltzing down the street with a big brick in his hand.

"Somebody want to tell me what the hell happened?"

Scraggs answered me. "I'll tell you exactly what happened. Your boys didn't tell mine how someone hammered a few nails in the tire of a car you were meant to drive. Our infiltrators found that out, but just a little too late to protect Joe Blow. If they had, they'd have gotten the someone before he had any chance whatsoever to take a brick to Joe Blow's head."

An agent said, "We'd figured the nail incident was in-house. Disgruntled employee."

I said, "Scraggs, what were we supposed to do? Arrest everyone I got fired?"

An aide started dabbing at my head, gently because she was an aide, not a graduate of medical school. I looked at all the downcast law gathered around. I said,

"I'm going back to my hotel. Please find the guy. I'm fine."

Scraggs got to push me in a wheelchair to his car. He never shut up the whole time. He lectured me, couldn't understand why I needed to get Rona Leigh this reprieve so bad that I was risking my life.

I said, "What's the matter with you? It's not Rona Leigh. It's all of them. Anybody who didn't get the fair shake they deserved. This is America, for Christ's sake, with liberty and justice for all, blah, blah, blah. Does it not *bother* you when you arrest someone who turns out to be innocent?"

"'Course it does. But I get more riled when someone's set free who's guilty. Just because a body maybe got a little overzealous, well, hell—"

"Overzealous? Some charlatan gives false forensic testimony to a jury? Since when is a man who commits a felony merely overzealous?"

"But to let someone off the hook? A killer who axed people to death?"

"Again, Scraggs, we're not letting anyone off the hook. You can't be sure she axed anyone to death if she didn't have a fair trial."

"You can't? I am."

"The evidence against her came from a witness who was a charlatan."

"But she admitted to the crime."

Here I go again. But I wasn't going to lecture someone who should know better. I said, "I kidnapped the Lindbergh baby. Arrest me. Then go and dig up that same charlatan and he'll tell a jury that I left my odor on the Lindberghs' front door. And while you're chatting up that so-called doctor, find out what's in it for him." I put my hands out. "Where's your cuffs?"

He rolled his eyes.

I said, "I'm overreacting because you're a disgrace to your uniform."

He pushed the wheelchair a little faster and didn't say another word. I fell asleep in his car. When we reached the hotel he woke me up. He said, "I can't tell you how glad I am you opened your eyes. You don't deserve a concussion."

The man was making nice because I'd injected a little guilt into his life.

He got me up to my room, sat me on the edge of my bed, got me two Tylenols and a glass of water. He took a couple himself. He said, "I don't know what's drivin' you, Poppy, but you have overstepped the bounds of common sense. You are actin' in an unprofessional manner. It's just as bad as my actin' in a cynical manner. So now I get to pass on some news to you. Gary Scott called us. Told us he wanted a restraining order against you. Said you threatened him with your weapon."

"He's nuts."

"Yeah, well, we know that. What're you about, Agent?"

This Scraggs was a stranger. That combined with a knock on the head is the reason, I suppose, I spilled to him rather than Joe. Rather than my shrink friend. I said, "I got a letter from the daughter of a man I prosecuted for rape in Florida. She was a kid then, and now she's an intern at Yale New Haven Hospital. She saved a lock of her father's hair. His DNA did not match the DNA of the sperm found in the victim's body. Her father didn't do it."

Scraggs sat next to me on the bed. He put his arm around my shoulder. He said, "I'm real sorry. But it happens, you know that."

"Shouldn't."

"Yeah."

"Can I get you anything else?"

"Nope. I just need to have a rest."

"If I can do anything—call me anytime."

"You already made that offer. The day we met."

"Today I mean it." He wrote his home phone number on his business card, put it on the bedside table, told me to take it easy, and left.

What I didn't tell him was that I knew the guy in Florida hadn't done it while I was prosecuting him. And back then I'd used all the arguments to support myself that the governor had used on me yesterday. Basically, the guy was scum, so what's the great loss?

Maybe I was no different from those women Vernon described on death row. I'd been hit by a bolt of lightning, and now I was pressed to make restitution.

I could not avoid the conversation the next day with my director. He wanted me back. I lied and told him I couldn't fly for a week, doctor's orders. But I would stay in bed until the execution. When it was over, I'd be back. What could he say?

∽

The most-used media word surrounding the upcoming execution of Rona Leigh Glueck was *circus*. From the Best Western, I watched the events unfold each night on the evening news, and *circus* was the right word. A tent went up, followed by several more, because Best Western, Holiday Inn, and the two other motels were not able to handle the hundreds of people arriving like ants attracted to a piece of cake at a picnic. Farmers rented out their harvested fields abutting the prison compound, and then, for small fortunes, they rented out their unharvested fields. Losing a crop to trampling proved cost-effective. About the time the flatbed truck carrying satellite dishes rolled in, the RVs descended, followed by little makeshift shacks manned by Mexicans selling food, drink, and souvenirs.

The anti-execution people were in the tents; the pro people were in the RVs; the day-trippers drove the pickups.

The biggest and sturdiest tent had been erected by CBS. Dan Rather, hailing from Texas, had warned his technicians to get a serious tent or they'd be sucking grit and so would their equipment.

The cardinal held an open-air mass in the public park in the middle of Gatesville. He brought his own security; the pickup trucks couldn't get close enough to drown out his sermon in English, then in Spanish, condemning the death penalty.

I ran into the people from *People* the afternoon of the execution, and they invited me to dinner that night. They'd had the foresight to make a reservation at the only restaurant in Gatesville that didn't seat people on stools at a counter. Turned out Rona Leigh had asked the warden if the photographer could take a picture of her after she was pronounced dead. She said she wanted everyone to know that dead was dead.

Frank said, "Shit, I couldn't believe our luck. We were sure the warden would say no, but he told us that the anti-death-penalty folks will see that Texas means business. Figured maybe they'd give it a rest."

The photographer said, "And our editor, he's beside himself. The first face of a dead body on the cover. 'Let the reactions begin,' he said."

Looked like she'd be on a *People* cover after all—one week after the cardinal.

I said, "Sounds as though Rona Leigh has given up."

They both looked at me. They couldn't have cared less about Rona Leigh.

I asked the photographer, "Is the warden limiting you?"

"Yeah. One shot."

"How many are you planning to take?"

He said, "I got a special camera FedExed to me yesterday. It's the Uzi of the camera world. I'll be taking pictures nonstop. One shot every second and a half. Special film. I can take eight hundred shots. Camera's got a silencer on it, too."

"You're serious, aren't you?"

He grinned. "I took a half-dozen pictures of you as you were coming in the door."

At the restaurant we all ordered the special, chicken-fried steak with okra, which we moved around our plates into varied patterns. I said to them, "You guys have never witnessed an execution before, have you?"

They hadn't.

"Well, that's why you have no appetite. I *have* witnessed a few, and that's why *I* have no appetite."

While we didn't eat they told me Rona Leigh would be going to bed as usual at 8 P.M. She would be awakened at eleven. They'd already taken pictures of her having her last meal at five. The meal she requested was probably not too different from the last meal she'd had before she was arrested. She wanted a Big Mac, fries, and a chocolate shake, more evidence that she had resolved herself to die. Takeout from McDonald's was not in keeping with what an angel would eat. Rona Leigh had accepted her fate; just like the governor, she knew God would not save her.

At eleven-thirty the moon was at three-quarters, with the kind of silver light you only find above the great plains of America. Once the media equipment came on, though, it was outshone.

❧

I stood in the doorway to the witness room with the warden. Through the window, the death chamber was exactly as it had been when I'd first seen it, except that a full IV bag hung from the metal stand with one piece

of rubber tubing hanging down loose, another strung
through the hole chipped out of the cinder block.

The families of the victims get the first row if they
choose. Gary Scott was front and center. The empty
seat next to him, between him and Melody's brother,
was for the governor. The warden told me the brother
had protested the arrangement but finally saw reason;
the widower was entitled to first choice. Melody's
brother had his head bent, his eyes closed, ignoring
the attempts at conversation coming from Gary.

The governor was the only one who hadn't arrived
at the prescribed time, and like me—at the warden's
discretion—he wouldn't be patted down.

There were two seats to the left of Gary and two to
the right of the brother. On Gary's side, Rona Leigh's
prosecutor and her arresting officer sat slumped, trying to act bored. On the brother's side, two witnesses,
Rona Leigh's last-minute choices—women from the
Christian Coalition who had been writing to her for
ten years. Their lips moved in prayer, their eyes shut
like the brother's.

Behind them sat Vernon, his hands on their shoulders.

The warden told me Rona Leigh's mother and sisters did not come. She had written a letter to her
mother asking "one last time" who her father was.
There was no response. The warden said, "As if the
woman had any idea who the father was." When Rona
Leigh knew that no members of her family would be
with her save her husband, she decided she wanted the
reporter and photographer from *People* to sit in the
family row and not with the three prison-assigned
newsmen in the back. The warden did not deny her
wish, so the photographer sat next to Frank at the end
of the front row. He'd have a good angle, Rona Leigh
full face to his right, her feet directly in front of him.

The other newsmen did not protest. One said to me, before he went in, "I'm tired of it. If I never hear another mother keening over her fresh-killed son, I'll be a happy man."

Rona Leigh also asked the warden if I could be there, and he told her he'd invited me himself. She could choose another. But there was no one else.

I would be behind Frank, in the row of cops and investigators who had been involved in Rona Leigh's case—bringing her into custody, collecting evidence, defeating her appeals. There were seven of them.

The Texas Department of Criminal Justice has a press secretary at all executions. His job is to go out to the media afterward and report the time of death and the prisoner's last words. He hands out a press packet covering the events of the prisoner's last day. He doesn't take questions. He used to, but the questions were deemed too morbid. I'd spoken to him earlier, asked him how many executions he'd witnessed. He said, "All of them."

Now he was talking to a guard in the corridor. His eyes kept darting back and forth, from his watch, to the door, to the witness room. "We used to just stand around like we were at a cocktail party, crowd up to the glass when it was time. But then there was this one prisoner, a young man, IQ in the sixties, fifties, maybe. He was tranquilized, but even so he didn't know what was going on. He started to cry when they tied his arms down because he liked waving at us through the glass. His family was waving back. So the chaplain whispered something in his ear and the boy said yes, he was going to ask Jesus if he could be the one to water the flowers that grew in the gardens of heaven. Then he started to sing a song, had to hum most of it, couldn't remember all the words. The song from his favorite TV show, that kids' show, *Mr.*

Rogers. His mother fainted. His sisters went down too; they didn't faint, their knees just buckled."

Then he excused himself. Told me he needed to hit the bathroom while he still had a few minutes. He walked as though his own knees might buckle.

Gary was trying to engage the men on his left in conversation. They ignored him just as Melody's brother had.

The warden approached me and told me to have a seat, the governor had arrived. Before he escorted Rona Leigh to the death chamber, he would escort the governor to his chair. As I walked in front of him, Gary gave me a big smile and raised his fist, pumped the air a couple of times.

A police escort entered the witness room, four Rangers including Max Scraggs. In uniform. He touched his finger to his hat when he caught my eye. They lined up against the wall.

We all stood when the governor entered the room. The warden took him over to Gary to make introductions. Gary shook his hand and said, "You can always count on my vote, chief." The governor stared at Gary's hair first, then his face. He hadn't paid much attention to the widower when he'd appeared on the local talk shows, I could tell. He expressed his condolences. Gary said, "Hey, what can I say? Me and Melody had us some damn good times."

The warden introduced him to Melody's brother. Up until that moment, the man had been slumped into his chair. Now he straightened and held the governor's shocked gaze. He said, in a strong and clear voice, "It is not too late to spare this woman's life, sir." Rona Leigh had an advocate with a direct line to the governor after all, and she never knew it.

The governor looked away from the brother, and at that moment he knew he'd made a mistake. But there was nothing to be done except to sit there in the gray metal folding chair between the two men, two men who could not look or sound more opposite.

Gary took over, leaned into him, and whispered in his ear. The governor pulled as far away from him as he could. The cops all watched, wishing they could go and get the big boss and yank him out of the room away from Gary Scott, just the way his aides had done when I'd crossed him.

The warden walked out of the witness room, leaving the door to the corridor open. A guard stood there, stiff as a board. It became still in the room except for the governor whispering to Gary. Whatever he said, Gary finally shushed.

The scene took on the feel of a wake except there was no body, just a window looking onto a peculiar bed rather than a coffin. We were all about to see someone enter and then watch that person be killed. Only then would we view a body.

The witnesses began to cough and shuffle, particularly those who had never experienced what was about to happen. The governor pinched the bridge of his nose, perhaps a way to keep his eyes covered.

The *People* photographer's hands were trembling. Frank patted his arm, whispering to him. Blurred photos would not do.

Then I noticed the new clock on the wall over the cot, a large clock with shiny black numbers and hands. It hadn't been there before. I looked at my watch anyway. In fact, everyone was glancing at their watches as if wishing the big clock was fast, its time somehow off. It was exactly correct.

At five minutes to twelve, two guards entered the death chamber and positioned themselves on either side of the cot. One of them was Harley Shank. His eyes were red, his face flushed. Then another guard escorted the nurse and a medical technician into the room. The nurse was short and chubby. She wore a high-waisted princess-style uniform, the skirt six inches above her knees. And a cap. She was young but she was old-school. She and the technician stood on the other side of the cot from the window and waited at attention. Their guard stood with them.

Outside the bungalow singing began, just a soft barely audible melody. The words of "Amazing Grace" became clear enough to make out, but they were quickly drowned out by a chant, increasingly louder, more raucous with each second that ticked on the big clock.

Kill her. Kill her. Kill her. Kill her. Kill her.

That was what Rona Leigh would hear as she lay dying. I wondered whether Melody Scott had heard the same.

The warden entered the death chamber. As soon as he'd planted himself by the side of the cot, we could hear the heavy footfalls coming from down the hall and the clank of Rona Leigh's chains. And then the words were called out: *Dead woman walkin'.*

With that, the *People* photographer gained total control of himself. I could see the tiny movement of his wrist.

Two more guards followed the warden in, and then the doctor, stethoscope swinging around his neck. A doctor whose job was not to save a patient's life but to watch carefully as a woman expired so he could declare her officially dead.

Then Rona Leigh stood in the doorway, wrists and ankles shackled, chin up, smiling. She saw the cot, its arms stretched toward her, and her smile disappeared. The cardinal was directly behind, and he was a spectacle: in full regalia, purple vestments, the color representing death. His hand was on her right shoulder. He must have squeezed her because she looked down at his hand and then moved forward, as did he, and we could hear again the clank of the chains and the swish of heavy silk.

It is difficult to walk with any sort of dignity with ten pounds of locks hanging from you and just a short length of chain connecting ankles to wrists, but Rona Leigh managed it. She didn't shuffle. With each step, she got her foot up off the floor.

She stopped at the edge of the cot, next to the warden, and looked through the window. She took us all in, and a wisp of a smile came to her lips. She said, "May Jesus rain His many blessings down upon you."

Gary shouted out, "God damn you to hell!"

The governor jerked.

A guard immediately stalked over to Gary and warned him to keep quiet or he would be ejected.

I looked back to Rona Leigh. She was staring at Gary. The chains clinked. Vernon began to sob loudly.

Her gaze went to him. She said, "I love you, Vernon."

Vernon choked out, "I love you too."

The warden came up to the glass and reminded us that we were to remain silent.

Rona Leigh's gaze shifted. Her eyes met the governor's. She said, "I appreciate your honoring me with your presence, sir."

From my angle, I could see his lips press together. He hadn't intended for honor to be part of his decision.

And through it all, the photographer's camera shifted left, right, up, down, catching it all.

Captain Shank took a large black ring of keys from his belt. He bent to unlock her ankle chains. He drew the chain out through her wrist cuffs, but they remained shackled together.

The technician smiled at Rona Leigh. He said, "Just

hop on up here for me," and he patted the table as if she were there for a physical.

She turned, faced the cot, and stepped up onto a metal stool. He took her two hands in his and steadied her as she inched herself onto the cot. Then he placed his palm between her shoulder blades and said, "Just lie back now."

She complied and he gently lowered her down, adjusted a little pillow behind her neck. The cardinal got right behind the head of the cot and put his hand on her forehead as if she were a child and he needed to see if she were running a fever. The two women from the Christian Coalition began to weep.

Shank jangled the keys as he freed her wrists. The other guards grabbed hold of her arms and legs and strapped them to the paddles. Then the belt across her shoulders: the warden made a gesture, and the shoulder strap was tightened. Rona Leigh called out, "My God, my God, why hast thou forsaken me?"

My stomach turned over. I had wondered at what point it would do that.

The cardinal put his other hand along the side of her face. The warden touched him, gave him a stern look. The cardinal stepped back.

Outside, ever louder, the words were coming out faster: *Kill her, kill her, kill her, kill her, kill her.* I looked down at my watch. Three minutes had passed since she'd entered the death chamber.

The technician tied a length of rubber tubing around Rona Leigh's upper arm. The nurse, who had stood as unmoving as a statue, hung the needle on a hook, bent over Rona Leigh's arm, and with her fingertips pressed a spot just above her inner wrist until she'd patted up a vein. Then she took a small bottle and cotton balls from her pocket and swabbed the spot she'd chosen. This step was normally dispensed with.

There was no point to preventing infection. But this nurse was going by her training, though I didn't think a course of study leading to an RN degree included execution procedure.

The nurse took up the needle and stuck Rona Leigh. Rona Leigh flinched. She was not sedated. The technician freed the rubber.

The intimacy of one human being killing another is not easily described. I could see tears coursing down the cheeks of the *People* man who would have to do the describing. Poor Frank.

The nurse attached the tubing hanging from the IV to the needle and then checked to see that the glucose solution in the bag was flowing down through the tubing and into Rona Leigh's vein. It was as if Rona Leigh were suffering from dehydration. The nurse and the technician went into their closet, and as soon as the door closed behind them, the warden said, "Rona Leigh Glueck, do you have any last words?"

Rona Leigh turned her head toward him and said, "Yes, sir, I do."

He waited but got no further response. His voice trembled. "Please say the words."

She said, "Lord forgive them, for they know not what they do."

I could hear Gary mumble something. I didn't know what it was, but the governor did. His shoulders seemed to pull inward. Too bad. Try as he might, he could not shrink away.

The warden stepped back and touched his cheek as if he had a little itch. That was the signal to the guard to go to the door of the closet and tap it three times. The cardinal went down on one knee. The clock on the wall read six minutes after twelve, as did my watch. Time had refused to stand still.

I watched for the first sign. It came in seconds.

Rona Leigh's fingers lost their flex as her lids dropped closed. Her lips parted. With the sodium Pentothal injected, she had been rendered unconscious.

Much louder now, a few bullhorns added to the decibels: *Kill her, kill her, kill her, kill her, kill her.*

And Gary took up the chant too. He sang out, "Kill her, kill her, kill her."

A guard rushed over, leaned over, and hissed in his ear. Gary said, "I have my rights!" The guard took hold of his shoulder, a judo restraint. Gary shriveled up a little, an involuntary reaction to the pain. The guard let go and went back to his post, leaving Gary wincing.

Rona Leigh's entire body twitched. Her chest rose up, higher and higher, then fell. The second chemical was coursing through her bloodstream. The pancuronium bromide forced her lungs into collapse as it paralyzed her diaphragm. Her chest rose again, the human will fighting asphyxiation. Her chest fell again, rose one more time, and then fell.

She was no longer breathing.

The doctor looked at his watch. I looked at mine. There would be no sign when the potassium chloride stopped the beating of Rona Leigh's heart.

The witnesses were paralyzed themselves during the two-minute wait.

Then the doctor walked to Rona Leigh's side, placed his stethoscope upon her chest, over her heart, and listened. He moved the instrument slightly to her aorta. He stood straight. The stethoscope swung against his lapel. He felt her neck with his fingers. I'd never seen that before.

He looked at the clock on the wall. He nodded to the warden and recited, "I pronounce Rona Leigh Glueck dead at twelve-o-eight," and then he said the date.

The warden ordered the drapes be closed. The

nurse came out of her hiding place. She looked to the warden. He nodded at her, and she began to remove the IV. A guard went to the side of the window and pulled the drapery cord. Nothing happened. The warden signaled to Harley Shank to help the guard with the drapes. But Captain Shank didn't move. His eyes were still on Rona Leigh. So the technician made a move toward the drapes.

That was when Gary leaped up out of his chair and shouted, "Take a whack at her for me, Melody. Take a couple!"

The governor stood, his eyes darting to the troopers. He was thinking one thing: Get me out!

Then Harley Shank clasped his hands tightly together. His knuckles turned white. Trying to control himself, I thought. His eyes narrowed. I followed his gaze to Rona Leigh. I saw the tiny tremor in her chin, her vulnerable little chin. Her lips parted very slightly and closed, and parted again, and closed the same way the mouth of a beached fish will.

Outside: *Kill her, kill her, kill her, kill her, kill her.*

Rona Leigh made a sound, a small one, strangled, a sucking sound. She was trying to breathe. Everyone came to their feet. She gasped for air. Gasped and gasped again. Breathed out. Gasped.

The *People* photographer stood and began snapping with a vengeance, no effort to hide what he was doing.

Rona Leigh Glueck had survived her execution.

8

There is only one word for what happened next: pandemonium.

Above us was Vernon, standing up on his chair. His arms were raised to God and his words came out in a roar: "Why do you make this din and weep? The girl is asleep, not dead. *Talithi cumi!* Girl, I say to thee, arise!"

Even though the endless events of the moments to follow seemed to happen all at once, there was a sequence, one action following directly upon the last, and I committed them to memory. The warden, triggered by the madness in Vernon's voice, calmly told the nurse to put the IV needle back in Rona Leigh's arm. She said, "But there are no more drugs. I used what I was given."

Still calm, but a little louder, he ordered Captain Shank to go to the cabinet in his office and get the other vials of drugs. Shank's eyes remained on Rona Leigh. Unable to take them off her, he backed out toward the door and fumbled at the doorknob.

The warden shouted, "Shank! Move!" Shank was gone.

Then the warden turned his attention back to the nurse. He said, "Girl, put the needle back in her arm."

She said, "It's no longer sterile."

I thought his eyes would bug out of his head. "Sterile? We're killin' this woman, you damn fool!"

The nurse looked down at the apparatus in her hands and threw it on the floor as if it were poison. It *was* poison. She became hysterical. The warden grabbed her and shook her.

Rona Leigh thrashed against her bonds. The cardinal grabbed hold of her shoulders and started to recite the Lord's Prayer.

Gary darted up to the glass and yelled, "Let me in there and I'll strangle the bitch with my bare hands!"

Then he made a beeline for the door. The nearest guard took out his gun and pointed it at Gary's face. Our eyes went from Rona Leigh to the gun. The Rangers and the rest of the guards drew their weapons. Gary yelled, "Go ahead, shoot me!" He pointed to the window. "Better yet, shoot *her!*"

The guard smashed his gun butt into the side of Gary's head. Gary went straight to the floor.

Rona Leigh vomited up her last meal from McDonald's.

The technician went into training mode. He unbuckled the shoulder and arm belts and pulled Rona Leigh up to a sitting position. He pounded her back.

The warden couldn't believe what he was seeing but knew he was fast losing control. He dashed out of the death chamber and came into the witness room. He stood facing the governor, who had turned to stone. He grabbed him and shook him the same way he had the nurse.

"Damn it, Governor, I got a thousand people outside waiting for word of that girl's death." He pointed down at Gary. "You see this fella? There's a lot more a him outside. They will storm my unit. It's up to you to help me here."

And the governor reverted to training too. He drew himself up and removed the warden's hands from his shoulders.

He said, "Bring the doctor to me."

The doctor, still in the death chamber, had turned to stone himself. The warden shouted, "Doc! Get out here right now."

The man didn't move.

"Doc! You fuckin' hearin' me?"

A guard shoved the doctor. He came out of his fog. He left and came into the witness room. The governor said to him, "What is the condemned woman's condition?"

The doctor glanced back through the window. Rona Leigh was collapsed in the technician's arms, shaking violently. "She is having seizures."

The warden said, "Any imbecile can see that."

The governor put his hand up. "Doctor, is the condemned woman going to die?"

"I believe she is dying, sir, yes."

Another huge convulsion shook Rona Leigh. A wet stain appeared in her lap. We watched the urine trickle down off the table.

The warden said to the doctor, "You at least got some kind of sedative on you till she does."

"No."

The warden looked to the door. "Where the hell's Shank?" But the tone of his voice showed he held no hope that new drugs would appear, that he could backpedal and set things right.

The governor said, "Under normal circumstances, Doctor, what would you advise for a woman in her condition?"

"A woman poisoned?"

The governor shut his eyes and then said, "Obviously."

"I would get her to a hospital, though I doubt a woman in the condition we are seeing would make it there."

The governor's voice was quiet, but we heard him over the chant outside. "Then do it."

The warden's eyes couldn't have bulged any farther out of his head. "Governor, are you out of your mind? How the hell can we take this woman to a hospital?"

"You call an ambulance, that's how. An *ambulance!*" Then he said, "Officers!" The Rangers came to attention.

"Full police escort. Set up roadblocks. Clear the highway of all civilian cars. One of you come with me, the rest get to work. I'm going outside to prevent a catastrophe. Let's just hope to God she's dead before the ambulance gets here and anyone finds out what happened." He took in the room. "No one leaves this room till I give the order." He looked at Frank and the photographer, with their little press cards hung around their necks. "Especially the two of you."

He headed for the door, the warden at his heels. They ran into Captain Shank. Shank said, "Warden, that refrigerator inside the cabinet was locked. Your wife couldn't find the key."

The warden's face was red as a beet. "It's too damn late anyway."

And then Captain Shank took in Rona Leigh. He said, "Lord have mercy."

The warden started ordering everyone around. "Who is the Ranger in charge here?"

Max Scraggs stepped forward.

"Commander, you are to see that we have an ambulance and clear the highway between Gatesville and Waco. You are to follow that ambulance to Waco and stay with the prisoner." Then he mumbled to himself, "Who's going with her?"

Harley Shank was right there. "I'll go, sir."

"All right, then, Shank. You will ride in the ambulance. You are to cuff your left wrist to the prisoner's.

And with your right hand keep your weapon pointed at her head. If she gains consciousness tell her not to move. If she does, shoot her. Go into the hospital with her, do not unlock the cuffs, I don't care what they're doin' to her. You will remain attached to the prisoner until you hear from me telling you otherwise. Do not dare to holster your weapon. There'll be Rangers all over, but you're my man and you don't leave her."

Shank reverted to training. He stood at attention. "Yes, sir." He took out a cell phone. He pressed one button.

It was taking four guards now to hold Rona Leigh down. Her eyes had rolled to the back of her head.

The warden said, "Where the hell'd the governor go?"

"He's waiting for you at the door."

"Tell him I'm coming. I need one more minute."

He took out a cell phone of his own, pressed one button, and ordered whoever answered to get every off-duty correctional officer to the Mountain View Unit.

Then he said, "Commander Scraggs, I need two uniformed Rangers with me to go outside for the governor's announcement. Make it look real official. And then see that he's taken home in a police vehicle so he doesn't get stopped at the roadblocks."

He said to the press secretary, "You go out and tell the crowd there has been a medical emergency postponing Rona Leigh's execution. Till when, you don't know. Just say—tell them Gary Scott has had a heart attack. Tell them an ambulance is coming for him, and as soon as it gets him out there will be an announcement from the governor."

The press secretary said, "Sir, I don't think—"

"No one's ever paid you to think, and we ain't startin' now. Go. Where's that Scraggs?"

"I'm right here. What you want has been taken care of."

"Good. Listen, we need all the personnel here you

can get. Don't know how much crowd control might be necessary."

"Already in motion."

"And you'll need—"

"There are a dozen vehicles on the way. They'll be following me. I'll be in the lead, ahead of the ambulance."

The warden told a guard to be sure the police vehicles lined themselves up along the driveway so they could follow behind the ambulance and the Ranger commander.

Cardinal de la Cruz came out of the death chamber to ask the warden if he could accompany Rona Leigh to the hospital.

"Eminence, you will stay here till things are under control and then you can go with me in my car to the hospital. Meanwhile, pray for us all. I have to tend to the people outside."

Rona Leigh made a loud gurgling noise and suddenly stopped thrashing. She lay still.

The doctor and the cardinal ran back into the death chamber and bent over her. The doctor said, "I believe she . . ." He pressed the stethoscope to her chest. She struggled to take in a breath and, once she accomplished that, threw up a projectile of blood.

Internal hemorrhaging was under way.

I went to the warden. I said, "I want to ride with Scraggs to the hospital. It won't hurt to have an FBI agent witnessing everything that's going on."

He looked me up and down. He said, "That there is the truth. C'mon."

He pointed to the door. I took one last look at Rona Leigh. The nurse was wiping blood from her face.

We found Scraggs in the corridor on his cell phone, trying to make someone understand that the governor would need a marked car to take him back to Austin.

"A marked car, goddamn it, with every light flashing and the siren turned up. Just see it's done." He flipped his phone shut.

I said to him, "The warden told me to go with you."

"Before or after you told him you should go?"

"After."

He turned on his heel, waving me on, and I followed him out of the building. The cruiser was already idling and we got in. We watched the warden and the governor walk out of the Mountain View death house, through the outside gate, and up the driveway. The two climbed on the platform set up just outside the drive alongside State School Road, where the gathered crowd was huge. *Kill her, kill her, kill her, kill her, kill her* fizzled, and then it stopped.

A whir and clicking of cameras filled the silence. The warden stepped up to the microphone, the governor shoulder to shoulder with him, but before he could speak the night was rent with the wail of a siren. The ambulance came flying down the road, high beams on, blue lights flashing, and took the turn into the driveway on two wheels before it screeched to a stop in front of the gate. Two paramedics leaped out, yanked a gurney out of the rear doors, and sped down the sidewalk.

Scraggs said, "Jesus, those fools'll kill her for sure. And themselves while they're at it."

Over the loudspeaker, the warden's voice was shrill and metallic. He said, "Ladies and gentlemen, we are taking care of an unexpected medical emergency. The execution of Rona Leigh Glueck has been postponed for one hour. The governor will speak to you shortly."

Scraggs turned on the radio, AM. We caught a newscaster mid-sentence. ". . . and the word I'm getting is that the widower of Melody Scott has suffered a heart attack. We will have the governor live in . . . according to the warden here at the Mountain View death house . . . in a few minutes."

The paramedics were out. They pushed the gurney back across the sidewalk surrounded by guards running with them, step for step. They loaded Rona Leigh into the ambulance. As ordered, Harley Shank's left wrist was cuffed to hers, and his gun was out.

The siren came back on. The ambulance drove around in a circle and pulled up behind us. Scraggs flipped on his own siren. I looked into the sideview mirror. Three cruisers were falling in line behind the ambulance. Scraggs hit the accelerator, and we took off through the gate.

The radio newscaster said, "The ambulance that arrived just minutes ago has left the Mountain View Unit surrounded by Texas Ranger marked cars. . . . Wait a minute . . . here is the governor now."

There was a little dead air and then the governor's voice came on, an echo of it coming at us from the outdoor loudspeaker. Scraggs turned up the radio volume. The voice was rock-firm.

"Ladies and gentlemen, I stand here before you to say that an unpleasant duty has befallen us. I must pass along shocking news, unprecedented news. The prisoner Rona Leigh Glueck, condemned to die at this hour for the murders of Melody Scott and James Munter, did not succumb to the chemicals that were injected into her bloodstream at twelve o'clock midnight. She is dying, but she is not dead. I have had no choice but to act in humane a manner as possible. I have directed that she be removed from this unit by ambulance to a hospital that will not be named. She will receive the medical attention she requires, and if she recovers she will be returned to Mountain View, where her sentence will be carried out.

"For the sake of justice, I can only hope she will be

executed as soon as possible if she does survive the . . . the failed attempt to"—Scraggs and I looked at each other—"to carry out her sentence. I humbly thank you, and may God bless America."

Over the radio, the crowd came to life, mostly with cries to God for mercy.

It was all drowned out by another siren. A second ambulance flew past us toward the prison, this one escorted by two Ranger squad cars in front and two in the back.

Scraggs, his eyes straight ahead on the road, said, "Maybe someone decided to take care of the widower after all."

Suddenly, the headlights behind us veered left and the ambulance carrying Rona Leigh shot past us.

Scraggs gripped the steering wheel. "What the fuck is he doing?" He smashed his foot down on the accelerator.

The radio announcer was describing the arrival of the second ambulance. He said, "Now no one will confirm whether or not Rona Leigh was in the first ambulance or if she's to be put into this one. . . ."

We approached an overpass, the entrance to the bypass that would take the ambulance to Waco. But the ambulance didn't turn into the entrance ramp, it kept going. I could see people standing on the overpass, poised. There were three of them.

I screamed "Max!" but it was too late. Concrete blocks hit the front end of our car. We went into a spin. The police car behind broadsided us. I caught one last glimpse of the taillights of the ambulance and watched them blink out. The ambulance was swallowed by the black night.

Another cruiser slammed into the one that had broadsided us, and we were sent spinning toward the concrete bridge abutment.

Scraggs and I got to listen to the intact radio during the long slow process of being pried out of his car. We would be black and blue over most of our bodies, but we were not killed. I knew right away by the Technicolor spirals all around my head that I'd suffered my second minor concussion in less than a week. Scraggs and I were jammed into each other by the newly concaved sides of the vehicle, plus the roof had lowered and the steering wheel had us wedged.

The first thing Scraggs said was, "Are you all right, Agent?"

I tried to get enough air into my squashed lungs to speak. I managed it. "Yeah, I am. You?"

"Yeah." Then he said, "Fuck me."

I said, "She escaped." I would have added, Fuck me too, but speaking had loosed a chain saw in my brain.

So he said, "Fuck me," again. Then, "How the fuck did they do it?" Then, "Fuck me."

The announcer on the radio was babbling wildly. "Again, I am saying this again, Rona Leigh Glueck did not die. She was executed but she lived! She lived through it. Her execution failed!

"She is presently being transported to a hospital, we believe in Waco. Apparently, the governor made that decision once the doctor in the death chamber determined she was still alive after the execution was over.

"Folks, the ax murderer Rona Leigh Glueck, who was to be put to death at midnight—eighteen minutes ago—was not . . . put to death. Rather she was, but she continued to breathe after the lethal injections were administered. There is no word as to her actual condition. We are trying to get someone . . . wait. . . ."

He whispered, "Is this my producer?" Then, into the microphone, "Ladies and gentlemen, I don't know if

I'm hearing this correctly. . . . Jeff, is that you? This can't be true. . . ."

Scraggs said, "I'm afraid it is, Jack."

A Ranger's face appeared, hovering over the webbed windshield. "Sir, can you hear me?"

"Of course I can."

"The Jaws of Life machine is on its way."

"Ain't any a you boys got a fuckin' crowbar?"

"Yes, sir, but we don't know the extent of your injuries, and we can't take a chance that—"

"There is no extent to my injuries."

"And your passenger?"

"She's fine."

"Commissioner wants to know who she is."

"Penelope Rice. FBI."

The Ranger looked at me. "You okay with our trying to get you out manually?"

I said, "Go to it."

In the ten minutes it took to wrench the driver's side door open, we listened to the newscaster and so did the guys with the crowbar, who kept pausing to shake their heads in disgust. Then the announcer went live to his man at the prison, who told us all:

"There is a vast amount of confusion here at the Mountain View Unit. The governor has been driven away. Rangers are arriving, van after van. The driver of the second ambulance has been telling anyone who will listen that he was responding to the call and only his ambulance was sent. There was no other ambulance. His was not the second ambulance, his was the first one and the only one. He has been taken into the prison complex by several corrections officers.

"Now, just when the witnesses began to file out of the death house, they were treated the same way: grabbed by the guards and several Rangers and taken back in, including Cardinal de la Cruz from New York. And I can tell you this—none of them much liked it.

"At this point, all we know is what you have already been told. For some extraordinary reason, the chemicals injected into Rona Leigh Glueck did not have the effect—"

He stopped. The original guy back in the station had the latest news. His voice was quaking.

"I am interrupting our man at the prison. We have just received word that . . . apparently the ambulance carrying Rona Leigh Glueck to the hospital . . ." He began mumbling to someone. He came back. "That ambulance has disappeared."

It was harder for me to hear him because of ripping steel and the buzzing in my brain. Essentially, a reporter in the caravan of police cars heading to the hospital said that the lead car, ours, was fired upon as the ambulance sped off. Several police cars crashed into each other, but as yet there was no word of fatalities or injuries.

Then dead air. Ripping metal. Chain saw making the noise it makes. My head was splitting. Radio again. There was to be a press conference; a spokesman from the Texas Rangers would be speaking in a few minutes.

Scraggs said, "Wish we had a TV. Love to see how poor Clarence is going to find his way through this one."

The crowbar managed an opening in the side of the car, but it wasn't large enough for Scraggs to fit through. They took their crowbars to my side. They got the door off, but when I tried to move I couldn't. Not without losing a foot.

"I'm wedged in." I pulled a little. I said, "Shit."

Scraggs asked me if my leg was broken.

"No, but it will be if anyone tries to get me out."

Scraggs said, "Then no avoiding Jaws of Life. Fuck me."

A cop said, "We got one comin', sir."

A very noisy machine. I thought my head might break in half. When Scraggs was freed he came around to my side of the car and talked to me while they put my side of the cruiser to the rack.

I said, "Scraggs, you don't need to stay. You've got a lot to do."

"I ain't leavin' till you're out."

"That's nice."

"Poppy, are you comfortable talking? Can you answer a few questions that are killin' me?"

"What?"

"Are you sure you're all right?"

"I can talk, Scraggs."

"Poppy, what the hell went down here? Somebody substitute water for the chemicals?"

"No. She couldn't have faked what she went through. And if she got smaller amounts than what was intended, a shitload of people are in collusion. Impossible. The nurse and the technician were a couple of robots from the system, not conspirators. Brought in from Huntsville. So that leaves antidotes. She was given antidotes over a long period of time so her system could withstand the poisons."

"Could that be?"

"No, but I can't think of anything else. All I know is she was able to resist the fatal effects of the chemicals. Soon as I get back to DC, to the lab I set up myself, I intend to find out what she got. That'll be while you're here figuring out how and who."

Scraggs caught my eye just as mine caught his. Neither of us could speak in that moment. I chose to be the one to fill in the silence.

"The ambulance. It was the governor who said to call an ambulance."

More silence. Scraggs filled in this one. "I think the governor was operating on whatever instinct he'd got left."

I finished his thought. "They got lucky, didn't they?"

"Yes."

"Whatever the plan had been to get the warden or maybe someone over him to call an ambulance proved unnecessary."

He said, "Fuck me." Then he looked up at the frantic cops. "I suppose we ain't got the ambulance yet, or you'd have informed me."

One of them was holding a cell phone to his ear. "'Fraid that's correct, sir. But we will. We got men with bloodhounds out, we got helicopters, and we got one helluva buncha infrared equipment all over the place."

He said to me, "How can anyone have pulled such a thing off?"

I smiled at him. "What you call your inside job, Scraggs."

The cop on the phone said to us, "We're doin' a head count right now, I'll tell you that. Soon as someone from that prison turns up missing, we'll know who."

I said, "He's already missing. The guard in the ambulance. I heard him volunteer to go. Harley Shank." I must have moaned.

"What?"

"I need a couple of Tylenols."

Scraggs said, "You sure your ankle ain't busted?"

"No. My head hurts."

"I thought the problem was with your leg."

"Actually, I can't feel my leg."

"Shit." Then he said, "Boys, you heard the Agent? You got that name? Harley Shank?"

"We got it."

"Poppy, who put him up to it?"

"The chaplain. He had the goddamn scripture set and ready to go."

"The husband?"

"Yeah."

He looked up again from his squat position. "Rona Leigh's husband accounted for?"

"Bein' questioned sir. Right now. Took him directly to Austin."

Scraggs said to me, "Our boys think just like the FBI, how about that?" He asked the phone cop, "What do we know about that boy in the ambulance? Shank."

"Chaplain's cousin, sir. Got him the job."

Scraggs and I made eye contact. I knew he'd say fuck me, and he did. Then he said, "Where the fuck can that ambulance have gone?"

I said, "Maybe it could fly."

"It probably could."

I said, "Did they get those people on the overpass?"

His brow knit. "What people?" The cops who leaned into my window were staring at me.

"Scraggs, the people who dropped the blocks."

I was the only one who'd seen three people drop the concrete blocks. Scraggs had been concentrating on his driving. He and the rest of the cops had assumed they'd been tossed from the ersatz ambulance. But then again, someone else had thought we'd been fired on.

I assured them that the blocks had been dropped from above. That sent a couple more cops to their cell phones.

Scraggs said, "We got ourselves a full-fledged conspiracy, don't we?"

"I'd say."

The front end of the car was lifted off my foot. I gritted my teeth and wiggled it. Squashed but nothing broken.

Not long after, a doctor at the Waco Hospital said, "Couple weeks on crutches, ma'am, is all. Wrenched real bad. Just stay off it."

I told him to dig out his Ace bandages and wrap my ankle up extra tight. I'd limp.

∽

That night, after he'd spent a few moments with his scotch in the library, the governor ordered everyone arrested who had witnessed the failed execution, including the police. Cooler heads prevailed, cooler heads who wondered aloud to him who then would do the arresting. He said, "Me." To lighten things up, the cooler heads wondered aloud if the cardinal would make bail. The governor told the cooler heads they were fired, but that was nothing unusual so the cooler heads persevered, suggesting to the governor that he would have to arrest himself. The governor announced he was going to bed and he'd deal with it in the morning.

However, the Texas Rangers did detain everyone who was in the death house, including the warden, including the cardinal. Even the corrections officers were detained, along with all the workers and the roused off-duty guards. Replaced by various people within the Texas Department of Criminal Justice, of which there are over a hundred thousand employees, the detained horde was conveyed to Fort Hood, where there was plenty of room. The cardinal was made to understand that it was necessary, and he counseled everyone else that they would just have to cooperate. They all did, too, except Gary Scott. He'd quickly recovered from the crack to his head. He needed a beer and he needed his lawyer. He wasn't given access to either.

9

When I got back to DC, my director was all abeam. "Poppy," he said, "your instincts run deep."

Then he went off on an ecstatic riff as if he were practicing for a news conference. "Because of you we end up with a legitimate presence in an investigation of even greater magnitude than the last Texas prison break. Don't have to barge through any doors insisting that the escapee must have crossed state lines."

I started to say that I was glad to be of help, so to speak. He wasn't hearing.

"Poppy, we're the ones who defined the direction this case should take because we had an agent right there. We had an agent who predicted that testing the syringe and IV line would certainly show the traces of the three chemicals used to execute a condemned prisoner."

"Actually, it was—"

"Even before that was *confirmed* we saved the Texas authorities a lot of time by eliminating tampering. Gave them a sharper focus. We've got a huge state police force who have had to come crawling to us for once."

I hated to burst his bubble. Drawing attention to the success of his agency was one of his jobs, the all-important political one. But he tended to get carried away when his personal security was enmeshed. "Sir, the only person we've eliminated was the UPS man who delivered the chemicals."

He said, "Please tell me the drugs were not delivered by UPS."

"Sorry."

He stopped his lion's walk back and forth in front of the giant window overlooking his kingdom. He stood behind his chair and leaned down on the back of it. "But the key is, they have the ambulance, and our guys found it before theirs did. So don't go making this out to be even more complicated than it is. You know as well as I do that people don't drop off the face of the earth. We'll find her."

"I think if we can—"

"She's on an island yet to be charted. Can't be a very big one because the borders were sealed so fast. We've got that chaplain, we've got good IDs on the guys in the ambulance, we're learning everything there is to know about Harley Shank. Also, three people lugged concrete blocks onto an overpass above a very busy highway. Someone will come up with something on them sooner or later."

I got directly into his face. "Sir, someone's received her and we have no idea who."

"Okay, so we've got our work cut out for us. Nothing new there. But we're all around her."

❦

Three days later, our work still remained cut out. No trace of Rona Leigh or the conspirators. But it was important that we'd found the ambulance. The fake ambulance.

Our dredgers located it at the bottom of the Leon River, three miles from where the river emptied into Belton Lake. At the lake itself, the Rangers found the remains of a campsite, an elaborate campsite several witnesses had noticed during the week leading up to the execution. Couple of guys with what they said was a boat under a blue tarp. Supposed to be working on the boat, but they decided to fish from the banks instead—feeling too lazy to try to get the boat in working order despite offers of help. They were generous with their beer supply and fellow fishermen enjoyed their company before heading along to their own favorite fishing spots.

The two men fished and fished, waited and waited, while their fake ambulance sat primed under the tarp and ready to go.

Most of the ambulances in Texas are old Cadillacs. This old Cadillac had been purchased on the Internet via a money order. In the investigation business, one of the most dreaded terms is *money order.*

The search of the campsite area was not unlike an archaeological dig. Under layers of dirt and leaves the Texas Rangers found hammers, screwdrivers, pliers, wrenches, drills, sanding devices, protractors, paintbrushes. They found more sophisticated items: a welding unit, a soldering machine, a drill press, and a compressor. And, obviously, a generator. Building an ambulance out of an old Cadillac is strikingly not a simple thing.

The ambulance was driven into the Leon River and sunk to its silty bottom eight minutes after I'd watched its taillights go out. The clock on Scraggs's dashboard had stopped exactly eight minutes before the one on the ambulance dashboard had done the same. The tracks through the swampy ground from where it left the road had been easy to find and follow. The ambulance never stopped until its front wheels were in the water, whereupon the occupants got out and transferred to another vehicle. Then the ambulance was pushed the rest of the way into the river.

The tire tracks leading back out of the swamp were left by standard-issue police van tires. Witnesses said they'd seen a police van in the area earlier. Yet another fake vehicle. Which left us with one really big clue: The conspirators were incredibly industrious and not short on funds.

The police that night had checked every car, truck, RV, motorcycle, bicycle, scooter, in-line pair of skates, baby carriage—anything on wheels. But they didn't check each other. Rona Leigh's private police van had clear sailing through the roadblocks while the entire highway patrol force, the Rangers, and a million good-time Charlies with rifles went hunting for an ambulance. All over the state that night, people being rushed to hospitals suffered setbacks.

The director asked me a question over and over just for something to ask: "How far a drive from Gatesville to the Mexican border?"

"Seven hours to Laredo, I know that for a fact. That would be direct, too. But even though it's a damn long border, all the crossing points were closed down way before seven hours post escape. More like seven minutes. Besides, sir, you can take a bath in the Rio Grande and no one bothers you."

"Is that so?"

"Yes. Rona Leigh is not in Mexico. If she's alive, she's got to be in some major medical center with a couple of brilliant doctors who were in on the escape. And we know that can't be. Sir, she was in bad, bad shape. So I don't know what to think. Whether she's dead or alive, the very clever people who sprung her have found as ingenious a place to hide her as their manner of saving her. We have to devote ourselves to figuring out the motivation for getting her out. Figure out the motivation, find your perp. Follow the money and all that. Last year, it took me two entire weeks to find out who was stealing the cardinal's money because his motivation was so unanticipated."

"Poppy, can there be any truth to the theory that she was spirited away? That she played no part in the escape?"

"No. She acted the part set forth for her. Rona Leigh would have done anything to stay alive, just like every other convict on death row. Even if it meant allowing herself to come within an inch of death. She'd risk possible death to avoid certain death."

He began pacing again. "With each day that passes, more and more people are using the word *miracle* to explain her escape."

"I know." The *People* photographer and Frank, the reporter, had chronicled the miracle. "Sir, I heard Dan Rather, straight-face, discuss the role of angels in her disappearance. He didn't say escape, he said disappearance."

My director sighed. "Switch to Brokaw. Rather lost his marbles years ago. Poppy . . ."

"Yes, sir?"

"How the fuck was this possible?"

"If I had her blood, I'd know."

Suddenly, he needed a little denial for comfort. "The blood was lost."

"No, sir, the blood was poured down the drain. But we have to stop worrying about how. We've got to concentrate on why. Then we'll get to who. After that, how."

"I know where our concentration lies. I thought we'd have a route when the ransom note arrived. I can't believe we don't have one."

"None of us can."

Offers to pay any ransom had come in from all over the world. Came from people who thought they'd be saving the life of an angel, not an ax murderer.

I stood up. I put my weight on my ankle. It felt like my dentist was drilling the bone. I needed the practice,

though. I smiled. "Permission to return to Texas and
find Rona Leigh Glueck. Ten days, max."

Another sigh. "The second the goddamned press
conference ends, go."

He hated press conferences. I loved them. Sometimes an astute reporter's question is one no one's
asked yet. Another profession where you can do something intelligent even though you flunked chemistry.

But no such luck. Once our representative gave the
findings on the syringe and the tubing—that Rona
Leigh had received enough poison to kill an ele-
phant—there wasn't a question from them that we
hadn't asked ourselves. The reporters' incredulity
matched our own. As in, "Her blood samples are *missing?*"

I spent a few hours with Joe before I went back to
Texas. We had dinner at my favorite restaurant. His
apartment. He re-created a Texas barbecue with
Stubbs barbecue sauce. Spike the cat finally became my
friend because he discovered how much he loved
brisket.

Post-sex talk is about equal to press conference questions when it comes to unforeseen illumination. Right
after Joe stretched and settled into his pillow, he said,
"Poppy, what didn't jibe?"

"None of it jibed."

"Think of the physical details. Rona Leigh walks into
the death chamber. From there, take each step she
took. Watch and listen."

I brought up images of each step she took, manacled
steps, then each step the others took once she was
through taking steps.

"Holy shit." I'd already thought of something not jib-
ing as it had been happening.

Joe said, "Oh, boy. What?"

"The nurse swabbed Rona Leigh's arm with alcohol."

I sat up and leaned on Joe so I could see his clock. Four-ten A.M. Two o'clock Scraggs's time.

I scrambled out of bed, located my purse, and found his card with his home phone.

A woman answered. "I need to speak with Max Scraggs."

She said, "You and everyone else, honey."

There was the smallest bit of fumbling, then: "Scraggs."

I didn't think to identify myself. "Max, I need to talk to the nurse."

"This you, Poppy?"

"Yes."

"You mean the nurse who would only kill Rona Leigh the once?"

"The very one."

"She's somewhere havin' a nervous breakdown is the last I heard. Talk to her about what? Let me do this, Poppy. Give me something. What do you want from her?"

"Ask her why she swabbed Rona Leigh's arm with alcohol before she stuck her."

"She swabbed her arm with alcohol?"

"That's what I said."

"You saw her?"

"Yes. And it has just now reentered my mind."

"But what dunce would do that?"

"A dunce following orders."

Before he could follow up the pause, I followed it up for him. "I know. Fuck me."

"Where the hell you callin' from?"

"A friend's. I'll be at the Holiday Inn in Gatesville tomorrow."

"You'll be at the Best Western, and you don't want anyone to find you easy, right?"

"Right."

"Man, I'm glad you're comin' back, Agent. We are at each other's throats here. Any voice of reason has flown out the window, so I surely would welcome yours."

"I'll call you when I get there."

I hung up. Joe said, "Who was that?"

I said, "Nobody."

He snorted.

⟡

I checked in with Delby before I got on the plane. I said, "I need you to call the police in Houston again."

"They're sure goin' to be sick of hearin' from me."

"There's a guy named Chuck who hangs out at the AstroBar. See if he's in any trouble. Tell them you need to know what anybody's got on him. Tell them you need that information immediately."

"They'll love that."

"Use Max Scraggs's name."

"Speakin' of same, I just talked to him. Wanted you. Told him you'd already left. Wanted to meet you at the airport. Told him he didn't need to, you had a car lined up. Insisted he had to drive you. Something urgent, he didn't say what. Told him, Okay. Okay?"

"That's fine."

"What the hell exactly is a Texas Ranger anyway?"

"State police. Elite section. It's what they call their homicide investigators, Delby."

"Know what they call state homicide investigators in my neighborhood?"

"Yeah, cops. Texans have the need to be noticed."

"How's your head?"

"Fine."

"Ankle?"

"Fine."

"Right. Take care, boss. I'll be manning the phone. Call me at home after eight if you need to."

Her kids were asleep by eight. But she'd never made the offer before.

"I appreciate that."

She'd already hung up.

The plane was late. Scraggs was hyperventilating. The first thing he said was, "We're questioning the warden this afternoon. He thinks it's just a visit to rehash the shit we've already rehashed ten times over. We wanted you to be there. Shake him up as much as possible. Scare the shit out of him so we can get to the bottom of this."

"The nurse was forthcoming, then?"

"She was. I want you there when we tell him what she told us."

When we walked into the warden's living room he was able to shake our hands and give us a friendly welcome, but his palm was wet. His wife sat squashed into one end of the sofa. He introduced us to her. Her eyes were red and she started crying again. She said, "My husband is going to lose his job, isn't he?"

Scraggs was not sympathetic. "We all of us surely deserve to lose our jobs, ma'am, and that's the least of our problems far as I can see. Agent Rice is here because we've decided we have to work together in the short time we got left till the governor fires us.

"We are here to talk about the nurse who injected Rona Leigh Glueck with the chemicals. What about her, warden?"

The warden's forehead wrinkled. "She got sent up from Huntsville just like the chemicals got sent up from there. Never laid eyes on her before that day."

"Did you notice she swabbed Rona Leigh's arm with alcohol before she stuck her?"

He thought. "Yes, I guess she did."

"You didn't think that was just a little bit ridiculous?"

"I didn't think about it at all till now you've brought it up."

I did sympathize.

"See, it's like this, warden. Turns out Vernon got to her. He asked if she would do something humane for Rona Leigh. He told her to swab her arm so that Rona Leigh would feel like she was just gettin' a little shot of penicillin. Keep her calm. Nurse told me she didn't see any problem with that. Figured if it would help to keep the condemned woman calm, why not? Told me she was willin' to go along with him, Vernon bein' a holy man and all.

"Warden, tell Agent Rice where Vernon Lacker is."

"I been through that enough, Scraggs."

"I'm afraid you'll never be through that enough. Tell her."

"There was nothin' to hold him on. You people said that yourselves."

Scraggs turned to me. "We questioned Lacker for two days. He and everyone else. Not a one of them seemed to have any idea what the hell happened. We couldn't connect Lacker to the ambulance, and there was nothin' else to connect him to. We told him not to wander far from home. Told us he'd be in the prison chapel prayin' when he wasn't sleepin' in his bed. We asked the warden here to keep tabs on him."

I said, "So I guess he's in the chapel."

The warden looked down at his shoes. "No, ma'am, he's not, but—"

Scraggs bellowed, "Is he sleepin' in his bed, then?" Scraggs didn't wait for an answer. "Tell the agent where he is."

The warden looked up at me. His wife was beginning to make a lot of noise into her wads of Kleenex.

"He asked if he could go on a religious retreat. To the meditation center out by Austin. I told him he could. My wife thought it was the best place for him. Good idea. He was attractin' a lot—"

Scraggs interrupted. "Was it a good idea?"

"No."

"So aside from the guard in the ambulance, we got one more man missin', don't we? I'm thinkin' they're on retreat together. Warden, tell Agent Rice who got Vernon a job here at the Mountain View Unit."

He seemed to be having trouble answering. So Scraggs answered his own question.

"The warden's wife got him the job, Agent. The warden's wife happens to be Vernon's cousin. Isn't that right, ma'am?"

She managed to squeak out some sort of unintelligible response.

"You want a job in the Texas Department of Criminal Justice, you got to be related to somebody. That's right too, ma'am, isn't it?"

She wailed.

"And who got the guard his job here at the prison?"

Now she sounded like a small dog barking.

"Vernon did, isn't that right?"

That woman could cry.

Scraggs said to me, "The guard, Corrections Officer Harley Shank, is this lady's great-nephew. Makes him Vernon's cousin, twice removed." Then he said to the warden, "If you and your wife don't want to spend the rest of your lives tillin' the soil like the girls out that window, then you think where your nephew and his cousin might have gone. Get the whole family to think. Where the hell would they take that girl? Where is that goddamned retreat?"

The warden's wife tried to speak. Her husband said, "Take a deep breath, honey."

She did. Then we were able to make out her words. "Maybe we could call his school."

"What school?"

"The school where he earned his ministry. They're his real family. We're family by name, but that's all. His branch was estranged—"

A very wide-eyed very young Ranger came running in. He said, "Commander, turn on the TV. No matter the channel. Hurry, sir."

The remote control was right on the coffee table. None of us moved. The Ranger grabbed it and hit POWER. He was partial to CBS, just like I used to be. I could tell how serious the situation was by the gay glint in Dan Rather's eyes. Dan was giving a dramatic explanation of what he was about to show us.

Copies of a videotape had arrived at the three major networks an hour earlier. They would shed light on the kidnapping of Rona Leigh Glueck.

Scraggs said, "Did he say *kidnapping?*"

We shushed him. Dan said the networks had agreed among themselves to notify the FBI. Whereupon the tapes were immediately confiscated. But the contents of those tapes were appearing on various Internet sites. Therefore, the FBI had decided the tapes should be shown on the networks in case the public could be of any assistance in locating the site where the original tape was made.

I said, "All that must have happened while I was in the airplane."

I got shushed.

Dan said he wanted to make clear that the tape hadn't been edited or altered in any way. He said, "This tape is authentic. The woman you will see is Rona Leigh Glueck."

His producer cut to the tape.

Rona Leigh was propped on pillows in a bed. She was dressed in white and all the bedding was white. The bedstead was hand-carved, sleek, and it was white-

washed. The wall behind the bed was also white. She
seemed to be floating in layers of clouds.

Her skin was white too, but it was a dull dead white.
Not white were the whites of her eyes. They were yellow and bloodshot. Her cheeks were sunken, her lips
dry and cracked. The only thing about her that was the
same as when I'd seen her last was the hair, the dark
mat of curls overpowering her little face.

Rona Leigh Glueck was alive, but just barely. She was
getting oxygen via tubes into her nose and a feeding
tube led into a cut in her neck, nourishment flowing
directly into an artery.

She wore what I'd have to describe as a white cotton
granny gown, prim, with a dainty ruffle at the throat.

A whisper of a smile came to her lips. She was strug-
gling to keep her eyes open. She tried to look directly
into the lens of the camcorder probably set up on a tripod, no shake.

She said, "Thank you, Lord Jesus," and her eyes
closed.

A man's voice, deep and clear, came from just outside the camera's range. Some of his words, certain
phrases, resonated like the bong of a heavy brass bell.
He said, "The time has come for ALL the world to
CELEBRATE. THE SECOND COMING OF CHRIST is
upon us. His KINGDOM ON EARTH is at hand. Although Jesus DIED FOR US ON THE CROSS and
although HIS HEAVENLY FATHER DESTINED that
He be EXECUTED in order to RISE AGAIN ON THE
THIRD DAY, the Lord God ALMIGHTY has not followed the same plan for his DAUGHTER. THE
SISTER OF JESUS CHRIST DID NOT DIE!

"Jesus Christ did as His Father asked. As has His SIS-
TER! She REMINDS us of what Jesus suffered and what
she has suffered and WILL SUFFER in order for us to
understand that all sin may be repented and FOR-

GIVEN! Repentance is the road to peace. Dear fellow
Christians, the LORD GOD ALMIGHTY has allowed
us TODAY, in this new CENTURY, in this great COUN-
TRY OF OURS, to witness the SECOND COMING OF
CHRIST, a WOMAN, the woman who lies before us.
We are truly blessed and we thank God IN HIS INFI-
NITE WISDOM for granting us such a gift for which
we are surely NOT WORTHY!

"AMEN. AMEN AND GOD BLESS AMERICA!"

The shot faded to black as the camera panned in for
a close-up of Rona Leigh's sunken-cheeked but serene
face.

The warden said, "Did he say the sister of Jesus
Christ?"

His wife slid off the couch in a graceful swoon. All I
could think of was the moment when I first stood in the
death chamber where Rona Leigh was to be executed
and had an image of crucifixion. How appropriate.

While everyone attended to the warden's wife, I
ducked out of the room to call my office. Delby assured
me that a tape was at the lab and it was being studied
right then. She got me through to a technician, who
said to me, "We'll need a few hours. Call us back,
Poppy." I hung up. Scraggs was watching me. I told him
to stop standing there and find out what school Vernon went to, that there was probably a diploma
hanging in his apartment, and then I decided I needed
to use the phone again. I needed reassurance.

I called Beltrán Cardinal de la Cruz. He was gracious. He was also cynical.

He said, "We were both used, Miss Rice."

"You feel certain she orchestrated it?"

"She was instrumental. I've visited many prisoners
sentenced to die. No matter how strongly I try to im-
press upon them that they will be going to a better
place so long as they take responsibility for their crime

and repent, they don't want to die. It's human nature, this will to live, one of God's gifts. But Rona Leigh Glueck was perfectly satisfied to meet her maker, as she put it. Because of my vanity, I forgot all I've learned of human nature."

It wasn't vanity. She'd charmed him. We are all subject to charm, but I didn't tell him that charm fucks us all up, even cardinals.

He said, "I saw small bits of anxiety in Rona Leigh that was not the same kind of panic you see in a prisoner's eyes who is about to die. The panic is animal. Her anxiety apparently reflected worry that the plan, whatever it was, wouldn't work. But her will to live allowed her to place huge confidence in whoever guided her through the days and events leading up to her execution. Her faith was not in God but rather in whatever team of culprits managed to spirit her away and conceal her.

"This is becoming a nightmare. Even the religious close to me want to believe that it was Jesus who saved her. They have no compunction about revealing this belief. And now, after this tape, I see the situation as downright dangerous.

"So Miss Rice, I will pray all the harder for you. I will pray constantly until you find her. So that the despicable use of God's love—God's grace—to serve her misguided means will be exposed for what they are."

The man was furious. Powerful men don't like to be taken. He'd given his crook of a bookkeeper one severe dressing-down before he sent him to the Hopis.

"Eminence, my concern has always been that Rona Leigh was deprived of a fair trial. Deprived of justice. But looking at Rona Leigh from your point of view, could her will to live have come from her not having committed the crime? Did she trust God to save her because she was innocent?"

He was silent. I waited. Then he said, so quietly, "God has given you time, Miss Rice, hasn't he?"

"I'm sorry. Time for what, Eminence?"

"Time to prove whether or not she was served by justice. Time to clarify to all of us whether she is a cold-blooded killer or a victim and, to yourself, whether or not the law was fair to her. If the woman is innocent, then when you do catch her, she may be saved yet again. May God forgive me for the judgment I have made based on my vanity."

"Eminence, all of us make—"

"Miss Rice, your mission, your life's work, is to see to others. It is what God means when he asks us to have goodwill. But do not waste your time seeing to me. I am not deserving. See to Rona Leigh Glueck. Find the truth. Bring her to justice, whatever that justice might be."

Exactly. Justice.

10

A new videotape would come every three days or so, and with each one another tube had been removed from Rona Leigh's body. She was healing, the effects of the massive chemical poisoning she'd suffered fast disappearing. Christian Web sites played the tapes over and over, and the Christian network emphasized the obvious influence of Jesus in her words.

In the second tape, Rona Leigh was able to put together a fairly efficient smile-and-wave combo. She said, "As the arms of Jesus enfold me in love, heed the words of my brethren," meaning the man behind the voiceover. He told us what we could see—that Rona Leigh was out of the woods, though still very ill. This is how he put it:

"Jesus has LIFTED HER up, breathed NEW LIFE INTO HER LIPS and will soon TELL HER when to begin conveying His WORDS OF SALVATION." He did not refer to her as Rona Leigh Glueck. He called her the Daughter of God and, like her Brother in Christ, Jesus, she would take on the sins of the world in order to save it. The *New York Times* refused to capitalize *she* and *her* when referring to Rona Leigh; all the newspapers within the Bible Belt did.

By the third tape, she managed to speak for about a minute. The vehicle for her message was in the tradition of Jesus, a parable, uplifting, a lesson in kindness, honor, and truth with just a touch of warning for doubters woven through:

"A man came to an intersection. He relied on luck to choose the right road, the one that would lead him to his destination. He did not think or consider with the intelligence and cleverness he'd been blessed with. And so he came to another intersection, and yet another, then another, only to realize the last had been the first. He'd been traveling in circles. And so I say to you, every road does not lead to God. In order to be redeemed we must work to find the road and pray with all our heart and soul that we might choose the right one. This is the Divine Plan of our Lord and Savior. Under His direction and guided by His will, I will help all believers to find the right road. It is the word of the Lord."

I could detect Vernon's style mixed with someone more authoritative yet still genuine. It was someone who had performed a physiological feat no less spectacular than a miracle. When Rona Leigh finished speaking, the mystery man came on again with his rising and falling crescendo, to give Lazarus the credit for interceding with God so that Rona Leigh would rise from the dead.

I decided, even with so little, maybe I could get a psychological profile from my buddy the shrink. But I could only reach his assistant, who said he'd been called away to head up an emergency conference on the effect of memory cells on something or other that I didn't quite get. He was momentarily unavailable. He'd left orders that he was not to be disturbed with any calls. Translation: He was in Vegas.

I asked Delby to get me everything available on Vernon Lacker. When I checked my e-mail an hour later it was all there for me.

Vernon came from a holy family. Both his parents

were circuit preachers, no church, no flock to call their own. Once Vernon was born, his father continued to make his rounds through Arkansas, Missouri, and parts of Mississippi and Tennessee, while Vernon's mother stayed home, taught her son the scriptures, and helped him to memorize them. At three, he could recite lengthy passages and his gift drew worshipers to his home, where he and his mother offered a Saturday evening service on their front porch intended to prepare them for the greater devotion required by the Lord the following day.

His mother became pregnant again, and when Vernon's father learned the news he stayed on his circuit, choosing to return home to another wife, choosing his other children over Vernon and the new baby sister. Even though he lived only 150 miles away, what with his new name and social security number it took years for Vernon's mother to track him down. When she found out that he was a bigamist, she had him arrested. Bigamy is no small matter in Arkansas. Eventually, as a young teenager, Vernon visited his father in prison. And so arose his interest in the incarcerated.

He graduated from a small Baptist college in Louisiana with a degree in theology, his concentration prison ministry. His mother's cousin in Texas was married to a man up and coming in the Texas penal system and she got him a job: assistant to the chaplain at a minimum security prison for women. And when a jury a short time later sentenced a woman to death, he lobbied for the assignment at Gatesville. It was not difficult for him to get the position, because his mother's cousin's husband had been named warden of the new unit.

The only jobs Vernon ever held before his prison career began—if you can call them jobs—were two internships his senior year in college. One was with a

Reverend Raymond Tiner, who ran a correctional camp for teenage boys not far from the school. The other was with an Air Force chaplain at a nearby military base.

I decided to start with Tiner and then move along to the Air Force, which would be a lot easier. I called the school as the warden's wife had suggested. Administration told me that Reverend Tiner had retired years earlier and they didn't have a present address. But after his camp had closed, he'd served for a few years as pastor at the Church of Christ right in town. Perhaps the present pastor would be able to tell me where I could find him. After she gave me that number, I asked her if the school had taped any of his sermons or lectures, so she transferred me to the library. No, sorry, they had nothing.

Next, I called the Church of Christ rectory and told the present rector that I was with the college and that we were planning a centenary book with biographies of all our professors and instructors. Alas, we didn't have an address for Reverend Tiner. Alas, neither did he. So I asked about taped sermons and there were none that he knew of, but he put me in touch with the auxiliary, the Ladies in Christ. Some of the ladies had been members for many years, and perhaps one of them might know of a taped sermon.

I went through the same short series of lies with a Lady in Christ, who told me she didn't know where Reverend Tiner was but she was happy to say that some of the parishioners probably still had some sixteen-millimeter home movies of Reverend Tiner's holiday services, since they were so popular and drew people from miles around. She asked me why I was interested in them. I told her that when the centenary celebrations took place we would be showing old movies and tapes of faculty sermons. The Lady in Christ was more than happy to see what she could find. She'd get back to me.

So then I had Delby get everything there was on Reverend Raymond Tiner. She found some biographical material in a Christian *Who's Who*. He was born in Texas on the day a great hurricane destroyed Galveston. A very posh wedding reception was taking place in the top floor of a grand hotel sitting on a slight rise in the middle of the city. An hour after the storm struck, water had risen all the way to the ballroom and the guests sat on the tables, water swirling at their feet. One of them was pregnant and went into labor. Another of them was a doctor. He delivered Raymond Tiner in the eye of that storm.

Raymond believed he was delivered by God. After high school, where he never received a grade lower than an A, he attended and graduated from Princeton and then went on to Union Theological Seminary in New York, where he received a Ph.D. He made his way through a series of parish churches, including the Church of Christ in Louisiana, until he found what he felt was his true calling; he served as chaplain at a mental hospital for the criminally insane in Middletown, Connecticut. After a failed crusade to eliminate treating the patients' violent behavior through lobotomy, he headed to Louisiana and opened a school for incorrigibles, his work the forerunner of schools and camps that began popping up in rural America and became known as tough love facilities. Many of the schools, including his, were closed when young boys died trying to escape.

To ease his mind, Tiner found a welcoming retreat at the last working Shaker community in the world, located in New Hampshire. And there the trail came to an end. There was no record of what became of him after his departure from New Hampshire.

I found a number for the Shakers in New Hampshire and dialed. A young man answered. He told me he was in the process of joining the community, he and a friend, and that there was only one actual Shaker left. I told him I was an agent with the FBI and that I needed to speak with whoever was in charge, presumably the last Shaker. He said that would be Elder Charlotte. He told me he would ask her if she would agree to come to the phone. He added, "She's ninety-three years old."

I waited. He came back. "Elder Charlotte would like to know what, specifically, the FBI might want to speak to her about."

I said, "Specifically, I want to find out if she knew a Raymond Tiner some years ago when he was staying with your community."

The name meant nothing to him, but he delivered the message. A few minutes later, a soft voice on the telephone asked me, "And who might you be, sister?"

I said, "Is this Elder Charlotte?"

"Yes."

"My name is Penelope Rice."

"Ah. Penelope. Wife of Agamemnon. The great weaver of cloth. And of evidence, I would surmise." Very gracious. "Sister Penelope, here is what I wish to say to you. First and most important, if our society dies, we Believers do not wish to be remembered as chairs. More repugnant is the thought of our being remembered as an inspiration for Raymond Tiner's rogue society, which is based solely on his uninformed interpretation of our founder's philosophy, an utterly false interpretation."

I stayed calm, kept right on chatting her up. "How does his interpretation differ from yours, Elder Charlotte?"

"There is just one difference, and it colors all else. I

spent many hours debating him on this matter, but I could not sway him from his position and therefore was forced to ask him to leave. Our difference, I'm afraid, is that staggering."

"And did he leave?"

"Oh, yes. He went on to create his own society—I couldn't stop that—and I have no doubt they follow our historical and cultural traditions based on our founder's philosophy, *Hands to work and hearts to God.* He would live off the land and survive on the intelligence and ingenuity bestowed on the human race by God Almighty.

"His members, like ours, would no doubt be celibate, a choice God has given all of us. A choice for those of us who do not wish to procreate in order that we may dedicate our lives solely to God. We renounce our sordid propensity and ardent desire to copulate. Also, the time and dedication required to raise a good child precludes such a service. People outside don't understand—"

I interrupted as gently as I could. "Elder Charlotte, what else would you expect him to do, in terms of setting up a society of his own?"

She cleared her throat, and her voice was no longer soft. "Reverend Tiner will no doubt pray in our way. We allow the Holy Spirit to enter us, and then we express the Spirit through physical movement and sound. It is a form of prayer whereby we give our minds and bodies over to the Lord. If people think of our method of prayer as shaking, so be it. But we do not call ourselves Shakers. That is a slur. Our name has always been the United Believers in Christ's Second Coming. We are meant to be called Believers, which is how we refer to ourselves."

My heart dropped several beats. "Please repeat what you just said. Tell me again what the Believers believe."

"We believe in the second coming of Christ. But that is precisely where Reverend Tiner and I came to differ. He chose to follow a later interpretation of how the second coming should be defined. Our founder, an Englishwoman, *was* the Second Coming. She was God's Daughter and, like His Son, She died for our sins.

"But Reverend Tiner chose to go along with the Elders who led our society in the second century of our existence. They resolved that our founder was not the Daughter of God but rather a prophet who foretold that the Messiah would return again as a woman.

"Just as the Reverend Tiner is wrong, the twentieth-century Elders were wrong, but they came to see their mistake and returned to the teaching that we few continue to hold dear. Our founder was officially pronounced Messiah—the Messiah who carried out God's mission—when She overcame terrible trials and tribulations to found our society, to bring us from England to the United States, and to keep from being killed for her beliefs.

"If you find Reverend Tiner, he will look like us but he is not us. He fell away to watch for Her, to await the second coming, which, of course, will never happen. It happened two hundred years ago." Her voice began to tremble. "He took one of the two young men and three women we had adopted as children. The group would be the foundation for the renewal of the society on his imprudent terms.

"We true Believers haven't much time left. If the society dies with us we accept that. What Reverend Tiner has formed is not true. How can it be true when he has determined that his Messiah has just now come, that the Daughter of God, the Sister of Christ, is a *murderer?* A *beast?*"

I found my voice. "Why didn't you call the authorities?"

"To the authorities, I am a chair."

I offered my condolences and then the second I hung up I called the Church of Christ back and asked to speak to the Lady in Christ again. I apologized if she'd been getting a busy signal. I said, "I'm trying to reach so many of our former professors."

She said she hadn't called me back. She said, "I needed to pray before getting back to you. For guidance."

I said, "Is there a problem?"

"Well . . ."

"Did you find any home movies?"

"Yes, I did. Three. Three of our ladies took movies of their children when they appeared in Reverend Tiner's little plays. I have one of them. I watched it."

"You have it with you?"

"Right here in my hands."

"Are his words on the movies?"

"Yes. But the movies are the private property of the church, naturally. The thing is, one of our ladies works at the college and they just didn't seem to know about any centenary. And when I watched the movie, well . . . I mean . . ."

I started blathering away while I got on my cell phone and gave the signal.

I kept on blathering until she said that there was someone at the door and she had to go. Before she could hang up, I got to hear her scream as the agents broke into her house, relieved her of the home movie, and left.

I hung up and the phone rang. It was my friendly agent from Waco. "Northrup," he reminded me. Then he said, "We got him."

"Who?"

"The guy with the hammer and nails."

"Good. Who is he?"

"He's a cop."

"Oh, please."

"Want to meet him?"

"Sure do."

"Can you come up here right away?"

"I can. Why'd he do it?"

"Someone paid him."

"Well, no kidding. I meant, why did someone . . . ? Never mind. You don't know, do you?"

"No."

I drove the twenty miles to Waco, took me no time on the bypass, where someone had dropped concrete blocks on Scraggs's vehicle. I found my way to the Federal Building, where Northrup was waiting for me. "Guy's lawyer just got here."

Northrup took my elbow and hastened me down a corridor.

"This particular lawyer happens to require a check for twenty-five thousand dollars deposited into his personal account before he sees a client, and he won't see the client till after the check clears."

"How sticky was arresting this cop?"

"Haven't arrested him. He's just here for questioning. If he's arrested he's not going to lead us where we need to go."

"With the kind of lawyer he's got, I don't think he'll lead you anywhere."

"You don't know my chief."

Hadn't had the pleasure.

The door to the chief's office was open. Flung open, by the look of the lawyer. Northrup and I stood in the open doorway and watched.

The cop sitting in the chair wasn't in uniform, but he was a cop. He was in the middle of jerking his thumb toward the lawyer and saying, "I never seen this dude in my life. He's not any lawyer of mine."

The lawyer said, "Shut up. We are on federal property. We're in the offices of the FBI. We're bugged."

The cop said to him, "Who sent you?"

The lawyer slammed his briefcase down on the chief's desk. That always shuts a client up.

I said to Northrup, "If this office is bugged, why are we standing here eavesdropping?"

We walked in.

The lawyer said, "Is this the police?"

The cop said, "I'm the police."

The lawyer said, "I told you to shut up, you damn fool."

The chief jumped up and came around his desk to pump my hand. "A real honor to meet you, ma'am, a real real honor. Name's Brewster."

I said, "I'm glad to meet you, too, Brewster."

Then Brewster said to the lawyer, "I'd like to offer you the great privilege of meeting Miz Poppy Rice, visitin' us here from DC where she reconfigured our crime lab. Did such a good job runnin' the place they all got calluses from pattin' her back. Now she's our A-One investigator, and her car is the very one your client here chose to demobilize with the contents of his trusty tool kit."

The client said, "I ain't his client. And I never got near any FBI—"

The lawyer told him to shut up again, and the chief aimed me toward a chair. "Take a load off, Agent. Get in here, Northrup. Shut the door behind you."

I sat, Northrup stood guard.

The lawyer said to me, "It is indeed a pleasure to meet you, Agent. I have worked with your office many times, another great pleasure." He looked to Brewster. "Listen, can I speak with you people alone?"

Brewster said, "'Course. Northrup, take the detainee outa my office."

The detainee was very happy to get out of Brewster's office.

The lawyer said, "I am about to go through the necessary motions expected of me, and then I'm washin' my hands of whatever shit's comin' down here. That okay with you?"

Brewster looked to me. "Miz Rice?"

I said, "Your investigation, sir."

He stood up and stuck his head out the door. "Northrup, bring the perp back in."

The perp's voice came through the door before he did. "I ain't a perp." In the doorway, the perp continued protesting. "I have a right to call my union. I—"

Northrup yanked him into the room, told him to sit back down, shut the door behind him, and stood guard again.

Brewster said to the perp, "A representative of your employer, the Houston Police Department, is on his way. You can talk union with him when he gets here. Since he's runnin' a little late, maybe we can get to the bottom of this and then maybe he won't get here at all.

"First, real quick, I got a few intros to finish up. Miz Rice, this here gentleman with the briefcase is H. Johnson Medved, Esquire, who is representin' that little fella settin' over there."

The little fella, the cop, wearing all brown like a storm trooper, was way past six feet tall and had to weigh two-seventy-five, minimum. He stood up.

"I am a Houston police officer. My name is Richard Purcell."

The lawyer said to him, "Sit down. And how many times do I have to tell you to shut up?"

"You ain't got the right to tell me a goddamn thing."

So the cop and the lawyer went at it, and Brewster joined in helping the lawyer do as he'd asked, go through the motions leading to a point when the lawyer could desert the client he was hired to represent. I didn't see the percentage in that. I wanted to know if whoever hired the lawyer was the same person who hired the cop. Northrup was watching me, watching me think.

I scoped the office and was impressed to see the unexpurgated edition of the Random House dictionary on a stand in the corner. Even though this Texas department chief with the FBI was also a cowboy who liked to yell and was as capable of turning as beet red as the next guy, he saw the need to have a dictionary on hand and not just any dictionary.

I sidled over to the stand and, having taken my cue from the briefcase-smashing lawyer, I hefted the dictionary, held it chest high, and dropped it.

They all drew their weapons except for Northrup, who had obviously been head of his class in observation skills. The office door flew open and several agents, also with weapons drawn, flew in and froze in crouched positions just like in the movies. Jesus. Both the cop and the lawyer had their own guns pointed at the dictionary. Then they saw Northrup, smiling, arms folded across his chest. He said into the extraordinary silence, "Miz Rice accidentally dropped the chief's dictionary." He unfolded his arms. "But don't you move, ma'am. Allow me."

He came over and picked it up.

I said, "I'm so clumsy."

Everybody reholstered and took up previous positions.

I said to the cop, "What did you use to hit me over the head with? The same hammer you used to drive nails into my tire?"

The lawyer jumped up. "Don't answer that."

I knew he'd do that just as I knew his order would incite the cop further. The cop said, "What? Hey, you're

the one got laid out in Austin, ain't you? I didn't do
that. I'd never do such a thing. I ain't crazy."

Brewster said to me, "Agent, what say we cover one
thing at a time?" Then he said to the lawyer, "I want us
to all settle down and talk things out before our gal
from Washington creates some kind of international
incident."

International. Texans still think of Texas as an independent republic.

He sat, the rest of us sat, and I crossed my legs, ren-
dering them all momentarily speechless. While their
eyes were riveted on the eight or so inches of my exposed thighs, I said, "Mr. Medved, I want to know the
deal you intended to make when you walked in here.
Obviously, no one's under arrest, as my fellow agents
did not disarm your client. And since, according to
your client, he's not your client, I should think the
chief might want to make a deal."

Brewster said, "If I may, here is the deal. And for Mr.
Brown here, trust me, it's the *only* deal."

"It's Mr. Purcell," said the cop.

"Mr. Purcell, Mr. Brown, whichever. I would like to
know the name of the fella who paid you to put an FBI
agent's life in danger. Then I want you to use my
phone to make known your intention to resign from
the Houston Police Department this very day. Then I
will let you out of here and you can go into the nearest
church, get down on your fucking knees, and thank
the Lord God Almighty that things ain't worse for you
than that. If that deal don't appeal to you, I got an alternative."

Brewster looked to me. I used the same shrug as
Northrup.

He said, "I will use the power invested in me to arrest
you for a federal offense—the attempted murder of a

peace officer of the Federal Bureau of Investigation—
and I don't need to tell you the penalty for—"

The cop jumped up. "He only wanted to put a scare in
some guy screwin' around with his wife. Put a nail in his
tire. He lied. I didn't know a lady would be drivin' the
car, and I didn't know she wouldn't be from around
here, and I sure as hell didn't know she'd be FBI."

Medved reverted to shouting *shut up* again.

Brewster said to the lawyer, "We got a deal goin'
here. Let me finish." Then he went back to the cop.

"Since I'm not going to arrest you, here's what I expect you to do. Tell the people who made up the
wife-adultery story that you were fool enough to believe it, but you're not fool enough to harass a big-shot
FBI agent no matter how much they pay you. And I
want you to do it right now or you will find yourself in
some very deep shit. But just before you do, tell us—"

The cop said, "It wasn't the money. It was just a favor.
For an old friend."

The lawyer said, "He tells you the name and we're
out of here, is that it?"

Purcell decided to hurry and tell the name. "Tommy
Kego."

Brewster said, "Who is—?"

"Used to be a cop. Knew him in Houston. Retired."

"Where's he at now?"

"Little town outside Austin."

The chief smiled at Medved. "Counselor, I have only
one question for you, but I believe Miz Rice should
have the privilege of asking it."

I didn't get a chance to ask it. The lawyer had had
enough. "Ma'am, the man who asked me to protect the
interests of Mr. Purcell is a philanthropist who helps
out police officers in need and who prefers to remain
anonymous. I don't know the name Kego, and I am
not going to tell you my client's name. He has that

right. And there'll be no need for you to tap my phone because he doesn't speak to me directly."

I said to the lawyer, "Not to worry. He's going to speak to *me*. No one needs you to find out who he is. And I'd suggest, for your own good, you break your ties with your philanthropist and consider going back to handling dog-bite cases and water in the cellar."

The lawyer said, "Don't you threaten me, Agent. Officer Purcell is correct. I was here to protect his interests but not to represent him. However, I would suggest to him that he procure representation elsewhere as soon as possible."

He picked up his briefcase and headed toward the door. Northrup opened it for him, and H. Johnson Medved was gone.

Brewster said to Northrup, "See he's followed. See he's bugged. His office, his house, his garage, his car, his fuckin' dog. S'cuse my French, Agent. And find out who his fuckin' philanthropist is."

Exit Northrup.

"Now. What did you say your name was, Jack?"

The cop couldn't get his name out. He was hyperventilating.

The chief said, "Never mind. Your friend, this Kego? He got some clout?"

Cop managed a yes.

"Next time some nutcase wants you to do a bad turn for them, don't be influenced by clout. Just say no. Now, before you get the hell outa here, step into my outer office and my secretary will get you the outside line you'll be needin'. And make sure I get an invitation to your retirement party, you hear?"

Exit the cop.

Brewster sighed and looked at me. "I need a drink. Will you allow me to buy you a stiff one, Agent? By way of an apology from my office. We'll get the guy with the brick soon. But we've got to let this Purcell loose so he can contact Kego, and then we'll see where Kego leads us. Boys outside are primed to take care of that, as you pointed out to Mr. Medved, Esquire. Won't take but a day or two is my bet. So how about the drink?"

"Actually, I'm starving."

"Well, good. The place I got in mind serves a thirty-two-ounce porterhouse the likes of which never get exported outa the great state of Texas."

Maybe Texas actually *is* another country. They talk import-export.

I uncrossed my legs. "Sounds great," I said, to the top of his head. Dining with Texans was going to force me to renew my membership in a DC fitness center.

By the time we got to the restaurant, a seventeen-second drive from the Federal Building, Brewster had received news as to the present role of the retired Houston cop Tommy Kego, old pal of Officer Purcell, now a retired cop as well. Kego was a state appointee, appointed specifically by the present governor eight years ago and still serving on the Texas Board of Pardons and Paroles. The very board that turned down all of Rona Leigh's appeals for a reprieve.

Over our four pounds of cattle, the chief would interrupt himself every few minutes to take a message from his cell phone and then pass along the news. "Ya see, ma'am? Those boys on the parole board?" He waved his fork. "They don't like to be disturbed. They got a cushy situation for themselves and they been havin' a lot of trouble lately. It's in their best interest to keep killers movin' in a direct line from death row to the death house and just keep quiet about it all. They been havin' trouble stickin' with *no comment* lately because the press has been houndin' them so bad. They never figured gettin' hounded would be part of the job."

Three mouthfuls later, his phone would beep again.

The facts continued to roll in, and the Waco chief would chew and then fill me in. "Kego was a cop on the Houston force seventeen years ago when Rona Leigh was arrested at his precinct, though he was not the arresting officer and did not take part in the apprehension or investigation. After she was convicted, though, he got a big promotion within the department, a new job with more money and one hell of a lot more prestige than merely pounding the beat. Shortly after that he married the daughter of a rich doctor who catered to the up-and-coming of Houston.

"Doctor, name a Blake Redmon, relocated to Austin, and now he runs several a those factories where they zap your eyeballs so you can throw your glasses out with the garbage. This Kego continued to rise and rise in the department, and the minute the governor was elected he appointed Kego to the parole board."

Over dessert, the phone filled in more blanks. While we spooned upside-down cake saturated with goo that had to be one part butter to one part brown sugar to a third part some alcoholic compound, Brewster told me that the guy's father-in-law lived in the Texas equivalent of the Kennedy compound—big ranch outside Austin with a big house and a bunch of medium-sized houses for his grown children and their no-'count husbands and wives, including Kego.

Then he said, "So what we need now, Agent, is the connection. Need to know why this Kego worried about your presence. And we'll find out who knocked you cold, too, trust me. Kego couldn't count on a friendly favor for that. He had to hire a real piece of shit. We'll get him, I promise you."

He pushed his chair back a foot so digestion could commence uninterrupted by the pressure of the table edge on his large stomach. "But whoever's unhappy that you came pokin' around this Rona Leigh thing—

well, by now they know you're back and continuin' to poke. So whoever hired the piece of shit, he's presumably gettin' unhappier by the minute. Therefore, I would like to know your whereabouts at all times."

I leaned forward on my elbows. "I count on my assistant to act as my whereabouts. Her name is Delby Jones."

I gave him Delby's card.

He pulled his chair back up to the table, leaned over, took my hand in both of his large ones, and looked into my eyes, his own filled with concern. "I will continue to do my best to regain your trust, Poppy Rice. I hope you accept my apologies for what you've been through."

I removed my hand. "I will accept your apologies, and you'll regain my trust, as soon as you find a few more connections and see that whoever hit me over the head is behind bars."

I told him I loved the steak. I wondered if Brewster was his first name or his last. It was late when I got back to Gatesville.

I called Delby and told her to get what she could on Doc Redmon.

She said, "Tonight?"

"I'd appreciate it."

"Okay, I'll do that. Call the director so he quits bothering me. Dying to congratulate you."

"Okay."

He was still at the office. He said, "Poppy, I heard from the lab today. I don't know how you did what you did, but the guy in the church movie is the guy in the room with Rona Leigh Glueck making the videos. The voices are one and the same."

"Has Auerbach seen the movie?"

"Auerbach's in charge."

"Thought so."

"Your boundless commitment to this department will never fail to . . ."

When I got rid of him, the phone rang immediately. Delby again.

"Who's Fred Helton?"

"I don't . . . wait. Let me think."

"Take your time. I got all night. Not a single one of my kids has an ear infection."

"Fred Helton. He's Melody Scott's brother. He was in the witness room."

"Oh. No wonder he sounded like such a miserable dude. You feel like talkin' to him? He asked."

"Where is he?"

"He lives outside Houston, halfway to Austin. And a neighbor of his would like to talk to you too."

"A neighbor?"

"One of the jurors who convicted Rona Leigh. Helton said Cardinal de la Cruz advised him to see you. That cardinal's all over like shit, ain't he?"

"Cardinals obviously have more responsibilities than meet the eye. Give me Helton's number."

I would love to hear what that juror wanted to say. But before I could call Melody's brother, I had things to do. First, Max Scraggs. I got the same woman as last time. She recognized my voice, said, "Hold on a sec, Agent." I heard the sounds of bodies rolling over.

He said, "I'm here."

"Max, the FBI found the guy with the hammer and nails. Now don't flip out; they threatened him and let him go."

First I let him finish flipping out.

"I told you not to flip out. They want to follow his tracks."

"For Christ's sake, the man hit you over the head with a brick."

"Someone else did that."

"How would you know that?"

"I could tell. I had the pleasure of meeting him this afternoon in Waco."

"Who the fuck is he?"

"A cop."

"Sweet Jesus."

"He did it as a favor for another cop, the son-in-law of a doctor named Blake Redmon."

Silence.

"Do you know him, Max?" More silence. "You live in Texas, you've at least heard of him. What's the cop's name?"

"Can't say. If I do, your guys will be following him too, and your guys and my guys will end up shooting each other."

"Listen, Max, could you come up to Gatesville in the morning? We'll have breakfast, we'll talk, and then I need to use you."

"How?"

"Melody Scott, Rona Leigh's victim—her brother wants to talk to me. Him and one of her jurors. If they want to tell me something that has anything to do with the possibility that Rona Leigh may not have gotten the kind of trial she's guaranteed under the U.S. Constitution, I want the Texas law there with me."

"Poppy, if for some reason that I sure as hell can't figure out, you've got Blake Redmon interested in you, I'm not going to let you out of my sight. I'll be with you for breakfast."

"What's that mean?"

"We'll talk in the morning."

"One more thing."

"What?"

I told him who sprung Rona Leigh. Gave him the name and all I knew.

I doubt the man went back to sleep.

Delby called me. "Boss, my fax has been pourin' out some major shit. Here's the connection you're looking for. It's a humdinger. That forensic physician who testified for the prosecution against Rona Leigh? Dr. Glee? Dude name of Blake Redmon."

I think I said fuck me.

"Well, here's the story on that scumbag. This guy Redmon's daughter got knocked up seventeen years ago by your Houston cop, Kego. She was a kid just about to finish high school at the time. They ran away to Mexico and got married. So this doctor who never testified at any other trial before or since told Rona Leigh's jury he could smell her on the ax handle. Then, right after the conviction, Kego gets his reward, a big promotion. Real *real* big. That's because the Houston police department prides itself on being more successful than any other department in the state as to number of convictions and is especially proud of the number of death penalties, more than any other county in Texas and the rest of the U.S. too, for that matter.

"So basically, you're one rich doctor, your daughter has just participated in a debutante ball to the tune of twenty-five grand and suddenly she announces she's married to some bottom-of-the-barrel patrolman who has also knocked her up. What do you do? You agree to testify in a murder trial where everyone's crying for blood. You hand over that blood with your false testimony, and consequently the defendant never has a chance in hell for justice, but the prosecutor gets another notch in his belt and therefore your son-in-law gets a free ride to a prestigious level of law enforcement thereby ensuring that Daughter maintains her place in Texas society."

Delby took a breath and said, "Now that last bit's an oxymoron, right, boss?"

This is why I love, cherish, and honor Delby Jones.

She said, "So here's the rest. Soon as the present governor was elected, he appoints Kego, the son-in-law, to his present position on the Texas Board of Pardons and Paroles. Turns out the governor and this here Dr. Glee went to prep school and college together, and according to the brothers at Delta Kappa Shmappa the doc was the sole reason the governor made it through college at all. The doc called the governor, who was a legislator at the time, and asks for the entrée necessary to volunteer for Rona Leigh's trial. Only way the doc's ass stays covered now is for Rona Leigh's sentence to be carried out.

"So I'm thinkin' about all you told me, and the way I see it is the governor granted her a reprieve after all when he told the warden at Gatesville to call an ambulance. If he hadn't, the warden would have stalled around and Rona Leigh would have choked to death on her own vomit. Man, I love irony, boss. Or, as we call it in my neighborhood, findin' out somethin's been shoved up your ass without your knowin' it."

I said, "Delby, I am a great observer of ironic developments myself, but there are more pressing matters. Has this Redmon ever done anything illegal?"

"Honey, the guy has had more malpractice suits filed against him than a centipede has feet. And has never had to pay anybody a dime. Seems it's like this here: *You don't like I sent a laser beam so far into your eye you need a dog to cross the street? How would you like two broken legs so's you need a wheelchair to go along with the dog?* That's how he settles his malpractice cases. Some, anyway. I'm exaggerating just a little bit. But he's got a whole bunch of guys, led by his son-in-law, who back up threats he makes. The guy with the hammer and nails is entry-level. Whoever dropped a rock on your head is probably one rich fellow about now. Long gone unless he's a halfwit, sorry to say.

"Bottom line: Guy sold Rona Leigh down the river

solely for the advancement of his testosterone-heavy
son-in-law. Top line: Boss, long as you're in Texas,
watch out for pickpockets and don't drink the water."

"I won't. Delby, I have just one more thing to ask of
you."

"I got it right here." She gave me Redmon's phone
number.

The person who answered Redmon's phone identified himself as Staff.

I said, "Listen Staff. My name is Poppy Rice, I'm with
the FBI, and I need to speak to the doctor."

"Is this an emergency? It's quite late."

"I know what time it is."

He asked, "May I ask what this would be in reference
to?"

"I have a pain in my ass."

Staff put me on hold.

Dr. Redmon was all charm, all DEKE, the way the
boys are when their moms come to college on parents'
weekend and they have to hide the fact that they've
been placed on academic probation.

"Agent Rice," he said. "I understand you'd like me to
recommend a proctologist."

"Actually, I'm the one with a recommendation. I recommend that you deposit twenty-five thousand bucks
into your lawyer's checking account right away. Nothing
is going to stop my exposing you. I'm going to reopen
some of your most egregious malpractice suits, and I'm
going to get people with poor eyesight and broken noses
to sue you until you've got nothing left to your name but
a tongue depressor. I'm going after you. Be prepared to
hear a fellow frat brother tell the press he only faintly remembers you when you go looking for help from him.
And if you dare put anything in my way, if the numbskull
cops on your payroll come within fifty feet of me, you will
be arrested immediately. Tough choice, I know, but if I

were you I'd choose poverty over the Texas judicial system, because we all know. . . ."

The phone was dead. At what point he'd hung up on me, I didn't know. I didn't care, either, because he would get to hear it all again through more proper channels or I will eat dirt.

11

It was late. I was wired, but I forced myself to wait till morning before I called the Air Force chaplain who'd been Vernon's other mentor.

No explanations required. He told me he expected he'd be hearing from the FBI sooner or later. "It's about my student. It's about Vernon Lacker, isn't it?"

"Yes, sir, it is." I always call military officers *sir.* They especially appreciate that from a civilian. Loosens them up.

He said, "I can't tell you how much I liked and admired that boy. All of us who are connected with the school are devastated by the trouble he's in. Have you found him yet?"

"No. I'm wondering if you might have any idea where he might be."

"He is looking for his wife, I'd have to say. A crying shame. There was a boy not just interested in praising God but in doing his work. Agent, Vernon Lacker was a shy boy without a pulpit, but he carried out the work of the Lord in the most challenging place there is: prison."

The man should have heard his shy boy exhorting the witnesses to Rona Leigh's execution not to weep as she was only asleep. In Hebrew.

He said, "Sadly, of course, a prison chaplain of Vernon's sensitivity can be influenced and manipulated by his charges, as we have seen."

I said, "Perhaps manipulated by others as well. Did you know his second mentor when Vernon was your student?"

He coughed. "I did." He coughed again. Double cough means the human body is resisting what wants to come out of its mouth. But the Air Force man was a soldier. He carried on. "Reverend Tiner served as an adjunct, like several of us, but he didn't actually teach on campus. The boys went to him. He came to all our meetings, though. It was important for him that he have . . . input. What you are wanting to know is whether this fellow, with Vernon's help, orchestrated Rona Leigh Glueck's escape."

I would not have a coughing fit. Very steadily, I said, "Sir, what makes you assume that?"

"I have to tell you, Agent, my colleagues and I have spoken of little else, though only in hypothetical terms . . . at first, whether Vernon helped Rona Leigh escape, and then whether Tiner might have been involved. The Vernon we knew, though naïve, was so pure of heart we couldn't imagine he would do what he knew to be wrong. But Raymond Tiner had entered Vernon's life again when he married the killer. Last night I had dinner with a few of my colleagues. Old-timers like myself. That's when we admitted it."

"Admitted what, exactly?"

"Admitted we could no longer deny that the voice on the tapes might well be Raymond Tiner. We decided we must stop deliberating and, instead, pray for the capture of the condemned woman."

"Did any of you think of fingering Tiner, sir?"

I waited. Finally, he said, "Last night we did express to one another our collective desire to *finger*, as you put it, Raymond Tiner. But that would have been foolish because we have nothing to prove that he is the voice of the man on the tape. And we had to consider our thorough dislike of the man. He has been an evil influence on a boy we were once so fond of. We're only human and, deep down, we worry about what will become of Vernon, once . . . once this is all over."

"All right, sir. I can understand that." I couldn't. "But it will help me if I know as much as possible about Raymond Tiner."

"I can certainly tell you what I know. As I said, he was an adjunct here. He served as mentor to third-year students only. Vernon was entrusted to Reverend Tiner and was sent to the camp the man ran for incorrigible boys. Reverend Tiner invented the tough love movement, a movement having nothing to do with love but rather with cruelty and deprivation. The goal was to break the child's will. Easy to do when there is no one to advocate for that child. He'd have the boys lie down, and he'd play the music of the wind in swaying trees, the ocean waves, birdsong, things of that nature. And while he played his tapes, when he had the boys almost asleep, hypnotized, he'd clang a pair of cymbals together and shout, *Satan!*

"I told Tiner it was the kind of things the Communists in Hanoi did to our captured men. Men I served with."

Had to keep him on the main track. "Do you know what has become of Tiner?"

"Once Tiner severed his ties with us, I never heard anything about him until last year. Vernon called me periodically as he worked his way through the Texas prison system, always bursting with excitement over each promotion. But that all came to a halt. I did not respond in the way he'd hoped when he told me of his decision to marry the killer. I advised him strongly against such an irrational act. I reminded him of his training. How important it was not to become emotionally involved with the people who needed him. Who placed their trust in him. I told him it was unethical to do otherwise.

"It was a terrible conversation. He was calling me to ask me to perform the ceremony. He truly thought I would be happy for him. I made him realize that the opposite was true. All I could do was emphasize that what he was planning was a dreadful mistake.

"He said to me, 'But she's my girl,' as if this killer were a high school sweetheart.

"And after the deed was done, I never heard from him again except for a note telling me of the marriage and that Raymond Tiner had performed the ceremony. Tiner had entered Vernon's life again. In effect, he brought down a fine young man, involved him in what reflects his own madness. I suppose, then, that this is one piece of information that would be useful to you, Agent. Tiner was in the women's prison. He'd met Rona Leigh Glueck."

Where he perhaps had been bewitched as well.

"Sir, you never contacted Vernon after that?"

"No. My stubbornness, sadly, prevailed."

I asked him where Tiner might go. Say, if he wanted to start another camp or some religious community.

He said, "I'm sorry, Agent. The man was a closed individual."

"If you think of anything, if any of your colleagues at the school . . ."

He promised he would think and he would ask around.

A short time later, my director called me again. He wasn't going through Delby anymore. The capture of Rona Leigh Glueck had become a top priority.

"Poppy, we've got all the data we can get out of the

videotapes. We want you in on this. Can you get here today?"

I looked at my watch. Still early. "I'll be there this afternoon."

The airline reservations clerk I'd been dealing with now recognized my voice without my having to say who was calling. I ordered up two tickets. Scraggs had a right to be in on things too. I reached him on his cell phone. He was grateful.

When Scraggs spotted me at the airport, he put down his newspaper, stood up, came over, and took my overnight bag from me. He was stiff—made a little face when he stood. Takes a while to recoup after your car slams into a concrete wall. The handshake, though, was as solid as ever. "Never been to the nation's capital. Hope you'll be able to show me a few sights."

Wonderful.

❧

We arrived at the crime lab, and as I walked to the screening room everyone came out from behind their tables, up from their microscopes, turned off their Bunsen burners to welcome me back. I was damned proud of all of them.

Auerbach sat at the computer. He said to me, "Hey, Poppy!"

I said, "Hey, Auerbach!" and then I introduced Max Scraggs to all of them.

What Auerbach was looking at was blown up and projected on a movie screen. A dozen of us sat close by him: me, my director, Scraggs, a couple of technicians, various agents, Delby. Auerbach moved his arrow across a frame of the first video, across Rona Leigh's near-dead body and face until it set down on the headboard of the bed. *Click.* He zoomed in.

"The headboard is pecan, hand-carved." The arrow

meandered across the headboard. *Click, click, click.* He zoomed in until we were at the eye of his microscope. The grain of the wood looked like a sandbar. He said, "Fine wood from a tree forty-seven years old."

Click. The arrow settled on the blanket covering Rona Leigh. Auerbach said, "Hand knit, lightweight wool, worsted." Zoom and *click.* We were looking at ship's ropes. He said, "The sheet is linen. Homespun. The sheet, the pillowcase, Rona Leigh's nightgown. All linen, woven by two separate hands."

He spent ten minutes describing the difference in weave that showed him two people had contributed to the work. Scraggs tapped me. I whispered that there was no rushing Auerbach.

We spent a much longer time on the adobe wall behind the bed.

"There is a thin coat of whitewash over a type of adobe that is between 296 and 299 years old. Rona Leigh Glueck is in a mission built by North American natives under the direction of Spanish priests." We learned all we never wanted to know about how one can deduce such a thing.

The arrow flowed up and down over the wall. Auerbach said, "The adobe is incredibly preserved. There is no explanation at this time as to how it could have remained in this near-perfect state over such a long period of time. The makeup of the adobe shows us the mission was built in Texas. Rona Leigh is still in Texas."

The time had to come where I would interrupt. I said, "There's adobe in Mexico, too. In Arizona. California. How do you know—"

He was only a little short with me. "First, they don't bother preserving adobe in Mexico. And the adobe in Texas is different from the adobe in Arizona, which is different from the adobe in California."

Click, click, click. He fed us pictures of microscopic

comparisons of adobe. He pointed out the character-
istics of Texas adobe as compared with the others. We
were educated further.

He said, "She's in Texas."

Then he pressed a button. The screen went white
and the lights came up.

I got up and stood behind Auerbach. I asked him
how long he'd been sitting in front of the computer.

He said, "What day is this?"

I told him to go home, get some sleep, and not return to his office for twenty-four hours.

He refused. He said, "Don't make me miss something, Poppy."

I gave him a ten-second professional shoulder mas-
sage. I said, "Your muscles feel like a headboard made
of pecan wood." Then I asked, "So, Scraggs, how many
missions in Texas?"

"Two million, give or take a hundred thousand. I
don't know. There are a dozen official ones under the
U.S. Park Service, starting with the Alamo. Most of
those, like the Alamo, needed restoration; a couple are
in such good shape they've needed no work at all other
than to protect them. But none in the shape this gentleman has described, far as I've heard.

"Then there are many, many buildings and pieces of
buildings built by missionaries that are abandoned. If
that retired minister of yours is in one of them, fixed
up so that it's habitable, with walls that are intact, the
Rangers will find him. We've got the resources to locate every ruin in Texas in a few hours.

"'Course, we got an all-points bulletin out on
Tiner. . . . It's a bitch when there's no recent photo."

We had all despaired that the last photo taken of
Raymond Tiner was thirty years old. Now we were
using a frame from the Church of Christ lady's home
movie instead. That was only twenty years old.

I said, "Well, tell the Rangers there's a mission out there populated with people who know how to weave and sew and knit and make some very lovely furniture, and these people have some serious tools. They can refurbish a vehicle so it replicates an ambulance or a police van. They've got computers and webmasters who can develop and destroy a site in short order. And they sure as hell have medical people too, because whoever saved Rona Leigh's life is a genius. That is, unless God did it after all."

My director said, "Captain Scraggs, no word yet on what happened to her blood?"

"Was about to bring that up. I got word. About an hour before I left Texas this morning. The warden in Gatesville has known since the get-go what happened to the blood. Hushed it up. Had so many strikes against him, he felt he had to do something to save his skin. The blood samples were there all along, but they didn't match up to what the prison knew to be her blood type. Her blood had been replaced with someone else's. Harley Shank's. The missing guard."

The director said, "Jesus."

I said, "How come you didn't tell me?"

"Didn't want you jumping out of the airplane."

"That warden been fired yet?"

"He has."

Our chemical researcher's turn. She and Auerbach had changed seats. Took her awhile to get her data up. Numbers and x's and y's filled the screen. We followed the arrow as it went from line to line, unable to understand any of it. But her narrative was easy. That's because she'd gotten nowhere.

She said, "These are our conclusions based on no real data. We've looked at studies where rats were given minuscule amounts of potassium chloride, with the idea of building up these amounts slowly over a period of time to see how much they could tolerate. They couldn't tolerate any. Less than a thousandth of a milligram, and their little hearts came to a screeching halt. I'm sorry. That's it."

I said to her, "Don't feel bad. At least we know Rona Leigh isn't a rat."

Then I took a turn. These people had always worked best when they weren't relegated to a vacuum. I filled them in on the bizarre life history of Raymond Tiner and his influence on Vernon, as described by the Air Force chaplain. I looked to my sad researcher. "I don't have a lot more than you."

My director said, "Where the fuck do these nutcases come from?"

I said, "Texas." I turned to Scraggs. "No offense."

The meeting came to an end.

On the way back to the airport, I reminded Scraggs about Melody Scott's brother wanting to talk to me.

"You brought me to DC to thank me for a favor I didn't even concede, right?"

Cynical fellow, Scraggs. "I know it looks that way, but that wasn't the reason."

"Where's this guy live?"

I gave him the address Delby had gotten to me.

He said, "I know it."

I got on my cell phone and had Delby change our plane tickets from Waco to Houston. She made overnight hotel reservations and then I finally returned Fred Helton's call. He was relieved when I told him I would be happy to see him.

He said, "We saw you on television. After you were attacked during the escape. When I heard the rumors—that you were going to investigate whether or not Rona Leigh got a fair trial—well, maybe, finally, someone would listen to us."

"By *us,* you mean the juror as well as yourself?"

"Yes."

"Is tomorrow morning okay? Say nine?"

"It surely is."

Scraggs whispered, "What's the juror's name?" and I asked Helton.

He told me Candy Sinclair.

I mentioned I'd be bringing a Ranger, the one in charge of finding Rona Leigh. He asked me why I'd do that. And then he immediately excused himself for being intrusive. He said, "I guess you need protection, don't you, ma'am?"

"I guess I do. And I need a witness to hear what it is you've got to say. An official Texas witness."

He understood.

In Houston, Scraggs ordered a car. "No way I get in one of yours," he said to me.

We checked into the hotel, shook hands in the elevator, planned to meet for breakfast at the coffee shop at six-thirty, said good night. Business being business.

∽

At the appointed hour he was waiting for me, a pot of coffee already on the table. He was in uniform.

I said, "I bet they issue you great sunglasses."

"You know it." He took them out of his pocket and put them on.

"Godzilla would look sexy in those."

"I will take that as a compliment."

"Can you get me a pair?"

"No. But I can tell you where you can buy yourself a knockoff. Cost you."

He told me.

We ordered.

I said, "Scraggs, if Rona Leigh didn't get a fair trial,

if she was entrapped, I need a very serious report to that effect so that when you capture her—"

"Moot. You know what the penalty is for escaping prison?"

"A thousand years."

"Something like that."

"Maybe she wasn't in on the escape."

"You know better than that."

"Maybe she just trusted in God and he made good."

"Falls under the category of escape. C'mon, Poppy. Let me tell you a little story. Couple years ago, guy was scheduled for execution. When his date came up he was dying. Cancer. They didn't think he'd make it through the trip from death row to the death house. He did, but he lapsed into a coma. So they took him to a hospital, did God knows what to him, and managed to get him to a semiconscious state. Brought him directly back to the death house, and his sentence was carried out right then.

"Poppy, once we get Rona Leigh, she'll be executed in a matter of hours."

"Maybe she could be arrested in another state. If Tiner moved her to another state, one that doesn't have execution, she won't be extradited."

"He can't take a chance on trying to move her from their hidey-hole. Every state that borders Texas has the death penalty. Too risky to travel very far. And the reward keeps growing, besides."

"How much is it up to?"

"Half a million dollars for information. Those Shakers, or whatever they are, are going to be mighty tempted. Bounty's the same amount."

"Bounty?"

"Bounty hunters get the same half million for bringing her in dead or alive."

"You're joking, right? There's a bounty and there are bounty hunters?"

"Afraid so. Only hope not too many of them end up shooting each other."

"Scraggs, you know what a U.S. Marshal gets for finding her, one who's on the task force for capturing fugitives?"

"No."

"They get their crummy salary."

"Well, the Shakers won't turn her in. Harboring an escaped murderer and all. Tough to spend a half million when you're working on a chain gang. Anyway, it is not my job to see that wrongs are made right. I don't believe an innocent person should be put to death, you have to know that. But if she was entrapped, and I'm not sure where you're goin' there, I'm afraid I have no sympathy. The punishment still fits the crime."

"You're entitled to your opinion."

Our bacon and eggs were polished off.

Scraggs took up his hat and settled it on his head and then he put on the sunglasses. Outside he had a great big unmarked car.

"What is this?"

"A Lincoln. You got a problem with that?"

"Just open the door for me, Max."

We rolled out into the traffic, which slowed for us since the drivers could tell he was a big-cheese cop. We settled into the flat Texas sixteen-lane road. He asked me if I knew anything about the juror.

"No."

"I do. She's a cowgirl. She works on one of the new ranches northwest of Houston on a new highway goes to Austin. Fred Helton built one for himself not too long ago. They've become neighbors, but they ain't exactly on the same social level."

"She's a real cowgirl, then."

"Yeah. The highway we'll be on cuts through empty tracts of land whose former owners went bankrupt back during the oil bust. People who seen to that highway are the ones bought the land from the banks. Corrupt techno-rich boomers, not ranchers, is what they're called in some circles. Then they built farmhouses with twelve thousand square feet of living space. The houses always sit on the highest available knoll so they can be seen, even though they might be set back as much as a quarter mile from the highway.

"Every twenty miles or so, they stick up like sore thumbs. You'll see. So anyway, these guys brought in big herds of cattle. The more cattle you have, the more land you're telling people you own without having to give the numbers. Sounds less like crowing that way. Cattle require a good deal of grazing land, since one cow can pollute six square acres in about a week. Status symbol, so to speak. Then, to go with all the cows, these so-called ranchers needed cowboys. Sometimes, cow*girls*. Had to scour the rodeo circuits to find them.

"Juror's been interviewed all over the TV. TV people love her because she ropes cattle and wears fringe. And here's why else. I caught one of the shows she was on. She had on a fancy silk shirt very much strained by her mighty chestworks. She don't button the top three or four buttons, because if she did they'd pop off the minute she sneezed.

"Juror called for the execution of Rona Leigh. Real loud. Looks like her neighbor made a point of makin' her acquaintance."

As we left the city, the highway was lined with billboards advertising hotels and restaurants, the space center, resorts in Galveston. Through the power of advertising, I learned that I could call a bail bondsman at 1-800-WALK.

GOING TO JAIL IS YOUR BUSINESS.
GETTING YOU OUT IS OURS.

And anyone with a change of heart as to procreation could dial 1-800-REVERSE.

YOU STILL GOT LEAD IN YOUR PENCIL, DUDE.
DR. CRAIG WILL RE-START YOUR ENGINE.

The billboards advertising Viagra needed no further illumination other than the photo of Bob Dole, smiling like a kid in a candy store.

After the billboards, the new highway was bordered by empty grassy land with cattle grazing. Very scenic. I had to agree with Scraggs about the sore thumbs, though. The new houses were copies of Normanesque châteaus and Savoyard palazzos—multistoried Palladio-windowed mansionettes. There were Victorian atrocities like the one the Addams family lived in and spread-out villas meant to lie under the Tuscan sun, not under the one in Texas. Then there were houses representing a more contemporary school of architecture, with walls of glass brick acting as prisms, throwing rainbows over the rolling landscape.

All were bound together by the ubiquitous western fence stretching along both sides of the highway, broken only by huge ornate wrought-iron gates marking the long drives leading to each house. The names of the ranches were cast in the gates. We came to Fred Helton's address, the name of his ranch THE GUN AND ROD.

Scraggs said to me, "Now don't think this Helton named it that because we worship guns, as Easterners like to believe. Used to be an old shooting range around here as I recall, plus great fishing. The lake with all the fish belongs to one of these new ranchers."

We turned in and drove up the driveway. The late Melody Scott's brother went with contemporary.

Fred Helton and Candy Sinclair stood in the doorway. He looked just as sad and stricken as I remembered him from the witness room at Gatesville. The cowgirl was a bit long in the tooth, maybe late forties. Her skin was weathered and tan, her eyes bright blue, and her hair in a braid down her back, a rich brown with some wiry gray strands springing out. The shirt she wore was in the vein Scraggs had described. She looked like a Texan Sophia Loren.

Helton invited us to sit in an air-conditioned sun porch full of plants, with a crocheted hammock stretched out in a graceful swoop under a wide window. The cowgirl poured boiled coffee from a blue-and-white enameled tin pot. When Scraggs took a sip, he said, "Coffee don't have to drip through a filter and it don't have to come from Ethiopia either to taste damn good."

I asked for sugar.

Basically, Fred Helton was bursting with the need to spill his guts. He thanked us for coming, for enjoying his coffee, and then he looked down at the floor and he said, "I hope you don't mind my starting with a little background. I want you to see where I'm comin' from."

We let him go to it.

"My father was a cattleman. Sold off everything after the ocean of oil under his ranch was drilled free. Allowed me to go back to raisin' cattle all these years later, though people still consider me oil trash." A little smile came to his lips and then flitted away. "When Rona Leigh's execution date grew close, I came to believe I had a responsibility to made amends for some things in my family's life I am not proud of."

The cowgirl stopped him. "If you got some responsibilities, I got a damn sight more."

He didn't respond to her.

He said, "My mama got pregnant with my baby sister at forty-eight years of age. My brother and I were teenagers at the time. Everyone—family, friends, and especially my father—tried to talk her out of goin' through with it. We were all worried to death. Afraid we would be dealin' with a Down syndrome child the rest of our lives. Still, Mama was determined and there was no discouragin' her.

"So then here comes this beautiful blue-eyed blond-haired baby girl who spent the first hours after she was born cooing at all of us with such a sweet sound we named her Melody. How often I have thought since, Oh, for a Down syndrome child who couldn't sing!"

The cowgirl refilled his cup.

"When my sister got to be around fifteen, we started to pressure my father in earnest to do somethin' about her troublin' behavior. Criminal behavior. We didn't let up for two years. When she was seventeen, he decided to get rid of us—me and my brother—not her, which had been our advice concerning our sister.

"It was upon news of her marriage, when Melody turned up on his doorstep with her no-good scum of a husband, that's when he turned her out without a cent. Of course Melody kept coming back, kept crying to him for money, but he stood firm. He refused her. Told her to get a job. Go to college. Dump her husband. Then she could have all the money she wanted. Finally, he slammed the door on her, wouldn't let her past his doorstep. She knew he meant business.

"Then she was dead."

The cowgirl patted the back of his hand.

"My father called me up one day, called to tell us she'd been murdered. Me and my brother flew back to Houston, and the minute we were in our father's presence, he blamed us for what happened. 'I turned her loose,' he kept saying, over and over. 'Threw her to the wolves, and now my little girl is dead.' At the funeral, he told me he hoped I'd never have a fragile child, but if I did, I'd better listen to my heart when it told me to protect that child.

"Mama had to be hospitalized.

"The funeral was a travesty. I swear, every drug addict in Houston was there, cryin' their crocodile tears."

His own tears now were not crocodile.

I asked him, "Are your parents alive?"

"My Daddy died within a year after Melody. My brother and I each tried havin' Mama live with us. She was bitter; she was angry; she made our families' lives hell. She was clinically depressed, is what she was. We had her treated but she wouldn't take her medication. One day, one of many such days, she stormed out of my brother's house and sped off in her car. She was killed. Couldn't make a curve."

Candy had gone out, and now she was back with a box of Kleenex.

I said, "I'm sorry." Scraggs said the same.

"Thank you. All that is why I went to Gatesville. There has been enough of death, so I went. Killing Rona Leigh Glueck wouldn't change anything except to end yet another person's life. She was a teenager when she murdered my sister. She was, we've all learned, a fragile child. A very fragile child. She was doin' okay there in prison. I thought, just let her stay put. So when the governor said he would witness the execution I was happy to hear it, because at the last minute, I would have the opportunity to ask him for mercy. He wouldn't let me earlier, when I tried to see him. But my plea was to no avail.

"Ma'am, what if my sister had redeemed herself with my father instead of latchin' on to Gary Scott? I like to think I'd have forgiven her for the grief she caused us. But I never had such an opportunity. So instead I have forgiven her killer."

Max Scraggs said, "Mr. Helton, I don't see how you could. Your sister died for no rhyme or reason."

Helton said, "Oh, there was plenty of reason. My father could have told you what he thought the reasons were. And I know a few."

And then Fred Helton went on to tell us the same story that Chuck had told me in his truck, driving away from the AstroBar. When Chuck said everyone knew what Gary Scott was about, he was right. Gary was bent on creating a scenario in Lloyd and Rona Leigh's head that was dynamite.

"Gary Scott wanted Rona Leigh to understand that the woman she would find with James Munter was fixin' to move in on Lloyd. Gary Scott's the one who set those two kids up to die.

"I know this because I hired an investigator so I'd have a clear answer, a reason as to why my sister died. The reason is that Gary Scott lit their fuses.

"My sister had some money. She didn't know it. Our parents put money aside for all of us, hers in a secret trust. We made my father swear he would never tell her. We let her think she'd been cut out of my parents' will so she'd never have money ever. We thought destitution would turn her around. It didn't. Told us she didn't need our goddamn money.

"My brother and I beseeched our father to close down the trust, and he told us he would. When she was dead he said he should have used the money to care for her. To lock her up and have the ruin washed out of her brain. Man never stopped agonizing. But he was lying to us. He never closed the trust. If he had, I suppose he'd have lost the last bit of hope he was hanging on to—hope that she'd return to her family sorrowful and contrite. Ready to change her ways. Become the girl he'd hoped the little cooing baby would become.

"Melody's husband inherited that money. I was there when our lawyer informed Gary of his windfall. Around a quarter of a million dollars. Gary shouted out something that sounded like a pig call. Then the lawyer advised him to get a lawyer of his own because his former brothers-in-law would take every legal action available to prevent him from getting that money. So Gary hired a lawyer. A snake is not a stupid animal.

"It took him ten years to get his hands on Melody's money, and it cost me a damn sight more to keep it out of his hands for as long as I could. I learned that when he held the check in his hands, he started to cry. Overjoyed. Like one of those people on television who win the lottery. When his lawyer attempted to advise him of the tax consequences, he fired him. His lawyer called me to tell me that. Thought it might offer me some condolence.

"He bought the bar where he worked, bought a new truck, an RV. He drinks her money, he gambles it, he spends it on whores.

"Gary Scott may not be stupid but he's not rational either. What he is, he's a conniver. His conniving got my sister killed. After she died, I got to thinking about that pig call he made when he learned of the money she had. I'd expected stunned silence. That was when I knew he'd found out about the money earlier. He just didn't know how much."

The cowgirl did her wrist-patting again.

He said, "Damn my father. Once my sister was married, her husband would automatically become the trust's beneficiary. He knew that. But still he didn't have it revoked. It was his stubborn love for my sister that created the motive for her death."

He looked directly at me. "Miz Rice, you are the FBI.

You are meant to walk in my shoes. I can't walk any-more, I'm tired out. Rona Leigh was sucker-punched, set up to walk a deadly path. But she went on to achieve what my sister did not: redemption."

He looked at Max Scraggs. He said, "And you, sir, though I have all respect for you and the job you do, you can't do what I hope the FBI can. I hope the FBI can find her instead of you and take her to a federal prison where she won't be executed. Just keep her there.

"All this talk of closure is stuff and nonsense. Let her live. Killing her will not bring closure to me. But some-thing else will. What I want is for Gary Scott to be held accountable."

It was as if he and the cowgirl had rehearsed it all. She took her cue with those words.

"Ma'am, Fred has brought me to see the light. I have been asked and asked why myself and the rest of jurors did not take pity on a seventeen-year-old girl who'd lived one wretched life. Why we didn't sentence her to life in prison. I have been talking it out with Fred here. He has allowed me to see what I didn't see, didn't want to see back then. I tried to tell him no one could see past the crime-scene pictures, which will stay in my head forever. Couldn't see past the attitude of Rona Leigh, her laughin' at us, braggin' about killin' givin' her a sex thrill. Couldn't see past that doctor describ-ing how a little girl like that went about pulling the ax out of Melody, strugglin' with it so's she could hit her again.

"You are goin' to think we were a bunch of dumb-bells in there when I tell you we didn't know anything about Lloyd's turn on the witness stand as bein' part of a plea bargain. Well, we didn't. Nobody told us. And we *wanted* to believe what he had to say. Easier that way. Just, Here's the story, here's what happened, now let's get the hell outa this miserable place. I mean, we had no air-conditionin' and the bathroom was filthy. We were never asked to consider if maybe Lloyd was lyin'. Somebody on the jury said, 'I don't believe that guy.' Suggested maybe he did it while Rona Leigh stood out in the truck.

"But we ignored him. It would have forced us to think. We didn't want to think. We wanted to get away from those pictures and that damn jury room.

"Durin' the sentencin' phase, after we found her guilty and then had to go back to determine her sentence, we got more testimony from the doc. That's when he told us she left the smell of her hands on the ax. We laughed at him. In the jury room we were sayin' things like, He must've gotten a medical degree from Grasshopper U. We made jokes instead of deliberatin', and then our foreman says, 'Looks like the death penalty.' We said, 'Looks like it.'

"And so we sentenced her. We sentenced her based on a load of horseshit, and nobody sentenced Gary Scott to nothin'. I am seein' past those terrible pictures and now I'm thinkin', We all did that Glueck girl wrong. We never gave her a fair trial."

෴

Out on the road, Scraggs tried to be rational. "Poppy, killers are folk who have short fuses, like Fred there said. You and me know that. A whole lot of murders happen because a victim eggs on the killer. In this case, the victim didn't egg on the killer, her miserable husband did. But killing is killing. They still did it."

"We don't know that. What if Rona Leigh did stay outside in the truck?"

"Lloyd didn't want Melody dead; she did."

"So we got the testimony of a short-fused fellow in a plea bargain. And what kind of plea-bargain arrangement was that? He was sentenced to die too. What the hell happened there?"

"Judge found a loophole. Judge was considered a hero."

I opened my window. I needed real air, even if it was dry and hot. Scraggs shut off the AC and opened his window too.

"Max, how the hell can you stand living in this stupid place?"

"Every place has its stupid parts."

"I want to see Lloyd's warden."

"What for?"

"The story is that Lloyd confessed in prison to committing the crime himself. Let's go hear if that's true from the horse's mouth."

"I see no point."

"Then stay home."

"I'm coming. No way I'm dropping you off all alone in Huntsville."

We just drove along, listened to the wind instead of our voices. Then I needed to know something. "Scraggs?"

"What?"

"If you come to see things differently, if you become convinced that Rona Leigh shouldn't die for this crime . . . will you do anything?"

"What the hell could I do? I only do my job as I know it's meant to be done."

Stubborn man. I let it go. I was wrung out.

12

Scraggs called the warden, who told him he had all the time in the world for us. We drove back out of the city, north to Huntsville. Again, the cavalcade of billboards. In half an hour the buildings of Huntsville crept up over the horizon at exactly the point the biggest billboard of all welcomed tourists:

> VISIT THE MUSEUM OF THE TEXAS PRISONS—
> *Wonder at Old Sparky, the Country's First Hot Squat.*

The words were superimposed on a photograph of an electric chair constructed of a couple of two-by-fours and strung with BX cables.

I said to Scraggs, "I rest my case."

"Which one?"

"The one where I wondered how a rational person can live in Texas."

"DC is rational?"

He took the exit just short of Huntsville, and we headed out on a forty-mile trip to the new death row. The old one was bursting at the seams, 459 men, and there was no more room for construction in the city. Huntsville could only contain so many prisons, had to leave room for a Starbucks or two. A week before an execution, the condemned man had to be driven forty miles to the death house—still in Huntsville—from death row. The Terrell Unit had been built in suburbia.

Terrell was a bright and shining outpost of walls and towers and floodlights and razor ribbon. Every guard working the outer wall had a dog accompanying him. We went into the administration building and were escorted to the warden's office. All Texas wardens have mansions. Maybe his was back in Huntsville and he commuted.

His secretary was not a prisoner, wasn't in farm togs. She wore a navy blue suit and white blouse, greeted us with a big smile and handshake, and then apologized: Something important had come up, and the warden wouldn't be able to see us till later in the afternoon. "How would y'all like to speak to Lloyd Bailey's chaplain in the meantime?"

Was this an unwritten procedure? To be pawned off on the chaplain in hopes that visitors to the warden would pack their tack and go home after being bombarded by scripture?

Scraggs said, "What exactly came up? I just spoke to him a couple of hours ago."

She smiled harder. "Warden's nephew is in town unexpectedly. Warden is taking the opportunity for a few hours of duck hunting."

Scraggs seemed to find that completely acceptable.

I said to the secretary, "Excuse me, is the season terribly short?"

"What season?"

"Duck hunting season."

She laughed and winked at Scraggs. "You can always tell a hunter from up north. Agent Rice, hunting season is year-round here, no matter what it is you want to shoot. Now let me just ring for a conveyance. The chaplain's office is right around the corner."

Around the corner meant around the corridor cor-

ner. The conveyance was a golf cart. The driver wore
orange. Scraggs and I climbed in and I asked the prisoner, "What are you in for?"

"Fraud." He looked at me with tired eyes. "I meant
to give it back."

I said, "I know."

Scraggs laughed out loud.

White-collar criminals in Texas get to drive golf carts
so they won't lose their touch before returning to the
country club.

I asked him how he got the job.

"Minimum security holds a lottery. I won."

All Texas wardens have slaves of one kind or another.

I looked over at Scraggs in the backseat and smiled.
He gave me the finger. Now I laughed, guessed he'd
been wanting to do that for some time.

Lloyd's chaplain was not unlike Vernon Lacker in
that he was soft and calm, but he was quite a bit older.
According to the certificate on the wall, he'd graduated from the Christian Ministries of America, no
degree bestowed.

He had thick glasses and watery eyes. He welcomed
us and blessed us and then he said, "Warden told me
to tell you all I can about Lloyd Bailey. All he might
have said concerning Rona Leigh Glueck. Is that what
you came for?"

I said, "Yes."

He took off the glasses, wiped them off with a fold of
his shirt, and gazed into the ceiling. "Lloyd Bailey," he
said softly, as if he were perusing an invisible Rolodex.
"Lloyd told me first time I met him that he'd meant to
hang on to Rona Leigh for as long as he could, which
amounted to as long as she'd let him. He said to me
she was the one precious thing he'd ever owned in all
his life, even more precious than his chopper, which he

blamed for getting him into the trouble he was in. *Trouble* was what he deemed the crime of murder."

I said, "He referred to his part in the relationship with Rona Leigh as ownership?"

He smiled a little bit. "That's the vernacular among people like Lloyd Bailey. You've got a woman who's true to you, why, then you own that woman. There is a strong pride that goes along with it."

How nice. I thought that Gary Scott wasn't able to take much pride in ownership. I asked the chaplain how else people like Lloyd Bailey were alike.

"I'd have to say they're the world's biggest losers, ma'am. Low intelligence. Addicts. Ugly. Unloved, mostly."

"Are you aware of the plea he struck to avoid the death penalty?"

"Yes, ma'am, I am. I have just reviewed his file."

The warden may have asked this chaplain on the spur of the moment to fill in for him, but at some earlier time he'd had him review Lloyd's file.

Scraggs said, "Was he the kind of man who would have invented a new version of the murders to guarantee himself a life sentence rather than the death penalty?"

"I believe every man here is that kind of man. But when Lloyd was first arrested, he felt free to tell anyone who would listen that his victim deserved what he got. For stealing his bike and refusing to hand it back when confronted. Told everyone he gave James Munter a chance to make him happy. Lloyd never said anything about Rona Leigh taking part in the crime, told the police it was not the thing a real man would do when they'd asked him. But then, once the police convinced Lloyd that Rona Leigh, being a girl, a very young girl, wouldn't be sentenced to death no matter what, and that he would be, sure as hell, he eventually came to believe them. To believe that it was in his best interest to say he killed James because Rona Leigh made him do it and he only hit Melody the one time to put her out of her misery once Rona Leigh was through with her. But he couldn't get it right: Rona Leigh tried to kill her but Melody wouldn't die, Rona Leigh never touched the ax after all, Rona Leigh was out in the truck.

"His story changed again and again. Finally, he said Rona Leigh did it all. She went crazy, he said, and axed both the victims. He signed a witness report describing in great detail Rona Leigh's ferocity when she killed James with one blow and then attacked Melody with the intent to hurt her before doing away with her. The report ended with his saying the whole thing was her idea. He didn't even know for sure if James was the guy who took his bike.

"My understanding is that they made up a confession along those lines for Rona Leigh to sign, and she signed it."

"By 'they,' you're talking about the police."

"Who else would I be talking about? They're the ones feel the pressure. Made no matter in the end, though. Lloyd Bailey drew the death penalty. But he was to escape his execution." He looked to the heavens again. "Same as Rona Leigh, turns out, though in his case Lloyd died of prison-contracted AIDS. Or it could have been hepatitis, as so many of the men pass that on to each other along with the AIDS. They're puttin' cause of death as AIDS pretty much with every death here. Further humiliates the convict's family."

"What is the point in further humiliating the convict's family?"

"Feelin' is, you raise a child to be scum, you're likely scum yourself. We're in a paranoid and punishin' culture, ma'am."

I caught Scraggs's eye. He stared me down. "Reverend, did you get to talk to Lloyd personally?"

"Many times. He confessed to me as how he made up all that stuff up about Rona Leigh in order to live. In the infirmary, he told me how his plea bargain was all a lie."

"What was the truth? Did he tell you that?"

"Yes, he did. And I told him to repent not just for the crime but for not telling the truth to the court."

"Will you tell me what he said to you?"

"He said he killed James Munter and Melody Scott."

"Meaning he alone?"

"Yes."

"He said that Rona Leigh took no part in the killing?"

"That's right." He shook his head.

Scraggs said, "Did Rona Leigh and Lloyd carry on a correspondence?"

"She wrote to him, yes. Right till he died. But he couldn't read or write. His fellow inmates read the letters to him. I read him a few. He did send several letters back to her that he dictated to his cellmate."

"As far as you know, did her letters influence him?"

"Her letters were mostly reminders, descriptions of the sex they'd had."

Scraggs crossed his arms over his chest, his line of questioning over.

I asked, "Did you attempt to make Lloyd's revised confession known to the authorities?"

He smiled. "The revised confession of a condemned killer holds no weight with the Board of Pardons and Paroles. But God in his infinite mercy took Lloyd with him into paradise from a hospital bed rather than our death chamber."

"Dying of AIDS-related afflictions doesn't sound much like mercy to me, Reverend."

"Everything is relative, ma'am. I'd say a death certificate that reads cause of death is AIDS has a kinder ring than STATE-ORDERED LEGAL HOMICIDE."

"Death certificates for the executed really say that?"

"If you're executed in Texas that's what they say, and correctly so. When these men are executed, they show all the terror and fear that you or I would show if someone was pointing a gun at our heads and we knew we would be shot no matter how we might beg for our lives. The men plead with us. They cry and grovel and then they scream, all the while insisting they are innocent. They beg the warden, the guards—me—to understand they're innocent, or they're sorry, or they didn't mean to do it."

"In executions I've witnessed, the prisoners have been sedated."

"Where was that?"

"Florida."

"Not so in Texas. About half the time we're required to call in a cell extraction team."

He looked at me and saw he needed to explain.

"Group of corrections officers chosen based on the shape they're in, their strength. They come in and pry the prisoner out of his cell. In one case, we had ourselves a killer who truly should have been sedated. Not to calm him but to prevent him from his last slap at the face of the law. He insisted he wasn't going to let anyone kill him. Took a dozen men to drag him out of Terrell, and then on the day of his execution it took a dozen more Huntsville officers to get him out of the holding pen and on down the corridor to the death chamber. Corrections officer who's supposed to announce they got a dead man walkin' was too busy wrestlin' with him to say the words.

"In the end, he ripped the stitching in the bonds that tied down his arms. Men had to use their belts to secure him to the gurney. His last words amid the curses he hurled were, 'I almost did it. Don't none of you forget it either.' Then he spit out the key to his handcuffs.

"To this day, there's been no official explanation as to how he managed that."

"How do you think he managed it?"

"Extra key got made somewhere along the line. The prisoner's friends or family came up with the money."

Everywhere, always, money talks.

"Reverend, was Lloyd Bailey repentant? For the death of his victims and for his lies to the police and the courts about Rona Leigh?"

"I'm afraid, like most of the men you find here, he didn't know the meaning of the word *repent*."

"You said God took him into paradise."

"Yes. Because Lloyd Bailey was a victim. Because he'd been rendered senseless by drugs, by the criminals who make them available. It has been my observation that drugs first attack that part of the brain that makes a man a human being."

"Wouldn't God punish him for taking drugs in the first place?"

"No. Lloyd's upbringing denied him the capability required to know the difference between right and wrong."

This was one liberal chaplain. "Bottom line, Reverend, there was no remorse at all?"

He reached over and gently patted my wrist. "Do we feel remorse when we run over a possum?"

I'd never hit a possum. But I didn't mention the remorse I'd felt when I hit a squirrel a few months ago in DC.

I said to him, "Rona Leigh's chaplain married her. Became her husband. What did you think of that?"

"I wasn't surprised. She's a witch."

A witch.

"God in his infinite mercy has never found any mercy for her?"

"Probably accurate. She controlled Lloyd. She could have stopped him from doing what he did, but as I said, he was bewitched."

"You're saying she was responsible for his actions?"

"Yes."

Not so liberal when it came to lady killers. I said, "But she'd been rendered senseless by drugs just as he had been."

"A woman's constitution allows her to maintain her reason."

Scraggs stood up on that note. Probably afraid I'd take out my gun and shoot the chaplain. He thanked the reverend and told him we had to be on our way.

Out in the corridor, in another golf cart, Scraggs said to me, "Being a chaplain for the condemned is one unconventional job. He's been around psychopaths too long, Poppy."

"It's a good thing he's not around women. Probably would want them all crucified, the Jezebels."

⁂

The warden was big and beefy, just like wardens in old black-and-white prison films. I asked him how many ducks he'd bagged. He said, "A dozen, ma'am. Each 'n' ever' one fat as a Goodyear blimp. So what's the FBI doin' here exactly? Shouldn't all your forces be concentrated on chasin' down Rona Leigh?"

"The FBI is preparing for what's to be done once she's captured."

Scraggs said, "Texas Rangers are chasin' her down."

"Then I'm sure the Texas Rangers have told the lady what's to be done once she's captured."

"Lady figures she might not necessarily be captured in Texas."

The warden leaned back in his chair. "Ain't easy to get a dyin' woman through the international area of the Dallas/Fort Worth airport."

Scraggs said, "Ain't easy getting one out of a Texas death chamber."

Scraggs sympathized with my irritation at the chaplain, was taking it out on the warden. I appreciated his support. I cut to the chase. "Lloyd Bailey told your chaplain—and I wonder if he told you the same thing—that Rona Leigh Glueck took no part in the killing of James Munter and Melody Scott."

He grinned. "Man on his deathbed will say the damnedest things. Rona Leigh was Lloyd's woman. Maybe he felt less a man that his words put her on death row. Wanted to prop up his self-esteem."

"Did he say anything to lead you to believe . . . ?"

"He said a lot of things. Might have said the moon had cooties big as pigs. He was a sick man. He was dyin'. Man's word's not very reliable in such a condition. Lloyd had his chance in court. That's all that counts."

"As your governor so often points out."

"And rightly so. Now, ma'am, I have got a lot of backed-up appointments today. I can't tell you anything the chaplain hasn't already said. You mentioned you'd appreciate the opportunity to talk to Lloyd's former death row neighbors. They're long gone, a course. We execute three–four men, average, every month. Do the math, ma'am. But I got a few others you might be interested in.

"Four men are waitin' on rides to Huntsville now who knew Lloyd back before they graduated. You're welcome to talk to them. Give me the chance to make up for keepin' the FBI waitin'."

"You did make up for it. The chaplain was very helpful. But I would be glad to speak with those men."

"Thought so." He clicked his intercom. "Martha, darlin'? My car right out front? Good." He stood up, put out his hand, and we all shook.

We were driven across the prison yard.

I saw the four men. One of them recognized Scraggs. He said, "Hey, Scraggs, you still out there plantin' false evidence?"

Scraggs told him to shut up. "Lady wants to talk with you. I do not. Me and you were done talkin' a long time ago." Max's grammar mocked the criminals.

This prisoner and each of the other three said the same thing, using different synonyms: *Lloyd Bailey was a killer (the devil / a psycho / a piece a shit). I'm not. I was framed (set up / shafted / fucked over) by my lawyer (the jury / the judge / the prosecutor). I didn't kill (shoot / stab / strangle) anybody. I am a Christian. So listen, FBI (ma'am / angel / sweetheart), why don't you see about gettin' me a reprieve?*

I didn't say no, I didn't use synonyms for no, I just lied. "I'll see what I can do." Then I asked each of them, "Did Lloyd tell you that he killed both his victims and that Rona Leigh did not?"

I got: *Damn right. / You got that straight. / Sure as hell did. / Made me write it down.*

I asked the last one, "Why did he want you to write it down?"

"Couldn't write hisself. Too stupid. But he was so sick he couldn't lift a pen anyway. Had me put it in a letter to Rona Leigh's public defender."

"And you sent that letter according to his wishes?"

"Well, ma'am, it ain't like I went down to my local post office and mailed it direct. Letters go to the censors first. If that letter got outa here, I'm a pickle in a barrel of brine."

Scraggs and I drove back to Houston. "Scraggs, when you find her you'll take her back to Gatesville, right?"

"That's the law."

"Do you believe she's entitled to a new trial?"

"I believe the laws that steer our courts should be looked at a little closer."

"A lot of innocent people could die while that's happening."

He sighed. He said, "It's out of my hands."

"No, it's not."

He gripped the steering wheel a little more firmly. "I cannot be distracted from this job. Which now has become finding Rona Leigh Glueck and bringing her back to justice."

"You don't see your job as bigger than that? As a peace officer?"

"Not if I want to keep it."

I looked away from him.

Then he said, "How many kids *you* supportin', Poppy?"

Scraggs went back to Gatesville. Had to tuck in all those kids he was supporting. I stayed another night in the Houston hotel. The globe-trotting was getting to me.

⚬⚬⚬⚬

In the hotel room, I tried my British shrink again. He was back.

"Find her?"

"No, Doc. So what about rage?"

"What about it?"

"Can you become so enraged that you take on superhuman strength?"

He sighed. "No. You merely *think* you have superhuman strength. When you become enraged you are ready to take on the world. Enraged drivers leap out of cars so they can go and throttle the fellow who cut them off, only to be picked up by their collars and tossed to the side of the road by the big bully who rules it. Rage does not turn you into Superman."

"It only makes you act on impulse."

"Exactly. Yes. Poppy, people in this country watch too much bloody wrestling. They think a person can actually lift someone over his head, twirl him about, and throw him to the ground. The rage of wrestlers is, as we know, choreographed, but for some reason people have no inclination to believe that. Spoils their fun. I'm coming to understand Americans are taskmasters at avoiding reality. Do you think that's true?"

It is. I didn't tell him to go back to Liverpool. Because I'll never forget a rape victim who told me she was just such a confident person. She always felt that if she were ever accosted she would be so angry she would be able to turn on her assailant, kick him in the balls, and gouge out his eyes with her car keys. And then, unfortunately, the opportunity arose. Her attempt to fend the man off meant two black eyes and a broken jaw. For her, not him. One of her front teeth lodged in her windpipe and almost killed her. I assured her when she came out of surgery that because of the confidence she'd just described, she'd had the presence of mind to crawl across the parking lot to where he'd first hit her, pick up the three other teeth he'd knocked out, and put them in her pocket. Which meant the dentist on call at the hospital was able to stick them right back in along with the one they suctioned out of her lung. An awful lot of rape victims are reminded of their assault each time they look in the mirror to put in their bridgework. "That's not going to be you," I said to her, as she wept and wept.

The shrink said, "Penny for your thoughts, darling."

Ah, the British. Always too happy to soothe your soul.

"What about sexual frenzy?"

"What about it?"

"The killing of Sharon Tate."

He actually said "Ah-hah," like he was Sherlock Holmes. "Well, you see when Charles Manson and his followers killed those people in California, why, yes, they were all in a frenzy. Their act took on a passionate ferocity where the killers seemingly lost themselves in the joy of the killing, so excited by the violence they were perpetrating. One of Charles Manson's girls, the one who actually killed the actress, described to the police how satisfying it felt when the knife thrusts didn't hit bone. She stabbed her victim forty-five times, and about half the thrusts sank the knife up to the hilt. When that happened she said she felt satisfaction. So much satisfaction that when she hit resistance, bone— when her hand slid down the knife and she sliced herself—the pain of that did not stop her. She kept going for soft tissue. After she was arrested, the police took off the rag she'd wrapped around her hand and had to get her into surgery. Stitches alone couldn't put her shredded flesh back together."

"So what's your point?"

"I'm talking, once again, about religious ecstasy. I've discussed it with people. You can have superhuman strength in a sexual frenzy, but only if that frenzy is created in combination with religious fanaticism."

"Rona Leigh didn't find Jesus till *after* the frenzies."

"Listen, my dear, if you Americans continue to insist on the death penalty, why not use it only when the motive has to do with personal gain? If someone kills simply because she's a bad seed, programmed by heinous circumstances beyond her control, maybe that particular sort of killer deserves to be rehabilitated. Whereas—"

"Thanks, you've been a great help." I maneuvered myself off the phone. This wasn't about the death penalty. I was tired of explaining that. Now I was about to hit the sack when the phone rang. Joe.

"How did you know where I was?"

"I'll tell you later. There's an interview with the merry widower in *Time* magazine. It's just out, in case you missed it. I thought—"

I didn't even maneuver, I hung up. Joe would understand. I grabbed my purse, dug out my wallet, and went down to the lobby.

Gary even got a photo, big slick hair and all. Looked like he'd painted it with Kiwi shoe polish. I started reading the article in the elevator. There was an older photo of him too, taken at Melody's funeral. Two knots of mourners outside the church were separated by a few feet of empty sidewalk One group was stoic-looking, well tailored, heads held high. Fred Helton stood at its center. Gary was lost in the second group, newly cleaned up, though none of the men wore suits and all the women sported Rona Leigh hair.

In his interview, Gary mostly talked about how much he had looked forward to seeing his wife's killer caught and executed. How much he looked forward to seeing her die. He hoped that next time the drug that first puts her to sleep would be thrown out. He wanted her to feel her lungs when they wouldn't work, feel the pain of the heart attack that would kill her. Feel her life being stolen away the way Melody had.

I needed to talk to Gary Scott again. I called the AstroBar. I got a recorded message: *This here's the AstroBar. Come on down and drink to the capture of that bitch, Rona Leigh Glueck. On the house.*

I looked up the name GARY SCOTT in the Houston phone book and dialed. The Gary Scott I dialed wasn't Melody Scott's widower. It was an irate man who shouted, "Sumbitch! This is it. I'm gittin' me an unlisted number!"

I opened my laptop. I searched the Houston papers. In the last few days, Gary had been interviewed, or at least quoted, everywhere. I found that "Bad-Ass Houston" was still in business and they'd interviewed him as well. In their interview, his direct quotes were printed semi-phonetically. He told them:

I intend to enjoy watchin' that little piece a dirt die. When I'm settin' there while Rona Leigh is gettin' croaked one more time, I won't take my eyes off her till she's as dead as the two hundred armadillos between Gatesville and my bar. After that, I will close my eyes for just a second and enjoy what will happen next. [The reporter slipped in a little narrative line to point out that Gary had stopped talking long enough to slug down a bottle of Lone Star.] *That's when I'll be seein' Melody standin' and waitin' outside the Pearly Gates so's when Rona Leigh finally gets there Melody'll have an ax of her own. Right in her two sweet little hands. She will chop the livin' shit outa that two-bit whore. Whack her into a million pieces. Then Satan'll put the pieces together so's Melody can have another go. Melody will ax that whore right through till Kingdom Come.*

Repeating his lines for all he could get out of them.

I looked at my watch. I read the latest fax from Delby one more time. Then I changed into jeans, put on my new boots and my armadillo belt, stuck on the Stetson, and left.

⚭

The Friday-night crowd had shoveled itself into all available standing room. They happily passed beers over their heads to anyone who shouted out an order and then passed bills back up to the bartender. Gary wasn't doing the bartending. Good. They wore western gear, and the bar—being in Texas—meant that no one had a problem with the gun butts poking out from between waistbands and gut.

Music blared: Kinky Friedman and the Texas Jewboys singing one of their standards, "I'm an Asshole from El Paso." Kind of song a crowd can't help but sing along with. Most of them were.

I saw Chuck and threaded my way toward him. When he spotted me he came over and shouted into my ear, "You back?" as in *Whatcha doin', mowin' the lawn?* Wish I could get over that.

I shouted, "I'm back."

He shouted, "What?"

I shouted louder, "I want to talk to a few people who were here the night of the murders. Were you?"

"Hey, I been here every night for twenty years. But, honey, I don't think your budget is gonna get any of us to open up, especially me. What with Rona Leigh on the loose. We're all scared she's gonna show up and kill us all."

"Is that why Gary's not here?"

"That's it. Figured she'da been caught in two shakes of a cow's tail but the man was wrong. You people ain't gettin' the job done, if you don't mind my sayin'."

I shouted into his ear the contents of Delby's fax. Then I told him he was not a priority with the Houston police as far as his involvement in the beating of a certain loan shark Thanksgiving morning of last year, but that his name could be put at the top of their list with just a phone call from me.

This was the first that Chuck heard he was even a suspect in the crime. I could tell by the sudden slackness in his jaw. But he shored his face back up after a moment and he said, "That guy would shake down his own granny, rip off her fingernails if he needed a laugh."

"First, he'd have to get out of his full body cast, wouldn't he?"

The cowboy shrugged. Then he scanned the crowd. Every head was turned our way. He looked back to me. "My stock is way, way up. They're all wonderin' where I latched onto the fox." He picked a strand of my spiraled hair from my shoulder and gave it a little toss. Houston humidity had given it a great perm. "I think I got just the customers you're lookin' for. But they're hard up. They'll be welcome of a bribe unless you got something on them, too."

He felt hurt. Too bad. "I always pack a little slush."

He looked back to the crowd and crooked his finger at a couple slow-dancing, very slow-dancing. They weren't moving, just standing, hips pressed up against hips. The couple looked toward him. Chuck led me out the door and they followed.

The man's name was Stick, the woman's, Pinky.

He told them they'd all three get an early Christmas present, a damned good one, if they chose to tell me what was going down at the bar the night Melody and James were killed. All three. Chuck would have his cake and eat it too.

Pinky said, "What's the present?"

"Couple hundred for you two, couple hundred for me."

Pinky said, "Well, hell, just tell us where you want us to start from."

I said, "From the minute you saw something was up."

Chuck made a noise that was akin to *hee-haw*. He said, "Somethin' was up when Melody walked in the door. Hadn't been around in the last few days, but she didn't wait long enough for the black eye to fade out all the way. So she's flirtin' around here and there, and once she comes on that dude, James, she starts to rev up."

I asked if they knew James.

Pinky said, "Nah. I seen him a few times. He liked to stay by hisself 'cept when he was yearnin' for some female company. He got a ride with someone from the motel to the bar. No car. He didn't have any notion Melody was Gary's wife. But Melody made sure to stay right in Gary's line of sight, didn't she, Stick?"

Stick: "Sure as hell did."

Pinky: "Rubbin' up against James like a calf to a cow. James put his hand on Melody's butt and she didn't make any move to shift away. That's when we knew trouble was on its way."

Stick: "Next thing, the two a them are goin' out the door while he's still feelin' her up. Not that this was anything all that new for Melody."

Pinky: "'Cept this James was one real cute dude."

Stick: "Once they was out, Gary just kept handin' out Lone Stars, same as always, drinkin' a few hisself. Then he started lookin' at his watch, lookin' at it a lot, pacin' a little bit too, ya know? Mutterin' to hisself, sloppin' beer on the customers, watchin' the door. Hour went by, they didn't come back. That's when he knew Melody'd taken off with James, sure. A quick one out in the back of a truck is one thing, but he knew she was intendin' a whole night a fun. She crossed the line. Gary threw a towel at Chuck here and told him to take over."

Pinky took a pack of cigarettes out of her shirt pocket and offered them around. I declined. The three of them lit up.

Pinky: "Soon's he was gone, Chuck says to me, 'Hope he don't find 'em.'"

Stick: "But he did."

Pinky blew out a stream of smoke. "Melody drove

James to his motel room, one he rented at the weekly rate. His mattress was on the floor because one corner of the bed frame collapsed. He'd throwed the frame in the Dumpster outside."

I asked her how she'd come by that information. Chuck and Stick snickered.

Pinky pushed her chest out. "I been there one night. James was just a kid, see? Lonesome. He liked to make out is all. Fool around. He had a little fridge with bottles a beer in it. But see, his air conditioner didn't work. He didn't care. I cared. Nighttime, I got to have my AC. So I told him I'd be seein' him some other time, thank you all the same. Too bad his not havin' AC didn't bother Melody. Well, maybe it did. But she was there to get even with Gary, not to keep cool. For the black eye."

Stick: "So Gary comes back—he's gone about a hour hisself—tells some people Melody is fuckin' that cowboy in a motel and then he starts whinin' that he only smacked her, didn't mean to give her a black eye. Said he didn't deserve that kinda shit. So then he's drinkin' heavier and heavier, gettin' madder and madder, and finally he says to a few of us, 'Any a you seen Lloyd Bailey tonight?'"

Pinky: "Nobody seen 'im."

Chuck: "Nobody. Too bad. Lloyd used to come around, buy drugs from Gary. But once he'd took up with that hooker Rona Leigh, he let her handle the drug supply. Lloyd rather be with her 'steada hangin' out at the bar, which was fine with us 'cause Lloyd Bailey had one dangerous temper. Meaner 'n' a rattler on a hot skillet. A brawl's one thing, but Lloyd liked to cut."

Pinky hugged herself.

"Word came down later Rona Leigh'd struck gold that night. She got herself a stash of heroin from an old friend she used to do business with, gal who owed her. Lloyd and Rona Leigh were home shootin' up."

I asked, "What did Gary do?"

"Pinky knows exactly what he done. And I mean exactly."

Pinky put her nose up in the air. "Gary came into the back room of the bar where there's a phone. Where I happened to be."

Stick: "Where she happened to be givin' the former owner a blow job."

Pinky: "We was engaged."

Chuck: "You was engaged, all right."

Pinky: "Only way *you* could get a blow job, mister, is to hold a gun to a girl's head. And even then."

Me again: "What did Gary do?"

"He called Lloyd. Couldn't make Lloyd understand him at first. Here's why. See, I got a girlfriend who was friends with Rona Leigh for a while? She heard, after they finished their heroin that night, they cooked up a little crack and then followed up with a surprise dessert Rona Leigh come by. She'd bought a twenty-four-bottle case a cough syrup from a kid for five bucks. Dimetapp. Twenty percent alcohol is my understandin'. Makes it forty proof. She did it because Lloyd had a sweet tooth. Liked to make her man happy, 'cause Lloyd surely did do right by her."

Chuck: "'Cause a Lloyd, she was off the streets."

Pinky asked if I wanted to know what Gary said. Chuck said to me, "Ain't this girl some kinda idiot?" Then, to Pinky, "She wants to know or she wouldn't be throwin' hundred-dollar bills at us, would she?"

Pinky stuck her tongue out at him. Then she said, "Gary told Lloyd that James Munter stole his bike. Told him where to find James. Told him James was with his own wife. Said Melody informed him earlier she was goin' to fuck James, and once she was done she was goin' after him—Lloyd—next. He told Lloyd, 'See, my wife wants to have a ride on a good bike. Yours.'"

Chuck: "Ain't it just a sonofabitch?"

Out came Pinky's cigarettes. They all lit up anew. They were agitated.

"Then what happened?"

Chuck: "We all know what happened. Melody and James got theirselves axed to death. Lloyd did it. If he told Rona Leigh what Gary had said about Melody havin' the hots for him, Rona Leigh mighta gotten in a few licks. But I doubt he told her."

Pinky: "I doubt it too. I don't believe Lloyd woulda told Rona Leigh about that there part."

I asked, "Why not?"

Pinky: " He loved Rona Leigh."

They all took deep drags on their cigarettes. Stick said, "Pinky's right. Lloyd had no interest in makin' Rona Leigh jealous. And he woulda had no interest in Melody whatsoever. It was Rona Leigh he wanted, and he had her."

They smoked. They'd stopped looking at me. I said, "I want the rest."

So they eyed each other.

Pinky: "Well, I'm broke so what the hell? Gary called the cops. Wanted to get his wife in as much trouble as he could. Get her busted. Knew she didn't go anywhere without a couple joints in her pocket. I didn't hear that particular conversation. But after he called 'em, 'bout an hour, the folks stayin' out at the motel all came down here. They told us they had to get out 'cause, first, there was so much shoutin' and screamin' goin down they couldn't take it, and, second, the cops came, lotsa uniforms, and then plainclothes too, and those guys with the yellow crime tape. Knew somebody was dead."

They were taking deep drags on their cigarettes to

settle their nerves. Three pairs of shifty eyes all aimed at the ground.

I asked how Gary reacted to that. To the sudden crush of new customers who told him someone at the motel was dead.

Stick and Pinky looked to Chuck. He didn't say anything.

I slid my purse up tight over my shoulder.

Chuck: "Gary? Shit. Why, he smiled ear to ear. He got such a face on him, looked like a pig what found a private lake full up with wet mud."

Stick and Pinky nodded, and then Chuck said, "I believe we have a deal."

I loosened the grip on my bag. I unzipped. I counted out four bills and passed them over. Then I asked, "Why did Gary give Melody a black eye in the first place?"

They looked at each other. Stick shrugged.

Pinky stuffed her bill into the front pocket of her jeans. "Man, that's what *she* wanted to know."

Chuck: "Came cryin' to me too. Told me he did it for nothin'."

And I said to the two men, "Gary would have sacrificed any of you or your friends in there." I nodded toward the AstroBar. "It was bad luck on James Munter's part that he happened to walk in the door when he did. Now I have one last question."

All three gazed into my eyes. They were confused. I'd taken all the fun out of the deal.

"Where can I find Gary?"

⚭

Target practice is an acceptable diversion in Texas and, combined with that, Texans don't set much store in recycling aluminum cans and glass bottles. The entertainment inherent in shooting them is worth far more than a nickel apiece. And that is how Gary and a few friends were whiling away their Friday night, sitting shoulder to shoulder on beach chairs and firing away. There were six bottles standing on a sawhorse and a lot of spent casings on the ground. None of them was a good shot. They stopped shooting to follow the path of my headlights and watch my car pull into the field. I parked alongside the RV. Not only were the highway lights next to the lot bright enough to shoot by, I would have bet Gary needed black-out curtains to sleep.

Squinting did not help them to identify me. I walked up to Gary in his shooting chair and took off my hat. He jumped to his feet and looked me up and down.

"Hey, FBI, I am impressed by those boots. Got 'em off that ex-con in Gatesville, I'll bet."

A friend said, "FBI? Where?"

Gary told him to shut up.

He'd kept up his hair, which was solidly aloft, but he hadn't showered in a while and he needed a shave. His nails were dirty and his clothes looked slept in.

I said, "Think we can have another chat? I mean, if you're not angry over the last one."

He smiled. "I never carry no hard feelings, not my style. Sure we can have a chat." Then he said to his wide-eyed friends, "Go ahead and enjoy yourselves. Me and the agent are gonna have a chat."

Their eyes shone in the light.

I followed Gary up the steps of his RV. Once on the threshold, he stopped abruptly and turned. I was on the step below so we were face-to-face, no more than an inch between our bodies.

He smiled. "Make no mind on the mess." Gary had perfected one of those crooked smiles where only one side of his mouth went up, a semi-sneer somewhere between Elvis and Mick Jagger.

He stepped back, leaving me just enough room to

squeeze past him. He didn't expect me to stop in mid-squeeze, which I did. With my body pressed against his, I looked down into his eyes. I said, "This shouldn't take long," and then I moved into his living quarters.

There was floral-upholstered furniture in there, but all of it plus every bit of floor space was littered with empty cans and bottles. Gary and his friends outside had a lot more shooting fun at the ready. Mingled with the cans and bottles were the remains of food stuck to paper plates and plastic forks. I chose the chair covered with the least amount of trash, moved the pile onto the greater heap on the coffee table, and sat down.

I said, "Paper plates are always a good idea when you're having a lot of company."

"That's what the girls decided. Got to get them back over here, though, so they can bag the stuff and go find a Dumpster." He swiped the trash off the chair across from me and sat down too. "Like a beer, Agent?"

"Sure."

He reached over the side and made picnic sounds. There was a tub of ice next to him. He pulled out a bottle of Lone Star and tossed it to me. He got one for himself.

I held the bottle away from me and twisted the top off. It took awhile for the carpet to soak up the geyser of foam. I said, "Have we got a napkin, Gary?"

"We have."

He got up and went to the kitchen, which was partitioned off from the dining area by a counter covered with pots and pans. He came back out with a stiff, accordioned dishcloth. He handed it to me.

I said, "Don't the girls know about paper towels?"

"They do. Didn't get enough. Dumb bitches."

"How come you're not at the bar?"

"How come you can't find Rona Leigh?"

"You're afraid she's looking for you?"

"Never know. Got me a few guards. Aim to lay low till she's caught."

"How come you're giving interviews then?"

"Gave interviews the day after the execution, the execution that didn't take. Figured you'd have her in a hour. Shit. How much you pay for them boots?"

"Six hundred and fifty dollars plus another hundred to rush the order."

He made a sound of admiration.

I said, "But once I'm home, the only place I'll be able to wear them is a costume party. Maybe I was too impulsive."

Gary could recognize an insult. He put his own boots up and into the trash on the coffee table and changed the subject.

"My bar got a lot of publicity. I'm gonna have enough money to expand. I been lettin' my present establishment go. I got a down payment on a place uptown, paid for by all these newspaper people wantin' my account of the near miss on Rona Leigh. Dumb asses, let me tell you. I tell them all the same thing. Wouldn't have to pay me anything if they'd read the first guy's story. Once Rona Leigh is caught and I tell those reporters I talked to you, they'll pay me plenty, is what I'm thinkin'. And that is why I'm havin' this chat with you. So how 'bout you tell me what the hell it is you want from me, FBI."

I took a swig of freezing-cold beer. "I want to verify a couple of things. Things that could get Rona Leigh a new trial."

"What new trial?"

"If I find evidence . . ."

"Evidence ain't gonna do her a swill a good. When she's caught, she's gonna fry. Everyone says so."

"They don't fry prisoners anymore, Gary."

"Yeah. Too bad. I like the expression all the same.

When they got rid of the electric chair, they shoulda replaced it with an electric sofa. Kill off four at once. Save the state some money." He smiled. "New trial? You're crazy, honey. Me, I'm wishin' about now that there was no death penalty."

"Really? Why is that?"

"Rona Leigh got nothin' to lose. If she's of a mind, she really will come and kill me."

"But maybe she didn't kill Melody and James. Maybe she's not a killer. Maybe Lloyd killed them by himself."

"Not what she said when she made her confession."

"I have never seen a confession I trusted. Her condition—"

"Listen to me, FBI. You can't spring her. Parole board works on a deadline. It's passed. Once she's back in custody, they'll make themselves scarce. They ain't about to be woke up at all hours of the night durin' some killer's last hours. Rona Leigh's had her chance, the only one she got comin'. Y'all are wastin' your time. There ain't nothin' I could tell you, because everybody already knows what I done."

"What do you mean by that?"

"Here's what I mean. Melody was a whore, exactly like what you was insinuatin' back at the AstroBar. I wanted that bitch Rona Leigh to kill her. Believe me I did. But the thing is, what I wanted I never believed could happen. Not for a minute. Just wishful thinkin' on my part. Everybody knew that. I wanted maybe another black eye. Maybe a little hair pulled out. Few claw marks.

"But Rona Leigh or Lloyd or whoever goes and *kills* Melody. Maybe Melody deserved more than a hair-pullin', maybe not. But the thing is, it don't matter 'cause she went and got herself killed and Rona Leigh was right there, whether she swung the ax or not. So she deserves to die for what happened to Melody."

"Spending her life in prison wouldn't be punishment enough for her?"

"If she'da crippled Melody, maybe. Put out her eye. Slit her face. Made her ugly. But the two a them meant to kill her. When you use a ax, you ain't just whistlin' Dixie, you know what I'm sayin'? Melody's dead. So, an eye for an eye. I figure my Melody wants me to see her dead. You ready for another cold one, honey?"

"I am."

He tossed me a can this time. Drops of water splashed the front of my shirt.

I cracked it and then I said to him, "Gary, I think you're leaving something out."

"What might that be?"

"James Munter. An innocent bystander. Didn't even know Melody was your wife. Or anyone else's wife, for that matter."

He searched around the tub and came up with another beer for himself. He drank half of it in one swallow. "Shit. I admit I was a selfish bastard there. But like I said, I didn't think anybody'd get killed."

"Gary, why do you insist to people that Rona Leigh swung the ax even if Lloyd maybe did it on his own?"

"Because Rona Leigh was a pig."

"Like Melody?"

He looked up from the bottle. "That's right."

"Deep down, you feel Melody got what she deserved, don't you?"

"Yeah, that's right. Deep down, I do."

"But you wish none of it had happened?"

"I didn't mean for it to happen. Not the killin'. Those Christians you been seein' on the TV? Ones want Rona Leigh saved? They're a bunch of liars. They don't care about a killer findin' Jesus. What they like is to see some sex fiend who turns herself back into a virgin. Don't matter none what the sex fiend did, which was primarily to kill another sex fiend. They only took pity because Rona Leigh will never have sex again. She's married but still, she'll stay a virgin.

"That's the kind of person they want to save. A born-again virgin. Jesus said to the prostitute, 'Go and sin no more.' But people who got a head on their shoulders, the governor and the parole board and the like, they know once a sex fiend always a sex fiend. They recognize it. A sex fiend will contaminate you. Turn you to dirt. Best to get rid a them. Never met a man went to a hooker who didn't want to kill the slut right after."

"Is that so?"

"Ask 'em."

"I will. But I'll have to think of a delicate way to say to a man who's paid for sex, Did you want to kill her right after?"

"No, I meant ask the whores. They got the broken jaws to show you how close the dudes come to killin' 'em. FBI, I'm the real Christian here. And I'm goin' to heaven."

"What is heaven to you?"

"You know what heaven is."

"Since we come from different parts of the country, maybe we were taught different things about what heaven is."

"I don't know what they teach you back east, but here there's just the one Bible and the Bible tells us what heaven is. Heaven is a place where everybody's happy. You get to see all the people who died before you. Grandparents and so on."

"And then what?"

"I already told you."

"I'm sorry, I forgot what you said."

"Everybody gets to be happy."

Time to surprise him while he was feeling like a

heaven-bound Christian. "Gary, you knew about the money, didn't you?"

He looked down at his beer, patted his hair a bit, and then his eyes came back to me. "I did. Still, the truth is, I didn't put it all together till I got the news Melody was dead. When people came to the bar that night said somebody might be dead, my first thought which I couldn't help was, Piss and shit! If it's Melody, I am one rich cowboy."

"I find that hard to believe."

"Which?"

"That it wasn't before Melody was dead, not right after, that you thought about being a rich cowboy."

"FBI, I ain't gonna let you rile me this time around. I got a good conscience. I told you, I'm goin' to heaven. The Lord ain't leavin' me to starve out on a dry range, you can be sure a that."

"You figure you can fool the Lord with your lies?"

"Hey! What the hell do you know about it? You don't even know what heaven is. Fuck you, FBI. So why don't you get outa here and go outside and have a little fun with my boys out there. 'Cause maybe they might like to have a little fun with you."

As I walked by him, he tried to grab my leg but missed.

Outside, my car had four flat tires. Shot out. Gary's friends sat in the beach chairs watching me.

I walked over to them and stood behind the guy in the center of the row. I placed my gun one inch from his ear. I fired six times and shattered all the bottles. My weapon is very powerful, a real loud retort.

I came around to the front of the line of chairs, my weapon still in my hand. I raised it. "Whose pickup back there?"

None of them answered.

"Whose?" I yelled and pointed the gun into the face of the guy still holding his ear.

He pointed with his free hand. "Him." Guy on the end.

I pointed the gun anew. "Give me the keys."

He said, "What?"

I shouted, "Give me the goddamn keys."

He dug them out of his pocket.

I borrowed his truck for the night.

A local FBI agent saw to switching vehicles back around the next day. My car was still in the vacant lot but Gary's RV was gone.

13

Back in the hotel I had a message. Delby. Call her back. After hours, if necessary. Call her at home no matter what time.

This had to be good.

First I said, "How did you find me?"

First she said, "What time is it?"

"Two-ten."

"Oh. Wasn't easy. Joe told me."

"How the hell did he know?"

"Scary, isn't it? Ask him. That's if he's still talkin' to you. Pissed. Said you'd hung up on him."

"I thought he'd understand."

"Did. But figures you should have called him back by now."

"I intend to."

"How you sleepin', boss?"

"Like a rock."

"That's 'cause you're happy." The excitement in her voice had raised its usual melody several notches.

"So what's the scoop, Delby?"

"Scoop bein' the right word. Boss, you know the advice you gave me about insomnia? Took it."

She needed to stop for air. As if she were hyperventilating. I was very calm. "You taped Dan Rather?"

"Not quite. I decided to watch QV-whatever-it-is.

Shopping channel. They're on twenty-four hours. About an hour ago I maybe found out who can tell you where that mission is."

"Say what?"

"Stop now."

"Delby. Who?"

"The CEO of the shopping channel. Tonight they were showing bedroom furniture. The QV-something people were trying to get viewers to buy something in the middle of the night, like a bed. Figure insomniacs might get the notion a new bed would help. So they're showing this bed, saying it was hand-carved, blah-blah-blah. I'm admiring these beautiful white linens on it and I'm saying to myself, Now all this is damn familiar. I paid closer attention. Man, it looked a lot like Rona Leigh's bed, the one Auerbach showed us. So I turn up the volume. Saleslady says the furniture was made by the Shakers. She didn't say it was Shaker furniture, she said it was *made* by them. I figured you'd want to go right to the top, so here's the phone number of the shopping-channel CEO."

I don't know how she does it.

She said, "Meanwhile, the TV woke up my baby. I'm putting her on the phone. Tell her to go back to bed. She'll listen to you."

I told the child to look out the window and if the moon had gone to bed then she should too. That was the rule.

Delby took the phone. "Thanks, Poppy, she went to the window and now she's headed for her room. So we're even."

The CEO of the shopping channel was just as excited as Delby had been. He told me I was the first FBI agent he'd ever spoken with, so I shouldn't apologize that it was the middle of the night. He couldn't wait to tell all his friends. He offered to give me every single thing I might see on his shopping network at a discount.

I said I didn't need anything right then but to fax me all he had available on the Shaker furniture makers.

He said, "Hey, no problem. When do you need it?"

"Now."

"Now?"

"Yes."

I was sure he was going to tell me he'd have to get his mom's permission.

Then he said, "Sure. I can do that. Okay, then. But I should notify these clients of your request, right? It's only fair, I think. I mean, I like to—"

I said, "Fair? I am about to fax you a copy of a gag order. The agent delivering the original is probably walking up your driveway. This conversation never happened."

He said, "Oh, wow. Sweet. Cool—"

I didn't let him get to *awesome*. I told him to get a pencil so he could write down my fax number.

⟡

The New United Society of Believers in Christ's Second Coming had an address which happened to be a box office in San Yglesia, Texas.

Called up my map.

San Yglesia was a backwater on the Rio Grande. It was twenty-five miles south of Laredo. I'd practically been in their backyard.

La Missión de María en Cielo de la Ascención was built fifty years before La Mission San Antonio de Valero, more popularly known as the Alamo. But the Pamaya Indians living in what became San Yglesia preferred their own ways to what the Spanish priests were inflicting upon them, so before the mission was consecrated the Pamayas built a dam just upriver, and the first big storm that came along covered the priests' and their own huge labors with a lake.

A couple of centuries later, ten years ago, the family that owned the land decided to drain the lake and watched, shocked, as the Mission ascended toward the heavens just as its namesake had. They sold off what they thought was a crumbling pile of adobe and the fifty boggy acres surrounding it to Raymond Tiner. Tiner's offer was contingent on a report of the engineers he'd hired. The engineers came to find what he'd suspected, that the water had in fact preserved the mission; the lumpy mass was one-half loose muck that could be scraped off. The building underneath was sound. The engineers were awed by the fluke of nature—they didn't know about the rebellious and clever Pamayas.

Tiner spent his family's fortune making the building habitable, the land arable. There were several articles in a Texas newspaper about the holy man who resurrected a mission. A local priest wanted to reconsecrate it, but Tiner got a court order preventing him, on the premise that the mission hadn't been consecrated in the first place. The Pamayas knew what they were about in more ways than one.

Within a few years forty people lived in the mission, supporting themselves as the old original Shakers had: They were a capitalist venture using profits from their handiwork to maintain a farm, livestock, two sets of living quarters (one for men and one for women), a communal kitchen and dining hall, an infirmary, a pharmacy, and a hall for worship. They became entirely self-sufficient in very short order.

I called Joe. He knew by the tone of my voice to put off a squabble. He went to his files. The New Shakers living in San Yglesia were still there. Unarmed and peaceful.

He said, "They built a wall around the complex. Don't like to be disturbed. Very industrious folk who leave their neighbors alone. And unarmed, so we leave *them* alone. You're not joining up, are ya, honey?"

"No. They're celibate."

"I know. Hence the industry."

I didn't fill in what wasn't in his reports. That the complex the New Shakers lived in was a mission. Because if I shared what I now knew, the mission would be stormed. Rona Leigh had to live if a fair trial instead of the one she had were to determine her guilt or innocence and then render an appropriate sentence. Fair having nothing to do with whether or not she was a martyr, the daughter of God, Sister of Jesus. Rona Leigh dead would make her more a saint and martyr than she was already fast becoming. Tiner and his Shakers dead meant we'd have a lot of work cut out for us trying to find answers that they alone had. What we needed to do was go in there, grab Rona Leigh, get out with no loss of life to any of the conspirators, or to us— and then arrest everyone.

All we had to do was to gain the target. When least expected, when the guard was down, send in a minimal force, grab her, and get out. If my director felt we could get in and out he'd at least consider it. Not Joe. He wouldn't.

"Poppy, I appreciate that you suffer from insomnia, but couldn't this have waited till morning?"

I breathed softly into the phone. "I just needed to talk to you. To hear your voice." Then I told him I was sorry I'd hung up on him before. "I meant to say goodbye, but I panicked that I'd miss buying the last *Time* on the newsstand."

He said, "I wish you were here."

I said, "Me too," a lie.

I waited till morning to call my director. I asked what

exactly his plan was once we knew the whereabouts of Rona Leigh. "With me here and you there, I want to be aware of what's happening."

"Plan?" He was agitated. "Poppy, either there's a quick surrender or there's a bloodbath. We're talking about people who sprang and are now harboring a convicted ax murderer. The same people who tried to kill a few Texas Rangers by dropping concrete blocks on them from an overpass. Who could easily have killed *you* while they were at it. We obviously aren't pussyfooting around on this one."

"A lot of people will think you're crucifying Christ."

"Fuck 'em. If we're lucky, we can do it fast and quietly before any cameras arrive. But if the cameras find us, people will get to see us warn Rona Leigh and her buddies to come quietly. They'll see it on the news after whatever happens happens."

"And if she was kidnapped? If she had no part in the escape? What if she didn't commit murder?"

"Here's what you and I are committed to doing: Protect the innocent, not the guilty. She has been convicted of murder, and the people who got her out of the Gatesville prison are plenty guilty. And you're the one behind my crime lab. You say it's not possible for someone of her physique to do what she was convicted of. All right, then. If she agrees to come peacefully, I will guarantee her a reprieve so her case can be reopened. I'll have my man, or maybe your man, Joe Barnow himself, wield a trusty bullhorn as soon as we find her. If she's being held against her will, if she's been brainwashed—whatever—we'll have scoped the place so we'll know that. Hopefully, we'll be successful at getting her, or get her kidnappers, if that's the case, to surrender her and themselves as well."

"A bloodbath is the last resort, then."

"Of course, Poppy. Listen, we're all freaked out by

this, but no one has gone off the deep end. Where the hell is she, Mars?"

"Sir, what about the Rangers?"

"They'll be in on this. They weren't in on Waco. They'll be in on this."

"What if the Rangers decide they'd like to replay the Alamo, only win?"

"Because I will convince the Rangers and I will convince the ATF that a quick strike will do the trick."

"How will you do that?"

"I'm working on it. My job, remember?"

"And what if the Rangers locate her first?"

"Then Scraggs will call the shots. That's the arrangement. They won't be first, though. We will."

I reached Joe. We held the same conversation. His version included his complete trust in me. He said, "I'm not going to humor you. Soon as we know where she is, the place gets surrounded by your guys and us, and the Rangers if she's in Texas, where you've convinced us she is. We give them three minutes to come out. If they don't, we fire tear gas. A ton of it. Also smoke bombs, so even if they have masks, they can't see. We don't cajole them, we don't beg them, and most of all we don't do anything that gives the press time to get there."

"All right, Joe. So if they don't come out and you're forced to start firing even though they're blind as bats, how many killed on our side are you estimating?"

"Don't be sarcastic. I don't need it."

"Yes, you do."

"The answer is, None. Armed or unarmed, we're trying something new."

"What?"

"A gas. It makes you woozy. Not quite blotto. Then it dissipates immediately without affecting anything more than twenty yards away. It's fast. Absorbed through the skin. Those who are affected come right around. Couple minutes. With handcuffs on, is the idea. The only downside is that if you're woozy, anything you've just eaten you'll probably throw up. Hope someone comes up with vomit-repellent clothes real soon. I remember when I was a rookie patrolman a few lives back. First job was scooping up drunks out of alleys. You were always covered with vomit."

"Joe, this is a joke, right?"

"No, it's not. No different from the rationale behind tear gas. We'll just have to make sure they're refocused before we arrest them and read them their rights. I mean, they'll have broken the law. When you refuse to obey a police officer's command, the officer must interpret that as a threat. The immediate action an officer takes when finding himself in a life-threatening action is crucial in terms of the officer remaining alive. We're going to try this plan and then see what happens as far as legal action is concerned, which is what you're thinking, I know. But—high risk, high gain."

"Joe, you're talking complete bullshit. You're going to *gas* them?"

"We took the same risk with stun guns, if you think about it. Figured that would be unconstitutional for sure. Wasn't. This'll just be another test case."

"But what if they have explosive devices lying around. You can trip a switch even if you're woozy."

"Naturally we'll scope the place first."

"The Sister of Christ will spot you and warn them."

No comment.

"I wasn't being sarcastic this time. I'm just trying to—"

"Since when did you go from defending what's right to kidding around? Since when did you stop trusting me?"

"I trust you. But I'm worried. What if they've strapped explosives to themselves?"

"Another chance we have to take."

"The apostles all died for Jesus. That's not sarcasm either. I'm trying to make a point, to make you see—"

"Sweetheart, she ain't Jesus. Or his sister either. Period."

"Joe, is there any way to get someone inside?"

"Inside of what?"

"I mean, once we know where inside is? Talk to them. Talk to her. Get a guarantee for a new trial in writing. Offer to—"

"I don't have to tell you the penalty for escaping from prison. In Texas, it's probably torture."

"If she's innocent—even if she's not innocent and just suffered an inequitable trial—then she had the right to escape from prison seeing as how she was in the process of being executed. Well, not the right, but—"

"Damned straight, not the right."

"Maybe a human right. I wasn't talking legal rights."

I'd tired him out. He raised his voice. "Poppy, we've got a convicted killer on the loose who is influencing a lot of people. This is a new kind of deal. The situation is escalating. We want her alive so that we don't create a martyr. *You* want her alive because you think she might be a victim. The idea behind the plan is to keep her alive. What the hell is your problem?"

I told him I had a headache. I did.

⟡

Scoping the mission wouldn't take long.

I made a reservation on a flight to San Antonio. I'd have a two-hour layover before the next flight to Laredo went out. I ordered another ticket under another name for that one.

I'd stopped at a bookstore and bought a couple of

books on the Shakers. I learned that the Shakers were not only industrious, they were also pathologically hospitable. Because their creed instructed them to be so, and for practical reasons too, since they couldn't depend on offspring to promulgate their faith. They pretty much welcomed lost souls to their door by feeding them, giving them a place to sleep, and allowing them to see what the Shakers were about. Historically, the first thing they did of note was to set up a soup kitchen in the middle of Dublin during the famine. They saved more Irish lives than emigration did.

So basically, they offered people a productive life of industry and goodwill instead of sex. They simply felt children weren't the only thing a person could produce.

In the United States, they invented the flat broom and the washing machine; they created the first national seed catalogs, illustrating the little packets of seeds with the end product; they came up with treatments for illnesses and diseases that were later copied by the orthodox medical profession. And they experimented with drugs. They made salicylic acid, dried it out, and turned the powder into little concentrated tablets, which they'd discovered was an antidote to minor pain. Today, drug companies do the same thing. The Shakers were taking aspirin a hundred years before the rest of us.

They were capitalists who started out seeing if gardeners would buy seed from them, and when they made a fortune doing that, they moved along until they were mass-producing their trim, clean furniture. With that, they became totally independent—what they didn't grow or make they were able to buy. Business managers far ahead of their time.

When your sexual energy is suppressed, it doesn't just go away. It's displaced, as my shrink friend has assured me. And that explained the extraordinary ingenuity and wit of the Shakers. Too bad for them there weren't any more of them left on earth except one very old lady. I didn't consider Raymond Tiner's band of followers Shakers. According to the little old lady, they didn't count. They were misled, that was for sure. But they were topnotch capitalists all the same. Got a little sloppy, though—forgot to pull their product from the shopping channel.

I threw the books in the trash can at the San Antonio airport.

I'd never seen the Alamo but I'd certainly seen pictures. That's how I was imagining Tiner's mission, and that's exactly what it looked like.

I stood in the shade under the spreading branches of a live oak that had to be a hundred years old. It was on a little rise that had not been affected by the Pamayan flood. The mission itself might have been built by Disney; it was perfectly square-cornered, its outer layer of new adobe smooth and burnished in the sun. It was surrounded by an adobe wall twelve feet high, which meant no one could see into the grounds unless they chose to climb the hill to the live oak. A dirt drive maybe a half-mile long made its way from the town of San Yglesia to the mission.

On the other side of the mission, the snaking line of vegetation was the same as what I'd seen outside my window at La Posada. The Rio Grande was just a few yards from the rear wall behind the mission.

Two men were sinking thin metal posts every few feet along the top of the wall. The men were dressed alike. In the bright Texas sun, they wore white shirts, black pants, and gray vests. Black hats, too, exactly like

the photographs of the Shakers in the books I'd read.
I guessed they were getting ready to string barbed wire.

A car came down the road. There was a gate in the
wall, and it opened for the car. Two men just inside the
gate were also in Shaker clothes. The man who got out
of the car was not. I'd say it was Vernon Lacker.

I walked down the backside of the hill the way I'd
come up and went to the pickup I'd rented. The road
from Laredo skirted the hill. I'd parked the pickup just
off the road. I got in and drove into San Yglesia. The
town was a sleepy, dusty little place. The only part of
the mission visible from the town was the bell tower
looming over the walls. The wood houses facing the
street were dilapidated. The biggest one had a sign: SAN
YGLESIA HOTEL. I guessed there might be a vacancy.

I got my stuff and went in. A young woman behind
the desk was reading *Vanity Fair*. She looked up at me
and did a bit of a double-take. I said, "I'd like to check
in and stay for the night."

"Would you now?"

"Yes."

She got out some papers and spent quite a bit of
time trying to come up with a pen. When she did and
I'd checked in, I said, "Is there a way to get to the mission other than from the street out front?"

"You mean the temple?"

"The temple?"

"It ain't a mission, because a priest ain't been in it.
Fact is, they call it a temple, so we do too. Planning to
join, right?"

"I'm thinking about it."

"Honey, get a divorce instead. You want to walk out
on a bad man, fine, but don't think you'll be any hap-
pier with those folks. Some guy kicks you around, you
end up with a limp, 'course you leave. But those people, they work like dogs and they don't ever come out.

They believe in separation of the sexes. Don't exactly throw parties. You're too young and good-lookin' to be buried, if you don't mind my saying."

"Thanks for the advice."

"Best you just go on upstairs and freshen up. When you come down I'll have a nice little sandwich for you out on the porch. You can watch the wind blow the dirt and have a think about what you're doin'. I'll throw in a bottle of Lone Star, on the house." She handed me a big iron key. "It's the only one I got at the moment, so make sure you give it back when you check out. Gal who works here tomorrow won't think to ask."

I said "Okay," took the key, and thanked her. "If it turns out I want to stay a couple of days, will you have a vacancy?"

She laughed. "You can throw that worry away. Been on the road?"

"Yes."

"Listenin' to the radio?"

"No. It rattles."

"You ain't heard the latest on Rona Leigh, then?"

I felt a little lurch in my stomach. "No."

"'Nother tape come in. Got it right here in the VCR. Saved it for my friend. Care to see it?"

I did.

She gestured for me to come around the desk. She had a little TV on a shelf under the counter. She played the tape for me. Rona Leigh's voice was much stronger. The feeding tube was gone. She quoted from the parable of the Prodigal Son. Then she recited one of her own about the inevitability of goodness never being able to hide long. Then she said that even though she had not been willing to die for the murder of Melody and James, she would accept dying for Jesus, if that's what it took to pass along His Holy Word. "Just as I accept the thorns of Jesus' crown which represent his own bitter suffering, I also do not forget the crown's green leaves, symbolizing the hope I nurture for the reward awaiting me. After the darkness of the winter of my present life, I will at last enter the happiness of the eternal spring of heaven which blessed God grants me in his precious mercy."

Her words didn't reflect Vernon's anymore. They reflected Tiner's. She and Vernon had had no plan for her to enter the eternal spring of heaven.

She closed her eyes. That was the routine. Only this time she didn't need to close them. Her efforts hadn't wiped out any energy she had. She was still smiling.

Tiner's voice came over the serene shot of her lying there so contentedly, arms folded in a cross over her chest, her tiny hands relaxed. He said, "Our CHRIST AND SAVIOR knows that capture will soon be upon us. The LORD GOD has told me this. We will soon be TRAPPED within our GETHSEMANE. Until that time, the Daughter God has SENT TO US will continue to preach. Her followers INCREASE each day, a hundredfold. It is the WORD of the LORD!"

The video went black.

The clerk said, "My, my, my."

I said, "You're not on the Internet, are you?"

"Me? Nearest computer is in Laredo. Unless you want to go to the temple and ask the crazies if you can use theirs."

Nope. "Is there a phone in my room?"

"Yes, ma'am."

I went upstairs. The room was small, the ceiling almost too low for me to stand up, and the floor was tilted. The little window looked down onto the river, the banks only a few feet apart, much narrower and slower-moving than it had been in Laredo. I called the shrink, seeing as how he didn't trace his calls. I told him I needed a favor, needed him to find out the server of the Rona Leigh tape, the newest one. Told him I didn't have the facilities.

He'd seen the tape. "She's looking a bit stronger, isn't she?"

"Yes."

"Hold on, Poppy."

I heard him clicking around. He came back to me.

"Webtunes dot com."

"Thanks, Doc."

"As always, the pleasure is mine. Closing in, Poppy?"

"Maybe."

He was still clicking and then he stopped. "Poppy, Webtunes dot com is now off the Internet. You people don't waste any time."

My man Auerbach was watching. The FBI had shut it down and I'd gotten my answer from the shrink in the nick of time.

I hung up. I thought a shower before my sandwich would be nice. There was only a bathtub, though. I've forgotten how to take a bath. I washed my face instead.

I went back downstairs for my sandwich.

The clerk wasn't behind the counter; she was outside sitting at the table on the porch having a sandwich of her own. Mine was there too, with a napkin over it. I sat down.

I said, "Is there a store here that sells clothes?"

She looked me up and down. "Nope. Laredo. Jesse's feed store sells work clothes out at the opposite end of Main from the temple." She pointed. "That's all we got."

The sandwich and the beer fortified me. I got in the pickup and drove to Jesse's. I was officially accepting the no-walking philosophy of Texas.

Jesse sold me a short-sleeved jumpsuit, plus socks and work boots. He threw in a John Deere cap. I said, "Do you mind telling me if there's been any unusual action at the temple lately?"

He scrutinized me. He decided to answer, liked to talk. "I stay clear a them, ma'am. I'm a Christian, and sure as hell don't know what the hell they're about. Won't do business with them people. Not that they need my business. Everything they need they order on their computers. Deliveries all the time, stuff goin' in every day."

"So nothing especially out of the ordinary has happened?"

Scrutinized me again. "Who wants to know?"

"I do. I've been hired by a fellow to talk them into giving him his daughter back."

He started to clean his nails with a screwdriver. "Won't be the first time someone tried to do that. Daughter, huh? Usually somebody's here lookin' for his wife. If the daughter's over eighteen they'll tell you the daughter's got free will. They'll tell you that real friendly. Then they'll order you off the property. Call the authorities. Sheriff'll come down and tell you same thing they told you. Way it is."

"The man who hired me is willing to pay a lot of money to have his daughter returned."

"Your man's a fool, then. Ought to hire a few cowboys, go in there with their weapons drawn, grab her."

"Are the people inside heavily armed?"

"Ain't armed at all. Be easy as lickin' butter off a knife. Fact, tell your man to pay me. I'll do it."

"But how do you know they're not armed?"

"Been inside. See, at first they come to me. Till I decided they was just a little too cuckoo. Give me the heebie-jeebies. Only weapons they got in there are hoes. Nice hoes. Forged them right there inside the temple. They don't hunt. They're mostly vegetarians. Eat a chicken or make a lamb stew once in a while. They got no guns for huntin'.

"People tolerate 'em 'cause once a week they hold a

market outside the gate. Best produce you ever seen. Cheap. People come from miles around. Couple a Believers drive a truck up to the Laredo border into Mexico and donate the food. Do-gooders."

He wiped the screwdriver on his pants.

"But now that you mention it, they stopped havin' their market not so long ago. People keep comin' around, but the Believers tell 'em they don't know when they'll hold the next one."

"Nothing else?"

"Well, I'll have to think. I'm more than happy if I can help you get the girl back. Those people ain't healthy. Don't believe in the sex life. Husband and wife join up there, they got to agree to separate sleeping quarters. So, hey, at least that daddy a yours don't have to worry about his gal gettin' knocked up."

He laughed and coughed and took out a grimy little can, opened it, and plugged up his cheek with what looked like a wad of tar.

"Now I consider it, there's been *two* unusual things. One, closin' up the market like I said and, two, a police van went in there couple weeks ago, dead a night. Don't know what that was about. Musta shook 'em up. Those people go to bed when the sun sets and get up at dawn. My brother seen the van. He lives down that end a Main. He's border patrol, works third shift."

"Did he see the car leave?"

"Not that he said. I imagine it left. 'Less some cop decided to give up fightin' crime so's he can grow his own beans and do without women. I doubt that."

"So do I."

I thanked him for the clothes and the help.

I drove down Main. A curtain hung from every front window in San Yglesia, and every window framed a person holding the curtain back.

I passed the hotel and stopped at the drive that led

to the mission. The barbed wire was up. The tapes had to be worth a fortune. It isn't often you find live video of God's Daughter. I guessed Tiner would order his followers to fight the law or why the barbed wire? And he meanwhile would take off with the tapes, abandoning all of them to a pitched battle. It was about money. Which meant they might not have been armed previously, but they were now.

Rona Leigh and the New Shakers were about to be thrown to the wolves. If Tiner ended up in Venezuela a rich man—well, there are worse things. But if Rona Leigh and the Believers ended up dead, there would be renewed sanity status for all the right-wing militias refusing to disappear. Tiner had to be convinced his safest course of action would be to turn Rona Leigh over to the authorities, and my deal would be to give him a twenty-four-hour head start to disappear with his tapes.

And there would be no storming of the Alamo if everyone knew I was in there with them. They'd know I was in there as soon as the FBI interviewed my hostess at the hotel and Jesse at the feed store. I'd registered in my own name. As soon as they went into my room and found all my stuff. Far as I could see, I was the only authority who might arrange such a deal with Tiner. The idea would be to have Rona Leigh in custody before the mission was located, which would be very soon because, when Delby realized I didn't pass the information she'd given me to our director, she would do it. Goes with integrity.

What I needed was a policeman. I didn't want to just bring her into the local station. I had to feel out Scraggs. If he didn't see my point, I'd do it without a policeman.

I drove north to Laredo and used the phone in La Posada. I had a hard time reaching him. He was up the road somewhere in San Antonio. Where my trail got cold. I left my name and waited for my cell phone to ring. It did five minutes later.

He said, "Where are you?"

"Laredo."

"Laredo. I'm not the only one trying to keep tabs on you, Poppy. Your director is looking for you and losing his mind in the process. You found her, didn't you?"

"Don't be ridiculous."

"Then what the hell are you up to?"

"I need to talk to you."

"Talk."

"I need to see you."

"Why?"

"I want to compare notes."

"Poppy, tell me. Where is she?"

"Max, I need a good cop I can trust."

"Where is she?"

"I need your help."

"Okay."

"I'm in the hotel on the plaza. La Posada. Max, I need you to be on your own."

"Fine. Hour and a half. That means no stops along the way."

He hung up.

I left the hotel and went into the plaza and sat under a tree on a bench. In daylight the cathedral looked gray and scruffy. Whoever power-washed the hotel needed to do the same for the church. For an hour and a half, I contemplated my life while I ate coconut ice cream and watched Mexican Americans stroll or play dominoes. Me and the bench were at a defining juncture, I knew.

Scraggs found a parking spot just past the hotel. He was alone, and he didn't speak into his radio before he got out of the car.

I called out, "Max."

He turned and spotted me. I waved.

He wasn't just stiff the way he'd been in Washington. He was limping. When he reached me, I said, "I'm the one who's supposed to be limping. What's your problem?"

"It only looks like a limp. Doc just unwrapped my cracked ribs. If I walk this way it hurts less."

"You didn't look like a man with cracked ribs when they pulled you out of the car."

"I was being brave for you."

I liked this Scraggs, I really did.

I told him, "So sit down here on the bench and I'll go buy you an ice-cream cone."

He sat. I got the cone and brought it back.

He licked it. Three times. Then his head turned toward me and he said, "Where is she?"

"She's in a restored mission."

"We've checked every mission in the state."

"You missed this one. That's because it's a temple. Restored by the man who influenced Vernon when he was a student at a Bible college. He's founded a new religious order. An offshoot of the Shakers."

"The Shakers?"

"The chair people."

"I know who they are. This Bible school guy is really the one who got her out?"

"I'd say so."

"I'm not goin' to ask you how, Poppy. Just where. For Christ's sake, tell me."

"I'm getting to that part. But I want to do something that I know no one else will go along with. Except maybe you. Will you listen?"

"Fine. But while I'm listenin', I hope she's not runnin' out the back door."

"I don't think Tiner's letting her out of his sight.

Scraggs, what if we just go up to the door of the mission? With a warrant for Rona Leigh's arrest. She didn't cross a border, so Texas has jurisdiction. The people in the mission probably aren't armed. If the FBI finds her first, they'll say there are illegal weapons in the mission and call in the ATF. What makes sense to me is to avoid that.

"So Scraggs, let's just go get her. Me and you. We might have a little negotiating to do with them, but—"

"What do you mean, these people probably aren't armed?"

"I checked with someone who would know."

"How the hell long . . . ?"

"Max. Just since this morning."

"Okay, so what's the next step after these people tell us she's not there?"

"She might not be. They might have moved her. And if she's not there and the FBI or the Rangers storm the place and kill a bunch of peaceful farmers or whatever they are, then—"

"Peaceful farmers? Poppy, are you in the middle of a nervous breakdown? C'mon. It's still that letter, isn't it? From the daughter who showed you her father didn't rape anyone."

"No, Max. That letter drove me to taking action where none was being taken. Rona Leigh is just a small part of that action. She happened to be next in line, that's all." I picked up a shopping bag next to the bench. "I have something to show you."

I reached into the bag, took a roll of paper, and spread it out across my lap. Max decided to humor me, waited for me to tell him what I was doing.

"An architect designed the present layout of the mission. The temple. This is the blueprint."

"I almost don't want to know. But I'll ask anyway. Where'd you get this?"

"From a Web-site server."

"You didn't need much of a threat, right?"

"Didn't need anything except to identify myself and my job."

"I don't want to remember what investigations were like before computers."

"Me neither."

We looked at the layout. The entire first floor was labeled WORSHIP. An addition had been added to the back, a dining hall and kitchen. The loft where a choir was meant to sing hymns three hundred years ago had been expanded into an entire second floor with two dormitory wings on opposite sides. Males right, females left, big communal bathrooms for each group. In between, a tiny apartment for Tiner: sitting room, bedroom, office, and, next to him, a large guest room. Also a pharmacy and two infirmaries, one for the men, one for the women.

A second paper showed the layout of the outdoor grounds. Six outbuildings for animals and equipment, carpentry shop, business office, a garage. There were three gardens, labeled FEED, FOOD, and HERBS.

Scraggs studied it all.

I said, "Believe it or not, this is in keeping with documents portraying Shaker compounds that go back over two hundred years."

He said, "So we've got around forty people plus Rona Leigh."

"And Vernon."

"We don't know that."

"I know that. I saw him."

He swung around to face me, which made him wince. He said, "Then you've been seen, Poppy."

"I don't think so."

He looked into my eyes. "Arrogance'll get you killed.

And considerin' what you're suggestin', it could get me killed too."

"I was careful. We'll be careful."

"Careful. Here's what I think about careful. This bunch of people got a set of tapes worth a big load of money. They know we're closin' in. The guy in charge will bail out. Maybe already did. And that means—"

"See, Max. You're thinking what I'm thinking. We've got to close in while he's still there. We'll make a deal with him. We'll—"

"No. We have to follow the standard operation. Warn 'em to come out and tear-gas 'em if they resist arrest. If they really don't have weapons, that'll bring 'em out."

"Maybe they'll have masks."

"Poppy, come with me to Austin. Now. We'll fly up, be there in an hour. Tell the Rangers what you know. They don't want to kill Rona Leigh. They want her alive. They know how important it is. With all the hullabaloo, the governor has no choice now but to reopen the case. He'll do it, I promise you that."

"Don't bullshit me, Scraggs. No way. She'll be taken right to Gatesville and executed. With you or without you, I'm not going to let that happen."

"Then I feel it is my duty to protect you from getting yourself killed, thinkin' you're above the law. Let me tell you what you're up against. A boss who thinks maybe it's time to rein you in. And I would agree there. You got the boots, you got the hat, and you even got the right belt, but that doesn't make you some kind of one-man posse. I'm not about to—"

"Scraggs, listen."

"No, you listen. I've got a lot more to say. The governor's wife told us you quoted the Bible to her when you were in her home, that you must be one of them. The warden at Gatesville claims you taunted him about the expiration dates on the chemicals. You even joked about springing Rona Leigh."

"He joked, not me. And I taunted the governor's wife, so what."

"Here's the kicker, Poppy. The night of the escape, a couple of Texas Rangers including myself didn't see where the cement blocks came from that fell on us. We all figured they must have been tossed from the back of the ambulance. Now I surely do believe you when you say there were three people up on the overpass who dropped them, but the general thinkin' is, you couldn't have seen them either. General thinkin' goes on to say you must have known they were going to fall because you *knew* where they were going to fall *from*."

I said, "I was the one who came up with the nurse. Sterilizing Rona Leigh's arm."

"Yeah, you were. Interpreted as throwin' suspicion off you. Real reason I came down here, Poppy, is because I had to find you before anyone else. A warrant for your arrest is bein' put to press right now. The law says if I find you, I have to be the one to arrest you. Law also states I must protect myself, draw my weapon when I make an arrest. I'm sorry, Poppy, I have no choice here."

He drew his gun. He aimed it at my heart just the way procedures require. He stood up, and when he did, he grimaced. The broken ribs.

My eyes went from his to the barrel of the gun. The gun wavered just a little bit; then he held it steady. "Just come back with me and tell us what you know. Say you'll do that voluntarily. I'll believe you. We're friends, right? What we've been through . . . hell, Poppy, if you don't, your life will be over. A fine and dedicated life that—"

I put my hands together and swung a two-fisted backhand into his ribs. He doubled over and the gun flew. It hit the sidewalk and went off. I was already in a sprint. I got in my truck and was out of there.

I didn't have time to grab the architect's plans.

14

The Rangers wouldn't know where Rona Leigh was for as long as it would take them to find the architect. Hopefully, he was off designing a mosque in Khartoum. Of course, they could get lucky just canvassing. Then it would only take until some local historian said, "Hey, I know that place. It's the temple some cult dug out of a lake." Perhaps they wouldn't take such a person too seriously and give me more time.

I drove to San Yglesia. I wasn't stopped, and the town was as drowsy as ever.

I said hello to the hotel clerk, went up to my room, and left everything there. I took my bag out to the car with nothing in it but my new jumpsuit. If I needed a change, I wasn't going to wear a Shaker dress and bonnet. I came back down and told the clerk I was going to the mission and paid for an extra week's stay.

I said to the clerk, "Wish me luck."

She just shook her head.

I drove up Main Street to the gate in the wall, but I didn't need to get out and knock. The big wood doors opened for me. Beyond was a scene about as dazzling as the one Dorothy encountered when she looked upon Oz. Behind me, brown dust and dilapidation. Inside the gate, everything was green and ordered, each section of garden cordoned off by rows of flowers. The barns and

the outbuildings were whitewashed. It looked like half
the New Believers were working outside.

The guard Shaker came up to me. I said to him, "I'd
like to see Elder Tiner."

He said, "I'm sorry, Sister. If you're interested in joining us, I have to tell you that the Elder is not presently
welcoming new converts."

He seemed genuinely sad about that.

"I'd really only like to speak with him. I'd like to
speak to Vernon Lacker too."

He went from genuinely sad to genuinely appalled.
Like a child staring at a ghost, he said, "Who are you?"

"I'm Agent Penelope Rice, FBI. Vernon knows me."

He tried to keep control of himself. To the air, he
said, "She's alone." To me, "Please drive through." As
soon as I did, he pressed a remote control and the gate
closed behind me. I stopped and waited. Now when he
approached the pickup he had a weapon pointed at
me. Jesse the feed store man was wrong. The weapon
wasn't a hoe, it was a small handgun.

He said, "I would ask you to step out of your vehicle
with your hands in the air."

While I climbed out, he was still pressing his remote.
Six men appeared from the mission, guns drawn, running toward us. From the look on the guard's face they
couldn't run fast enough. This was something he
didn't do very often.

One of the men said, "Give me your weapon."

I did.

Then they took me inside, where my eyes adjusted to
the dim light. It was ten degrees cooler. The hall of
worship was empty, and even though the design was
classic Catholic church there were no Catholic accou-
trements. Only whitewash.

We went up to the second floor. They had me sit
down in a small reception room furnished with the fa-

mous chairs, a no-nonsense table, and one row of pegs across a wall. I didn't have a coat to hang. The men sat too, each one pointing his gun at me.

A man came through the door, dressed exactly like the others. There was no question, though, that he was the leader, the one in charge, their Elder. Raymond Tiner had terrific stage presence, an aura of authority. It was the way he seemed to float into the room. I stood up. The men rose, the guns rose. I put out my hand. I said, "I'm glad to meet you Elder Raymond. I'm Penelope Rice."

He waved at the men and the guns went down. A second wave, and all but one of them left.

He said, "You are blessed in our eyes, Agent Rice. You did what you could to save the Daughter of God. We had hoped you would manage it, but we have never faulted you for what, in the end, you could not do. The task was left to us."

"And how did you do it?"

He smiled. "You have discovered us. You have the instinct and ingenuity your profession requires. We are our Sister's liberators. But the Daughter of God is alive today through the intercession of Jesus Christ. A miracle. He alone is responsible."

"You managed it for him. How?"

"We facilitated His miracle. Jesus Christ revealed to us the means to saving Her life and then made clear to me that I must bring His Sister to my refuge once Her life was saved. Once the Lord raised His Daughter from the dead, we only followed his command."

"What was his command?"

"He asked that five people be at the ready, two to drive the ambulance and three to drop blocks from the overpass. And then God wrought another miracle. None of the five were caught. A gift. We successfully carried out what had been prescribed in His Holy Name."

"You know all of you here are in grave danger?"

"We had been in danger until this moment. We are now safe. The Daughter of God told us there would be a sign. A sign that would offer us relief from the threat of danger you speak of. You are the sign. The Child is safe so long as you are here, isn't She? Your people will not sacrifice you. And you know that, or you wouldn't be here. So let us talk. May I offer you some tea?"

Tea.

His body began to rock a little, up on the balls of his feet.

I told him how good a cup of tea sounded.

The two of us sat down and a female New Believer brought tea. She wore a bonnet. To me, the bonnet meant a human mind off-kilter. She left without looking anywhere but at the tea or the floor.

I said to Tiner, "Why is she wearing a bonnet? She's not out in the sun."

"A woman's hair is the glory of God. It is also a temptation. The Bible says it must be hidden from men."

"Jesus didn't say that, though. It's in the Old Testament."

"That's true."

"Mary Magdalene dried Jesus' feet with her hair."

"Do you read the Bible?"

"No. I remember it from pictures in the Bible stories for children that my grandmother gave me."

He chuckled. "There is something about tea that calms us and turns our talk inward. Are you enjoying it?"

It tasted like ragweed. "It's very good."

"My favorite. Chamomile, but without the element that makes you sleepy. What is it you have come to say, Agent Rice? As God has sent you, it is my duty to take your words with great seriousness."

"I came to you to ask you to let me take Rona Leigh with me. Let me take her into custody, federal custody.

She won't go back to Gatesville. She will have a new trial. Despite her confession, despite her thinking otherwise, Rona Leigh might not have killed the people she was accused of killing."

He sipped at his tea. He mused. Finally, he said, "Wrongly accused. That would make even more sense. I mean . . . as to why God chose these terrible circumstances for Her. She has suffered. If She was wrongly accused, She has suffered even more mightily than any of us could ever know."

"Elder Raymond, if you allow me to take Rona Leigh, you can leave these premises first. With the tapes."

He blinked. "But I have no tapes. As soon as we make a tape, we send it to the media. We don't need to keep them. We have their Holy Source."

"You would be paid handsomely for those tapes."

"I imagine I would be. But there are none. We do not mean to profit from the second coming. When divine inspiration fills the Daughter of God, we film Her as She speaks His Words. None of us have any need here of personal fortune. We survive comfortably. Now that we have done the duty prescribed to us by the Holy Father, nothing could give us more joy and happiness. Certainly not money. We have been fulfilled."

His face was completely serene, like a sleeping infant's. I'd followed the money, and there was no money. A first. Time to pay especially close attention.

"Agent Rice, I feel momentous gratitude for your goodwill toward the new Christ Child. Still, the Lord has deemed that I should be responsible for Her, not you. I know it is hard for you—for anyone—to believe all that has come to pass has been solely for the glory of God. But it has. My last task on earth is to protect the Sister of Jesus Christ for as long as I can. We are all prepared, as were His apostles, to accept the consequences of our actions. There is no Judas among us."

I forced down a swallow of tea. "Then it makes sense that God sent me, doesn't it? Rather than your task coming to an end, the task will next lie with me. Once it is beyond your means to protect Rona Leigh, I will. And then you will live to bear witness to her and to the miracles you have experienced."

He started rocking again. "That is a possible interpretation as to why He sent you. But I am convinced He sent you to protect His Daughter here in this place just a bit longer than we'd hoped. I think I understand exactly why you are here. Why Jesus has led you to us. Because as long as you are here, there will be no Armageddon. With you among us we will be safe. The police, those who govern—no one will want to see anything happen to you. And as long as nothing happens to you, nothing will happen to the Daughter of God."

"Reverend Tiner, once I am seen as secondary to their goal, we might all be killed."

"If the Lord chooses Armageddon for us, so be it."

"If you let me take Rona Leigh now, Armageddon will not take place."

"I wish the Christ Child could be kept with us for a very long time. But no, the manifestation of Her second coming will occur. Many will be called, few will be chosen. What you ask me to do is not what I have heard from the Lord God. He says that we care for a great treasure, His Child, and that we should fear neither danger nor death. And since the Lord justly chastises us with His whips, we try, with His aid, to stand ready to receive the blow from that mighty hand. Having magnanimously granted us the present life, He retains the power to deprive us of it at any moment and in any manner.

"Sister, we are prepared."

I sipped at my bitter tea. Rona Leigh had trusted these people to do God knows what to her in order to survive the infiltration of poisons into her blood. She was able to convince herself that this was her only chance to live. She took the chance. A matter of faith, as Vernon had described faith to me. But not faith in God. Faith in science. In people who are able to take the sleep-inducing elements out of chamomile tea. I knew damn well that Rona Leigh was not about to welcome Armageddon.

I said, "May I speak to Rona Leigh?"

He put his cup down. "But of course. She sees you as Her friend. And you remain Her ally, as anyone can see. God blesses you for that. I presume you intend to try to convince Her to go with you. If she chooses to do that, then everything changes. She is the Daughter of the Lord. She is the Second Coming. I recognize that Her desire is our command. But I must warn you, Agent Rice: To think you have such a power is inaccurate." He looked at his watch. "She is receiving medical treatments for the next twelve hours. You won't be able to speak to Her until tomorrow. For now, it's best if someone familiarizes you with our home here. It will be your home until I decide that you are no longer safe."

"You intend to keep me here against my will?"

He ignored the obvious. He stood. "I believe you will be more comfortable discussing the circumstances you have entered into with someone you have come to know."

He blessed me before he left. His one henchman stayed. He had remained standing quietly in the corner with his weapon pointed at the floor, but now he raised it. He led me back out to the grounds in front of the mission where Vernon was waiting, a plastered-on smile contorting his face and dampness in his eyes.

Vernon shook my hand, blessed me in the name of the Lord, drew me a few steps away from our Shaker guard, and whispered, "You've got to help us." Then, in a bright voice, "Let me show you the Temple of the Second Coming, Sister."

We walked.

He lowered his voice again. "He wants to save the world. He can't do it without the martyrdom of Rona Leigh. We'll all be killed but him."

"How will that save the world?"

"The people will rise up, and he will lead them."

"How will he do that if he's dead? If there's a slaughter, he will not survive."

"He will be sure to avoid death. Miz Rice, I have known this man for a long time. He is a gifted visionary. He has proven intellectual abilities. He is filled with genuine religious fervor and at the same time a practical wisdom. He has long been a recipient of revelations. Now he will survive to carry out his vision of a kingdom as emissary of the Lord."

"You're saying he intends to lead a religious revolution?"

"Yes. He believes people are willing to follow his providential guidance into the kingdom. And of course they will. He has been the instrumental factor in creating the path for the Second Coming of Christ, which is now upon us according to His teachings."

"What did he base his plan on, the fall of the Shah? Does he think he's another Ayatollah Khomeini?"

"Miz Rice, perhaps you are not far wrong. The Ayatollah overthrew who he saw as the devil. In the eyes of the people, both men saw to a miracle. Reverend Tiner's miracle is continuing on millions of television screens. His followers will happily defend him and depend on his providential guidance. How could they not? He has seen to the rescue of the Daughter of God from the chains of bondage."

I tried to keep my voice at a whisper. "He saw to some of it; you saw to the rest. Vernon, how had you planned to get your ambulance there? Before the governor did it for you?"

He stopped walking. He scuffed at the dirt with the toe of his shoe. "The nurse. I—" He started walking again.

"You awed the nurse."

"We believed that if I'd called out for an ambulance, Harley and the nurse—hopefully others—would have backed me up."

"Vernon, you don't believe any of it, do you?"

"No. I am a selfish man."

"You went along with everything to get Rona Leigh out."

"Yes." A tear trickled down his cheek. "Ma'am, I could see that, as he aged, Reverend Tiner was no longer keeping to a steady course. His rudder—his love of the Lord—deteriorated into something else. I have tried to tell him Rona Leigh does not want to go back to prison to die, but that she shouldn't die here either. He just smiled when I said that, as though I were a young student again in need of his help. So I've prayed. And you are the answer. You and your hopes for a new trial for her. What can we do?"

"We can think. That's about it. We have to think fast and come up with something before we hear the sound of the helicopter rotors. If I arrest her on a federal charge, she'll be in our custody, not theirs. It's the only hope she has."

We walked along the paths of flowers, and the New Shakers just kept on hoeing as though we were invisible. Harley Shank hoed too. He did not look up at me. Then Vernon said, "Elder Raymond says you may talk to her in the morning. You have to convince her that what you say is her only hope. I will pray until then that we do not hear the sound of helicopter rotors."

I became roommate to twenty other women. The sister who had served Tiner and me tea took me to the women's sleeping quarters after my talk with Vernon. It looked like Bemelmans's drawings of Madeline's bedroom at the orphanage: two long lines of neat little cots. At the front of each cot, a trunk on the floor and, again in the Shaker tradition, pegs all around to hang their things. The tea sister told me it was an honor to have as a guest an apostle of the Lord's Daughter. They were all happy I was going to speak with her. Among them, only Sister Emily was allowed that privilege.

I inquired as to who Sister Emily might be.

"Sister Emily is her nurse and stays with her all the time." I would, in fact, be using Sister Emily's bed.

She put my bag in the trunk and said, "It's dinner-time."

I looked at my watch. Five o'clock. She asked if I would like to join them or if I'd prefer a tray brought up. I would join.

"Come, then."

In the dining room, the men sat on one side of the room while the women sat on the other. Men served men and women served women.

Across the front of the room on a platform was the head table, where Elder Raymond sat with two of the men I'd first seen running at me with semiautomatic weapons. Vernon was there too, and there was a chair for me. The woman told me that, as a guest, I would be at the Elder's table even though I wasn't a man. Then she whispered, "When the Sister of Jesus is well enough, we will have the blessed privilege of sharing our meals with Her. How we look forward to that day!" Her cheeks were flushed with excitement.

Dinner began with grace, a sermon from Raymond

Tiner that lasted an hour. Tiner's theme was trust in the Lord, who will never fail to help and reward. He knew people were going to need to trust somebody when the helicopters began spinning overhead, creating their uniquely mind-shattering racket.

Huge platters and bowls were passed around, the food abundant and tasteless. Farm-fresh vegetables boiled into oblivion. No one's appetite had been deterred by the goings-on, they ate till all the food was gone, heaping piles of it on their plates a second and third time, never speaking. Tiner spoke. To me. He told me that after dinner they would have their prayer service and then retire. I was welcome to join the service. I looked to Vernon. He told Tiner he chose to pray in private.

The Believers went downstairs in their two gendered lines. On the main floor of the mission I stood aside, watching them as they drifted into a kind of spiral, their leader at the center. Tiner's chief guard stayed close by me. Once formed, the spiral began to move and a noise rose out of it. At first, I looked around to see if there was a CD playing. I didn't know what the noise was. Didn't imagine it could possibly be a human sound. It was an unearthly moaning and whining, a little chanting mixed in, a grating singing punctuated with discordant squeals.

The spiral's movement speeded up and then, as if someone had pulled a string connecting the figures forming it, the whole thing began to vibrate. Each of its parts trembled spastically as though invisible hands had descended to clutch every Believer around the middle and shake them like rag dolls. The noise grew louder, more raucous. The rag dolls began throwing their arms up in the air, and each began to grab at his own face, his chest, the women their breasts. The noise expanded. It's not that it grew louder, it grew wider. I imagined Vernon upstairs, lying on his cot with a pillow over his head. That's what I wished I were doing. Then they hurled themselves to the floor, heaving and tossing, all but Tiner, who picked his way across the bodies and disappeared through a door.

Religious ecstasy.

If the feds stormed the place during prayer service, all they'd need was a big net.

It took a long time for them to wind down. Prone on the floor, they gasped for breath until they were somehow able to drag themselves to their feet and climb back up the stairs, sweating, exhausted. The guard gestured with his gun for me to follow them.

There was a communal shower at the end of the bedroom, and the women stripped, went in, and turned on the water, trying to stay awake in order to clean themselves. Then one by one they took a towel from a peg and dried off their bodies and their five-o'clock-shadowed heads. There is an advantage to not having hair when you don't have the energy or time to dry it. They wore bonnets not to hide their glory but to hide their baldness.

The women took nightgowns down from the pegs and were asleep before their heads hit the pillows. There was a nightgown hanging from Sister Emily's peg. I assumed it was mine. I took a shower too. I plugged in my hair dryer and turned it on. None of them budged. It wasn't even completely dark yet. I stood by a window and watched the sun set behind the river.

15

"Hi." Wave, smile.

She'd gotten back even more color since yesterday's tape. The video camera was on a tripod in the corner of the room.

What could I say but the same? "Hi."

"I never expected to see you again."

"Nor I, you."

"I'm supposed to be dead, right?" She laughed.

"How are you feeling?"

"Much better."

As I went to sit down in the chair by the bed, she patted the mattress. "Please sit here so I can hold your hand."

Why not?

"Miz Rice, how I wanted to touch you when I realized the great effort you were making to give me a chance at life."

"Rona Leigh, do you know how they did it?"

She giggled. "Oops. Now don't you go making me laugh or I'll knock my IV out."

"Rona Leigh, do you know how they did it?"

"Who?"

"The Believers. How they got you out."

"Well, yes, I think I do."

"How?"

"Trust in the Lord."

"How did the Lord reward that trust? What instructions did he give them?"

She sighed. "The way I understand it, Vernon and Harley added things to my food. Gave me pills to take. Wouldn't let me eat certain things, includin' a few of my favorites. Vernon told me it was like getting the polio vaccine. He said, *Like when we were kids and the doctor gave us little cubes of sugar with the drop of pink vaccine on it.* 'Course, I didn't tell him I never been to a doctor in my life." She smiled. "See, it was a vaccination. They vaccinated me against the lethal injection."

"That's impossible."

Bigger smile. "Well, here I am. Little worse for wear is all. You can always ask Sister Emily. She's got more of the details."

Sister Emily sat sipping lemonade, writing in a notebook in the corner of the room. She was keeping a log of Rona Leigh's health manifestations. She didn't look up at me.

I said to the woman, "Are you a chemist?"

Her eyes lifted. "I'm a healer. In service to the Lord."

"But you studied chemistry."

"No. There is a chemist among us. I assist him by taking care of the Sister of Jesus and informing him of my findings."

Rona Leigh said, "Hey, Miz Rice. I thought you were here to visit me, not the nurse."

"Yes, I am."

A little wrinkle formed at the bridge of her nose. "You don't look so good, ma'am. You got a headache?"

"Rona Leigh, there is no time. I need to say something you won't want to hear."

"And you're afraid you'll spook me, right?"

"Yes."

"Don't you worry. I am in the hands of the Lord. His Son, my Brother, is at my side."

I looked into her face. Rona Leigh had one of those sweet little chins that makes an attractive woman girlish. Vulnerable. *An Elizabeth Taylor chin* was how my stepfather once described it. Apocalyptic breasts but that little bitty chin. I was noticing Rona Leigh's chin, I think, because she was working so hard to make it jut out as far as it could go. And her lips were pressed together. She'd braced herself for what she would hear from me.

"Rona Leigh, do you know who called the police to report a disturbance at the motel the night of the murders? Do you know who called them again, on the same night, to tell them where to find you and Lloyd?"

"Yes, I do. I have learned Gary Scott did that."

"Gary Scott set up you and Lloyd to assault two people who'd done nothing to either of you."

"You might say so. But—"

"Did you know that Gary told Lloyd that Melody had her sights set on him?"

"I have learned that too."

"Was it true?"

"Lloyd never knew the girl."

"Then why did Gary say it?"

"He figured Lloyd wouldn't rough her up if he knew she had took notice of him."

She bit at a fingernail.

"Do you know people think Gary said those things to Lloyd because he knew you would hurt Melody?"

The chin went soft again. She was relieved. She'd been worried she'd hear something she didn't already know. Then there came an ever-so-slight flare of the nostrils.

"Poppy, Gary Scott is evil. A drug dealer. If Gary told Lloyd that Melody had the hots for him, Lloyd never said anything like that to me. Makin' me jealous was not somethin' he'd do. Wasn't that kind of boy. I did not know Gary or Melody Scott. I'd been to the bar but I never seen her before that night. I told you, I took direction for those murders from Satan. When I held the ax, I didn't even know what I was swinging at. This was not your premeditated murder."

"Do you know Iago?"

"What's that?"

I asked, "What if Gary deliberately used Lloyd to drive you into a jealous rage? Make you so angry you might even kill her?"

She sighed. "Maybe you didn't understand what I just got through sayin'." Her voice became deeper, a tone I'd never heard before, not in our conversations, not on TV with Dan Rather either. "Gary Scott had a wife who was messin' around. And he couldn't do a thing about it. Couldn't control her. Couldn't keep her out of other men's beds. Couldn't keep her from gettin' herself murdered, turned out.

"See, what I did, I gave him public shame. And guilt too. Gary may be the scum of the earth. He may have tried to do what you say he did. That wouldn't surprise me. But Gary is wrong to blame himself for what I have wrought."

"Are you aware that Gary knew he would inherit a substantial amount of money if his wife died?"

Her gaze took me in. For a minute I thought she was going to ask me to repeat what I'd said. She hadn't been aware of any such thing.

"Rona Leigh, you didn't know that, did you?"

Now the voice went back to its usual chirpy pitch. "I did. I heard he inherited money."

"But you hadn't heard that he knew of such an inheritance before she was killed."

"Can't remember one way or the other."

"Rona Leigh, do you have a recollection of that night?"

Her eyes seemed to grow dark, and again there was a heavier sound to her voice. "I told you and told you. I was drugged and I was drunk and Satan resided in me. I know it's hard to think I could've done what I done for no sensible reason. But there was a reason: the Devil. The child who was treated with evil committed evil back. Then the child became an adult and the evil was banished because the adult accepted Jesus as her Lord and Savior.

"I can't explain why some other child who was put through what I was don't grow up to kill for no sensible reason, but that's what happened to me. But see, now that me is *gone.* I'm *freed.* Freed because I found Jesus, and that's the honest and simple truth. Accept Jesus and He will bestow great gifts. I have learned that firsthand, and I can only say, Thank you, Jesus, thank you.

"Miz Rice, Revelation, chapter nine, verse one: *And there appeared a great wonder in Heaven; a woman clothed with the sun, and the moon under her feet, and upon her head a crown of twelve stars.* . . . . I am that woman. Can you pass me my glass of water?"

The glass was on the table next to the bed. I would pass it to her rather than respond to the announcement as to who she was. Sister Emily watched her and made a note, presumably, as to how much Rona Leigh drank.

"Rona Leigh, when Lloyd testified against you, how did it make you feel?"

She rolled her eyes so I'd be sure to see she would only make light of my questions. But there was a sharp little glint there all the same. "I remember bein' happy to see him again. He had no choice but to bear witness to my crime."

"No. He bore witness in order to save his skin. Not

an unusual thing. That, combined with other circumstances, leads to reasonable doubt that you are guilty. There is the possibility you can be retried, a determination that can be made in an appeal to those who wield the power to do it, those with power outside the state of Texas. And if a second jury also finds you guilty but considers the mitigating circumstances surrounding your crime, your sentence might well be commuted to life.

"Rona Leigh, let me take you with me. Tell Elder Raymond—"

Her face took on the mask of a stern grade-school teacher. She shook her finger at me. "You are aimin' into a blind alley, ma'am. Leave this place . . . a new trial? A life term? I ain't doin' it, so forget about it. Elder Raymond saved my life. I came closer to death than maybe anybody before me. I will abide with him. Maybe he can hide me forever here, who knows? We will listen to what Jesus tells us, and He ain't told me to leave."

The grammar she'd learned to dazzle the likes of Dan Rather had been abandoned in order to dazzle her followers glued to their TV sets.

She took a balled-up napkin from under her bedcovers. She unwrapped it and whispered, "Look what I got." She smiled, and instead of a grade-school teacher I was looking at a child in grade school. "Here, Miz Rice, have some fudge."

I looked down at the chocolate squares. Rona Leigh was looking at Sister Emily. The woman's head was on her arm, her eyes closed. She was snoozing. Rona Leigh whispered again. "Vernon sneaked 'em to me. Go ahead."

She popped one in her mouth. "Made with the cream from the cows in the yard. C'mon." She pointed to Sister Emily and snickered.

Rona Leigh claimed she'd never been a little girl.

She'd be one now. I felt completely powerless but, at the same time, resigned. I couldn't exactly drag her out by her hair. She'd made her choice. Rona Leigh held out the fudge. I took a piece. It tasted a little gamy.

A light show behind my eyes started within seconds. And when it did, Rona Leigh sat up straight and watched me. Somehow I knew to slip down to the floor rather than fight the descending black curtain which would mean falling off the bed; I couldn't afford yet another concussion. During the seconds of slipping when I was able to think about warding off a concussion, I was able to wonder what she'd dabbed on all the fudge except for her own piece. I was able to feel furious, to feel humiliated, but still I was aware of my priorities. I grabbed onto the blanket and hoped it would ease my landing. It did. I leaned against the bed and put all my strength into staying upright.

Rona Leigh's face above me was blurred. I tried to keep my eyes open. She got out of the bed. She took off her nightgown. Then she started to undress me. It wasn't easy for her. I was a dead weight.

While she worked she talked to me.

"Poppy, darlin', I have a clear recollection of the night Lloyd and me killed those two people. I remember standin' there while Lloyd and James was yellin' at each other about some damn bike and I got real sick of it, so I went out and got Lloyd's ax outa the truck. Sliced my hand. I told Lloyd to hit the guy. He thought I meant with his fist but I says, No, with the ax. First Lloyd said he only needed his fists, but then he saw the blood, my blood, and he just yanked that ax away from me and killed James with one swing."

She had on my underwear.

"It wasn't till then that me and Lloyd even seen Melody. Guess when she first heard us bashin' at the door she went off and hid in a corner. So we see her hidin' wrapped in a sheet. We seen her 'cause when Lloyd killed James she screamed. Dumb bitch. I hated her. I remember hating her. I didn't know who she was or nothin', I just hated her because she was screamin' and makin' my head pound. So I grabbed the ax and I went over to her and I swung it at her. Lloyd tried to stop me, but I told him to get outa my way. I remember thinkin', Look here at what I'm doin', everybody. Me! I'm killin' this bitch! If Lloyd could kill somebody, then so could I. *I am goin' to kill somebody* is all that was goin' through my head. I just swung away. She kept beggin' me to stop, too, but I didn't stop."

It was the desire for power, for control, for dominance that had given her the strength.

My eyelids closed. I wanted to stop hearing and just sleep. She slapped me across the face.

I looked at her. She was in my clothes. She squatted down and brought her face down to mine. "Poppy, killin' her was like my favorite kinda sex. Like when I'm all hot and the guy's dick is right on the edge a goin' in, like he's all primed, and then instead of just goin' in, he waits. He makes you wait, and you start beggin' for it, and he still doesn't go in, and you beg some more and when you least expect it, *bang!* He just rams it in as hard as he can so's your whole body gets jarred. Then he takes it out and he stops and gets you beggin' all over again and finally, *bang!* He rams it in even harder.

"You know that kind of strength a guy can have over you? Gettin' you to beg? Well, that's the strength I had over Melody. And after she quit beggin' it wasn't fun anymore. That's when I stopped. She wasn't dead, though. Lloyd had to put her outa her misery."

She put on my shoes and stood up. Towering over me, she said, "You awake?"

I was, but I couldn't answer. So she hit me again.

"Behind all of it, though, is that Gary Scott. He used me and Lloyd to kill his wife so's he could get her money. I murdered that girl, I surely did. So did Lloyd. But so did Gary, how do you like that? Only thing is, *he* gets rich and *we* go to jail. The son of a bitch.

"So here's another thing I want to tell you. One more thing before you maybe die. . . . Now mind, I hope you don't die, but there won't be anything I can do about it. So maybe this'll be the last thing you'll hear from Rona Leigh Glueck. When I had that needle in my arm, when the witnesses were watchin' me die, the plan was for Vernon to do everything in his power to get the warden to call me an ambulance. That was goin' to be the trickiest part. But he never had to. The governor did it for him. The governor! Soon as the governor gave me that little reprieve, Harley called our ambulance.

"I didn't need you after all, did I? But thanks all the same."

If she hit me again, I never knew it.

But I didn't die.

⌒⌒⌒

I woke up in one of the little Madeline beds. I was wearing a nightgown. I could hear them all downstairs. They were in ecstasy. Sister Emily was in the next bed. Another sister sat in a chair between us. She was feeding Emily soup.

They both looked at me.

I said, "She's gone, isn't she?"

They didn't answer.

I tried to sit up. I couldn't.

I got fed soup too.

Then I said, "I have to speak to Elder Raymond."

"He is in prayer."

"When he's finished, then."

"He intends to speak to you, Sister. When prayer is finished he will come."

Except for feeding me soup and home-brewed ginger ale, they ignored me. I looked at my wrist, but my watch was gone. Rona Leigh had taken that too.

"What time is it?"

A sister said it was eight in the evening. Whatever it was Rona Leigh had spread on the fudge had knocked me out all day.

The sounds of Shaker prayer came to their slow conclusion. Then the women appeared in the doorway and dragged themselves into the showers. They collapsed into their beds, ignoring me.

Elder Raymond came in, carrying an oil lamp. My nursemaid got out of her chair and he sat in it. He asked Sister Emily and me if we were feeling better.

Sister Emily said, "Yes."

I said, "She bolted, didn't she?"

"She was led out of the Garden by God. I cannot do Her work for Her. She will do it alone until She calls for me. Then She will have my help again."

"Listen, Tiner, you have to get word out to the authorities that she's not here. You must prevent what is going to take place any minute."

"Oh, but it *is* taking place."

"What?"

"We are surrounded by vehicles. They have brought in cranes. There are sharpshooters in the cranes. I am negotiating with them."

It was so hard to think.

"You see, Miss Rice, in this world, there is a bond between you and everyone who crosses your path. God intends that. The FBI and the ATF agents have been sent to us by the Lord. There is a reason God chose them to accomplish His purpose. Our souls are one."

"God wants all of you to line up like sitting ducks?"

"We must not get bold with the Lord. We must trus
Him and not demand that He save us. His purpose i
only that Rona Leigh be saved, and He accomplished
this before the law arrived.

"I have learned that no matter how difficult you
situation is, there is an answer and it will be revealed
Patience and prayer will always bring the answer."

He said, "You must sleep. In the morning, you can
advise me as to how I should deal with the people out
there."

"You're seeing to it that she has time to get as far
away as possible, aren't you?"

"Yes."

"What did she give me?"

"You can ask Sister Emily in the morning, once you
are both rested. But feel assured that it was at the directive of our Blessed Father."

I couldn't help myself. I fell asleep again.

꧁꧂

At dawn, the bustle woke me up. I watched the women
dress and then they left. Emily was not in the bed. I
drank the glass of juice by my bed.

I washed my face and put on my jumpsuit from the
feed store. A new guard was outside the door; he
helped me maneuver the stairs. The old one was probably feeling the effects of his own piece of fudge.

I was taken to Tiner's office. The first thing Tiner
said to me, in a voice high with joy, was, "We have word
of the doings of the Lord."

I waited.

"Yesterday, I gave Vernon permission to find and
protect his wife while she goes about Her Father's business, the work of saving souls. Vernon's own work has
been started. The bar in Houston that Gary Scott owns
burned to the ground in the early morning hours

Vernon has seen to scaring off the man who so wants God's Child dead."

"Vernon got himself to Houston and burned down Gary's bar?"

"Apparently."

"No, he didn't. Did Rona Leigh have any money?"

"No. God is all she needs."

"God? If she didn't have money, she acquired it. Rona Leigh used the only way she's ever known to acquire money. Then she got herself to Houston. Where's Gary Scott?"

He blinked a few times. "The authorities are looking for him."

"They'll find him when they sift through the ashes."

I went to the window. Three cherry pickers were in place, two buckets each. There was a sharpshooter in each of the six buckets. The cherry pickers had the names of the local utility company stenciled on their doors, and the agents were dressed like linesmen. I planted myself at the window long enough to be sure they knew I was definitely in the mission.

I turned to Tiner. "You can't let all these people die. You made a mistake. You were misguided. You can beg God's forgiveness. But there is a legal price to pay, and now you have to face that."

He smiled. He said, "We must see that the Sister of Christ has all the time God chooses to make available to Her through us. We will hold the ramparts as long as we can with the same fortitude Vernon showed when he distracted the enemy."

I said, "I don't feel well. I need Sister Emily."

He became concerned.

"You must return to the women's quarters and lie down. I will send her to you."

The guard led me back. I wondered why the ATF hadn't gone with the helicopters. To avoid attention,

obviously. To keep the media at bay as long as they
could.

I smelled clean morning air. No gas yet.

Sister Emily sat with several women sitting by a window with bowls in front of them. Oatmeal. I pulled up
a chair.

She said to me, "I'm sorry you're still feeling ill. I
you feel you need something to calm your nerves, we'll
get it for you."

"I think I pretty much need some of your breakfast."

She smiled. "Yes. You're hungry. I certainly was."

She asked another woman to fetch me a bowl of oat
meal.

I said, "Who is the chemist?"

Her voice was full of pride. "Brother George."

"He's here?"

"Of course he's here."

"How did he do it?"

All the bonnets turned to me and then away.

Emily said, "The Lord inspired our brother to devise
what was necessary. He records everything. I help him.
If you are interested, he will show you his records."

There is no fortifier like oatmeal. While I polished it
off, I said, "His records are about to be blown to
smithereens if we all don't put our hands in the air and
walk out of this building."

One bonneted head came up. "As long as we hold
out, we keep the Christ Child alive. She is out in the
world carrying forth Her Father's will, and She'll con
tinue to do so if we remain valiant."

"How are you valiant if you're burned alive?"

"Elder Raymond says that they will not do that to us
not after the debacles that have come before."

Another sister leaned toward me. "And Elder Raymond has also informed us that Vernon in his duty as
husband has destroyed Gary Scott's livelihood last

night. As a warning. To stay away from the Christ Child when She comes to show Herself."

I asked Emily why Rona Leigh had drugged us and left against Elder Raymond's judgment.

She said, "The will of the Lord is to be trusted, not questioned."

A shock is always a good move. I said, "I'm pretty sure that Rona Leigh set Gary Scott's bar on fire. She did that right after she killed him. They just haven't found his remains yet."

All the bonnets were up.

I kept on chatting. "I wouldn't be surprised if she goes after a few other people as well. Witnesses at her trial, maybe. The jurors. Her mother. She is not out there saving souls, she is exacting revenge."

At first, there was nothing from them, no reaction at all. Then one said, "You blaspheme. The tapes made of the Daughter of God are saving a thousand souls a minute. Her presence on earth, once She reveals herself, will save nations." She stood up. "Come, sisters, it is time for prayer."

All of them but Emily went downstairs to pray. Just as the strains of the first chants and rantings drifted up to us, the sound of a bullhorn drowned it out. The first rule of engagement was upon them. The warning.

In quiet but stern tones, the Believers were advised to come out unarmed with their hands over their heads. The voice said the federal government had a warrant for the arrest of Rona Leigh Glueck.

The voice announced that they had another federal warrant for the arrest of Raymond Tiner, suspected of aiding and abetting the escape from prison by Rona Leigh Glueck.

Then the state of Texas came on. They had warrants for the arrests of Vernon Lacker and Harley Shank.

Everyone else in the mission was advised to surrender as they were all under suspicion.

Emily's eyes darted from mine to the window. She got up and looked out.

The Rangers handed the bullhorn back to the feds. The voice said that the agent Penelope Rice was to be released immediately.

Immediately meant they would give the Believers ten minutes at the most. Then they'd do whatever they thought was best to save me. And after that . . .

I said, "Sister Emily, they'll throw tear gas very shortly."

The praying from downstairs became a loud jangling of ecstatic voices.

Emily found that more of a distraction than my words. She said, "I must join in the beseeching for the safety of the Daughter of Christ." She made her way to the stairs and I followed, both of us holding the wall for support. Downstairs, Emily wobbled into the snaking spiral.

The Believers snuck glances at me from the corner of their eyes. They were faking ecstasy, unable to concentrate. Elder Raymond stopped the service. They were relieved and they were scared, too. He told the men to set up the dining benches. They did and he gathered his followers before him, men on the right, women on the left.

He stood, arms raised. "The Lord has commanded Vernon to turn himself in to the police. He is in custody for the destruction of Gary Scott's bar. Therefore God alone now commands His Daughter's duties. He has revealed to me that She is dying. She is in Gethsemane. The Child does not have long. But we are not meant to die here, in a blaze of gunfire. We are not a cult. We are a revival. As disciples of the Daughter of God, the Sister of Jesus, we are soldiers of Christ. I am not afraid to be a leader to Her blessed disciples from the inside of a prison. A prison is where our Divine One served God for seventeen years. I intend to serve Him there for as long as that. Serve Him until I die. Join me and we will begin a life of continuous prayer.

"You are free to leave. All of you. Or you can stay and pray with me until they come and arrest us."

No one moved.

Tears came to Tiner's eyes. He said, "Now we must stand up and pray from the depth of our souls. We must make ourselves the embodiment of prayer. The power of prayer has sustained our great effort thus far. It is all we have left now to sustain Christ's Sister in Her journey into darkness."

The benches were put back, weapons were leaned against the wall. The spiral formed and in a few seconds took on a life of its own. The Believers became one thing, a growling animal, a hissing snake, Elder Raymond in the center of the undulating coil. And that mass of what was now true ecstasy contained one genius of a chemist.

I walked past them, past the line of guns and out the mission door into the bright yard. My hands were as high as I could reach. I felt the snipers concentrating on me, the hum of the cherry pickers moving into position.

I reached the gate. As deliberately as I could, trying not to tremble, I brought my right hand down and pressed the switch in the wall. The gate opened.

A swarm of bodies descended on me, lifted me off my feet, and carried me down the road to the lead van, about as big as the late Gary Scott's RV. I was hustled inside. It was filled with tracking devices and radar equipment.

They tossed me into the sectioned-off back of the van with two female Texas Rangers, who scanned me with sonar and then yanked off my clothes just to make sure there were no bombs strapped to my body. They also made sure there were none hidden in any body cavity. I was not surprised.

They gave me green scrubs to put on and then took me out and a technician did a full-body X ray. Then I was cuffed.

During the entire procedure, no one responded to the string of commands I hollered at them. I screamed that I wanted Scraggs, I wanted the chief FBI agent, and I wanted Joe Barnow. I wanted whoever was in charge.

And once the people I was calling for knew I wouldn't detonate, there they were, three across in front of me. Scraggs was the loudest, shaking a big paper in my face. I didn't understand him at first. He kept saying something about pinpoints. Finally, I could make it out: "Pinpoint her. Pinpoint her. Tell us exactly where they've got her." The paper was the architect's plan.

Joe stood over me, but he didn't know what to do in the face of Scraggs's incessant shouting. So he just put his face down to mine. "Just answer him, Poppy. Pinpoint her."

Everything began to spin. I knew I had to shout louder than Scraggs. I did. "She's not in there. She's been outside for forty-eight hours."

Scraggs said, "Bullshit. We're goin' in." His finger pointed into my face. "And somebody arrest *her*, goddamn it."

One of the women who searched me told me I was under arrest and while she was reading me Miranda the van came alive. Everyone was suiting up, grabbing canisters, masks. Not Joe. He squatted down. "She couldn't have gotten out."

"Night before last. Just before you got here."

I looked toward Scraggs. "Max."

He looked down at me.

"I'm telling you the truth. She's out. She got herself to Houston, where she killed Gary Scott."

They all gaped at me, including Scraggs. He said, "Who says he's dead? Every police officer in Texas is looking for Gary Scott."

"Then I hope they're using sifters. He's mixed in with the ashes of his bar."

Scraggs just shut his eyes. He believed me.

"Max, the people inside the mission are praying, if you're wondering what that racket is. They pray real funny. They pray till they drop and before they drop they hurl themselves around like a gang of lunatics. Give them fifteen more minutes, get on your bullhorn, and tell them to come out. They won't be able to come out, though, because they'll be collapsed on the floor. So you just go in, pick them up, and carry them out.

"Don't kill the people in there, they're misfits. That's all they are. They thought they were saving the life of Christ's sister. They think that now. They will not fight you. But there's a man there whose name is George, a chemist, that's all I know, and he'll tell us how he saved Rona Leigh from execution. You can't kill him; we need him.

"I'm sorry, Max. She's not there. She did it again. She's gone. She slipped right through my fingers the same way she slipped through yours."

Scraggs, very softly, said, "Fuck me."

Then Joe said, "And while you're at it, Scraggs, unarrest this agent, or you'll look like the biggest idiot in Texas since"—he thought—"since the Dallas chief of police let his friend Jack Ruby into the station so he could eyeball Lee Harvey Oswald."

Joe said to me, "You look like hell warmed over.

You'd look like hell warmed over even without the black eye. What happened?"

"She hit me. She poisoned me. She'd have killed me except that those people in there saved me."

16

A week later, my director held a meeting at the crime lab. Scraggs was there representing the interests of the state of Texas. Our chemist held us all rapt.

She said, "The New Shaker chemist, George Billings, came from a stern Pentecostal family and grew up praying. Praying to the exclusion of everything except eating, sleeping, and studying. Then he came to spend more time studying than praying. He was a genius. He won scholarships to great schools here and abroad. He studied, specifically, violently aggressive criminals and produced a Ph.D. thesis that is, to this day, held in the highest esteem.

"Dr. Billings was gay. When he came out of the closet as a young man, his family held a funeral for him. His empty coffin is buried in a cemetery in Oklahoma. Poppy Rice has characterized the New Believers as misfits. Sociologically, misfits are always in search of a family. Raymond Tiner only asked George Billings that he be celibate. The sexual preferences of the New Believers didn't matter to him. Only their sacrifice to God.

"George Billings worked independently—free agent—for years before he joined the society. He synthesized chemicals for other biochemists. He flourished financially by simplifying other people's jobs." She glanced up from her papers. "Now you won't want to hear this part . . ."

My director whispered to me, "I haven't wanted to hear any of it."

". . . but his chief client for many years was the FBI crime lab. Of course, Poppy Rice came aboard, and one of the first things she did was to see that this lab accomplished its work in-house."

She delved into her papers. "Billings's premise was that the constitution of the human body contains elements and receptors that can elicit violent behavior. He became a student again. He read, he studied. He learned that violently aggressive people—high-rate offenders, killers—are more likely than nonoffenders to have neurobiological anomalies. Their behavior centers on uncontrollable impulse; we have all observed that. Billings's findings showed that violent criminals have slower heart rates and far lower levels than nonoffenders of specific neurotransmitters like serotonin, dopamine, maybe epinephrine, others. . . . You get the idea."

Lots of sidelong glances.

"In addition, he came to believe—and this is supported—that violent offenders also have a complexity in their metabolic abilities that is not understood. There are sociopaths who have difficulty or are completely unable to absorb minerals, specifically manganese and possibly selenium, zinc, cobalt. . . . Which brings us to potassium. It is the most common mineral of all and can be transfigured into a huge number of compounds and derivatives, including potassium chloride, an extraordinarily deadly substance.

"Mineral absorption requires carrier proteins to move the minerals through the intestinal membranes. Billings was on his way to proving that violent offenders had abnormally low levels of these carrier proteins

Tiner extrapolated and concluded that the violent constitution of Rona Leigh Glueck was created specifically by God for his own purposes. And so it was left to their chemist to enable that purpose.

"Rona Leigh was treated in such a way as to temporarily rid her body of carrier proteins to prevent a fatal absorption of potassium chloride, and at the same her heart was chemically trained with L-dopa to beat very slowly without her suffering any lack of oxygen to her brain. In the death chamber, her heart almost stopped, but it did not stop completely.

"She did not absorb enough potassium chloride to kill her, though it was certainly enough to kill a human being with a normal metabolic constitution. And the process to rid her body of what she did absorb was begun the minute she was put into the bogus ambulance. Actually, Billings made clear to Tiner that the time it would take to get Rona Leigh into the ambulance after she'd been injected might prevent them from saving her. But the risk they would incur in having Harley Shank, the guard, give her something in the death house—that was one of their scenarios—would be greater than the risk in not treating her at all during those minutes. Billings concluded that they would have to rely on prayer during that gap."

She looked up from her papers again, smiled a little, and shrugged.

"As we know, she was restored to health." Our chemist paused and then said, "Brilliant."

But why wouldn't God's plan for his daughter be anything but brilliant?

She picked up the papers from the podium and patted them together in a neat pile. Then she said, "Finally, I want to conclude by saying that in the nineteenth century criminology was a branch of medicine. Scholars were on the verge of accepting biological ex-

planations for crime. But that study was abandoned
when Hitler showed us that racism alone can lead average
people to unequivocal violence.

"Perhaps now we can reconsider. Yes, there are many
factors that bring about violent behavior and racism is
indeed one of them. But also a simple chemical imbalance,
just like any other chemical imbalance, can
create antisocial behavior in one person and an utter
devastation of the brain in another, as with Alzheimer's
disease, while the rest of us show just the usual effects
of simple aging."

She held up her stack of papers. "If you want details,
specifics, formulas, studies, the mechanics of the whole
operation, these pages are only the beginning. The actual
notes are voluminous though crystal-clear, thanks
to the talents of one very patient chronicler"—she
flipped through the stack—"Sister Emily."

We all had lunch together, and Scraggs told us that
what was left of Gary Scott did not weigh as much as
the six little puddles of melted lead the Rangers pulled
out of their sifters. A five-gallon jug of gasoline plus a
building made of old dried wood will do that.

Joe leaned over and said to me, "Five gallons of gas
weighs more than the ax."

Then Scraggs said, "Rona Leigh left us a note in the
mission. Taped to it was a lock of her hair. The note
said"—he pulled a copy out of his pocket— "*This here is
a relic. Build my church upon it.*"

I thought the chemist would choke. She said,
"You've got a lock of her hair?"

Scraggs said, "Yes, we do."

I really hoped some cop back in Texas hadn't lost it

⌒⌒⌒⌒

That afternoon, my director brought me into his office
for a head-to-head. He said, "At the minimum, no more

ieldwork. You're behind a desk until the poison is completely out of your system and the concussion is healed
and the Ace bandage is put to rest."

All right.

"Poppy, you turned the FBI crime lab into a work of
art. Single-handed. My gratitude knows no bounds.
Now I've suggested the minimum to you, but I'd like to
ask you for a bit more. I know it's a cliché but, Poppy,
you need a vacation."

Nope.

As it turned out, he'd prodded Joe. Joe offered me
his cottage on Block Island without him in it. "'Course
I'd rather be with you gazing at the sunsets while we
fish for stripers."

I told him I'd take a rain check.

He said, "My Poppy Rice rain-check file is getting
mighty full."

So sweet as always.

Delby seconded both of them and felt free to add
her own opinion. "Go to that place. That island. See
what the world is like outside because you haven't been
outside in a damn long time. Go with Joe. Give the
man a chance. Give yourself a chance. See if you're in
love with him."

I said, "Delby, what has love ever done for anyone?"

She thought. "Nothin'."

We both laughed. I was starting to feel better.

⌘

The dragnet created by the U.S. Marshal Service swept
around the world and came up empty. They told me
that in almost all cases a fugitive will turn to family or
friend. Rona Leigh never had either of those.

There was no sign of her, not anywhere, and she
didn't turn up to kill any law officers, or jurors, or her
mother, or the johns who mistreated her, or anyone

else. There had been one sighting, a sighting that too
place within an hour of Rona Leigh's offering me
piece of fudge: In Nuevo Laredo a gringa prostitut
was seen exchanging her services for a ride to Hou
ton. The guy who gave her the lift would never turn u
to offer us leads because the clientele of prostitut
tend to keep a low profile.

My friend the shrink said to me, "All of it is so i
triguing. Tiner was the perfect personality for the ro
of the maligned guru. He encouraged his followers
project their fantasies upon him. He was asexual, r
moved, empty of personality, only able to fe
satisfaction via a crowd of worshipers, absorbing the
energy. Classic.

"But as to Rona Leigh, who knows? Maybe she'
never kill anyone else. Maybe she zeroed in on Gar
Scott because he epitomized all the men who abuse
her when she was a child. All the men who used her
satisfy their own needs, though they knew such trea
ment could only destroy her. Or perhaps h
represented all that was perpetrated upon her by a sy
tem that doesn't rescue a child like Rona Leig
Glueck. Maybe a swift sharp revenge has cleansed he
Maybe she's starting a new life. In which case her po
soning of you, Poppy, was merely what she was force
to do in order to survive."

He wasn't there when she'd cracked me across th
face.

I said, "Maybe she zeroed in on Gary Scott becaus
forced her hand."

"And, pray, what might that mean?"

"I told her Gary knew he would inherit a lot
money if his wife died. She hadn't been aware of that

He was silent for a moment. Then he said, "My ver
dear Poppy, might I suggest a one-session counseling
meeting for you? I know just the gentleman in Wash

ngton. He'll give you the magic bullet you need to
override any guilt. I know you'll appreciate that kind
of practicality."

But I already had a counselor. I called Cardinal de la
Cruz.

He didn't let me off the hook. He said, "Miss Rice,
all of us forced her hand. From her mother, to the father she'd never heard of, to the school system who let
her pass through without seeing to an obviously mistreated child, to a prison system that no longer bothers
rehabilitating teenagers. And I forced her hand with
my naïveté."

⌖

Before Vernon Lacker's trial began, I tried to speak to
him but he wouldn't see me. I talked with his lawyer,
though, a court-appointed attorney. He explained to
me very carefully that the DA had a confession.

No kidding.

I checked in with Max Scraggs fairly regularly. He
said he expected the body of Rona Leigh would turn
up when we least expected it. Wishful thinking, and he
knew it. He was hugely depressed.

So was I. I've always had a hard time opening up a
new closet before shutting the old one.

And Joe just kept battering me. "I'm tellin' ya,
honey, try a few days of breathing air full of salt. A few
mornings of heavy fog and the echo of buoy bells.
Evenings just listening to the waves plopping onto the
beach. . . . Man, it's magic. What d'ya say? Give your
brain a break."

Tempting.

I had bad nights. But Bobby and the rest of security
had orders not to let me come in to work at 2 A.M.
Bobby said to me, "I take my break at 2 A.M. Anytime
you're awake then, just call me and I'll meet you at

Starbucks. We'll shoot the breeze." I took him up o
his offer a couple of times. Bobby knows more abou
what's going on in the world than Dan Rather any da

⟨∽∽∽⟩

On the first day of Vernon's trial I was passing th
metro station on Pennsylvania Avenue. The sky wa
dark; it had been raining since dawn. When it's rain
ing, my driver leaves me off at the corner fifty feet fron
the FBI entrance. On Pennsylvania Avenue, rain mean
he'll need an hour to extricate himself from the tra
fic. Better I get a little damp than have the driver s
tied up.

I was just about to go into my dash mode when
woman came out of the metro and fell in step besid
me. She was holding out an audio cassette. I glance
down at it and then I took a better look at her, DC se
retary type, dressed neatly in a sky blue suit and a
unbuttoned black raincoat. Shoes nice but not terribl
expensive, short pretty auburn hair. And new Ralp
Lauren sunglasses, a pair I'd been considering becaus
they reminded me of the Texas Rangers issue. Tw
hundred and sixty-five dollars. Very pricey for a secre
tary, and she was wearing them in the rain.

She thrust the cassette into my chest and said, "G
this to Vernon's lawyer."

Her face was pale, she was a little on the thin side o
slim, and it took me a full five seconds to recognize he
because I'd never seen her forehead before.

I don't remember taking the cassette from her but
did. What I do remember is drawing my weapon an
screaming at her to freeze, while she slipped amid th
crush of rush-hour bodies all dashing through th
downpour. I fired into the air just in case the sho
might get everybody to drop to the ground so I coul
fire a second round into her back.

Nobody dropped to the ground, they just cringed, and I hoped the bullet wouldn't come down and pierce one of their stupid skulls. A very loud explosion went off in the middle of the street. That dropped them. I managed to shove the gun back in the holster, get out my cell phone, and punch in my emergency code before a gang of good Samaritans bowled me over and sat on top of me till a couple of transit cops came running out of the metro and reached me neck and neck with Bobby.

He squatted down and tried pulling people off me.

I said, "Bobby, Rona Leigh Glueck just ran into the metro."

He said, "Motherfucker," and got on his own phone as he took off.

I shouted at him, "Reddish brown hair, blue suit, black raincoat . . ." and then I stopped. It would do no good, and I had to get everyone off me. Once the cops knew who I was, I told them to quit worrying about the need of a bomb squad. The explosion was an M-80 that Rona Leigh had tossed into the road before flying down the metro steps.

She'd managed the perfect stage: picked heavy rain, the perfect *in obscura* moment, created a distraction, and danced the final dance—disappearing into a convenient hole in the ground. Rona Leigh had found a job and she'd obviously become an expert. She made drops for pros.

I was almost as impressed by the action to follow. The metro station, the streets all around it, the streets at all the stops the trains departing the stations were heading for—full of cops. But about as futile as firing my gun. Her wig made it all the way to Bethesda. She'd tossed it into one train but didn't get in herself. Instead, she went through a little doorway set into the concrete wall of the station that opened into a tunnel.

It was locked was what the poor transit police kept insisting.

The blue suit was in the tunnel. So were the sunglasses. She'd sacrificed them. All that probably happened in the time it took me to get to my office and collapse into my desk chair, wet, a mess, my knee bruised. Delby said to me, "Tell me it wasn't really her, boss."

"Sorry. It was. Different chin, though, now that I've had a chance to think."

"Poppy, nobody believes it. Just Bobby. They're all sure you flipped out."

"Do you believe me?"

"You know that, for sure. Still, you got trouble ahead."

That's when I became aware of the bump in my pocket. "Delby, have we got an audio cassette player?"

"'Course. This is the FBI. We got everything."

She went out and came right back with one.

I got the little cassette out of my pocket and dropped it into the machine.

Delby said, "I get a feeling this ain't gonna be John Cougar Mellencamp."

The first sound we heard was a door opening, and it was followed immediately by Gary Scott's voice. "I'm closed, sugar. Meetin' an old flame. Come back another time."

Long pause. Just the whir of the tape.

Gary said, "What's that?"

Another pause. "Oh, no. No!"

Then he said, "Jesus Christ. Hey. Please. Please."

There was a gunshot, a scream, and then the sound of Gary's body hitting the floor. He wasn't dead though. She'd just dropped him.

He groaned. He pleaded with her. "Rona Leigh, I didn't do anything. Listen to me, you gotta under tand. . . ." He groaned a little louder. "My leg. Damn, my leg. Listen, I'm bleedin' bad here. I can't—"

Rona Leigh said, "Shut the fuck up, you piece of shit."

Her voice, unmistakably, but with the sentiment and language she'd suppressed for seventeen years until the day she bolted the mission, leaving Jesus behind.

There was another shot. Gary howled like a dog.

Rona Leigh said to him, "I want you to die happy. You are going to be glad to hear what I come to tell you. See, Gary, I read that you believe I didn't suffer when they tried to execute me. Well, you'll be glad to know I did. I was drownin'. I was tryin' to breathe, tryin' to scream, but I couldn't get no sound out like I couldn't get no air in. I was bein' choked, suffocated, same as if there were two hands squeezin' my neck. Then I had some kind of mountain crushin' down on my chest. Felt like my insides were ripped apart. I knew I was gonna die, even though I didn't want to. *I didn't want to die.* I suffered plenty. Just like you. Except you're gonna die, aren't you?"

Then she shot him again.

Delby left the office.

Rona Leigh fired three times more, and Gary was gasping and crying and moaning all at once. There was a rustling on the tape, a bag—the sound of a shopping bag or a grocery bag opening. Gary tried to speak. I could barely make out the panic-stricken words. He said, "What are you doing?"

Then he found the strength again to shout, "No, no, no!" and begged her not to do it, kept begging her until there was a loud thump—the first swing of the ax hitting home.

I listened to Rona Leigh Glueck ax Gary Scott to death.

Then she repacked the bag, and there were footsteps

and the splashing of gasoline that went on and on, until finally a match was struck, followed by the *whoosh* of the flame and then her steps running. The tape ended.

I went to the outer office where Delby was sitting, blowing her nose.

She looked up at me. "Where'd you get it, boss?"

I told her.

That was right when my director came in to find out what the hell was going on, so I told Delby she'd better go off and have some coffee. No sense in just sitting there while I played the tape again.

⁂

Vernon Lacker would not be tried for the murder of Gary Scott. There would be another venue for him, aiding and abetting the escape of a convicted murderer. The jury, I knew, would take pity on him. Juries will do that. After all, he was bewitched. Also, he thought he was in genuine service to the Second Coming of Christ, an unauthorized mitigating circumstance that carries a lot of weight in the Bible Belt, which was why there was also so much talk of mercy concerning Raymond Tiner and the New Believers.

⁂

Joe flew me up the Atlantic coast to Block Island in his little Cessna. He'd been overjoyed when I told him I didn't want to be there alone, that I wanted his company. Most of the cockpit was taken up by his oversized cat carrier containing Spike, who yowled, pissed, and vomited.

I could tell the days to come—full of fog and salt air—would be ever so relaxing. Probably should have gone to Vegas with the shrink.

Please turn the page for an exciting sneak peek of
Mary-Ann Tirone Smith's next
Poppy Rice thriller
SHE'S NOT THERE
coming in April 2005 from Pinnacle Books!

1

I stood outside on the long wood porch. The morning sun had burned off most of the haze. The day would be warm but not muggy. Maybe the curl I had to my hair, far more fanciful than usual, would calm itself. Long spiraling tendrils sticking to my mouth are not as adorable as *Vogue* magazine would have people believe.

I could see Joe's cat, Spike. Actually, his fat, furry, marmalade tail, upright in the high grasses a few yards away. He was happy. Hunting. Then eating. He'd eat most of the game he snagged, leaving just the internal organs in a little pile for us right in front of the door. I'd been forewarned, so I always managed to step over the gift rather than in it. Joe has great respect for these acts of generosity so he doesn't mind the cleaning-up part. Joe is attached to this old tomcat, who yowled during our entire two-hour flight from Washington to Block Island. The yowling was nothing compared with the stench of the prodigious amounts of urine, doo-doo (Joe's term), and vomit Spike produced. Joe told me not to worry—there was a guy at the landing strip who would clean his plane.

"Fumigate it too, hopefully."

No comment.

"Maybe you should add a little Dramamine to his kibble."

Joe put the plane into a steep bank.

I took one of the bikes leaning against the side of the cottage and walked it up the grass-matted path to the unpaved road. I was thinking. It's Bastille Day. This is the kind of thing I've had on my mind during the few days spent away from my FBI chores—*It's Bastille Day, how interesting*. When I'd admitted such a thing to Joe he said, "Told you so." I'd forgotten one of his many exhortations on the pleasures of his hideaway: "The best part of Block Island is its ability to turn your brain cells to mush," a sensation I was positive I could not experience. And I was surprised it could be true of Joe Barnow, chief field adviser for the ATF, a brilliant and aggressive fellow when it came to serving justice. I never dreamed he'd be right. But there I was, thinking about Bastille Day and not much else.

The sound of Joe's little Cessna replaced the stillness all about me. He was off for a few hours on an errand. I shaded my eyes and looked up. The sun was dazzling. Climbing into the sky, Joe tipped a wing at me. Spike raised his head above the weeds and looked up too. So maybe Joe was tipping his wing to his cat.

I got on the bike and bumped along till the track merged with Coonymus Road, which led toward the old harbor on the other side of the island. The first half mile of Coonymus wasn't paved. The rest of it was, but barely—a network of gaping fissures and a mass of potholes. Block Islanders don't patch the asphalt all that often unless the state of Rhode Island really pushes them. They don't like tourists racing all over the place in cars. Tourists should walk. Joe bragged that you would walk the perimeter of the island in eight hours. That had me worried. I'm a city girl. Hearing that, I'd felt trapped before the plane ever took off from Dulles. But the sea did not trap me. The world

seemed expanded, in fact, and I liked the place more
and more each day, mushy brain cells and all.

I navigated through and around the obstacle course
that was the road, guiding the handlebars with my right
hand and holding the mug of coffee in my left. I took a
sip whenever there was a smooth stretch. Look, Ma, no
hands. Imagine that—me being giddy. At one point I
stopped on a rise, one of the highest points on the island: a hundred and fifty feet above sea level. I looked
north across the landscape dotted with restored farmhouses and new million-dollar vacation homes. Joe told
me the natives had done the restoring and then sold off
their surrounding acreage to developers for a ton of
money. He said the only difference between Block Island
today and Block Island twenty-five year ago—besides the
fabulous new "cottages," including his own—was that the
islanders no longer drove beatup red Ford pickup trucks
with the mufflers hanging off. Now they owned Cadillac Escalade EXTs—"they come with leather upholstery
and Bose sound systems"—silver being the most popular
color, with gold detailing of their own design and the ca-
pacity to haul 8,500 pounds, though there was nothing
to haul and no place to haul it. "This used to be an island of fishermen whose wives farmed their own food
and raised cows."

"So what do they do now?"

"Whatever they want."

The low coast of Rhode Island lying almost flat on
the horizon twelve miles across the Atlantic was
blurred. The haze still hung over the mainland. Washington was probably 97 degrees in the shade with a
humidity just shy of rain. Ha-ha on them. Block Island
was as remarkably beautiful as Joe had promised, hills
and vales and young trees, none high or full enough to
obscure the view. I would have to ask him where the
real trees had gone. A tiny breeze blew one of the ten-

drils that had escaped by scrunchie out of my mouth.
I got the bike moving again.

I passed the Pleasant View, a rickety farmhouse not restored but reconfigured into a B&B. The view from the
front was the road to the town transfer station; from the
back, "a stand of hoary willows and soggy bogs" was how
Joe had put it. Then the poet had smiled at me. "There's
always going to be the other side of the tracks, no matter
your paradise." I thought, I suppose so.

No one was up and about yet. At this particular B&B,
most tourists slept far later than I was able to; Joe said
the Pleasant View clientele were heavy drinkers who
missed the last ferry and had very little money left over
after an evening at the Club Soda. They crashed there,
four cots to a room, $25 a cot. "Block Island had many
facets," he had said by way of explanation, when we'd
driven by the first time and I'd asked, "What's that, a
flophouse?" And so I learned that one of Block Island's
many facets was a metaphorical railroad track.

Gulls were swarming a hundred yards past the Pleasant View at the corner of Coonymus and Center Street.
(Not seagulls. I had learned from Joe, that the *sea* in
seagull is redundant. "There are no gulls in Peoria," he
said.) A cemetery was at the corner there, an Indian
cemetery, mostly little rocks sticking up here and there
to mark a body. No headstones in the traditional sense.
Someone had put up a small sign asking those passing
to remember the souls of these departed Narra-
gansetts, the first inhabitants of Block Island, which
they called Manissees.

"Then why is the road by that lighthouse called Mo-
hegan Trail then?"

"Because that's the place where the Manisseeans
pushed the invading Mohegans over the bluff and into
the sea."

Oh.

When he showed me the cemetery, Joe said, "The Manisseeans are extinct, of course." Of course. Then, "There are a few slaves buried here too."

"Slaves?"

"They were leased."

Leased? I'd started to say, but he'd turned my attention to another point of interest. Many facets, indeed.

Now, gazing at the swirl of white birds, it took my mushy brain cells a few moments to recollect that bees swarm, not birds. There were dozens of them, and more were coming in from all directions. They made a god-awful racket, worse as I came closer. They did that kind of thing on the harborside when the fishing boats dumped out leftover bait. Just not this many. The gulls' wings were flapping so rapidly I could hear the beating over their raucous cawing.

They were circling above something lying in the crossroads in front of the cemetery. I slowed just enough to keep the bike from falling over. Where Center Street met Coonymus lay a lumpy mound. It was white, almost as white as the gulls, and it shone in the bright morning light. I couldn't make out what it was in the blinding glare of the sun. I came to a stop, put my feet down, and once again had to shade my eyes with my free hand. Then I got the bike moving again, pedaling closer, scaring off all but a few particularly brazen birds.

It could be a beached seal, I thought, its color washed out by the sun. Joe and I had come across one on a deserted west side beach. But how could a seal wash up here, so far inland? A good *mile* inland. Obviously, it wasn't a seal. The mush was clearing from my brain; I knew what I was seeing.

The mound was a body. Or was it two bodies, intertwined? I pedaled closer, No, it was not two bodies, it was an overweight adolescent girl, naked, her large

limbs wrapped grotesquely around her torso. This was
not typical rigor mortis: it was at if every muscle in her
body had cramped and spasmed and then stayed
spasmed. I stopped the bike. She was entirely naked. A
few shredded edges of her clothes—the waistband of
her shorts, the collar of her T-shirt—lifted in the
breeze. A very big girl—from the camp, I thought. Joe
had mentioned something like that, not too far away.
She was not one of the four campers we'd seen yesterday at the harborside, walking down the ferry ramp
amid the day-trippers. This was a different girl.

Her long lovely strawberry-blond hair fanned out
from her terribly twisted face.

I thought three things in a row: First, she was dead;
second, Joe hadn't come upon her; third, the gulls
hadn't drawn blood. The first meant there was nothing
I could do for her. The second meant she'd been lying
there for a very short time. The third, she'd been dead
too long for the gulls to make a meal of her. Gulls do
not hesitate when a fisherman tosses a fish he isn't interested in, but if he simply drops it at his feet, the gulls
are out of luck. By the time he packs up and leaves, the
fish is no longer suitable. Put it together and she'd
been killed elsewhere—at least an hour ago, probably—and dumped here.

I got off the bike and let it fall, forgetting I had a coffee cup in my hand. It fell, too, and smashed. The gulls
screamed and, disappointed to begin with, reversed direction. So did I. I ran back to the B&B and threw
open the door. The proprietor was right there, about
to go out herself. Joe had dropped in to say hello to
her on our first day and to introduce me. She'd given
him a big hug and ruffled his hair like he was five years
old. Aggie.

Now Aggie smiled at me and said, "Hey, honey,
c'mon in. I was just about to go see what the hell was

erturbin' the gulls"—she squinted at me—"but first
'm goin' to have to ask what's perturbin' you? You
een a ghost?"

She wore a housedress, the kind I suppose you can
uy only in a Wal-Mart. Instead of the top two buttons,
rhinestone brooch was holding the front of the dress
gether.

I said, "Don't go out there. Just call that cop in
wn."

"What cop?"

"The one from Providence. There's a body out in
he crossroads."

She hustled to the window. "I don't see no body."

"Aggie, where's your phone?"

She pressed her face against the glass, craning her
eck. "Whose body? Not one of ours, I hope."

"A girl. A girl from the camp."

"A girl? Dear God! What, was she hit by a car?
)amnable tourists. I'm always the first to say—"

"I know. Aggie, the phone."

She came away from the window. "Don't you worry
ow, I'll call over to Tommy's. Forget about that state
op. Hung over at this hour." She was probably right.
'd met him the day before, on duty for the summer
eason. He was completely played out. Tommy was the
sland's constable.

Aggie picked up a table phone from behind her
ounter and set it in front of her. She dialed and
vaited. She looked up at me. "All bloody, was she?"

"No."

Then Aggie spoke into the phone, slowly and clearly,
he way a persons talks to someone suffering from de-
hentia. "Jake? Now Jake, honey, this is Aggie . . . *Aggie*.
ou listen to Aggie very carefully. Get Tommy. Tell him
> hurry up to my place. Pronto. We got an emergency.
ell Tommy it's an *e-mer-gen-cy*. So what did Aggie say we

got, Jake?" She waited. "That's right. Good boy. An *e-m* *gen-cy.*" She hung up. She said to me, "Jake'll understa enough to get him. Tommy'll come up here by way the crossroads. Hope he don't bring Jake along." I'd m Jake. He lived with the constable. Jake was particular deranged. *No,* Joe had said. *Autistic.*

The pitch of the gulls' cries had ratcheted up ma decibels. Aggie headed toward the window agai "Buncha new gulls are headin' in. I was hopin' none my guests would wake up for a while. That way I c tell 'em they missed breakfast. Won't sleep throug that kind of racket, though." She glanced nervously the stairs behind her. Again, she asked me, "Hit by car, was she?"

I started to say no to her question. The body wou have been far less gruesome if it had been hit by a c if there were blood all over her. Blood is normal, a co torted musculature is not. So this time I said, "Yes." worked. She cringed and pulled away from the vie out the window.

My guess was that a drug or combination of dru had killed the girl. There had been no wounds or a signs of asphyxia, nothing around her neck, no mark Some drug—or else a mix of several—had devastate her central nervous system, violently contracting ever muscle. What drug or drug's might cause so torture a death I had no idea. I depended on my crime lab t answer questions like that. I wished I was one of thos people who could honestly say, Where do the kids g this stuff? I already knew the answer. They get it fro hard-core addicts who sell drugs vto make money t buy drugs for themselves. Where the addicts get th drugs from is always the more imperative question, on Joe Barnow is paid to figure out.

Aggie said, "Goddamned tourists drivin' around her like we was Boston. Least they're killin' their own."

My look stopped her short.

"Sorry, Poppy. Joe would understand. And you bein' his guest and all, I figured . . ."

Joe would understand? Block Islanders felt a big affection for him. Joe goes to the island in winter too. Spends long weekends whenever he can. When island kids get sick, he flies them to the nearest mainland hospital, even through blizzards. Well, they may have accepted him, but they were sure wrong to think he'd concur that it was better for a kid from the mainland to die of an overdose than a local kid to die from appendicitis.

Aggie said, "A couple of those girls have been here, partyin' with my guests. I had to call the camp to come get them. Drunk. Young. Say, Poppy, would a cup of tea settle you some?

I tried to muster a reassuring smile. "No, thanks, Aggie. Another time."

She tilted her head a little and started for the door. "I hear Tommy's truck."

I stepped in front of her. "I'll go. That way, if your guests do wake up, you can try to keep them from going down Coonymus. For now."

"Well, you and Tommy come in then, have some tea. After."

I went out the door. The constable's pickup appeared over the rise, the old red variety. Not a native, I supposed. No land to sell. He stopped just short of the crossroads, rolled slowly forward, and parked, damaging any sort of tire tracks or debris left by whoever dropped the body. He wasn't used to this kind of thing. In one of Joe's many riffs about the glory of Block Island, he'd told me there was no crime. "No skunks, no snakes, no fences, no banks, no lawyers, and, best of all, no crime." The elderly constable had volunteered to enforce town statutes, that's all.

Tommy got out of the truck and stood next to t
body. I walked toward him. He put his hands on l
knees and bent down to have a closer look. Then
became aware of me. He stood straight again. He sa
"You the one found her, miss?"

"Yes."

He squatted all the way down. It wasn't easy for hi
He stared at the dead girl. He pushed a strand of h;
off her face. Her mouth was open as far as human ja
allowed. She'd died screaming. What drug could
that?

The constable pulled himself back up to his fe
"Thought I should confirm the death. By the look
her, no need bothering to feel for a pulse. She's gon

"I think you should call the state trooper."

He was staring into my face intently. He knew
should, too. He sighed. "I'll have to stay with the bo
I don't have one of those car phones. You drive a sta
dard?"

I could, but more damage to the scene wouldr
help.

"Tommy, why don't I have Aggie call him?"

He squinted. "Trooper don't answer his pho
much before noon anyway."

"Isn't there another trooper with him?"

"Officer Fitzgerald takes the phone off the hook.

"I'll go. I'll ride my bike."

"All right, then. Best you do that. And miss?"

"Yes?"

"Notice anything strange around here? Seen ar
thing before Aggie called me?"

"No."

He looked up at the gulls and then back at m
"Been dead long enough to put off the birds, I'd sa

I didn't tell him I agreed. Since I arrived, I'd ke
mum about what I do for a living. I don't enjoy bei

conversation piece. Now Tommy had nothing more
o do or say. He was not a policeman, he was the equiv-
lent of a meter maid. He knew he had to wash his
ands of whatever had happened to the girl and leave
nings to the police, even if the police consisted of a
nan, the likes of Officer Fitzgerald. Francis X. Fitzger-
ld of the Rhode Island State Police. Fitzy, Joe had
alled him. Plus there was a rookie supposedly learn-
ng the ropes.

The constable lived at the intersection down where
'enter crossed Old Town Road, halfway to the harbor. I
eached it in minutes and slowed at his house, which had
 little addition attached to its left side. Literally at-
ached—a shack was nailed up against the house that
eemed as though it were pulling away. Jake lived in the
acked-on shack. He was standing on the sandy
ntrimmed lawn, which was littered with electrical
quipment, fiddling with a pair of BX cables. Jake was a
avant. Joe told me at Christmastime he wired the whole
sland. Tourists returned over a period of a month to see
is decorated tree at the harborside made entirely of
iled-up driftwood and so bright with lighting you could
nake out the glow from the mainland, his display of
inging angels strung above the town hall, and Santa and
is sleigh plus all the reindeer led by Rudolph arched
cross the nearest rise of cliff.

Jake watched me, his eyes directed at the front bike
ire. I called out to him. "Everything will be all right.
'ommy will be back soon."

I got a response. "Would not take . . ." and he
ouched his chest. Jake didn't use names or pronouns,
.ccording to Joe. Then he turned away and looked
lown at his cables, twisting them again.

"He'll be back soon."

I raced down Old Town Road to the harbor and
urned into a little side street Joe had taken the day be-

fore. A sign in front of a small cottage read RHODE
LAND STATE POLICE SEASONAL. It was not a convention
police station, just a temporary trooper's residence
ramshackle wood-frame house that served as an offi
too. It looked deserted. If it was deserted, I'd try t
clinic at New Harbor. Maybe I could get the doctor
look at the body. Hopefully, he'd know what to do
far as getting someone official out to the island. J
had picked one hell of a day to go dashing off to t
mainland.

I threw down the bike and ran up onto the trooper
porch, opened the ripped screen door and knocke
waited, and knocked a little harder. I thought I sa
movement over at the window. I let the screen sla
shut, stepped off the little porch, and went to
Trooper Fitzgerald's haggard, scowling face was u
against the glass. I jumped. He gaped at me. The ma
was not wearing a shirt. I banged directly on the wi
dowpane, hoping it wouldn't break. Maybe hoping
would. He grimaced. Then he shouted at me, "Ho
on, goddamn it."

He disappeared and I went back to the door. After
few minutes I pretty much started bashing on it agai
a vicarious bashing of the idiotic man himself. Finall
he threw the door open and stood there on the oth
side of the screen. His eyes were red and watery. H
had a shirt on now; he was buttoning it. His fly wa
open. He ran his fingers through his dirty hair.

Finally he said, "This better be good." He narrowe
his eyes. "You're that ATF guy's latest, aren't you?"

I decided to act as though I'd never seen him befor
"Are you the trooper?"

He smiled. "No. I'm Blackbeard the pirate."

I smiled back. "Oh. Well, there's a dead girl lyin
on Coonymus Road, twenty yards down from the B an
B. But she needs a police officer, not a pirate." I turne

ward the porch steps. The hell with him. I'd have to
ke over myself. I knew I wasn't meant for vacations.

"Don't move." I turned back. "What dead girl?"

"I wouldn't *know* what dead girl. She's quite over-
ight. I'd guess she must be from the camp."

"What the hell was she doing?"

"Doing? You don't understand. She's dead. She—"

"I mean, what *did* she do? Step in a pothole and
eak her neck?"

I said. "She was naked."

"Naked?" He started ripping through his hair again.
hit."

"Tommy's with her. He's the constable."

"I *know* who Tommy is. Listen, she wasn't just spaced
it, was she? That so-called constable sure as hell
ouldn't know the difference between croaked and
gh."

"I would."

"Would you? Your boyfriend teach you a few things
e that?"

Two tourists, running along the road, looked over. I
id, "Officer, the area needs to be cordoned off before
me jogger heads up toward Coonymus."

"Yeah." He zipped his fly and shoved the screen door
en. I stepped back in time not to get hit with it. He
oked toward the joggers. "Goddamn show-offs. Want
eryone to notice their tight little asses. Sight of some
ad girl might get a few of these nutcases off the high-
ys."

Highways.

Then he mumbled something about his rookie gone
trolling and how he would have to find him. He said
me, "Go in my office and call that slob that runs the
and B. Tell her I'll be there in five minutes and not
go near the body. Not to let any of those derelicts
o stay with her near the body either. Then call Doc

Brisbane at the clinic and tell him to get the hell up
Coonymus Road with his van and not waste any ti░
about it."

He stomped down the porch and went to his car░
was unmarked. He got in, started it, and shot off do░
the road.

I did what he'd asked me to do, went inside a░
found his phone. First, Aggie. She told me the gue░
were all on the porch, didn't want to miss anythi░
"Too scared to go near the body, though," she sa░
"Not to worry. Tommy covered her with a blanket,░
it's really all right, Poppy."

No, that wasn't all right. Extraneous fibers now░
place.

I dialed the operator and told her I needed Dr. B░
band and to put me through right away; it was░
emergency. Block Island had a local operator, and ░
call would go faster through her than if I dialed my ░
through information. It didn't occur to me that░
speaking with her meant the entire island populati░
would know about the dead girl in a few short minu░

When she got me connected, I told Brisbane's nu░
who I was and said I needed to speak to the doctor. S░
said, "Is Joe all right?" I didn't think I'd met her ░
she knew my connections. I said no, and she cut me░
before I could say anything else. "Sorry, the doc is s░
ing a patient." Whether *I* was all right or not did░
seem to matter.

"Listen, it's the state trooper who needs the doc░
And he needs him now."

She said, "Fitzy? What's he got, the DTs again?"

I told her about the dead girl and where her bo░
was located. The nurse said, "Omigod. I'll get Doc░
there now."

I went out, climbed on my bike, and headed back░

ward Aggie's B&B. Uphill. Took me a bit longer that it had to come down.

The maddened gulls were still circling and squawking. I stood my bike up next to Tommy's pickup, near the body. If Trooper Fitzgerald had half a brain, was even a marginally competent police officer, he'd have a fit over the blanket.

Tommy was between the body and Aggie's front porch, making sure none of her guests got adventurous. A couple of them were taking pictures.

We heard a roar. The car Fitzy had gotten into was not flying up Center Street. It screeched to a stop behind the pickup. The screech made the gulls even more crazed. The noise they made sounded like human screaming. The B&B's guests put their hands over their ears. Fitzy wasn't driving, the rookie was. He looked about twelve. I'm getting old, I guess. My stepfather used to say things to motivate himself, like, "You're as young as you feel." I was thirty-five. Last few days I'd felt eighteen. Right now I was a hundred and two.

Fitzy dragged himself out of the car, turned, and gave the rookie a dirty look. The rookie quickly emerged and slammed the door smartly shut. He stood by the car, stiff and tall. His uniform was immaculate, the trousers creased, the hat starched into perfect shape. He was also very nervous. His eyelid was twitching. He put on his sunglasses.

The constable walked toward us.

The state trooper said to him, "Okay, fella, what's the story here?"

The gulls were still screaming. Banshees rather than humans. Tommy said. "What?" Fitzy looked up at them, and I swear just his look along sent the whole flock a little higher into the air. Tommy nodded toward me. "Lady here had Aggie call me. Found this body."

Fitzy was still looking into the sky. "Can we do anything about the freakin' birds?"

Tommy said, "No."

The trooper shook his head. Then his eyes took in the blanket. He scanned the scene. "What's with the broken cup?"

"Figured the lady dropped it."

He raised his voice. "Figured? Well, you should've gotten me instead of coming out here to figure things. Why the hell'd ya cover the body? Jesus."

Fitzy grabbed a corner of the blanket. Tommy reached out, but there was nothing he could do to stop him. Fitzy threw the blanket off the dead girl. He went white. Now his voice wasn't so loud, though he let out a string of curse words. "Holy goddamn fucking shit." He turned to the rookie. "Johnny, get me—"

Johnny, staring at the body, was sagging. He turned his head and vomited his breakfast.

Fitzgerald said. "Wonderful." Then he looked at me. "How the hell come *you're* not throwing up? Don't tell me you're with the ATF, too."

"FBI."

"Oh. FBI. Well, that's good. That's real good. Maybe I can just get my commissioner to turn over whatever the hell happened to this girl to the FBI and leave me be."

The trooper went to his car and came back with two cellophane envelopes. He squatted down on his haunches and placed one over the dead girl's right hand. Then he taped it closed. He tried to move her other arm. It was rigid. He stood back up. He would leave it to the coroner. The trooper stuffed the second envelope in his pocket.

As he laid the blanket carefully back over the body so that every inch of her was covered, he said, "Damage is done." My instinct was to tell him not to do that, but he had a point about the damage having been done. Not unusual anyway. When someone comes across a dead body with no clothes on, that person will often throw a coat or jacket over the victim or run to the nearest house, not only to call the police but to get a blanket. The Rhode Island coroner would have to cope. Suspicious death; he'd have to pick out the blanket fibers. Tommy and I watched as, very gently, the cop bent over and went about straightening the edges.

With Tommy distracted, the guests from Aggie's had been creeping closer.

Trooper Fitzgerald stood, put his hands on his hips, and yelled at them. "What the hell are you people starin' at? Get back up on that porch or I'll arrest every goddamn one of you." Then he said to Tommy, "You too, old man. You disturbed any evidence we're gonna be wishin' like hell we had. And the road is covered with your tracks. Plus now we have my own tire tracks and we got the FBI's . . . bicycle."

Tommy said to him, "I saved any evidence. The birds might have started pecking at the body if I didn't cover it." Now the trooper's face showed frustration in addition to anger. He took a big breath, about to hurl another insult, then the distant sound of a siren filtered in through the gulls' screaming.

Fitzgerald said. "What the hell is that, the CIA?"

Tommy said, "It's the doc."

"Good. Hope he's got some Maalox."

Then he squatted down again. He lifted one end of the blanket, exposing just the dead girl's horrifically contorted face. He looked closely at her and said, "Poor kid. Someone sold her some real bad stuff." Not too terrible a man after all, perhaps. I went over and squatted down too, right beside him. He turned his head to face me. "You an investigator or a pencil pusher?"

"Investigator."

"Okay then, Agent. She was killed somewhere else and dumped here, wasn't she? Killed sometime last night, wouldn't you say?"

"I'd agree entirely with that assessment."

"Good."

"What would you like me to do?"

He looked into my eyes. "Just knowin' you're here is enough for now."

I have a friend. He's a shrink, a good one. He'd translate Fitzy's words to me—in addition to the expression on his face—as *reaching out*.

Reach out, Fitzy, you've got me.

About the Author

Mary-Ann Tirone Smith is the author of seven previous novels, including *An American Killing*, which was chosen as a *New York Times* Notable Book. She has lived in Connecticut all her life except for two years in Cameroon, where she served as a Peace Corps volunteer. She is currently at work on the fourth Poppy Rice book.

<u>BOOK YOUR PLACE ON OUR WEBSITE</u> <u>AND MAKE THE</u> <u>READING CONNECTION!</u>

We've created a customized website just for our very special readers, where you can get the inside scoop on everything that's going on with Zebra, Pinnacle and Kensington books.

When you come online, you'll have the exciting opportunity to:

- View covers of upcoming books
- Read sample chapters
- Learn about our future publishing schedule (listed by publication month *and author*)
- Find out when your favorite authors will be visiting a city near you
- Search for and order backlist books from our online catalog
- Check out author bios and background information
- Send e-mail to your favorite authors
- Meet the Kensington staff online
- Join us in weekly chats with authors, readers and other guests
- Get writing guidelines
- AND MUCH MORE!

Visit our website at
http://www.kensingtonbooks.com

Grab These
Kensington Mysteries